DASTARDLY DEEDS DOWN ON THE FARM

4 COZY FARMYARD MYSTERIES

DASTARDLY DEEDS DOWN ON THE FARM

4 COZY FARMYARD MYSTERIES

CYNTHIA HICKEY
LINDA BATEN JOHNSON
TERESA IVES LILLY
JANICE THOMPSON

YOU are the reason we do what we do here at Barbour Publishing. We promise that we will always use our God-given talents to produce content with you in mind—and that we will remain biblically faithful, no matter what.

Thank you for being the heart of our business.

Print ISBN 979-8-89151-224-5
Adobe Digital Edition (.epub) 979-8-89151-225-2

Cover illustration by Begoña Fernandez Corbalan

Published by Barbour Books, an imprint of Barbour Publishing, Inc., 1810 Barbour Drive, Uhrichsville, Ohio 44683, www.barbourbooks.com

Our mission is to inspire the world with the life-changing message of the Bible.

Printed in the United States of America.

HOG WILD

BY CYNTHIA HICKEY

CHAPTER ONE

The sound of a rooster's crow jolted me awake, my body stiff from a long day of hard work on the farm. The scents of hay, warm earth, and manure filled my nostrils as I pushed out of bed. My bare feet hit the cool wooden floor as my gaze landed on the clock—5:02 a.m. The morning routine called, and it always started with feeding the hogs.

I pulled on my royal-blue rubber boots with the bright pink flowers, shrugged into my denim jacket, and stepped outside. The dawn light stretched across rolling pastures, painting the sky in hues of deep purple and soft gold, the air crisp with the beginning of autumn. I took a deep breath and indulged in my favorite view: the farm early in the morning.

Something felt off as I headed for the hogpen after filling a bucket with feed. The usual grunts and snuffles were absent. An unnatural stillness hung over the farm, and my pulse quickened. I increased my pace, my boots kicking up loose gravel.

The pen gate hung ajar.

My stomach dropped.

"Oh, no." I fumbled with the latch. It seemed to work fine, not broken. I entered the pen. The bedding inside showed evidence of having been slept in. But hoofprints dug into the dirt, and the wooden railing bore fresh scratches, as if something large had been dragged out without permission.

"Red? Big Red?" I called for my prize hog.

None of my hogs answered. I groaned and poured the feed into the trough before setting out across the farm in search of Red and his harem.

If the silly thing got hurt, he'd never win another blue ribbon. I hadn't spent years raising the thick-headed, stubborn hog for him to vanish into thin air.

My steps faltered. What if someone had taken him? After all, the latch worked just fine. As smart as Red was, he couldn't open the gate himself.

Who would steal him? Dickins Hog Farm has been in the town of Oakwood, Arkansas, for decades, passed down through the generations until finally coming to me. My farm is an icon. I had to be mistaken. Still, the niggling feeling persisted that more than the hogs simply wandering off had occurred last night.

I walked to the creek where hoofprints let me know my hogs had been there. My heart rate relaxed a bit as I followed the tracks. "There you are." I smiled to see my hogs wallowing in the mud. All except Big Red. I clicked my tongue, then called out again. "SOOO-o-oeeyyy, Red."

No answering snort. He wouldn't have voluntarily left his girls.

Heart in my throat, I grabbed a thick stick and prodded the five sows toward home. I'd need help in finding out what happened to Big Red. Hopefully, someone at Hank's Feed and Supply in town could help.

Once the sows were back in the pen and happily eating, I grabbed the keys to my old Ford pickup. The engine rumbled to life. I spun gravel, racing away from the farm.

Oakwood isn't the kind of town where things go missing. Sure, people have their squabbles and small-time gossip runs rampant, but outright theft? Very rare. If someone had taken Big Red, I'd get him back—one way or another.

Main Street had started waking up when I drove in. Through the door of Millie's Diner came the scents of fresh coffee and warm pastries. The neon light in the window of Hank's Feed and Supply flickered on as I parked out front.

I opened my truck door, my booted feet hitting the pavement with force. Oakwood isn't a large town. Someone would know something. I shoved the door to the feedstore open.

"Whoa." A man jumped back to escape being hit, then grinned in recognition. "Shelby Dickins."

"Caleb Thornton. When did you get here?" He'd left me high and dry after high school to attend veterinarian school, at least that's how his leaving felt to me. He didn't call or text. He didn't say goodbye. Instead, he disappeared like a fugitive.

He was taller than I remembered, his broad shoulders filling out the dark flannel that stretched across his chest. A morning shadow of stubble dusted his jaw, and his usual easygoing smirk was absent as he steadied me with firm hands, those remarkable dark-blue eyes boring into mine.

"Last week. I'm the town's new veterinarian." His nose wrinkled, and his gaze dropped to my feet. "You still have the hog farm, I see."

"What?" I glanced down to see manure caking my boots. "Oh." I rushed back outside and scraped them clean on the curb before reentering the store.

Of all the people to run into, Caleb was not one I expected. I never thought I'd see him again and wasn't sure how I felt about seeing him now. He'd broken a seventeen-year-old girl's heart ten years ago.

"You all right?"

I jerked straight and whirled to face him. "You scared me."

"Sorry. You looked upset when you came in the store." His brow furrowed. "Were you in a hurry to run someone over, or is there an actual emergency?"

"Big Red is gone."

"Who is Big Red?"

"My prize-winning hog. He wasn't in his pen this morning."

"Gone as in. . ."

"As in missing." I crossed my arms. "I think he was stolen. The gate was wide open." My voice cracked. Red was the closest thing I had to a legacy. I couldn't lose him.

Caleb's expression shifted, all traces of teasing gone. "I remember him now. You've had him from a piglet. I remember how much he means to you. I'm sorry."

A flicker of something unreadable passed across his eyes. A shadow of the history between us. The weight of unsaid words hung in the air. I shook them off. I didn't have time to wade through emotions I'd worked to ignore.

I squared my shoulders. "I don't need sympathy. I need help finding my hog."

He studied me for a moment. "All right. Let's find Big Red."

And just like that, we were in it together whether I liked it or not.

"Good morning, Shelby." Hank smiled from behind the counter. "Need feed so soon?"

I marched to the counter. "Someone stole Big Red."

He took a step back. "Stole him? Are you sure?"

"Absolutely. The gate was open this morning. I found the sows down by the creek. No sign of Big Red." Tears stung my eyes.

"Why would someone steal him?"

"He's worth a lot of money, Hank. He's a prized stud with a long line of prized hogs in his lineage, not to mention all the awards he's won. Will you keep an ear open for me?"

"Of course I will. You should head over to the sheriff's office and file a report. The sooner you get the word out, the sooner you'll find him. Can't miss entering him into the fair this year."

No, I couldn't. "Thank you." I hurried outside, Caleb on my heels. "You don't have to go with me to the sheriff."

"I said I'd help you."

"Why not meet me at my farm in an hour? I'm sure you have things to do." I climbed into my truck. "You can help me search for clues."

"All right. See you then." He climbed into a newer-model truck and backed away from the feedstore.

I hadn't meant to be rude, but my priority was finding Red in time to enter him into next month's fair. I didn't have time to figure out how I felt about Caleb returning.

The sheriff's office was housed in a metal building near the diner. I drove across the street and parked. Renee Barker, a girl I went to school with, smiled at me from the receptionist's desk.

"I need to see the sheriff."

"I'll see if he's available." She spoke quietly into her phone then said, "You can go on back. Have a good day, Shelby."

"You too, Renee." I headed down a short hallway and entered a room on my right.

Sheriff Owen Lincoln, a round man only a few inches taller than my five-foot-five, turned his attention from his computer to me. "What can I do for you, Shelby?"

"Someone stole my hog." I hitched my chin. "I need you to find out who."

"Slow down. Tell me what happened."

I started with carrying the feed to the pen and ended with finding the sows. "Hogs can't open gates."

"Sure they can. Pigs are smart."

"The latch is too high, Sheriff." It had been installed that way specifically so the animals couldn't open the gate themselves. "Are you going to help me or not?"

"I'm going to need some proof, Shelby. If the animal hasn't returned by suppertime, call me and I'll send a deputy out."

"That's hours away!" Anything could happen to Big Red. My eyes filled with tears again.

"Now, don't go and start crying on me." He looked stricken. "I've got more to deal with than a missing animal. I said I'd send someone out if the pig doesn't return, and I will."

"Thanks." I sniffed and left his office, ignoring Renee's question of whether I was all right.

Of course I wasn't. I'd lost something very important to me. I wouldn't be able to concentrate on anything until Big Red was safely back in his pen.

CHAPTER TWO

My truck rumbled as I pulled into the long gravel driveway of my family's farm. My conversation with the sheriff still rankled, despite the familiar scent of hay and damp earth.

Near the hogpen, two people waited for me. Caleb stood with his back against a post, arms crossed over his broad chest and a cowboy hat tipped just enough to shade his eyes. Boy, I loved the way he looked in a cowboy hat. *Stop it, Shelby. You can't think of him like that.*

Beside him, my best friend Rosie twisted the hem of her flannel shirt, her lips pressed into a tight line. "Why did I have to hear about Big Red from Renee?"

"I'm sorry." I gave her a quick hug. "It happened this morning." Renee didn't waste any time spreading the news. "Let me show you what I found."

I showed them how the gate had been left open. "See? No way Red could've let himself out. The latch is too high." I showed them the grooves where someone dragged him from the pen. "Big Red wouldn't have gone willingly. He doesn't like most people."

"You missed these." Caleb pointed to the ground. Muddy boot prints too large to be mine.

Whoever had been here hadn't just passed through. They had stopped. Walked around. Studied the area. My heart pounded. "I need a dog."

Caleb and Rosie glanced at me in unison. "That's random," Rosie said.

"No, I mean it. A dog would be a good security system. No one would get on my property without a dog alerting me."

"Okay." Caleb nodded. "I can take you to the shelter later. I agree with you that someone took your hog. I also questioned a couple of your neighbors on my way here. Both reported seeing a dark-colored, older-model truck with a trailer pass this way late last night."

"They were both out that late?" A lot of folks around here drive an old truck with a trailer.

"Feeding livestock, they said. They also said the truck moved slow, as if hauling something heavy, and drove with its lights off."

Rosie glanced between us. "This doesn't sound random."

My jaw tightened. "No, it doesn't."

Caleb narrowed his eyes. "You have any enemies we should know about?"

I snorted. "Enemies? Only if you count those with a jealous streak because my hog is always winning ribbons." I glanced down the road. *Where are you, Big Red?*

"Who would you have on a list of jealous competitors?"

"Travis Reed, I guess. He's my biggest competitor. But why would he steal Red?"

"Look, y'all." Rosie waved a scrap of green-and-black flannel fabric. "I found this on a nail on the side of the wellhouse."

I took the scrap from her. "I don't have a shirt this color." I'd definitely be looking for someone wearing a green-and-black flannel shirt missing a piece.

"Anyone else who might not want your hog in next month's competition?" Caleb pulled my attention back to him.

"Where's Luke?" Rosie asked.

Luke Brenner, my part-time farmhand, was taking a few days well-earned time off. "Vacation."

"Would he have a reason to want Red gone?" Caleb scowled. "Usually, crimes are committed by someone close to home."

"Why would he? Without the money Big Red brings me from competitions and stud fees, I wouldn't be able to pay for his help."

The crunch of tires on gravel turned me toward the road as a deputy's car drove up. "The sheriff said he wasn't sending anyone unless Big Red didn't show for supper."

"He must've changed his mind." Caleb leaned back against the pen railing. "Looks like Dave Helton."

Caleb's rival from high school. Both had wanted the position of star quarterback. Dave hadn't liked that Caleb took first string.

"Be nice." I stepped forward to greet the other man. "Thank you for coming, Dave, but I wasn't expecting you."

"I came when I heard about your hog." He smiled, a look of admiration in his eyes.

Caleb huffed. Yes, the two had also competed for me.

I ran Dave through the clues we'd found and handed him the torn fabric. "I found the sows down by the creek. No sign of Big Red's prints, and they would've been very visible."

"The neighbors mentioned a truck and trailer?" He glanced at Caleb.

"Yep. Except for the truck not having lights on, they didn't think twice about seeing it."

Dave wrote on a notepad he pulled from inside his jacket. "I'll head down to the creek and look around anyway. I'll let you know if I find anything."

"Caleb is taking me to the shelter to find a dog. You have my cell phone number. Thanks again, Dave." I smiled, eliciting a grunt from Caleb. I had to admit to enjoying his slight show of jealousy. "You want to come, Rosie?"

"No, I've got to get to my shift at the diner. I can ask around if anyone has seen your hog." She tossed Dave a wave, her cheeks turning pink when he smiled and waved before marching toward the creek. How had I not noticed her infatuation with him before?

"Do you think the whole forty-eight hours thing pertains to animals?" I asked, buckling myself into Caleb's truck.

"As in finding them alive during that time?" He raised his eyebrows. "I don't think whoever took Red plans on killing him. What purpose would that serve? If I had to make an assumption, I'd say they intend on keeping him until after the competition so you can't enter him."

"We need to find out who's signed up. We might find Red on one of their properties."

"When is the deadline?"

"The end of the month." Which meant not everyone had signed up yet. Still, it gave us a place to start. "Thanks for coming with me. Being a vet, you'll be a good judge on what kind of dog I should get."

"I said I would help you." He smiled and pulled up in front of a cement building that housed the local animal shelter. "We're friends, remember?"

Right. Friends. Once I thought we were more than friends.

A cacophony of barks greeted us as we entered the building. On the off chance someone had found Red and brought him here, I headed for the section where they housed animals that weren't cats or dogs. Of course, everyone in Oakwood knew Big Red, but I still had to check. He wasn't there.

I joined Caleb in a fenced area where he was sitting on the grass and had three dogs in his lap. I laughed as they knocked him over and licked his face. "You want me to pick one of these ferocious beasts?"

"They're the best ones here." He untangled himself and got to his feet. "Lovable, but they'll provide the security you need."

How would I pick just one? I sat on a cement bench and waited to see whether one of them would come to me.

The mixed-breed brindle kept glancing my way. Finally, he came and sat in front of me, his dark eyes focused on my face.

"You're quite the mutt, aren't you?" I patted his head. "Beautiful, but what are you?"

"Shepherd, lab, and maybe a little pit bull." Caleb sat beside me. "He's a good boy. Healthy. About two years old. We can stop by my office, and I'll check him over. You have three days to bring him back if you find out he isn't a good fit."

"Wanna come home with me, Mutt?" Why hadn't I considered a dog a lot sooner? "I think he'll be a great addition to the farm." If I'd had him, Big Red would still be locked in his pen.

Tears threatened to choke me again. What if I never got my friend back?

Caleb patted my shoulder. "We'll find Red, I promise."

"Don't make promises you can't keep." He'd broken them before. I stood. "Come on, Mutt. Let's go home."

We made a quick stop at the vet's office where Caleb gave Mutt a clean bill of health and I tacked a notice to the bulletin board about Big Red. My note stood out among advertisements for dog sitting and puppies for sale.

"Let's grab a couple of burgers before heading back to the farm," Caleb suggested.

"Don't you have something to do?"

"Not really. I don't officially start work here until tomorrow, and I'm hungry."

"If I remember correctly, you're always hungry." I stifled a grin, not wanting him to think I'd forgiven him for dumping me ten years ago. "I could use something to eat. It is suppertime." My throat clogged again at the realization Big Red wouldn't be waiting for his feed and shoving the sows out of the way with his bulk until the trough was full.

Caleb went through the drive-through of a local burger shop, purchased food, then handed me a bag before tossing a patty into the back seat for Mutt. "Before I leave the farm, I want to make sure the dog will stick around if left outside."

"He'll be sleeping inside with me." I bit into the juicy mushroom cheeseburger.

Caleb frowned. "I thought he was going to be a guard dog."

"He is. He can do that from inside, can't he?"

"Fine. We'll stop at the mercantile and get a doggie door if you want."

"You don't have to. You've done enough today. I really do appreciate your help, though, and a doggie door would be great."

He reached over and wiped something from the corner of my mouth, his gaze softening. "You had some ketchup."

"Oh. Uh. . ." Not knowing how to respond to the emotions whirling in me, I took another bite of my burger.

By the time Caleb left, the sun had started to set, the hogs had been fed, the chores were done, and I sat on the front-porch steps with a glass of tea in one hand and Mutt sitting next to me. "I wonder how you'd get along with Big Red. He can be jealous, you know."

Mutt's ears perked up, his dark gaze on the road.

"Do you see something?" I strained to see through the deepening dusk.

An engine rumbled in the distance. I really should've already started questioning folks. Instead, I sat on the porch and missed my hog. Tomorrow would be different. Tomorrow, I'd pound the proverbial pavement and badger everyone in town until someone told me where Big Red was.

The sows in the pen didn't snort and snuffle as much as usual. They missed him too.

Don't worry, girls. Your man will be home soon. I wouldn't stop searching until he was.

CHAPTER THREE

The next morning, I coerced Rosie into going with me to pay a visit to Travis Reed. "You've got time before you have to go to work. What if he's dangerous? Do you really want me to go alone?"

"Fine." Rosie flounced against the back of the truck seat. "But if we get murdered, I'm going to kill you."

The drive didn't take long. Soon we pulled into the winding drive of a sprawling estate, a testament to Travis' family's wealth and long-standing dominance in the livestock industry. My farm seemed like a speck of sand in comparison.

Travis came around the corner of the house as I got out of my truck. A grin spread across his face. "To what do I owe this honor?"

"Oh, hush. I know you heard about my hog going missing. You wouldn't happen to know anything about that, would you?" I planted my fists on my hips as Rosie stood just behind me.

Travis grinned. "Now, Shelby, that's a serious accusation. Are you saying I stole your pig? His voice dripped with mock innocence. "I have plenty of my own."

"None as good as Big Red."

Rosie leaned around me. "It's mighty convenient that Shelby's main competitor suddenly has one less problem to worry about a month before the biggest competition in these parts."

He laughed, shaking his head. "You ladies always assume the worst. I didn't take your pig, Shelby. I don't need to. I've got my own entry, and it's better than anything you could bring to the table—even Big Red."

I narrowed my eyes. "Who is it this time? You usually bring in stock from out of town so no one sees your entry until the last minute."

"Wouldn't you like to know." He smirked and turned toward the barn, acting as if he'd already dismissed us.

I wasn't letting him off that easily. "Listen, Travis. If I find out you had anything to do with this, I'll make sure the whole town hears about it."

He stopped and looked back over his shoulder. "You do that. In the meantime, good luck finding that hog of yours."

I followed him to the barn, my boots kicking up dust. "My pen was locked up tight. Somebody opened the gate and dragged Red out. You have the most to gain by him not competing."

"Yeah." Rosie glared. "You've pulled some dirty tricks before, Travis, but this? This is low."

He chuckled. "I don't have time for this. I've got my own hog to tend to—entered it fair and square, like everybody else. I can't help it that you didn't take the proper care needed."

My hands curled into fists. The man was too smug. He knew something. If he took Red, he thought I wouldn't be able to prove it. I was going to make sure I did.

"Come on, Shelby." Rosie tugged on my arm. "Let's grab some breakfast from the diner."

Travis waved as he entered the barn. "Goodbye, ladies."

Ugh. The man was insufferable. "Okay. We need to formulate a plan to find Big Red in time."

"Do you think we can?" Rosie climbed into the truck.

"Caleb seems to think someone is holding him until after the competition and then he'll show up."

"That doesn't help you."

"No, it doesn't." I shot another glare toward Travis' barn, then turned around and headed to town.

"How do you feel about Caleb returning?" Rosie tilted her head.

"I haven't thought about it. I have other things on my mind." *Liar.* I thought about it a lot. Lost sleep over that thinking the night before. Truth was, I didn't know how I felt about his return.

"Hey, Rosie." The hostess of the diner, Macie, led us to a booth. "I'll be back to take your order. Sorry about your pig, Shelby."

"Thanks. Can you keep an ear out for any mention of him?" I opened the menu, my gaze landing on biscuits and chocolate gravy.

"Well..." She leaned closer. "Folks are saying Travis is sure to win the competition now."

"No whispers of who might've stolen Big Red?"

"Not yet, but you know this town. Someone will slip eventually." She left to seat a group of four.

"A three-hundred-pound animal cannot simply disappear." I sighed and leaned against the booth. "I should go back to Travis' tonight and snoop around."

"That's trespassing!" Rosie's eyes widened.

"So?" I shrugged. "It's also illegal to steal. His farm is the biggest around, with plenty of places to stash my pig. You'll help me, right?"

Her shoulders sagged. "Yes, I'll help. I feel like we're still in high school and you're getting me in trouble again."

"Those were the good ole days." I grinned and ordered the biscuits and chocolate gravy when the server came to take our order. Then I sobered and asked Rosie, "Do you know where the competition records are kept?"

Rosie shook her head as Caleb spoke from behind me. "I do." He slid in beside me. "I've got a buddy who works at the county clerk's office. I bet he'll let us have a peek."

"You think so?" I tried to scoot away from him without being obvious. I couldn't eat with him sitting so close.

"I'll text him right now." He pulled out his cell phone and typed, then motioned the server over. "I'll take the special. Three eggs over easy, hashbrowns, and sausage. Oh, and coffee."

"Aren't you supposed to be working?" I asked.

"The office doesn't open until nine. My first appointment isn't until nine thirty. I've got time. What have the two of you been up to?"

I filled him in on our visit to Travis'. "He knows something."

"Shelby and I are going tonight to snoop around." Rosie grimaced.

"Absolutely not." Caleb's face hardened. "It could be dangerous. Hold on. I've got a text." He glanced at his phone. "My friend said come to the back door of the courthouse tonight and he'll let us in."

I arched a brow. "How is that any different than going to Travis'?"

"We're invited, for one."

"Well, it's a good thing you don't have the authority to keep me from doing anything." I smiled as the server brought my breakfast.

"I could tell the sheriff." He shot me a sideways glance.

"You won't."

"No, I won't." He sighed. "Guess I'll have to go with you then. As backup."

I shrugged. I did ask for his help.

Later that night, I met Caleb behind the courthouse, where a man let us in a side door. "You know, I could get in serious trouble for this," Caleb said. "Where's Rosie?"

"She opted out. Said she had a rough day." I stepped back as the stranger waved us inside.

"Shelby, meet Alan." Caleb introduced me, and we followed Alan into a small office.

"Thank you, Alan," I whispered. "We wouldn't ask if it wasn't important."

Alan sighed, rummaging through a file cabinet before pulling out a manila folder labeled *Livestock Competition Entries*. "Here it is, and hurry. Mind you, there's still time to enter, so not all entries are listed yet."

I flipped through the pages, scanning the names. Most were familiar, farmers and ranchers I'd known for years, but. . . "This is a new entry. Someone who has never entered before." I turned the file around. "Who is Mason Duggar?"

Caleb peered at the page. "I have no idea, but it says here that he's entered a hog in the same weight class as yours."

My gut twisted. "That's quite a coincidence. I mean. . .he could be the guy. I don't really believe in coincidences."

"Why would you say that? Big Red can't be the only hog his size in the county," Caleb asked.

Alan crossed his arms. "Mason's not very well known around here yet. Moved to town a few months ago. Does odd jobs, mostly farmhand work."

I glanced up. "Where?"

"Recently he's been working for Travis Reed."

My breath caught as I met Caleb's gaze. I slammed the file shut. "I bet Travis made Mason steal my hog."

Caleb frowned. "You sure about that?"

I shrugged. "Maybe. I wouldn't put it past him to have someone else do his dirty work." I tapped the folder. "This entry is just a smidge under three hundred pounds."

Caleb exhaled. "What are you gonna do?"

"I'm gonna prove it. And when I do, Travis Reed is gonna wish he'd never messed with me."

"Right now, you're both going to leave," Alan said, replacing the folder. "If someone sees my light on, they'll come to investigate. I should've left the office hours ago." He ushered us out, locked the door, and made a beeline for his car.

"Now what?" Caleb asked, walking me to my truck.

"I pay a visit to Mason Duggar and the butcher, Carl Brunner."

"Why Brunner?"

"Because he's also entering the same weight size. One of those competitors has Big Red." I opened the driver's side door and climbed inside. Of course there were more competitors than just us two or three, but Travis was the only one I've had run-ins with in the past.

Caleb closed it for me, then folded his arms on the doorframe. "When do you want to visit Travis' farm again?" His eyes glittered in the light of a streetlamp.

"Tomorrow night. Ten o'clock. Be at my place or we leave without you."

He stepped back. "I'll be there."

Mutt greeted me on the porch when I arrived home. I scratched behind his ears. "Everything okay here?"

He answered with a woof.

"Good boy."

Since Rosie and I had been interrupted at breakfast and not had time to formulate a plan on getting my hog back, I pulled a pad of paper from my desk and sat at the kitchen table. I wrote down Travis Reed's name and Mason Duggar's. The only other clue I had was that a truck and trailer had been seen on my road the night Big Red disappeared.

I chewed on the end of my pencil. Maybe tomorrow night would reveal some more clues. I hoped so. I had a farm to run and a hog to find and found myself torn between the two. Work couldn't suffer. I had Luke to help care for the livestock, but they were my responsibility.

What a time for him to request time off. I frowned. Did he have an ulterior motive? Could Luke have taken Big Red and needed the time off to find a place to stash such a large animal?

The pigs were used to him. They wouldn't have made a giant fuss at his presence in the middle of the night, especially if someone lured my hog with food. I added him to my list of suspects.

Maybe I was getting somewhere.

Tomorrow night might reveal what I needed to do next.

CHAPTER FOUR

Carl Brunner stood behind the butcher counter, a short, barrel-chested man with thinning hair and permanently red-stained fingers from years of handling raw meat. Normally, he was steady-handed, moving through his shop with the confidence of a man who knew his craft. Today, he seemed off—his hands trembled slightly as he wiped them on his apron and avoided eye contact as Rosie and I approached.

"Ladies."

Rosie leaned against the counter. "You all right, Carl? You look like you've seen a ghost."

He fumbled with a wrapped package of meat, nearly dropping it before setting it aside. "Just busy. What can I do for you?"

Before I could answer, the door behind us jingled. I turned as Caleb strolled in, his presence as effortless as ever. He had that easygoing charm, hands in his pockets, his dark green T-shirt snug against his frame.

"This is a surprise." I arched an eyebrow. "Don't you ever work?"

He grinned. "Came to pick up supper." His gaze flicked to Carl, who visibly tensed.

Carl wiped his hands on his stained apron again. "Yeah, give me a second." He turned and shuffled toward the back.

"Something's not right." I glanced at my friends.

"No kidding. That man is skittish." Rosie kept watching where Carl had gone.

When he returned, he clutched a small brown paper bag. He thrust it into Caleb's hands as if it burned his fingers. "There. That's it. Now, if you ladies aren't buying anything, I've got work to do."

I leaned on the counter. "Heard you're entering this year's hog competition."

"Yeah, so? No crime against that."

"In the same division as me."

He paled. "Again, no crime in that."

"It is if you took my hog so you could win."

He snorted. "Big Red won't always win, Shelby. Someday, someone else will. Have a good day." He returned to the back room before we had a chance to leave.

Outside, Caleb laughed. "You haven't changed a bit. You've still got a real knack for walking into situations that smell like trouble."

I frowned. "I went on purpose. You've got a knack for showing up at the perfect time."

"Maybe I like being where you are."

My face heated, and I hurried to my truck.

"He still likes you." Rosie wiggled her eyebrows once we were driving toward the diner where I'd promised to return her.

"So? I've got other things to take care of."

"You still care for him."

"Do not."

"Do too."

We laughed as we reverted back to our high school ages for a second. I sobered. "I never stopped, Rosie, but he dumped me. Not the other way around. Let's focus on what's really important right now, okay? Finding Big Red."

"You still going to question Mason?"

I'd filled Rosie in on what happened at the courthouse the night before, and she'd informed me that Mason Duggar was a regular at the diner. "Yes, why?"

She drew my attention to the front door of the diner. "He's here." She pointed.

I parked a few spaces away from the door and followed Rosie inside. She headed for the kitchen to start her shift while I made a beeline for the table where Mason sat. "Hello."

He jerked his gaze from the menu to me. "What do you want?"

"Heard you're entering the competition."

"What competition?" With precise movements, he folded the menu and laid it on the table in front of him.

"Are you entering a hog in this year's competition?"

"Yeah, so?"

"You wouldn't know anything about my missing hog, would you?"

"I'm new around here. Wouldn't know your hog if it bit me on the rear end."

I described Big Red.

"He sounds nice. I bought me one from over in Clayton County. Ain't he a beaut?" He pulled a photo from his pocket. The black-and-white hog was almost as large as Big Red.

I waved away the approaching server. "You work for Travis Reed?"

"Yes, and I was ready to order my food." He glowered.

"You sure you haven't seen any sign of my hog?"

His eyes widened. "You think Travis stole him? No, I ain't seen no sign of your hog. Why would Travis steal yours when he's got his own?"

"To better his chance of winning." I crossed my arms.

"Hmm. Maybe so, but I don't think he did. Now, can I order and eat in peace?"

I stared at him for a moment, trying to determine whether he was lying or not. The way he met my gaze straight on led me to believe he spoke the truth. "Sorry to have bothered you." I guess I could scratch his name off my suspect list.

Later that night, Rosie and Caleb and I parked a football field's length from Travis' farm and made our way to the edge of his property. The scent of hay and manure hung in the night air as we crouched behind the tree line.

"Can I say, again, that this is trespassing?" Rosie clutched my arm.

"Consider it investigating." I adjusted the flashlight in my grip.

Caleb chuckled. "Remind me again why I always let you drag me into these things."

"You volunteered." I waved them forward, wishing we'd brought Mutt with us to watch our backs.

We crept along the edge of the property, keeping to the shadows the best we could. The barn loomed ahead, its doors slightly ajar. My heart pounded as I reached for a handle and carefully eased the door open.

Inside, something metallic added to the normal odors of hay, manure, and livestock. I swept my flashlight around the space. Nothing seemed out of place until Rosie nudged me and pointed.

A large meat hook hung from the rafters. Beneath it, the floor was damp and a few strands of coarse, dark, almost-black hair clung to the hay-covered floor.

My stomach twisted.

"Tell me that isn't what I think it is," Caleb murmured.

"You're the vet," Rosie said. "You tell us. But I think we found where Big Red ended up."

I whirled to face her. "Don't say that!"

A creak sounded from the loft above us.

My blood ran cold. Someone was up there. I flicked off the flashlight and gripped Caleb's arm. "We aren't alone."

A shadow shifted. Then I heard the unmistakable click of a shotgun being cocked. "You shouldn't have come here. Who's down there?" someone called.

Caleb stepped forward, shielding me with his body. "Just some folks admiring the livestock. Didn't mean to intrude."

A tense silence followed, then we heard the unmistakable sound of boots descending a wooden ladder. "Should've known it would be Shelby and her friends." Travis stepped into the light.

His face looked drawn, his eyes shadowed with something unreadable. He didn't point the shotgun at us directly, but he didn't lower it either. "You lost?"

I forced myself to appear casual. "Depends on what you mean by lost. We're searching for answers."

He exhaled through his nose and glanced at Caleb, then Rosie—who gripped her flashlight like a weapon. Finally, his gaze shot to the meat hook hanging near the rafters.

I followed his line of sight. "What was up there, Travis?"

"I don't know."

Rosie made a noise in her throat. "Oh, come on! We aren't leaving until you tell us."

He rubbed a hand over his face. "I got a call from Carl Brunner a few nights ago. He asked if he could use the barn to process something—said he needed privacy. He paid me in cash. That's all I know."

I narrowed my eyes. "You didn't see what he brought in?"

He hesitated. "I saw a trailer pull in, but I never looked inside."

Rosie threw her hands up. "Seriously? A man asked to use your barn in the dead of the night to process something, and you just let him?"

He shrugged. "I don't ask questions I don't want to know the answers to."

My gut told me he was lying, or at least wasn't telling the full truth. Before I could press him further, a sound outside the barn made me freeze.

Footsteps.

Heavy ones.

A shadow passed over the narrow gap in the barn door.

My fingers tightened around my flashlight. Rosie sucked in a breath. Caleb shifted to a fighting stance.

The doors swung open, and Carl Brunner stepped inside holding a gun. His earlier nervous demeanor was gone. His gaze was hard, his grip steady on the weapon. "Y'all should've stayed out of this."

I kept my voice calm. "So, it was you."

Carl's gaze flicked to me. "You don't know what you're talking about."

"Really?" I tilted my head. "Because it's starting to appear as if you had something to do with Big Red's disappearance."

His jaw tightened. "I don't have your pig."

I studied his features. He didn't seem like he was lying, but he *was* hiding something.

Caleb spoke next. "Then what is this all about?" He gestured to the hook and bloodstained floor.

Carl hesitated for half a second, just enough time for me to catch the flicker of uncertainty in his expression.

I took a slow step forward. "Did you butcher something here? Or did someone else?"

"You're out of your depth, girl."

"Then explain it to me."

His nostrils flared as he glanced at Travis. "You should've kept your mouth shut."

Rosie crossed her arms. "If you don't have Big Red, then where is he?"

Carl's mouth twisted. "You think I know?" He let out a bitter laugh. "You're barking up the wrong tree."

"If you didn't take him, then why try so hard to scare us off?" I narrowed my eyes. "How did you know we were here? Did you follow us? Who killed something here?"

His shoulders tensed, and I suddenly got the feeling that he wasn't trying to cover up my pig's disappearance. He was trying to keep us from finding out something else. I was willing to bet that something was a whole lot bigger than a stolen prize hog.

Caleb must've come to the same conclusion. "This isn't about Big Red at all, is it?"

A long silence stretched between them, then Carl shook his head. "No."

The tension in the barn changed.

My skin prickled. "Then what is this about?"

"You don't want to know." Before anyone could react, he took a step toward the door and bolted.

"Hey!" Caleb lunged, but Carl was fast. He ducked outside and disappeared into the dark.

I sprinted after him, Caleb on my heels. By the time my eyes adjusted to the night, Carl was gone.

The night was silent again, save for the sound of crickets.

"Well," Rosie said, "that could've gone better."

Caleb nodded. "We need to find him before he disappears for good."

My mind raced. Carl was scared. Not of us, but of whatever secret he was trying to protect.

Yes, Big Red was missing, but I was sure of one thing. There was something way bigger happening here.

And I planned on finding out what.

CHAPTER FIVE

Mutt's growling tugged my attention away from watching the coffeepot. I frowned, not being a morning person until I'd had my brew. Only then did I feel fit to care for the livestock and begin my day. The sun hadn't even risen yet. "Go on out if you want to."

He barked and dashed out the doggie door. When his barks increased, I opened the door, half expecting to see him chasing a rabbit.

A sheet of printer paper fluttered from the doorjamb. With my heart in my throat, I yanked it free and read, "Some pigs aren't meant to win. Stay out of this."

Not meant to win? Big Red had won the last two years. I crumpled the paper in my fist. It was just a note. Just a stupid note.

Except it wasn't, was it? The words stared back at me, bold and threatening when I smoothed out the paper and read it again.

I set the note on the counter and ran my hands through my hair. My stomach twisted in knots. I wasn't easily rattled. Life on the farm had made me tough, but something about this felt wrong. This wasn't just competition drama. Something bigger was at play, and I'd ended up smack dab in the middle of whatever it was.

A knock at the door made me jump. My heart settled when Mutt's tail wagged. I yanked the door open.

Caleb's eyes widened. "What's wrong?"

I grabbed the note from the counter and thrust it at him.

His expression darkened as he read. His easygoing demeanor hardened into something serious. "Who wrote this?"

"If I knew, I wouldn't be standing here trying to figure it out," I snapped. "Sorry, I just— Want some coffee?" I turned and poured myself a cup. "What are you doing out here before the sun comes up?"

"Had an emergency at Higgins' place. I saw your light on and thought I'd see if you needed any help before I headed to the clinic." He handed the note back. "You should take that to the sheriff. Or I could, if you want me to."

Letting people do my job wasn't my strong suit. I'd been on my own for too long, but it did feel nice to have someone care enough to want to help. "No, but thank you. I'll take it in once I've taken care of things here. I'm supposed to meet Rosie for breakfast."

"Okay." His gaze searched my face. "If you're sure. I don't like you out here alone. Not after this."

"I'm not alone. I have Mutt, and Luke is in the apartment over the garage."

"Where was Luke when this note was left?" He arched a brow.

"Uh, he's still on vacation."

"Uh huh. Be careful, Shelby. Please don't do anything foolish."

"You know me." I grinned around the rim of my cup.

"Yes, and that's what scares me." He looked as if he wanted to say more but turned and left instead.

At eight a.m. I entered the diner. My gaze searched the room for Rosie. Spotting her in a booth in the corner, I headed that way. "Guess what happened to me this morning?"

"What?" She peered over her menu. I really didn't understand why she bothered to look at the thing. She'd order the same thing she always did. Biscuits and gravy.

"I got a note." I pulled it from my pocket and slid it across the table.

"Ooh. This is scary." She lowered her voice. "Don't look now, but Mayor Simmons is sitting in the booth behind you with Travis. I said don't look," she hissed as I started to peer around the seat. "Keep your voice down so they don't know we're here."

"When did you become Nancy Drew?" I smiled and quickly scanned the menu, choosing strawberry crepes.

"I didn't know the mayor and Travis knew each other well enough to share a meal."

I shrugged. "Everyone in town knows Travis." I personally couldn't care less whether the two of them hung out occasionally or a lot.

"You understand me, right?" Simmons sounded urgent. Maybe I did care whether the two knew each other well. "This needs to be handled. No surprises."

"Yeah, I got it. I told you it would be taken care of." Coldness laced Travis' response.

"Good. Someone will pay dearly if it goes down wrong."

My mind raced. Handled? Was this about the fair or my hog? Was the mayor involved in whatever was going on? Before I could dwell on it further, a familiar voice interrupted my thoughts.

"Mornin', ladies." Caleb strolled up to the booth like he'd been invited, his lazy grin in place.

"Let's get out of here." Mayor Simmons stood and glared our way before tossing money on his table and marching from the diner.

I rolled my eyes. "Do you ever not show up uninvited?"

"Where's the fun in that? Scoot over." He squeezed in beside me. "I called in a breakfast order for me and my tech. It isn't ready yet, so I thought I'd come see what the two of you are up to."

Rosie didn't hesitate to fill him in on the short conversation between Travis and the mayor. "Sounds suspicious, right?"

He shrugged. "Could be about anything."

"Or it could be about Big Red." I crossed my arms. "Why aren't you waiting for your food at the counter like the other pickups?"

"The view is better over here." He grinned.

"You're insufferable."

Caleb chuckled.

Rosie laughed. "Caleb, do you really have an order to pick up, or are you here to stare at Shelby? Because you haven't looked at the counter once."

My face heated.

Rather than be embarrassed by Rosie's comment, Caleb laughed harder and waggled his eyebrows at me. "You two behave." He slid from the booth and went to retrieve his order.

"He really does like you, Shelby." Rosie dug into her breakfast the instant the server set the plate in front of her. "I do believe I saw stars in his eyes."

"Hush up." I wasn't blind to the way he looked at me, but as I said before, I had bigger things to worry about.

After a day of mending fences and checking on a pregnant sow, I sat on my front porch, a glass of sweet tea in my hand and Mutt at my feet. I'd dropped the note off at the sheriff's office. He still seemed to think Big Red would mosey out of the woods one day fine as rain.

I shook my head. The man would be no help. As for the note, he chalked it up as a prank by someone happy that they wouldn't have to compete against me. Could be, but I didn't think so.

A pall hung over the event I looked forward to each year. Without my hog to enter, I didn't think I'd attend the fair at all. Red wasn't just a pig, he was my friend.

Mutt got to his feet, the hair on the back of his neck standing at attention. He growled deep in his throat.

I set my glass down and slowly stood, my eyes peering through the darkening night. A shadow passed the hogpen, circling the enclosure before heading for the barn. Past the barn, I thought I saw more movement. I retrieved a baseball bat I kept inside the front door as protection and crept after the closest intruder.

CHAPTER SIX

"Who's there? Identify yourself." I raised the bat.

The figure stopped. A beat of silence stretched between us before he stepped into the light.

Luke.

His gaze landed on the bat, then on Mutt. "That's not a very nice way to welcome back the hired help, Shelby."

"Why didn't you let me know you were returning early?" I lowered the bat.

"I didn't think I needed to. I do work here, don't I?"

I muttered something not very nice under my breath. "Come inside before I do bash your head in. There are some things I need to fill you in on."

"Where's Big Red?"

"That's one of the things I need to tell you." I refused to think Luke had anything to do with my trouble. If I couldn't trust my hired help, who could I trust?

With one last glance past the barn where nothing moved any longer, I followed Luke into the kitchen. "Coffee or tea?"

"Neither. I'm good." He sat at the table, eyeing Mutt. "When did you get a dog?"

"A couple of days ago. Don't worry. He knows you're okay now. His name is Mutt." I refilled my glass with tea and sat across from Luke.

I took a deep breath and told him about someone stealing Big Red. "I'm hoping to find him before the fair, but it isn't looking good."

"Are you sure he isn't in the woods?" Luke crossed his arms. "He does like to go out there."

"I looked. Plus, the ground clearly showed he was forcibly dragged from the pen. He also wouldn't have left his harem." I studied him for a minute before continuing. "When I spotted you tonight, I thought I saw someone else past the barn. Did you come alone?"

He frowned. "Yep. Stashed my bag in my apartment and went to check the animals."

"Who would take my hog, Luke?" I set my glass down hard enough for some of the tea to slosh over the rim.

"Travis would be my first guess. He's always wanted Big Red, but it isn't like he can enter him in anything. Your hog is well known around these parts."

"Caleb Thornton, the new vet, thinks Big Red will be returned after the competition." I sure hoped he was right. "A neighbor saw an older-model truck pulling a livestock trailer the night Red disappeared."

"That could be half this town."

"Yes." I sighed. "See? It's been a few days, and I'm getting nowhere. The sheriff isn't very concerned about a missing animal."

"Now that I'm back you'll have more time to search. I'll ask around at some of the other farms. If anyone has seen Big Red, they'll let me know."

"Thank you. It's good to have you home." I placed my glass in the sink and went to bed.

The next morning, as I fed the hogs, hurried footsteps sounded behind me. "Miss Shelby."

I turned to see Jake, a lanky seventeen-year-old who used to help out once in a while, running toward me.

"You're not gonna believe what I saw this morning." He bent over, hands on his knees as he tried to catch his breath.

I wiped my hands on my jeans. "You going to tell me, or do I have to guess?"

"Heard your prize hog was missing. You know that abandoned farm past Route 7? I think your pig is locked in a trailer there. I mean. . .it looks like Big Red. Yeah. I'm pretty positive."

"You sure?"

"Promise. It wasn't just that though. The guy drivin'. . . Something about him gave me the creeps. Never saw him before. He was in a beat-up truck, kinda rusty. Anyway, I don't think he's from around here. He dropped off the trailer and split."

"Mind if I ask what you were doing at that farm so early this morning?" I tilted my head. "Did you see the hog with your own eyes?"

He cleared his throat. "Uh, me and a couple of the guys spent the night out there. Yeah, I saw the hog."

They were up to no good was my guess. "Thank you, Jake. I'll check it out."

The boy darted off, and I called Rosie. "Want to visit an old farm?" I told her what Jake had said.

"That farm has been abandoned for years," Rosie said. "Nobody has any business being there."

"Exactly." A sense of unease crawled up my spine. "You going with me or not?"

"Be at your place in ten minutes." She hung up.

"Shelby?" Luke approached a few minutes later as I closed the barn doors. "I've called the vet. One of the sows hurt her hoof. I think she's got a nail wedged up there, and I can't get it out."

"Show me." I waved at Rosie when she pulled up and pointed toward the hogpen. "Might be a while," I called to her.

The sow did have a nail in her hoof. I tried to pull it out with my fingers but couldn't. "How did she step on a nail?" I glared at Luke.

"Don't look at me." He held up his hands. "I just got back last night, remember?"

"Try to find out, please." I forced my voice to remain calm as I walked the perimeter of the pen. No lumber, no tools, no other nails. So how had she stepped on one? I turned to greet Caleb as he strode toward us. "Hello."

"Hey. Let me take a look at you, girl." He knelt down in the muck and lifted the sow's leg. "That's gotta hurt." He pulled a pair of needle-nose pliers from his bag and soon had the nail removed, medicine applied, and the sow's foot wrapped. He pushed to his feet. "She'll chew the bandage off in a bit, but it should stay on long enough for the medicine to do some good." He replaced the pliers in his bag. "It isn't like you to let your animals get into danger."

"No, it isn't." I crossed my arms. "I have no idea how that nail got there, but I'm guessing someone is trying to run me off my farm. First, Big Red. Now this."

"That's kind of jumping to conclusions." His brow furrowed. "Why would someone want to do that?"

"Prime real estate. I bet if we asked some of the neighboring farms, they'd say things were happening to them too." I had a feeling, and I'd learned a long time ago not to discount my feelings. "Now, if you'll excuse me, I have somewhere to be. Please send the bill for your services."

He marched beside me as I went to join Rosie. "Where are you going?"

"Just checking something out."

"Again. . .where?"

"A haunted farm." Rosie grinned. "Wanna come?"

"No, he doesn't." What was she playing at?

"Sure." Caleb put his bag in his truck. "I don't have another appointment until after lunch."

I groaned and climbed into the truck. "Get in if you're coming."

Rosie squeezed into the back seat, leaving the front seat for Caleb. "This should be fun."

I doubted it.

"Why are we going?" Caleb clicked his seat belt into place.

"A kid named Jake said he saw Big Red in a trailer on the property." I drove as fast as I could without getting pulled over.

The road to the abandoned farm narrowed into an overgrown dirt path, trees pressing in on either side. The property was in worse shape than I remembered when I'd gone there as a teen for parties. Thank goodness those days are behind me. If my grandmother hadn't gotten me into the youth group at church, I might've taken a very wrong path.

The barn roof had caved in, the house's windows were shattered, and weeds had reclaimed what was once a front yard. But there was no sign of a hog trailer or any other trailer.

We climbed from the truck, and I scanned the area. The place felt wrong. The kind of wrong that made the hairs on the back of my neck stand up.

I took a step toward the ramshackle barn when a gunshot shattered the stillness. *Dear Lord, protect us* was my thought before Caleb tackled me to the ground. The impact knocked the wind, and the prayer, out of me. I barely registered the weight of his body shielding me as another shot rang out.

"Stay down!" he ordered.

Rosie dashed back to the truck and dove inside.

I twisted my head, trying to spot the shooter, but the tree line was too dense. Whoever was shooting at us had good cover. We'd walked into a trap. "Who's shooting at us?"

"Don't know, don't care at the moment," Caleb growled. "We're leaving. Now."

Another shot kicked up dirt inches from us.

Caleb hauled me to my feet and dragged me back to the truck. He shoved me inside, slammed the door, then ran around and jumped into the driver's seat. He floored the gas pedal, flinging gravel as we sped off.

We sat in silence, except for the rough sound of Caleb's breathing. He kept a white-knuckled grip on the steering wheel. I thought I could hear his teeth grinding.

Finally, he shot me a sharp side look. "You wanna tell me what you were thinking?"

I stiffened. "Excuse me?"

"Running off to an abandoned farm in the middle of nowhere. You could've gotten one of us killed."

"I didn't know someone was going to shoot at us!" I glared. "I was following a lead."

"You aren't a detective, Shelby. Would you have gone even if you were aware it could be dangerous?"

I didn't answer, because I couldn't honestly say I wouldn't have. I'd have done almost anything to get Big Red back.

His voice dropped, quieter but no less intense. "You have to stop putting yourself in danger."

I hitched my chin. "I can handle myself."

"No." He shook his head. "You aren't invincible, Shelby."

Rosie shifted in her seat. "Well." She forced a laugh. "At least we got out in one piece, thank the Lord."

Caleb glanced in the rearview mirror. "You're as bad as Shelby. Do me a favor, okay? Pray before you make a rash decision to run off following a lead."

I stared out the window, my heart still pounding. Had someone lured us into a trap?

CHAPTER SEVEN

What's this?" Luke picked up the scrap of flannel I'd found the night I discovered Red missing.

"Rosie found that snagged on the pen railing." I handed him a cup of coffee. "Any idea who it belongs to?"

His face scrunched in concentration. "Seems like I've seen it before." His attention focused on me. "Why are you scratched up?"

"Oh, we went to that abandoned farm past Route 7 and someone shot at us. Caleb tackled me."

"That place?" He dropped the fabric back on the counter. "I saw lights out there a couple of nights ago and went to investigate. No one is supposed to be there. I saw a man wearing a shirt that could match this. I didn't see his face. He had his hat pulled too low and it was dusk."

My fingers tightened around the handle of my mug so tight I thought it would snap off. "You're sure? We went out there because I was told a trailer with my hog in it was seen."

"Yep." He nodded. "The man, I'm positive it was a man, carried a sack of feed from that rundown barn to an old truck. Looked like he was in a hurry too."

"Why would someone store feed at a property that hasn't had livestock in years?" I sat at the table. "I sure wish you could've seen his face."

"It could be some drifter, I guess. Maybe it wasn't a feed sack but a bedroll. Either way, make sure you keep your doors locked at night."

I swallowed hard, the coffee souring in my stomach. What if we'd run from that property when there might be a clue in the barn? Some sign that Big Red had been there? I needed to go back, but to do so could be suicide. Even Rosie would do her best to stop me from going. There had to be another way to find out whether my hog had been there.

"Will you go there with me?" I put my best pleading look on.

He frowned. "And get shot at? No thanks."

"This time they wouldn't be expecting us."

He exhaled heavily. "Okay, but let's make it quick. If I get killed, I'm going to haunt you."

"Deal." I jumped to my feet, called for Mutt to follow, and sprinted to my truck. No one could sneak up on us with my dog keeping watch.

Luke grumbled the whole way but stayed by my side when I stopped the truck and headed for the barn. "I'll go first." He squeezed between the door hanging from rusty hinges and the splintered door frame.

After a quick look around, I followed. The barn had so many woodpecker holes in the walls, my eyes didn't need to adjust to the dim light. Only two stalls still had walls and doors. I headed for the closest one. Nothing. Not even moldy hay.

The second stall had relatively fresh hay and a shiny chain attached to a hook. Nearby lay a pile of a few-days-old pig manure. I just knew Big Red had been here.

"Found some hog feed!" Luke called from the back of the barn. "I think we have enough information to light a fire under the sheriff."

I doubted it, but it didn't hurt to try. "Come on." We needed to leave before whoever left the feed returned.

As I drove down Main Street after dropping Luke off at the farm with Mutt, I spotted Mayor Simmons entering the diner. Since the last time he'd been there I'd caught an interesting snippet of conversation, I decided to have an early lunch.

Rosie rushed to meet me. "What are you doing?"

"Snooping." I jerked my head to where the mayor sat. "Can you get me closer without him seeing me?"

"Yes." She led me the long way around the room then pointed to the booth next to his. "Hide behind the menu." She shoved one at me. "Carl Brunner is heading this way." She raised her voice. "I'll be back in a few minutes to take your order, ma'am."

I hid a grin behind the menu. I started to feel a lot like Nancy Drew with Rosie in the role of Bess. I couldn't wait to tell her about what Luke and I had found in the barn.

Brunner flopped down across from the mayor, causing the seat to shudder and me to lift my menu to hide all but my eyes. "What's so important that I had to come now?"

"Shelby Dickins is this close to finding out something she shouldn't." Simmons held his fingers an inch apart. "Shooting at her doesn't seem to have frightened her off."

"I tried to scare her enough to stop nosing around, but I'm not sure I succeeded. We may have to get more drastic."

"No one needs to die, Brunner."

"She asks too many questions," the butcher hissed. The clanking of a spoon against porcelain punctuated his statement. "If she finds out what we're up to, we'll be ruined."

"Then pick up the pace on running the farm owners off their land."

Brunner snorted. "I thought you had control over this town." His voice turned smooth, dangerous. "If the girl doesn't back off, take the hint, we'll have to. . .persuade her."

I clapped a hand over my mouth to muffle my gasp. They were after my land—and property belonging to other farmers in town.

"I don't want this getting messy," the mayor said.

"Too late for that, Mayor." The booth shifted again as Brunner stood. Without a glance to where I sat, he marched from the diner.

How was I going to leave without the mayor seeing me? Feeling foolish, I hunched low, slid from the booth, and took the long way around the diner again and ducked into the small hallway where the restrooms were. From there, I shoved open the side door and stepped outside.

It was Brunner who had shot at us. The sheriff would have to do something now. I marched to my truck and sped to his office.

"I need to see Sheriff Lincoln, please." I slapped my hands on the receptionist counter. "It's important."

"It always is." Renee frowned and picked up her phone. "Shelby Dickins here to see you, sir. Says it's important." She listened for a moment and then hung up. "He said he can give you five minutes."

"That's all I need." I stormed into his office and crossed my arms. "I overheard the mayor and Brunner plotting to harm me. Brunner shot at me yesterday. Rosie and Caleb Thornton were with me and can verify that what I'm saying is true. Also, I found evidence at the old Foster farm that a hog had been held there recently. That's also where I was shot at."

His chair squeaked as he leaned back. "Pretty sure there are No Trespassing signs posted on that property. Also pretty sure they say trespassers will be shot."

My mouth dropped open. "That's legal? Besides, I didn't see a single sign. If there used to be some, they've been removed. Aren't you going to do something? Bring them in for questioning?"

"Did they specifically say your name?"

"Yes. Shelby Dickins, to be exact. Since I'm the only one with that name around here, it has to be me they were talking about."

"I'm sure the two men are only frustrated because of your meddling, but yes, Shelby, they'll be brought in for questioning. This is a serious allegation." He folded his hands on his desk. "Anything else?"

"What about my hog?"

"My deputies and I are keeping an eye out. He'll turn up. Good day, Shelby."

I backed from his office. That was it? No assurance of sending a patrol car by to check on me? To make sure I was safe? Was the sheriff involved in whatever Simmons and Brunner were messed up in? I needed to alert my neighbors that someone wanted their land.

With nothing else to keep me in town, I headed home to finish the jobs I needed to do. I didn't leave everything to Luke. With hogs, chickens, a couple of horses. . .there was always work to do.

When the sun began to set, I carried a glass of sweet tea to the porch as was my nightly routine as long as the weather permitted. I'd just sat down when Caleb's truck pulled into the drive. I went inside to fetch another glass.

"Thanks." He smiled when I handed him the drink.

I motioned for him to sit. "What's up?"

For a long moment he sat there and stared at me without speaking. "Something is bothering you. What is it?"

I told him of the conversation I'd overheard. "It rattles a person to hear that someone is out to get them."

He reached over and took my hand.

"What are you doing, Caleb?" I shifted in my seat to see him better in the growing dusk. "I never expected to see you again, and now here you are, stopping by every day."

"I know." His shoulders slumped.

Silence stretched between us, heavy with things unsaid. Finally, he spoke again. "I shouldn't have left like that, Shelby. I did the easy thing for me, but. . ." He shook his head. "I was very wrong."

I let out a short, bitter laugh. "Yeah, you were." The hurt in my gut was like a punch.

"I never stopped thinking about you."

I stiffened, wishing I could say I hadn't thought about him. But I had. A lot.

"Not a single day has gone by where I don't wonder what would've happened if I hadn't left like that."

Tears stung my eyes. "You don't get to just come back and say that, Caleb."

"I know. I don't expect you to forgive me overnight, but I need you to know that it was the biggest mistake I ever made."

I swallowed past the lump in my throat and stared into my glass of tea. "I don't know if I can do this again."

"Let me prove to you that I won't make the same mistake twice," he said softly.

"Is this why you're helping me find my hog?" I searched his face in the dark.

"Partly. I also couldn't go on if something happened to you. I'm here because I care and want to keep you safe."

I slipped my hand from his. "I can take care of myself. I have for years." My hand trembled as I lifted the glass to my lips.

"Shelby?" Caleb stood and set his glass on the small table.

I followed his gaze to see something big lumber toward the hogpen. "Big Red!" I leaped from the porch and ran to wrap my arms around the pig's neck. The remnants of a rope rubbed my wrist. "Looks like you chewed through this." I could barely see through my tears. "Come on, boy. Let's get you into the light."

Caleb followed us to the barn where he gave Red a quick checkup. "He seems fine, other than a bit smaller than I thought."

"I've got time to fatten him up before the competition." I tilted my head. "He couldn't have been held far from here, Caleb. Not if he was able to find his way home so easily."

"Where could he have been held within walking distance?"

I scrunched my mouth as I thought. "The old house where my grandparents lived while building this one. It's a small log cabin, one room, used for storage now." I locked Red in the barn, called for Mutt, and raced for the edge of the property.

Soon I was staring at a chewed rope next to a bed of straw in the middle of antique furniture and boxes. Stealing Big Red had been a tactic to make me want to give up and sell out.

It wouldn't work. It would take a lot more than that to run me off.

I turned to Caleb. "Let's bring down Simmons and Brunner."

CHAPTER EIGHT

The next morning, after making sure Big Red was being closely watched by Luke, I gripped the steering wheel of my truck as I drove down the winding dirt road leading to my neighbor's farm. Dust kicked up behind me. I reached over and patted Mutt. "Folks might not like to hear what I'm going to tell them, buddy, but they deserve to know the truth."

My first stop was the Jennings farm where Old Man Jennings sat on his porch, a shotgun resting across his lap like an old friend. His eyes were sharp beneath the brim of his hat as he watched me approach.

"I figured someone would come round sooner or later," he said before I finished telling him about the mayor and Brunner. He gestured toward a scorched patch of grass near his pasture. "That there was no accident. Ain't been real dry, but somehow my field caught fire. Way out here. Imagine that."

I frowned. "You think someone did it on purpose?"

He let out a bitter chuckle. "I don't think. I know. Same as you knew someone stole your pig."

"What are you going to do?"

"Sit here and fill them with buckshot if they show their faces. I ain't selling out, I can tell you that."

"Neither am I. If we all keep an eye out for each other, we'll get through this."

"I reckon we will. Where you headed next?"

"Ella McBride's place."

"Give a holler before getting out of your truck. She's a bit skittish."

"Thanks." When I parked in front of Ella's one-story ranch house, I honked the horn, called out my name, then climbed out of the truck.

I found Ella in the barn rolling up a length of barbed wire. She glanced up and brushed sweat off her forehead with the back of her arm. A rifle rested against a stall. "Howdy, Shelby."

"Ella." I leaned my folded arms across the top of the stall door. "I found Big Red."

"That's good."

"Supposedly, someone had him out past Route 7, then stashed him in my grandparents' old cabin."

"You don't say." She set the wire aside and wiped her hands on her denim-clad thighs.

"Yep. Also overheard the mayor and Carl Brunner talking about taking over the properties around here."

Her face darkened. "I'd like to see them try."

"Old Man Jennings said someone set fire to his pastureland. Anything strange happening around here?"

"Yep," she said, her voice tight. "Last week someone slashed my tires. That same night, a few of my cows went missing." She squared her shoulders. "It ain't no coincidence. If you see the mayor again, you tell him I ain't gonna be run off my land."

Why hadn't I heard about the fire or the missing cows? Had I been so wrapped up in my own problems I wasn't paying attention to others'? Guilt flooded through me.

By the time I visited the last farm, the pattern was clear. Families had been experiencing thefts, property damage, even financial pressure with bank loans suddenly getting denied. Mysterious buyers offered to pay off debts in exchange for land. The mayor wasn't only trying to take my home, he was running an entire operation, trying to force people out one by one.

This wasn't just about me anymore. It was about the town of Oakwood.

My stomach growled as I pulled up to my ranch, reminding me I hadn't eaten since breakfast. Caleb leaned against my porch railing like he belonged there. The moment I stepped out of my truck, his sharp gaze swept over me, taking me in like he was assessing whether I was all right.

"Let me guess." I closed my truck door with a little more force than necessary. "You're here to remind me that what I'm doing is dangerous."

He nodded, his expression serious. "Yeah, and to tell you that you shouldn't be doing this alone. Word is getting around about you asking questions. I'm worried."

"You have a job. I have a job." I crossed my arms. "I can also take care of myself."

He exhaled sharply, running a hand over his jaw. "I know you can, but that doesn't mean you should."

Something unspoken stretched between us, something heavier than concern over the case. His fingers curled around the railing. "I'm not letting anything happen to you." He pushed away. "I brought steaks. Hope you're hungry." He marched into my house without waiting on me.

"Come on, Mutt." Hungry or not, the livestock ate first. I fed Big Red, more grateful than I could say that he came home, then fed the sows. As they snuffled and snorted, I thanked God for my pig's return and prayed for safety while I tried to prove what the mayor and Brunner were up to. "And Lord, give me patience and wisdom where Caleb is concerned." I didn't want my heart broken again.

The sound of tires on gravel pulled my attention to the road. Sheriff Lincoln and Mayor Simmons exited the sheriff's car and came my way.

Within seconds, Caleb came out of the house and stood by my side.

"What can I do for you, Sheriff?" I did my best to look nonchalant despite my heart threatening to beat through my throat.

"Well, Shelby, here's the thing." The sheriff crossed his arms across his paunch. "It has come to Mayor Simmons' attention that you are accusing him and Carl Brunner of unscrupulous deeds."

"If shooting at me fits that description, then yes."

"Why would you think that, Miss Dickins?" The mayor looked shocked.

"You really should hold your meetings in private, Mayor. I'm sure I'm not the only one who heard you and Carl conspiring at the diner."

Something flickered on his face that had me taking a step closer to Caleb. Caleb rested his arm lightly on my shoulders. "Anything else, gentlemen?"

The sheriff cleared his throat. "Have you been harassing the neighbors over this silly quest to prove Carl Brunner stole your pig? Which I've heard has returned home as I said it would."

"I've only been warning the other farmers that someone is after their land. Since you've heard so much, I'm sure you're also aware of the trouble each farm has had."

"Yes, and we are looking into those complaints. It is not your job, Shelby. Stick to hog farming and leave the crime investigation to me." The sheriff spun and marched back to his car followed by the mayor.

Before getting into the vehicle, the mayor gave a cool smile over the hood of the car. A smile that reminded me of a shark's grin and looked every bit as deadly.

"Steaks are done." Caleb's arm dropped.

"Let me get cleaned up." I headed for the bathroom and washed the grime of chores off my face and hands.

By the time I returned to the kitchen, a steak, a baked potato, and a salad waited for me. "This looks great, thanks." I sat down and stared across the table. "What's the occasion, Caleb?"

"I thought we were starting fresh in getting to know each other."

I really did not want to start that conversation. I cut into my steak. "Do you think the sheriff is in cahoots with Simmons and Brunner?"

A shadow crossed his eyes. "Maybe he's simply digging for enough evidence to make an arrest."

"He did tell me he would bring them in for questioning, and it's my word against theirs. Next time, I'll record any conversations I overhear between him and Simmons."

Caleb dropped his fork with a clatter. "You've got Big Red back. You don't plan on selling out. Can't you let it go until the sheriff finds the evidence he needs?"

"I don't believe Sheriff Lincoln is competent enough." The steak was cooked medium rare, just the way I liked it. "This is good."

"Thanks." He picked up his fork. "Since you aren't going to let this go, what's the next step?"

I grinned. "Back to helping me?"

"Seems I don't have any other choice." His eyes twinkled.

A flash of lightning, then a boom of thunder signaled an approaching storm. "I wasn't aware we were going to get rain."

"Yep." Caleb reached for his tea. "Gonna pour for at least an hour."

"Great! I love storms." We ate quickly and did the dishes, me washing and Caleb drying.

Thankfully, he didn't bring up the topic of us again. Instead, he asked questions about the town residents and how much Oakwood had changed—or rather, how little it had changed in ten years.

I scooped a handful of suds into my palm and blew them at him.

"You're asking for it, Shelby." He wiped his face right before I blew some more.

He scooped up suds and placed them on my head. "Cute hat."

"My hair!"

He laughed and popped me with the dish towel. "Why don't you go sit on the porch. I'll bring out some tea and we'll watch the storm roll in."

"Sounds great." I hurried outside as another flash of lightning rippled across the sky.

Caleb joined me and handed me a glass of tea before sitting next to me. After several minutes of silence, I turned to him. "Why are you so quiet?"

"Just listening." He lifted his glass to his lips.

"To what?"

"The only thing worth listening to. You."

Wow. I didn't know what to say, so I chose not to say anything.

Luke waved on his way to his apartment, reaching his door before the first raindrops fell.

"I thought about leaving Oakwood once," I said softly.

"Why didn't you?"

I shrugged. "My parents died, leaving me the farm, and Big Red was born. . .too many things to keep me here. I can't imagine leaving now. This is home."

"I don't regret leaving, Shelby, only the way that I left you. I've always wanted to be a veterinarian. I couldn't stay here and get my schooling."

"How does it feel to be back?" I held my breath, waiting for his answer.

"Like I've come home." He reached over and cupped my cheek.

I leaned into his touch and closed my eyes, realizing for the first time how lonely I'd been working the farm alone. But was I ready to forgive him? My eyes popped open. I wasn't sure.

Caleb leaned toward me as if he planned on kissing me. I closed my eyes in preparation.

The window behind me shattered.

Mutt yelped and hid under the table.

Caleb shoved me to the porch floor and, once again, shielded my body with his. "Stay down. Someone is shooting at us."

"Shelby!" Luke leaned out his window. "You all right?"

"Good. Stay inside." I crawled to my front door.

Caleb grabbed my foot. "What are you doing?"

"Getting my gun." Once inside, I reached into the coat closet and pulled out my .243. By now, Caleb and Mutt had joined me. I peered through the hole in my shutter, ignoring the crunch of glass under my feet.

"See anything?" Caleb asked.

"No. It's too dark." The lightning and thunder had moved on, leaving behind heavy clouds and rain. I didn't think I'd see anyone unless they stepped onto the porch. I doubted that would happen.

"I don't want you staying here alone, Shelby."

"I'm not alone. Luke and Mutt are here."

He stretched out on the sofa and crossed his arms behind his head. "I'm camping out here. If anyone wants to get to you, they have to go through me first."

God, give me strength. And remember that patience and wisdom I prayed for? Send that quick.

CHAPTER NINE

The next morning, I woke to find Caleb already gone and a note saying he'd been called out on an emergency. Good. I still wasn't sure how I felt about him crashing on my sofa, and the early morning hour wasn't a time to dwell on such things. Especially not before coffee.

I stared out the kitchen window. My yard was little more than a marsh with standing water and mud. Doing chores wouldn't be easy this morning.

After sliding my feet into knee-high rubber boots, I stepped onto the front porch and took a deep breath of fresh, crisp, early autumn air. Mutt woofed behind me. I turned to see another sheet of paper tacked to my door.

With trembling hands, I pulled the paper free. The first note had been ominous. This one was bolder and more threatening. Humidity left the paper damp, smearing the ink—but the message was clear. I read it out loud. "Sell before it's too late."

The words were scrawled in jagged handwriting, pressed hard enough to nearly tear the page. A chill ran down my spine. Whoever left this clearly wanted me to feel cornered. It wouldn't work.

This property had been in my family for generations, and no one would bully me into giving it up. I gripped the note in my fist. I needed a plan to get a confession out of Simmons or Brunner or both of them. If I confronted them and they thought I had no way of getting free, they might tell me everything. This time, I'd be smart enough to tape the conversation and leave my phone where it could be found if something happened to me.

The property on Route 7 was the perfect place to meet. All I needed to do was get the word out, and the diner was the perfect place for that to happen.

I quickly did my chores, changed my shoes, and dashed to my truck as rain started to fall. At this rate, I'd need a boat to get around my property.

At the diner, I stepped inside, caught Rosie's attention, and jerked my head toward the restroom. She nodded and held up a finger to let me know it would be a minute. Strolling as casually as possible so as to not attract attention, I entered the ladies' room.

Rosie joined me five minutes later. "Sorry. I had to wait until my break. I've got fifteen minutes. What's up?"

I showed her the note. "We need a plan to catch them."

Her eyes widened. "What kind of plan? This is already so dangerous, Shelby."

"It won't end without a taped confession." I refused to be deterred. "Either help me or I do it alone."

She released a heavy sigh. "What do you want me to do?"

"Start spreading the word that I'm thinking about selling."

She shook her head. "No one will believe it."

True. I scrunched my lips. "Okay, how about that I'm willing to pay for information about who's harassing the farmers? I can pay out of my winnings if Big Red comes in first. Say that I'll pay one thousand dollars for information and for anyone with said information to text me."

She narrowed her eyes. "A thousand dollars for every person who texts you? How much are the winnings?"

"It's a small competition. Only ten thousand dollars, and no, not everyone who texts me gets money. Only credible information that can be proven." I smiled. This plan would work. I knew it would.

She crossed her arms. "And how am I supposed to spread this news without being obvious?"

"Just gossip with the other servers a little too loudly so someone else hears. The word will spread quick enough." Oakwood was a regular gossip mill.

"Fine. I don't like it, but I'll do it." She glanced at her watch. "I've got to get back. Are you wanting breakfast?"

"Sure." I followed her from the restroom and headed to an empty table.

Carl Brunner came down the short hallway a few minutes after I sat. He carried a wrapped parcel of meat. Shooting me a glare, he pushed through the swinging doors to the kitchen. I couldn't help but wonder whether the meat he delivered came from the poor animal butchered in the old barn at the Foster farm. Thank goodness it wasn't Big Red.

I ordered biscuits and chocolate gravy then sat back and watched as Rosie flitted from one server to the next. Several gazes settled my way. I ducked my head to hide a grin. Word would indeed spread as fast as a wildfire during a drought.

Carl exited the kitchen and paused, glancing at Rosie. Catching him staring, she jerked, then headed in the opposite direction. He shot me another glare and left the diner. My plan might be working faster than I thought if he'd overheard something.

Once my order was delivered, I ate quickly, paid my tab, and rushed home. Rain continued to fall.

Luke met me as I pulled up and handed me a rain poncho. "Someone cut the hogpen fence."

I frowned. It couldn't have been Brunner. He'd been at the diner the same time I was. The fence had been intact when I'd fed the animals that morning. "Let me put my boots on." I sloshed into the house. When I joined Luke at the pen, I asked, "Where were you and Mutt?"

"I'm guessing we were in the barn." He stretched a length of fencing, then held it while I hammered in a rebar. "Big Red tore a hole in his stall, and I was busy fixing it. I think he wants back out here with his girls."

"It's not safe for him out here." Not until after the competition anyway.

We repaired the fence, and I went to change into dry clothes while Luke did the same. I made coffee and headed to my office to do some work on the farm finances. Not my favorite job, but someone has to do them.

I lost track of time but thought maybe an hour or so had passed before Mutt's bark startled me away from the ledger in front of me. "What is it, boy?"

He dashed for the front door.

I followed. My heart stopped as I caught a glow through the window. The barn was on fire, and Big Red was inside. I slipped my feet into my boots, grabbed the rain poncho I'd hung on the front porch, and took off at a run.

Halfway to the barn, my boot caught on something. A second later, I found myself face down in the muck, my mouth filled with gritty mud. I lay there, stunned, waiting to be able to breathe again.

My jeans clung to my skin as I pushed myself up on shaking arms. I stood and tried to take a step. The mud sucked at my boot, refusing to relinquish me. Frustration surged through me. I didn't have time for this!

I pulled my feet from the boots and grimaced as my stocking feet sank into the cold muck. Mutt, able to move quicker than me, barked and pawed at the barn door. I quickened my pace the best I could, wishing for the rain that had left my yard in such a state as flames licked the far wall.

As I reached the door, Red's frantic squeals sent my heart into overdrive. "Get Luke, Mutt. Go on!"

He took off like a shot toward the garage apartment.

Without hesitation, I yanked the barn door open and rushed into the barn. Heat instantly stung my skin. Smoke burned my eyes, but I forced myself forward, keeping low. Big Red's stall was in the back, close to where the fire was spreading the fastest.

My vision blurred as I fumbled with the latch. It was jammed.

Coughing violently, I grabbed a nearby tarp and wrapped it around my hand, using it to shield myself as I wrestled with the latch. It finally gave way with a loud creak, and Red burst out, almost knocking me over in his panic.

I stumbled back, guiding him toward the exit as a beam crashed to the ground, sending embers flying. The heat was unbearable now, pressing against me like a living thing intent on devouring me.

I barely made it out before the barn groaned under its own weight and collapsed in a fiery explosion of wood and ash. I fell to my knees, coughing, my lungs screaming for air. Big Red butted me with his head, snuffling in my ear.

Moving to a sitting position, I watched as the flames consumed my barn. This was no accident. There was no way a fire could have started without help.

"You okay?" Luke crouched next to me.

"You said you fixed the stall." I glared up at him. "The latch was stuck. I almost didn't get Big Red out." I pushed to my feet, not caring that there was another layer of mud on my jeans and hands. "What took you so long to get out here?"

"I was in the shower." His brow furrowed. "I didn't hear Mutt until I got out. I got dressed as fast as I could."

"Seems suspicious to me." I marched toward the house and the water hose.

"What are you saying, Shelby?"

I turned on the faucet. "Call the fire department."

"No, you're accusing me of something. Say it."

I whirled, almost spraying him in the process. "Sounds suspicious, is what I said."

"I cannot believe that you would think such a thing about me." Pain clouded his face. "Why didn't I let Red chew his way out of the barn and take off? Why bother fixing the sow pen if I wanted to run you out of business?"

I aimed the hose on the smoldering remains of my barn. "It doesn't matter. What's important is that I got Red out safely."

"If you think I could do this, then fire me. Right now."

I stared at him. "I'm sorry. I'm. . .upset." Scared, frustrated, and a whole lot of other things. "Please call the fire department."

"I already did." Caleb came up behind me and took the hose from my hands. "I wasn't going to leave you alone tonight either. I'm sorry I wasn't here sooner, but a horse was having a difficult time birthing her foal." He handed the hose to Luke and wrapped me in his arms. "What happened?"

"I don't have proof, but I think someone set the barn on fire to get rid of Red and/or me." I sniffed against his shirt. "They almost succeeded."

"Let's get you warm and dry." He led me to the house as sirens wailed in the distance.

"I need to be here for the fire truck."

"Luke can handle things out here." Inside, he gave me a gentle push toward the bathroom. "I'll make some coffee."

With a nod, I headed for the shower. As the water streamed over me, I let the tears fall. Maybe I wasn't cut out to face men like Simmons and Brunner. Maybe I should step back and get out of the competition. If I did, they might leave my farm alone.

No, it was the land they really wanted. Why? There was plenty of farmland in the state for purchase. Why bother us in Oakwood? I shrugged and turned off the water. Convenience, I supposed.

I also owed Luke an apology. Of course he didn't set the fire. He loved my animals as much as I did.

Clean and dry, I joined Caleb in the kitchen. The mug of hot coffee warmed my hands as I sat at the table.

"You sure you're okay?" He sat across from me, a worried gaze locked on me.

"I'm fine. Where's Red?"

"I put him in the garage with some feed."

"Thank you."

"I heard about the rumor going around town."

I jerked upright. "Brunner was at the diner when Rosie was talking about it. He must be the one who set the fire. He's the one who shot at us. He failed to scare me off then so tried again tonight."

I shuddered, realizing how close I'd come to death. These men needed to be stopped—and it was up to me to stop them.

CHAPTER TEN

I've got a date with Dave Helton tonight," Rosie said. "Want to go with me to buy something to wear? I've been wanting to go into that new boutique in town."

I cradled my cell phone between my ear and my shoulder as I shoveled manure from the hogpen into a wheelbarrow. "Give me two hours to finish up here and shower."

"Great. See you then!" Rosie hung up.

My phone slipped, and I grabbed it with my dirty gloved hand before it landed in the muck. Grimacing, I wiped it off on my jeans and slipped it into my pocket. Excitement for an afternoon of shopping with my bestie filled me. It had been a long time since I'd shopped for something other than necessities.

I shot a sad look to where my barn had stood, now nothing more than ash and charred lumber. Someone would pay dearly for setting it on fire. I jabbed the shovel into the ground and sloshed my way across my sodden yard to the house.

When I arrived at the Main Street Boutique, Rosie waited on a bench out front. She jumped to her feet as I parked behind her car. "I saw the cutest dress in the window."

I opened the door to let her go in first. "Before you tell me about it, I have to tell you that someone set my barn on fire last night."

"What?" She gasped.

"Yep, but we're all fine. Now tell me where the two of you are going on your date."

"Okay. If you're sure you're okay."

"I am."

"We're going to a nice Italian restaurant in Birdwell. I looked it up online and saw photos of diners. Some of the women wore dresses." She grinned. "It'll be nice to wear a dress that isn't my work uniform."

"You wear dresses to church all the time."

"This is different."

I shrugged, not seeing the difference at all. Spotting some cute jeans with pearls down the sides of the legs, I left Rosie to search for her size in the cranberry-colored dress she'd spotted.

"Psst."

I glanced around for the source of the sound.

"Psst. Shelby."

I bent to see Rosie hiding in the rack of sweaters behind me. "What are you doing?"

She pointed toward the window. "Go look."

"What? Why are you whispering and hiding?"

"Go. Look."

I shrugged and went to the window. Mayor Simmons and Carl Brunner stood on the street. The mayor glanced left and right, then gripped Brunner's arm and dragged him into an alley.

"Come on. We have to follow them." I dashed out the boutique door. "Get out your cell phone."

"I left it at home." She panted behind me.

I slipped mine from my pocket and handed it to her.

"Yuck. What is on this?"

"Manure. Shhh. We don't want to be seen or heard."

"This is hog poo?"

I turned and grinned into her shocked face. "It's organic. You like organic."

"I'm not using this." She thrust it back at me. The phone dropped to the sidewalk and cracked. No matter how hard I pushed the camera button, the screen remained black.

Great. "Guess we aren't taking photos or recording a conversation now." Shaking my head, I shoved the damaged phone back into my pocket and peered around the corner of the alley. The two men stood too far away for us to hear what they were saying. We needed to get closer.

I pointed at the dumpster about twenty feet away.

Rosie shook her head.

I rolled my eyes and sprinted for the dumpster. Once there, I waved for her to come over.

She shook her head again and stayed where she was. Fine. She could go get help if I got in trouble.

I still wasn't close enough but managed to catch some phrases such as "Foster barn" and "no witnesses." Then something about the plan falling apart. Brunner said it was time to cut their losses.

"No." The mayor's answer reached me loud and clear. "I've worked too hard. I'm not stopping until it's finished."

Brunner mumbled something else.

Oh, I wished I had a way of recording them. That would give me the evidence needed to convince the sheriff these two men were up to no good.

I shifted, inadvertently kicking aside an aluminum can.

The men stopped talking and scanned the alley. I held my breath and shrank back, making myself as small as possible as they slowly approached the dumpster. Rosie, bless her, made a clatter outside the alley, drawing the men in that direction and giving me the opportunity to sprint down the alley and out the other end.

I met up with Rosie at the boutique. "Quick thinking back there."

"Thanks. Can I get my dress now?" She tilted her head.

"Yes, and I'm buying a pair of jeans."

When we finished at the boutique, we headed to a local burger joint for lunch. I'd suggested the diner, but Rosie said she had enough of it at work. We ordered and chose a table outside, something we wouldn't be able to do in a few weeks when winter arrived.

"Is Big Red ready for the competition?"

"He's gaining weight like a champ." I leaned my elbows on the table. "I think the fire last night was set deliberately."

"I'm so sorry. Insurance will cover it though, right?"

"Yes, but not for a while. Red is in my garage for now."

She lowered her voice and leaned forward. "Do you think Brunner did it?"

"Yes, and I don't think our plan worked. I haven't received a single text."

"It was a good idea anyway." Her eyes widened at something behind me.

I glanced over my shoulder to see Carl Brunner walking past the burger shop only a few feet away. From the stormy look on his face as he glared our way, I felt certain he'd heard at least part of our conversation.

"Good afternoon, Carl." I smiled.

He marched past without saying a word.

Later that evening, Chinese takeout in hand, Caleb arrived as he'd done the last few nights. "How was your day?" His smile faded as I told him about eavesdropping on the mayor and the butcher.

A muscle ticked in his jaw as he opened the boxes of food. "I really wish you would let the sheriff handle this."

"I don't think we can trust the sheriff." I scooped some spicy chicken and rice onto a plate.

"On what grounds?"

"On the fact he did nothing to find Red and didn't believe me when I told him it was Brunner that shot at us. Any ethical law enforcement officer would at least consider that I might be right and keep an eye on me for my safety."

He chose chow mein over rice. "This is too dangerous, Shelby."

"Yes it is, but the mayor has to be stopped. This town needs to know what kind of man he is. Who they voted for. Why don't you run for sheriff?" Oakwood could use a man like Caleb looking over its citizens.

"Don't change the subject." He pushed his food around on his plate.

My phone buzzed in my pocket, startling me. I couldn't read the text through the crack on the screen, so I pushed the buttons until I hit the one to have the text read to me. A computerized voice said, "If you want to know what they're up to, be at the Foster barn tonight. Come alone, or you'll regret it."

A chill slithered down my spine. That message did not sound like someone with information. It sounded like a trap.

"You are not going." Caleb's gaze bored into mine.

"You can't tell me what I can and cannot do, Caleb. This might be my best chance to uncover the truth of what's going on."

"You must have a death wish." His eyes flashed.

"No, but I have no intention of going alone. I'll have Dave Helton come after his date with Rosie. He can stay out of sight and step in if things go bad."

"When they go bad. Not if." He crossed his arms. "He's on a date with Rosie?"

I nodded. "She's liked him since high school, but he didn't date nice girls back then."

"What happened to your phone?"

"Rosie dropped it because it had manure on it." Which reminded me that I was using the phone while I ate. Gross. I got up and set it next to the sink so I could wash my hands.

While I did, I searched the yard outside the window, half expecting to see an intruder up to no good. The only things left to destroy of any importance were the house and garage. *Spare me, Lord.*

Not seeing anything, I rejoined Caleb at the table. He stared at his plate of food, then gave a long exhale. "Fine. I'll be going with you tonight. What time?"

"The text said to go alone. I thought I'd take Mutt."

"I'll stay out of sight like Dave, but you are not going with only a dog to protect you."

I started to remind him that he couldn't give me orders, before realizing his surly attitude came from fear and a desire to keep me safe. I reached across the table and placed my hand over his. "Thank you."

"So, what's the plan?" He pulled his hand free and picked up his fork. "The message didn't say what time."

"We'll go right at dark. Get into place before anyone else shows up." I gave him Rosie's phone number. "Text her, please, and have her give the message to Dave. Tell him not to say anything to anyone, not even the sheriff."

"Do you think he'll not say anything?" Caleb typed into his phone.

"If Rosie asks him, then yes. I saw the way he looked at her when I reported Big Red missing that first day." If I was wrong, I'd still be facing the sheriff. Either way, I hoped to end the mayor's reign of terror tonight.

"I also want you to carry my phone so you have a way of communicating if you have to." He handed his phone to me.

"What about you?"

"I'll use my work phone." He dropped his napkin onto his plate and handed me a fortune cookie. "Maybe this will say that a change of plans tonight would be a good thing." He smiled.

"You'd like that." I laughed and opened my cookie. My laugh halted as I read, "Pushing forward with a decision could have disastrous results."

I thought Caleb would bust a rib laughing. "That's even better than I'd hoped for."

"Good thing I'm not superstitious." I tossed the slip of paper onto my plate. Stupid fortune cookie. "You can stop laughing now."

"Oh, I missed you, Shelby." He wiped tears from his eyes. "I forgot how much fun you are. Frustrating, but a lot of fun."

"Hush." I got to my feet and started clearing off the table, keeping my head down so he wouldn't see my smile. I had to admit to myself that I'd missed him too.

"I pulled up the Foster farm on Google maps." Caleb tapped my arm. "There's an old logging road that runs along the west end of the property. That's where I'll park my truck. It's far enough to be out of sight but close enough for me to come to your aid. I'll let Dave know that's where I'll be."

"What if the mayor comes that way instead of the main road?" I would if I knew about it and was showing up to confront the person determined to bring justice on my head.

"I'll make sure to pull off the road enough so I can't be easily seen." He gave my hand a gentle squeeze. "I've got you, Shelby. I promise not to let anything happen to you."

I prayed that was a promise he could keep.

CHAPTER ELEVEN

Be careful." Caleb stopped me as I reached for the truck's door handle. The look in his eyes, the way his gaze landed on my lips, told me he wanted to kiss me. I wanted him to.

Instead, I leaned over and planted a tender kiss on his cheek. "I will be." Before I did anything rash, I bolted from the truck and called for Mutt to follow.

The dog's presence at my side dispelled some of the fear as I made my way through an overgrown field toward the shadow of the barn in the distance. When I reached the edge of the slightly less overgrown area surrounding the barn, I stopped, looked, and listened. Since Mutt seemed more concerned with a mole hole than anything else, I suspected we were alone out there. For the time being.

The barn loomed before me, dark and silent, its wooden structure worn from years of exposure. Most of the time, I loved old barns. This one seemed malevolent, intent on harming me. I rubbed my arms as the cold night air pressed against me, my breath coming in small, visible puffs.

After an hour inside the chilly barn, I stomped my feet to warm them. There'd been nothing. No movement, no voices, no sign that my plan was working.

Doubt settled in my chest. Maybe this had been a mistake. What if they didn't show? Or worse, maybe they'd figured out what I knew and changed their plans.

I exhaled in frustration and snapped my fingers to get Mutt's attention away from the mouse he'd cornered. This was a complete waste of time.

I reached for the door handle. Mutt's ears stood at attention, his dark gaze on the door as the distant rumble of an engine broke through the stillness. I sent Caleb a quick text. "They're here."

Headlights flickered through the holes in the barn walls. I pressed my eye to one as a black sedan pulled up, its tires crunching on gravel. The doors opened in unison.

Mayor Simmons stepped out first. The glow from the car's interior lights cast a sharp outline of his face. Calm. He adjusted his coat, his gaze scanning the area before settling on the barn. He marched toward it, then entered.

I slipped my hand into my pocket and pressed the record button on the small device hidden there.

Carl Brunner followed, larger, more imposing. He shut the barn door behind him with a little too much force, cracking his knuckles as he stepped toward me.

My stomach twisted. I put a hand on Mutt's head to steady myself.

"I didn't think you'd have the guts to show up here alone." Simmons voice came as smooth as silk. "You're a brave girl, Shelby Dickins."

I hitched my chin up. "I suppose I should thank you for the compliment."

Brunner chuckled. "What are we doing here? You've snooped long enough, Shelby. So long that you've become a nuisance that needs to be gotten rid of. A pity really, but I'll definitely benefit from you being gone. You have no family. No one to inherit your farm. It'll go on auction fast enough."

"You'd like that, wouldn't you?" These two weren't expecting any trouble. They were relaxed, confident.

A sharp glint caught my eye. Metal in Brunner's hand. A gun.

Panic surged through me. "You're going to shoot me?"

"I've offered you ways out of this, Shelby," the mayor said. "You've refused to see reason. Don't despair. Your beloved hogs will take care of your body easy enough."

I spun on my heel, trying to sprint away from them, but I wasn't fast enough. A rough hand clamped around my wrist, yanking me backward. I let out a strangled cry as I stumbled, my shoulder slamming against Brunner's chest.

"Not so fast." He tightened his grip.

Mutt growled and lunged.

Brunner brought up his gun hand. "Call off your dog, or I'll shoot him."

"Down, Mutt. Sit." I forced the command past my fear-clogged throat.

I fought to free myself, twisting and kicking, but Brunner was too strong. His arm locked around me like an iron bar. Panic shot through me, my heartbeat a wild, erratic drum in my ears.

Then, a blur of movement.

A sharp thud followed by a grunt of pain.

Brunner staggered, his grip loosening as Mutt latched on to the hand holding the gun.

I barely had time to register what was happening before a figure emerged from the shadows.

Caleb was a force of motion, his fists landing with brutal precision. Brunner reeled from a well-placed punch, stumbling back against the wall and dropping his gun. I leaped forward and snatched the weapon from the dirt as Caleb turned his attention to Simmons.

The mayor reacted fast, reaching inside his coat. Caleb was faster. He caught Simmons by the lapels of his coat and slammed him against the barn door with a loud crack. The man slid to the floor.

"You want to try that again?" Caleb growled, his voice low and dangerous.

Simmons struggled, his expression shifting from shock to fury. "You're making a mistake, Thornton." He tried to get up and failed.

"I don't think so."

Brunner recovered. His face twisted in rage as he lunged toward Caleb.

"Caleb, behind you!" I raised the gun but didn't shoot for fear of hitting Caleb.

He turned just in time, blocking Brunner's wild punch with his forearm. They grappled, fists flying. Brunner was bigger, stronger, but Caleb faster and more precise. A brutal right hook sent Brunner staggering again.

For a second, I thought we had the upper hand. Then Simmons moved.

His hand dipped into his coat again. This time he succeeded in pulling out a gun.

"Caleb!"

Before the shot could ring out, Caleb grabbed me, pulling me into his arms and twisting, shielding me with his body. His arms locked around me. The smell of leather and faint cologne filled my senses.

Headlights once again flared against the barn. Doors slammed. Feet pounded.

Dave's voice cut through the night. "Drop the weapon, Mayor."

The mayor froze, the light from the car catching on the gun in his hand.

Rosie entered the barn, a rifle in her arms. "Now." She aimed the gun at the mayor.

For a moment, things were at a standstill. The tension crackled like an electric current.

Simmons let the gun slip from his grasp. It fell with a thud onto the floor.

Brunner groaned, blood trickling from his split lip. Dave wasted no time slapping cuffs on him while Rosie kept the mayor from running. She glanced my way, looking wonderful in her new dress and heels, brandishing a rifle. "Now this is what I call a date."

Caleb let out a slow breath, loosening his hold on me. "You okay?"

I turned slightly. Our faces were close. Too close. My pulse hadn't slowed, but I wasn't sure if it was adrenaline or the warmth of Caleb's arms still around me.

"Yes." I cleared my throat.

His gaze searched mine for a moment, something unreadable flickering behind his eyes. Then, with a sigh, he released me and stepped back.

As Dave, with Rosie still holding her gun on the mayor, hauled the two men toward the cruiser, I finally allowed myself to exhale. It was over. "Come here, Mutt. What a good boy." I stooped to his level and wrapped my arms around his neck. "This was the perfect time to disobey me."

"Come on, Shelby." Caleb took my hand. "Let's go home."

He draped his coat around my shoulders.

"Now you'll be cold."

"I'm fine." He smiled, his gaze dropping to my lips again.

Was he going to kiss me now?

Dave cleared his throat behind us. "You two can come to the station in the morning to file your report. I think this night has been long enough."

"Sorry about interfering with your date with Rosie." I stepped away from Caleb.

"Don't be. She said she had a blast." He grinned and gave a salute. "I'd give y'all a ride to your truck, but my back seat is full. Good night."

"Good night." Caleb took my hand again and led me across the field. "I almost lost you tonight, Shelby. If I hadn't followed you. . . If I'd waited until I actually heard something dreadful, I might be standing over your body right now."

"Nope. Simmons planned on feeding me to my hogs." I shuddered.

"There's a thought."

"At least I'd be part of things I love." I stifled a laugh, feeling a bit giddy now that the danger was past.

"Are you sure you're all right?"

A giggle escaped me. "I think I might've been more frightened than I thought."

He opened the passenger-side door to his truck. He studied my face for a moment, then planted a kiss on my forehead. "You're amazing." He helped Mutt in beside me, closed the door, and headed for the driver's side.

We made the ride home in silence, each of us lost in our thoughts. As the adrenaline that had coursed through me faded, I realized just how much trouble I'd been in and that God had saved me from what could've been a horrible ending.

Not only had my life been in danger, but Caleb's too. My shoulders slumped. God's Word says He looks out for the foolish. Well, hello, here I am. Still, it was over, the mayor and Brunner would go to jail, and no one had to die.

And I had my hog back. I leaned my head against the seat. Tomorrow would be another long day. The sheriff's office and phone calls to the insurance company.

I straightened as we neared my farm, surprised to see Sheriff Lincoln waiting on my porch. He marched toward us as I got out of the truck. "I owe you an apology, Shelby. If I would've listened to you, tonight might never have happened. Dave called me and told me about Simmons and Brunner meeting you in the Foster barn." He frowned. "Which was a very foolish thing for you to do, by the way."

"I didn't see any other way." I grinned. "I've already had a conversation with God about my foolish ways, thank you."

"You running off hog-wild could've gotten you or someone else killed." He drew a breath sharply through his nose. "But no harm done. I'm glad you didn't die, Shelby."

"Me too, Sheriff." I handed him the recording device, then watched as he headed for his squad car. He turned before opening the door and tapped his fingers against the brim of his hat. I waved and climbed my porch stairs, wanting my bed more than anything at that moment. When Caleb didn't follow, I turned to face him. "Aren't you coming in?"

"No need." He gave a crooked grin. "You aren't in danger now from anything but yourself."

"Oh." I had gotten used to him being there.

Luke rushed toward us. "I got worried when you were gone so long, and I called Rosie. Glad to hear things are over."

"Me too. Good night, boys." I entered my home, closed the door, and leaned against it. Yes, I was happy to know that justice would be served, but now Caleb didn't need to protect me. He wouldn't be coming around all the time.

What had started out as an annoyance now filled me with sadness to know it had also ended. "Well, at least Big Red can join his sweeties again." I had no reason to fear someone kidnapping him or harming him to keep him from taking home the prize money.

After a quick shower, I climbed into bed, pulled up the covers, and stared at my ceiling. I again gave a prayer of thanks for the safety of everyone I cared about. Life could now return to normal.

Mutt jumped onto the bed and curled up beside me.

"Okay, boy. You deserve the bed after saving me tonight."

He pressed his wet nose into my neck and licked me.

"I sure am glad I adopted you." I couldn't imagine him not being here. At least I still had one man in my life. No, two. I had Big Red.

I fell asleep dreaming of a blue ribbon.

CHAPTER TWELVE

One morning three or four days later, Mutt's barking woke me. The sound of multiple engines outside drew me to the window. My mouth fell open as vehicle after vehicle drove in behind a truck pulling a flatbed trailer full of lumber.

What in the world? I quickly tugged on a pair of jeans and buttoned a flannel shirt over the T-shirt I'd slept in. A glance at the clock on my nightstand had me in high gear. I hadn't slept until eight a.m. in years.

Hopping toward the door, I tugged on one boot, then the other before racing outside where Caleb pointed and shouted orders. "What's going on?" I asked him.

He turned with a grin. "The town is so excited not to lose their farms to the mayor that everyone got together to rebuild your barn."

"But—but—"

"Is Shelby Dickins at a loss for words?" He put a hand to his chest in a mocking gesture. "Never thought I'd see the day."

I had no idea how to express the myriad emotions flooding through me. These were my people. My friends and neighbors. Even folks I barely knew had shown up ready to work.

Men unloaded lumber, hammers, and buckets of nails while women set up tables and piled them with food. Children ran through my fields and around the hogpen.

As the sun climbed higher, the sounds of construction blended with laughter and conversation. Caleb and a few others worked on securing the main beams, their shirts soaked with sweat while Dave and another group focused on reinforcing the roof structure. At one point, Dave attempted to lift a plank that was clearly too heavy for just one man. He stumbled backward, nearly landing on his backside. A round of applause and hearty laughter erupted from the crowd.

"Maybe stick to writing tickets, Deputy," Old Man Jennings teased.

"Ha ha." Dave laughed and shook his head.

Sheriff Lincoln arrived with a cooler and passed out bottles of water and soda to the workers. "Gotta keep the town hydrated. Got a minute, Shelby?"

Nodding, I followed him to my porch. "Don't tell me the mayor escaped custody." I grinned and tilted my head.

"Nope, but Brunner says he knows how to. I'm checking on you is all. You doing okay after all. . .that?"

"I couldn't be better, especially today."

"You did the town a service. I regret that I was too thickheaded to see what was right in front of me." He swiped a bandanna across his perspiring forehead. "Warm day for this time of year. Perfect barn building weather."

"Yes, it is." I turned to help Ella McBride carry a heavy box full of food to the tables.

"I remember coming out here as a kid," Ella said to me. "Your grandparents were always having some sort of get-together or church social on their property." She started unpacking the box and spread checkered tablecloths on each of the tables placed for us to eat at. "Those were some of my favorite days as a kid. A group of us would wander off and play in the creek."

I remembered days like that too, when I'd spend the summers here on the farm. It was when I fell in love with the hogs my grandparents raised. "The town's help means more to me than I can ever say."

"You're one of us, Shelby. Always have been." She patted my shoulder. "Let the men know we'll be eating soon, would you?"

I strolled to where Caleb was sawing a board in two. "Food's about ready."

He straightened and sniffed. "I can smell the barbecue. I'll let the guys know it's time to clean up." He smiled. "You'll have a barn by nightfall."

"I can't believe it." Tears filled my eyes. "Thank you, Caleb."

"Wasn't me. Folks were already talking it about a couple of days ago at the diner. I'm not sure who started it, but most of the town thought it was a great idea."

"I'll pay everyone back for the supplies when I get my insurance money."

"I don't think that's expected, but I'm sure it would be appreciated. Save me a seat next to you at a table." He flashed another grin and marched to where the other men worked, leaving me to return to the cornucopia of food.

Slow-cooked pork and barbecued ribs, cast-iron skillet cornbread with crispy golden edges, freshly baked pies of every fruit imaginable, baked beans simmered with brown sugar and bacon, potato salad, coleslaw, the list went on.

I stepped aside as the men converged on the tables. They were the ones who had spent the morning working while I wandered around feeling useless.

"What's wrong?" Rosie stood next to me, a slice of cornbread dripping with honey in her hand. "Aren't you happy?"

"Very happy. There isn't anything for me to do to help. I'd only be in the way working on the barn."

"You can help clean up after everyone has eaten." She grabbed a sturdy paper plate. "Go on. Eat."

I laughed as a little boy around six years old peered from under one of the tables. Then he reached out and snatched a cookie off a plate before hiding again. A woman wandered around, eyes searching the crowd. His mother no doubt. I pointed to the table.

She smiled and nodded, then lifted the tablecloth. "Come eat something other than cookies, Wyatt."

After everyone had eaten and the barn was complete other than a coat of red stain, music played from someone's truck radio, a mix of country and bluegrass. One of the men who had worked on the barn pulled a guitar from the trunk of his car.

Someone turned off the radio. The strumming of the guitar took its place.

An older couple started dancing near the barn, swaying to the music. Before long, others joined in. I exhaled slowly. For the first time in a long time, the weight on my shoulders didn't feel so crushing. Things would be okay now.

Caleb joined me, handing me a glass of sweet tea. Our fingers brushed briefly, a small, fleeting touch.

"This is way better than anything the city ever had to offer," he finally said.

"I can't imagine a life other than this simple country one." I took a sip of my tea.

"I'm glad I came back." His gaze lingered on me. "For more reasons than the lifestyle." He twirled a finger in a loose strand of my hair. "Better go clean up my tools."

As the celebration wound down and the last of the guests trickled away, I found myself needing a moment to breathe. I wandered to the hogpen, feeling at home with the grunts and snuffles. "What do you think, guys? Isn't the barn pretty?"

I eyed their shelter. Might be time for an update. I leaned against the railing, my gaze scanning the property, noting other things that could be modernized. I might have money left from the insurance now that I didn't have to pay for the labor required to build the barn. Or, I could use the winnings from Big Red.

Of course, he might not win. Eventually, another hog would take the number one spot, and that would be okay. Big Red would go on to sire a lot of winners before I retired him to simply enjoy life.

Caleb passed the barn and stopped near the fence line, sleeves rolled up. A dim lantern light cast long shadows as he hammered a nail into a broken plank.

I hesitated before stepping closer. "What are you doing?"

He didn't look up right away. He gripped the fence post, testing its strength, then finally met my gaze. "Making sure you don't lose anything else important."

The words settled between us, heavy with meaning. Did he mean himself as one of those important things?

This wasn't just about the fence. It was about the barn, my home, my sense of safety. It was about me. I was the something important, and he was the one who didn't want the loss.

"Thank you."

He nodded, then went back to work as if it was the most natural thing in the world. I stood there for a moment before going to make coffee, a silly grin on my face.

After the arrest of the mayor, I'd missed Caleb. Then he'd shown up today with the whole town and still worked fixing things that needed fixing.

Someone had left half a cherry pie on my counter. I cut two slices and set them on plates while the coffee brewed.

I waved out the back door at Luke, who headed to his apartment. "Here." I gave him the pie plate with the last slice.

"Thanks." He jerked his head to where Caleb worked. "Why is he still here?"

"Found some things he thought needed doing." I set the plates and coffee cups on a tray and carried them to the front porch before calling Caleb over. "You've done enough today. Enjoy some rest."

"Thanks." He sat and dug into the pie. "You ready for the competition next week?"

"As ready as I can be. Red is back up to his optimal weight. Now that I have a barn, thanks to you, I have a clean place to put him once he's had a bath." I blew into my coffee. "When is the trial for the mayor and Brunner? I forgot to ask."

"Both of their trials are set to happen about a month after the competition, I think. With the mayor out, you've one less competitor."

"I don't think he really intended to compete. It was all a ploy to get under my skin. Take my focus off where it should be so he could work on his evil scheme to take over my farm and surrounding ones." I took a sip and burned my tongue.

"You'll receive a letter, Shelby. You'll have to testify."

I cringed, thinking of the stack of mail on my desk that needed to be dealt with. "I've let some things go lately while I focus on the competition." And tried to figure out what, exactly, was happening between me and Caleb.

CHAPTER THIRTEEN

I watched Big Red eat in the livestock tent. The aroma of fried food and popcorn mingled with the scents of animals, hay, and manure. Shouts and screams filled the air as folks rode the carnival rides and played games.

I reached into the pen and brushed a smidge of dirt off Red's rump. "Don't go getting dirty. I'll be showing you soon."

My stomach twisted in knots despite having done this before. If my hog won for the third year in a row, he'd be in high demand for making little pigs.

I strolled the livestock building, noting the competition, then moved to the chickens, bunnies, calves. . . Every kind of farm animal had a showing. Some of them were for sale. I stopped and studied a caramel-colored calf. "You're an absolute doll." I did want to grow my cattle herd, and she would be perfect. A glance at my watch had me retrieving Red and heading to the tent where I'd show him.

"Will you hold this for me?" I handed Caleb my phone. "The judges won't be happy if it goes off when I'm up there. I could turn it off, but I'm expecting a call from the insurance company, and you can take it for me if it comes in."

"Sure. Good luck." He gave the lopsided grin that sent my heart flipping.

After the judges had viewed Big Red from every angle and I'd walked him around the floor several times, we waited to find out who would be the winner. My palms sweated. Red plopped down and promptly started to snore.

Mason Duggar laughed while keeping a firm hold on the collar of his pig. "Wish I could be as relaxed as Red."

"The limelight means nothing to him." I grinned. I knew we'd done well. If not first place, then second, which still meant a nice-sized check.

Sitting in the first row and being very supportive was Caleb. Next to him sat Rosie. Dave stood at the back of the tent in plain clothes. Still, anyone looking would know the deputy stood at full attention.

I narrowed my eyes when I noticed the sheriff pass by the tent entrance. Not that it was uncommon for law enforcement to be at the fair, but they both looked on edge. I kept my smile in place and motioned my head toward Dave.

Caleb turned in his seat then back to me and shrugged. A moment later, he joined Dave. His spine stiffened, and he shot me a stricken look. Something had happened.

"The runner-up is Mason Duggar and Chunk." The judge's voice pulled my attention to the stage. "And this year's winner is. . .Shelby Dickins and Big Red!"

The place erupted in applause, and the judge handed me the trophy and an envelope containing the check. A young woman hung a blue ribbon on Big Red. I held the trophy high.

Caleb gave a thumbs-up from where he stood.

The applause halted. Laughter turned to gasps, cheers into frightened murmurs, as the crowd shrank into their seats.

I glanced over my shoulder.

Brunner.

A coat too large for his frame barely hid the jail clothes underneath. The man was dirty, disheveled, and armed. The gun in his right hand wavered a bit, but his gaze stayed locked on me. "Nobody move, nobody try to be a hero, or she dies right here on this stage." He swung the gun toward Caleb and then back at me when Caleb took a step forward.

"Give me the money. It's mine. I earned it," Brunner said with a sneer.

The check crumpled in my hand from my tight grip. My palm perspired around the trophy.

"Who should it be first, Shelby? Your boyfriend, your best friend, or the pig? Or maybe someone in the audience." He waved the gun like a madman.

Caleb moved again.

Brunner grabbed me, using me as a shield and pointing the gun at my head. I dropped the trophy. He backed up at a snail's pace, taking me with him.

"It isn't cash, Carl. It's a check. With my name on it." With my eyes, I pleaded with Caleb not to move again.

"That's why you're going to cash it for me." He exited the tent. "Start running. We'll lose them in the crowd."

"Don't hurt anyone. Please." I darted past the Tilt-A-Whirl, then the Ferris wheel. People parted like the Red Sea before us. No one seemed to notice the gun in Carl's hand.

"Whether anyone gets hurt is all up to you." He panted behind me. "Okay, slow down. Don't think about running off, or someone dies."

I stopped and faced him as he leaned against a food truck to catch his breath. There had to be a way to escape him without anyone else being harmed. I glanced at the envelope in my hand. No way would I cash it for him.

"Okay, let's go." He waved me on.

"Go where, Carl?"

"My truck is waiting at the far gate. You're going to drive us to the check-cashing place on Fourth Street. Move it."

I'd seen Carl's truck. An older-model Chevy without airbags. The idea filtering through my head would be dangerous. I might not survive, but everyone else would.

I quickened my pace, wishing the man behind me would suddenly have a heart attack or a stroke or something. The way he gasped for air gave me hope.

"There's my truck." Carl tossed me the keys. "Make it quick."

I climbed into the driver's seat and put on my seat belt. I stifled a grin when Carl failed to put his on. I prayed my crazy idea would work.

Traffic was light since most of the town was at the county fair. I drove the speed limit, hoping the sheriff would be following. How would they know which direction we'd gone? I should've thought to leave some kind of a trail.

Maybe some people had seen us racing through the crowd and noticed which gate we'd gone out of. It wasn't much, but it might be enough. *Please, God.*

"You're awfully quiet for a chatty woman." Carl frowned.

"You aren't really someone I care to have a conversation with."

"Might as well. We've got ten minutes."

I rolled my eyes. "How did you escape?"

"That's a good one." He chuckled. "I slammed the guard's head into the bars of my cell when he brought my breakfast. In a town this size, there aren't a lot of people in the jail. I got out easy."

"And the mayor?"

"Thought about bringing him with me, but why? The ten thousand dollars you have won't last me long. Why share?"

"Hmm." I turned onto Fourth Street. Rescue hadn't arrived yet. I racked my brain for another idea.

"Once we cash the check, you're going to drive me to the next town. I'll release you there and head for Mexico."

“Why are you sharing information with me?” I shot him a sideways glance.

“Passing time.” He shoved his door open before I cut off the truck’s ignition. “No funny business. You cash the check; we step outside; you hand me the money. Simple as that.”

“Will this place be able to cash a check this size?”

“I think they will once I persuade them with this.” He waved his gun.

The girl behind the counter looked bored as she flipped through her phone. She didn’t sit upright until Carl slammed the gun on the counter.

“This woman is going to cash a large check. You’re going to do that for her.”

I slid the envelope across the counter.

The girl removed the check. “I can’t cash this.”

“Who can?” Carl growled.

“The manager.”

“Is the manager here?” His face darkened.

“Yes.”

“Get him. . .or her!” He shook his head as she dashed away. “Stupidity at its finest.”

I really wanted to hit him with the stapler on the counter but doubted I could make it knock him out. I had no other choice but to keep following orders. For now.

The girl returned with a man in his mid-to-late twenties. In his hand, he carried a stack of hundred-dollar bills. “This wiped out our safe,” he said, handing me the money.

“I’m sorry. I really am.”

“Enough with the pleasantries. I’m sure they called the cops.” Carl gripped my upper arm and dragged me outside. Then he let me go and held out his hand. “The money.”

I handed it to him with a sigh, then got into the truck and put on my seat belt. I could implement my plan soon. My heart threatened to beat free at what I intended to do. I pressed the gas pedal and rocketed us down the highway.

"Take the interstate," Carl ordered.

"I don't like driving the interstate," I said.

His eyes narrowed. "You're up to something."

I put on my most innocent expression. "What could I possibly be up to, Carl? You are clearly in control here."

"That's right, and don't forget it." The gun lay on his lap now instead of being clutched in his hand.

Now was my chance. I pressed the accelerator and headed for a grove of saplings. The truck barreled through them and came to a jarring stop against a large oak. My body snapped forward, the seat belt keeping my head from slamming into the steering wheel.

Carl wasn't as lucky. Since he wasn't wearing his seat belt, he was hurled against the dashboard.

I fumbled to free myself. When I succeeded, I climbed out the driver's-side window and landed in a heap on the ground. Once I caught my breath, I limped in the direction of the road.

"I'm going to kill you, Shelby Dickins!"

Carl's shout spurred me to go faster. If I could get to the highway before him, I could flag someone down.

Blue lights flashed from the road, coming up fast. I jumped out and waved my arms. "Here! I'm here."

The cars came to a halt just feet from me.

A sound split the air. The sharp crack of a gunshot.

For one horrifying moment, I thought I'd been shot. I gasped, my body frozen until I realized it wasn't me. I turned to see who had fired the shot.

Brunner staggered back, a dark stain spreading across his shoulder. His gun wobbled in his hand as a sharp cry of pain ripped from his throat.

Sheriff Lincoln stood next to his car. "Drop the weapon, Carl."

Carl dropped it.

"Shelby."

I jerked, then turned to see Caleb.

"You okay?" Worry creased his forehead.

I swallowed, my pulse still racing. "Yes."

He held out his arms, and I rushed into them. A wave of relief and disbelief crashed over me. I let out a breathless laugh, my hands shaking. "Carl has my money. It's in the glove compartment of his truck. That way." I pointed to the path the vehicle had made as it plowed through.

"I'll get it." Dave jogged in that direction as an ambulance wailed to a stop next to the scene.

"Big Red?"

"Rosie is taking him home. Which is where you need to be." He led me to his truck and gently helped me inside.

"How did you find me?"

"The Quick Cash place called the sheriff." He brushed the hair away from my face. "He had Dave go to the interstate, but my gut told me you went this way. Luckily, the sheriff listened."

"I'm pretty sure your gut had some help from above." I leaned my head back and closed my eyes. Already my chest hurt from the seat belt.

"Why is Carl's truck in the woods?"

"I crashed it in order to get away. It's the only plan I could think of." I opened my eyes and turned my head to see him better. "Carl said he would release me at the next town, but I didn't want him to get away."

"With your money." Caleb laughed.

"That too." I smiled and sat up as Dave arrived with my winnings. "There's a pretty little cow I want to buy with part of this."

"What about the rest?" Caleb climbed into the truck.

"Some repairs around the place, paying people back for the barn supplies." I waved away the EMT, promising to go to the clinic. After all, they were busy trying to keep Carl alive.

"You've got a bump on your head and a bloody lip." Caleb turned the key in the ignition.

"I didn't hit anything."

"You must have. I felt the bump when I smoothed back your hair. I'll drive you to the clinic."

"Okay. My ankle hurts from climbing out the window."

He laughed again. "You're something else, Shelby. Never a dull moment around you."

"That's what my father always said." I hoped my parents would be proud of how I'd kept the farm going. With the help of a prize-winning hog, of course.

CHAPTER FOURTEEN

Since Oakwood grasped any chance to celebrate, the pastor called out from the pulpit on Sunday morning, "Today, we celebrate Shelby Dickins and her unrelenting pursuit for truth and justice. Not only did she save her hog, but she saved our town by bringing down Mayor Simmons and Carl Brunner. Shelby, this town owes you a debt of gratitude." He smiled over at me. "Now, let's pray and go to the picnic."

With Caleb at my side, we followed the crowd to the town square, which had been transformed into a festival of sorts. Long tables covered in checkered tablecloths sagged under the weight of homemade dishes. The scents of fried chicken, roasted pork, and warm apple pies hung in the air, mingling with the crisp autumn breeze.

"Wow." I took it all in. "I thought there were a lot of people at my barn raising, but this must be the whole town."

"Looks that way." He placed his hand on the small of my back and guided me to the food line.

Children ran between the adults, weaving past the clusters of people who had gathered to exchange stories about the scandal I'd unraveled. The downfall of Simmons was the talk of the town, but so was I. I couldn't get through the crowd without someone stopping me.

"You really did it." Mrs. Wilson from the bakery beamed, gripping my hand. "That no-good crook finally got what was coming to him, and it's all thanks to you."

Mr. Brant, the oldest resident of Oakwood, gave a knowing nod. "You've got more grit than a sawmill, Shelby. Your folks would be proud of you."

My eyes teared up at their praise.

Even Mr. Greenley, the grumpy owner of the hardware store, grunted something that might've been approval. " 'Bout time someone shook things up around here."

I tried to brush off the praise with a smile, but inside, a warmth I hadn't expected filled me.

As I reached for a plate of peach cobbler, a hush fell over the crowd. A murmur passed through the townsfolk. I followed their gazes to see Caleb standing in the center of the gazebo behind the microphone.

"Shelby." His voice rang out, steady but warm. "I've been wanting to do this for a while now, and I figure there's no better time than when the whole town is watching."

A few chuckles rippled through the gathering. My heart beat too fast for me to focus on anything but the man behind the microphone.

"I wounded you deeply ten years ago. It was a decision I've come to regret, and I want to make up for breaking your heart. You're stubborn, independent, and you've got a real talent for getting into trouble." A grin split his face as the crowd laughed again. "But I also know you've got the biggest heart of anyone I've ever met. Underneath your tough exterior anyway." His lips twitched. "So, with the whole town watching, I want to ask, would you go on a real date with me?"

The crowd seemed to hold its collective breath. All eyes locked on me. The moment stretched, thick with anticipation.

Heat rushed to my cheeks, but despite the way my heart raced, a smile tugged at my lips. This wasn't some grand gesture just for show. Caleb meant every word.

"Yes," I whispered. Then, realizing he couldn't hear my answer, I spoke louder. "Yes, I'd love to."

A cheer rose from the crowd, whistles and applause ringing through the air. Someone clapped Caleb on the back. Rosie, standing a few feet away with Dave, cupped her hands around her mouth and let out a loud, playful whistle.

"Well, shucks," she drawled. "You always manage to get yourself into the thick of things, Shelby, but at least this time you found yourself a man instead of more trouble."

More laughter from the crowd. I rolled my eyes but couldn't stop the grin spreading across my face.

Caleb moved to my side and leaned in. "Dinner tonight?"

I tilted my head, still grinning. "You think because you made a big public show that I'm an easy yes?"

His smile turned smug. "You already said yes. You can't take it back now."

I laughed. "Fine. Dinner it is."

After the picnic, I spent a few hours cleaning the hogpen. Red and his girls were great listeners. "Am I being silly going out with Caleb again? I mean. . .he does seem to have changed from the boy I once knew." Snorts were their answer, so I petted Mutt, who sat right outside the pen. "What do you think, boy? Am I being stupid to give him another chance?"

Mutt barked and lay down, his head resting on his paws.

"Was that a yes or a no?" I shook my head and kept working. Maybe I was overthinking things. Why not just enjoy the now after days of danger? Rely on God to lead my life in the direction it was meant to go.

I propped the shovel against the hog shelter and went inside to shower and change. Yes, I would wait and see.

Now I had the opportunity to wear my new jeans and a frilly white blouse with a soft blue sweater that matched my eyes.

I stepped onto the porch as Caleb turned into the drive. I fairly skipped to his truck, feeling a lot like the teenage girl who had done the same thing so many times before.

He drove to a quiet spot near the river. "I hope you don't mind. After my announcement today, all eyes would be on us if we went somewhere public."

"This is perfect."

A blanket was laid out on the grass. Lanterns cast a soft glow over a picnic basket.

"Nice."

"You're worth it."

The evening passed in easy conversation and laughter. We talked about everything and nothing—our childhood misadventures, things we'd done the last ten years, dreams we never admitted out loud, and the silly quirks of Oakwood's residents. Stars twinkled overhead while the river hummed a quiet, steady tune in the background.

I leaned back on my elbows. "I never saw this coming."

"Didn't see what?" Caleb turned to face me.

"You."

He smiled and reached out, tucking a loose strand of hair behind my ear. A gesture that made me roll my eyes when seen in books or movies. But when he did it, I felt special.

The space between us shrank. Caleb leaned in and brushed his lips softly against mine. Slow, lingering, and filled with a quiet promise of something more.

When we finally pulled apart, I let out a small laugh. "You really don't give up, do you?"

"Not when I know what I want."

And just like that I knew this wasn't just another misadventure, another fleeting moment in a town full of gossip. Something for folks to talk about.

This was something real.

And for once, trouble had led me to exactly where I was meant to be.

Cynthia Hickey is a multi-published and bestselling author of cozy mysteries and romantic suspense/thrillers. She has taught writing at many conferences and small writing retreats. She and her husband run the publishing press Winged Publications. They live in Arizona and Arkansas, becoming snowbirds with three dogs. They have ten grandchildren, who keep them busy and tell everyone they know that "Nana is a writer."

www.cynthiahickey.com

THE DARK SIDE OF THE MOO

BY LINDA BATEN JOHNSON

CHAPTER ONE

Dad!" I was shocked to see a slumped, deflated version of the man I considered my rock. He wore overalls and work boots and leaned against the doorframe with eyes downcast.

I grabbed his hand and pulled him inside my apartment. "Is Mom okay?"

"She's fine. It's the cows."

"What does the vet say?"

Dad collapsed into the only chair in my living area and stared at his hands. "Ben's baffled."

"Ben would be." I grabbed myself a kitchen chair. "Could you ask a different vet?"

"No. Ben's been our animal doc for years. I don't understand why you dislike him."

"Personal." I leaned forward and squeezed Dad's hand. "What's wrong with the cows?"

"Respiratory thing. I'm hoping your university learning might save the farm."

"You want me to come home? Now?" Only two weeks remained for my master's program, including the defense of my thesis. Not good timing.

"Liv, your schooling is important, but this is. . ." Dad let the words trail off. "I'll go to the john while you think about it."

My father represents the fourth generation of the Olsen family operating Friendly Farm, a dairy with a sterling reputation. Judging from his fatigue, Dad had driven from Wisconsin after the morning milking.

I emailed my supervising professor and my neighbor that there was an emergency at home. Dr. Graham Armstrong hadn't been overly helpful in the past, but he'd know I wouldn't leave campus unless absolutely necessary.

I packed my clothes, made sandwiches, and thought about questions for the trip home.

Dad smiled when he saw my bag. "Thanks, Olivia."

I knew it was serious when he called me Olivia rather than Liv.

"Want me to drive while you fill me in?"

"Sure." He started down the stairs with my small suitcase.

I locked the apartment and followed with my computer bag filled with research and notes.

Once I cleared the Minneapolis traffic, I glanced at my dad. "Talk."

"Been about a month that something's been wrong. You can tell when a cow doesn't feel well."

I nodded. "I know a couple of signs. They stretch their necks forward, and their ears are droopier than usual."

My dad grinned. "Knew you'd understand. You followed me to the barns as soon as you could walk."

"And you told me, 'Liv, if you're going to be in the barns every day, you might as well work.' You taught me so much."

"Now it's your turn to teach me. We need you to use your book learning to find out what's going on. If we don't get an answer, we'll lose the farm."

"Is this more than sick cows?" Since I was driving, he could talk without looking me in the eye. Mom and Dad never discussed money with us kids, so we never knew the status of the business.

"Cost of feed is up, milk contracts are down, and we've updated major equipment. We redid the piping and holding tanks last year, and I needed a new tractor. Have to farm to have food for the animals. Everything hit at once." He quit talking.

I let the silence grow as long as I could. "Do you want me to look at financials too? That's not my strong suit. You should ask your tax man."

"Prefer not to. You're welcome to check the books, but we want you to concentrate on the herd, since dairy cow nutrition is your field."

It was, but my research is specific to dairy food supplements, and I feared my college focus might not help. "I'll do what I can."

Dad stared at the road. "Isn't natural for parents to rely on their kids. Kids should depend on their parents. Your mom and I only asked because the farm is your inheritance."

"How bad is the cow problem?"

"Bad. One died, and Ben's quarantined about ten due to tainted milk. Our annual open house is Mother's Day weekend. Your mom believes the event could make or break us. You know she sells her eggs, jams, jellies, and crafts, and we book farm-experience visits. Those farm vacations for city folk are pure profit. But to stay afloat, we need other money-making endeavors. With the cow sickness, local shops are shying away from selling your mom's food and craft items. Guess they can smell disaster."

"Dad, it's not just you. The big dairies are forcing out the small holders all across the United States."

"I know, but now it's personal. I had to ask for credit at the feedstore, something I've never done in my whole life."

I knew that must have been difficult for my proud, self-sufficient father. When I turned down our country road, the sun shed its last rays on Friendly Farm, a home to generations of the Olsens. Twin brown silos with silver bowl caps stood next to the red barn and the milking building, both with white-trimmed windows and doors. Our home, a rambling one-story with a full basement, was beyond the silos but not beyond the aroma of manure. Dad always joked that the smell of manure is the smell of money. Our farm still had the unique aroma but might not have the currency.

Mom wiped her eyes with the hem of her apron when she saw me. My mother is plump, not heavy, and her hair is the same straw color as mine. I got her wide mouth and blue eyes, but my eyes require glasses. She wrapped me in her arms and squeezed tightly. "Thanks, Liv."

I relaxed into her embrace. Mom gives hugs freely, and those on the receiving end remark on her gentleness and softness, but our family knows her as a fierce, protective, determined woman.

"Let's get you something to eat." Food is Mom's remedy for everything.

"We had sandwiches," I said, "but I'm sure you have a cake or pie in the kitchen."

"Both. German chocolate cake or apple pie, and I have oatmeal raisin cookies in the jar." My mother bakes when she's stressed, and everything she makes is delicious.

I patted my stomach. "I've been sitting at a computer most days. I'll have to limit myself, but I will have some pie."

My dad opted for cake, and Mom prepared our sweets while Dad and I took the bags to my room still regaled with high school memorabilia. Mom couldn't bring herself to remove my souvenirs, something I'd vowed to do. I wouldn't tackle it this visit, because the priority would be the cows and the farm finances.

I awoke to the smell of coffee and noted the time, three a.m., the hour life on a dairy farm begins. Out of habit, I dressed in work overalls and filled a thermal mug with black coffee.

Mom and Dad were spreading feed in the troughs when I reached the barn. The milking equipment gleamed after being washed with a disinfectant soap followed by a chlorine mixture rinse. My oldest brother, a medical equipment sales rep, used to joke that our dairy barns rivaled hospital operating rooms for sterilization. Frank Jr. now lives in California, and my other brother, Tim, is a navy man on the Atlantic coast. The three of us grew up helping on the farm, but neither of them loved it like I did.

Their careers and family demands prevented frequent visits to the home place, and dairy farmers rarely take vacations. I visited each brother between university terms and kept in touch via texts and calls. Working shoulder-to-shoulder with them growing up forged a special bond.

When my dad whistled, the first group of Holsteins moved in orderly fashion to the milking stations on both sides of the building. Our family names each cow, and I noticed Millie, Cora, and Agnes missing from the first group. I saved a sample of the trough food, not expecting to find anything amiss, but it was a reference point.

While Dad supervised the milking process, Mom and I walked to the field where the quarantined cows grazed.

"They're off their feed," Mom said. "Breaks my heart. Look at Millie. She's too tired to even greet us. Their milk was thick and yellowish. We dumped it all, sterilized everything, and started again. We're hand milking these ladies."

"Any improvement in the milk?"

"No. Ben tries something new every time he comes. He always takes blood samples and nose swabs for testing."

"How about another vet?" My heart ached at the sight of the lethargic cows.

"Your dad's loyal to a fault. Ben's partner, Noah Reed, seems good. His wife works at our dentist's office in Eau Claire. Her name's Wren, like the bird. Fits her. She's a tiny thing. Liv, would you ask your dad to let Noah check the cows?"

"Me?"

Mom gazed at the barn, then faced me. "I've tried. Your dad can be stubborn."

I nudged her shoulder. "He is a dairy farmer, and you have a similar stubborn streak. That trait made you a successful team."

Mom ignored my comment. "I need to go to Eau Claire for fabric and decorations for the open house this weekend. We can stop by the vet's office and confirm Noah and his wife will attend. Ben 'forgot' to tell them about the invitation last year."

"Sounds like Ben. We could stop by the dental office too. You could introduce me to Wren, and we can suggest to her that Noah examine the sick cows during the open house. That would be the perfect time. And I'll pay Noah's fee. Then Dad and Ben won't know."

"Not like me to do anything without telling your dad." Mom rubbed the back of her neck. "But I think Ben's missing something."

I pointed to the cows milling aimlessly. "They need to be milked. We could send a milk sample and a portion of their food to my supervising professor and ask him to have the university lab do an analysis. I'm sure Ben checked both the feed and the milk, but this would give us a second opinion."

"What would that cost?" Mom asked.

"I'm sure they'll do it as a favor, since I'm a grad assistant. I'll grab some sterile containers and cold-pack bags."

We headed to Eau Claire after morning chores. Mom drove while I confirmed the university would process the samples for free. Then I called Ben Wimble's office and learned both he and Noah were out and not expected back until afternoon.

Mom turned on Main Street toward the dental office. "Let's see if Wren is close to her lunch break. Maybe she'll be able to join us."

I'd wanted to get the packaged samples to the Fast Package office but didn't mention it. Neither of my parents were behaving normally. Friendly Farm has weathered problems throughout the years, but Mom's question about testing costs made me curious about their money situation.

"This is it," Mom said. "Reception is downstairs, dental offices upstairs."

Wren sent word that she could join us for lunch, so we clock-watched until a petite lady with almond-shaped brown eyes and shoulder-length black hair with red streaks appeared.

The woman reached up to give Mom a hug, then turned to me. "I'm Wren Reed, and you must be Liv. You look like your sweet mother. I can do lunch, but I have to take some molds to Fast Package first. We don't make our crowns here. Could we grab something at Tilly's Sandwich Shop? It's next to the shipping place. June, I hope you're going to ask me to do something at your open house. I'd hate standing around while Noah talks to farmers all day. Should I drive? Oh, I can't. Noah dropped me off today." Her voice was high-pitched, and she flitted from subject to subject as her name suggested she might.

"Perfect," I said when Wren paused. "I have a package too, and I love Tilly's."

The three of us squeezed into the truck's front seat, and Wren talked nonstop on the way to Fast Package. After sending our parcels, Wren and I joined Mom at Tilly's. She'd claimed a red vinyl booth toward the back of the sandwich shop, and waters with lemon slices were already on the table.

Mom tapped the menu. "Special today is chicken salad on a croissant. That's what I'm getting."

I held up two fingers, indicating I'd have the same.

"Okay for me too," Wren said.

Mom wasted no time after the server took the order. "Wren, Frank and I have used Ben Wimble for years. Noah's been out from time to time, but nothing regular. Our cows are off, and I, well, we"—she inclined her head to me—"would like for Noah to check them."

I reached for my water glass. "I'll pay Noah's fee. My dad would consider it disloyal to Ben to ask for a second opinion."

"I'm sure Noah would be happy to help, and I wouldn't worry about loyalty where Ben is concerned, as he's not always honored his word. When we bought into his business, we were promised an equal partnership. It hasn't worked out that way. Noah's discouraged. He'd like to leave and open his own practice, but Ben told him the contract is binding for ten years. Ten years! I'll be old and gray in ten years. And Ben assigns my Noah all the distasteful chores and the cantankerous clients. Ben keeps the easy tasks for himself. I am not a Dr. Wimble fan!"

I hadn't expected that outburst. I wondered if Ben had said or done anything that made her personally dislike him as much as I did. I'd save that question for another day. Mom discussed open house duties, and Wren agreed to be in charge of hayrides. She'd look fabulous in overalls and a broad-brimmed hat, and her enthusiasm was guaranteed to convince families to ride on hay bales on a flat trailer. The ride is hot and dusty, and hay sticks in your clothes and scratches your arms and legs, but people eagerly pay for the experience, some more than once. With sociable Wren in charge, I knew the event would be a moneymaker.

CHAPTER TWO

At the open house, Ben Wimble glad-handed me as if he hadn't seen me in years even though we'd been together in the barn the day before.

"Liv!" He squeezed my hand in both of his.

I pulled away from his viselike grip. Many people considered Ben handsome with his broad shoulders, trim physique, thick black hair, neatly trimmed beard, and dark, deep-set eyes. I didn't. His eyes bothered me. He squinted, as though he needed glasses or was plotting something. I leaned toward plotting something. I couldn't put my finger on it, but the hair on the back of my neck stood up anytime he was within ten feet. He'd been flirtatious with me—more than once—when he was engaged to my best friend Sharon. Since he'd never exceeded boundaries, and she was head-over-heels in love with him, I hadn't said anything. His actions today made me wonder if I should have.

Ben moved closer to me. "You can't avoid meeting me at your own farm."

I lifted my chin. "I can avoid spending time with you."

His eyes narrowed into slits of onyx. "Your parents need me at Friendly Farm." He grinned. "Well, as long as they own it."

Before I could ask what he meant by that, Dad entered the barn with Ben's wife. Sharon greeted me as effusively as her husband had.

She gave me air kisses on both cheeks, careful not to muss the bright red lipstick she always applied carefully. From junior high to the present, I've secretly admired how she administers her lip colors with a thin brush, using the tiny mirror on the side of her lipstick container. Sharon's voluptuous figure was accented by a wide belt, and her shoulder-length hair appeared slightly tousled, although I'm sure she sprayed it with sufficient product to keep it from moving. She'd been my best childhood friend, but because of my prejudice against her husband, I'd avoided her and Ben since their marriage.

That wasn't fair to her, so I plastered a smile on my face, determined to be kind. "Good to see you. I hoped you'd come to our open house."

My simple goodwill greeting lit up her face as if I'd offered her homemade ice cream.

She reached for my hand. "May I help at a table or booth?"

"Absolutely," I said. Her eagerness and our lack of volunteers meshed perfectly. "Come with me. Mom's fussing over the activity schedule now. We have to sandwich open house events between the milkings and chores, so she'll appreciate your offer."

I hated to miss today's conversation between my dad and Ben, but Mom had worked herself into a real tizzy about this open house. My dad said they had money problems, but Ben's remark about the farm made me wonder if a successful event today was vital to their financial survival.

Sharon placed her hand on my shoulder and gave it a quick squeeze. "Liv, we were great pals in high school. What happened to us?"

"After you met Ben, you focused on him and I left for university. We drifted apart, didn't we? And then you married, in a truly spectacular ceremony."

"The ceremony was more spectacular than our marriage. Liv, I need a friend. Can I confide in you again?" She continued, "Our marriage has changed, and now I think Ben's hiding money from me. I don't understand what's going on."

"Whoa, my friend. Let's get our assignments from Mom, then you can explain that bombshell."

Sharon nodded, and we walked to the house in silence.

"I rounded up a volunteer," I said softly as my mother held a phone against her ear.

Mom hung up the phone. "Bouncy-castle folks are five minutes out. Sharon, I need a hug. We don't see you nearly enough."

Sharon stepped into Mom's embrace. "June, I'm yours for the day. Tell me what to do."

Mom released her and glanced out the window. "Why don't you two meet the bouncy-castle people? Tell them it goes in our front yard, and then you can set up the face-painting booth and the craft-sale table under the tree. Adults will buy while the children jump. Oh, there's the bounce truck with Noah and Wren right behind them."

"We'll talk to the bouncy-castle people, Mom. I know you'll want to talk to Wren about the hayrides and the thing Noah's doing."

Sharon linked her arm through mine and continued with her marital woes. "Ben's up to something. He sneaks out at all hours and hangs up the phone when I come into the room. I don't know what to think."

"That is puzzling." I signed the delivery sheet and pointed to the spot for the red-and-blue inflatable.

"Ben says he has a business thing going on that he can't discuss. He says, 'I'm' going to be rich soon—not 'we're' going to be rich. It's always 'I' and not 'we.' Ben and I haven't been to dinner by ourselves for over a year. I don't think he wants to be married, at least not to me." Sharon stopped to suck in a deep breath.

I avoided commenting by pointing to the folding tables leaning against the tree. "Let's set these up. Sharon, I may not be the right person to give marriage advice, since I'm twenty-eight and single. But I can lend an ear while you work through this."

"He won't go to counseling. He won't talk to me. I'm ready to give up."

The set of Sharon's mouth told me how upset she was. She didn't want advice, just someone to listen. We decorated the tables and placed some of the cow figurines, toys, and jams and jellies on one table, leaving a spot for ticket sales for the bounce castle and face painting.

"We should probably put items for restocking under the table. Should we go to the house?" I asked.

Sharon nodded. "I'm meeting with our pastor to get his advice. I supported Ben through vet school. I thought things would be rosy after he finished, but he's still insisting I be frugal. Liv, your mother has a gun!"

I was only half listening to Sharon, but the word *gun* got my attention.

"Mom! Wait up!" She was on a direct course from the house to the barn. "Mom? What are you doing?"

"Getting this gun out of the house. We keep it in the barn in a gun case, but the lock broke. It's fixed now, and I want it secured for today and in the barn where it belongs."

Sharon and I fell in step behind her as she made her way to the barn where Ben, Noah, Wren, Dad, and our neighbors Albert Wagner and his son Doug clustered around my favorite cow, Trudy.

"What's wrong?" I asked.

Dad blew out a breath in frustration. "She's like the others. Came on real quick. None of us know what to make of it. Have to move her before our visitors start arriving."

"I'll take her out, Frank." Noah took the lead from my father's hand and gave me a nod, letting me know he'd examine the Holstein. "Mind if I look her over?"

Ben shook his head. "I treat the Olsen cows."

"Just curious, Ben. I'm not trying to steal a customer," Noah said.

"We'd appreciate that, wouldn't we, Frank?" My mom held up the pistol. "What's the combination for the new lock?"

"Same as everything else, 0731, your birthday. I don't dare forget that." Dad's halfhearted smile didn't reach his eyes.

Wren linked her arm through her husband's. "I'll walk with you. I don't have anything to do until the gates open."

Noah grinned down at his wife. He was about a foot taller than she was, and he shortened his stride so they could walk at the same pace. Wearing a starched plaid shirt and jeans, Noah looked more professional than our official vet, Ben, who'd chosen lightweight running pants and a stained Grateful Dead T-shirt for his attire today.

Sharon and I moved toward Doug, our constant companion in high school who'd never left the area. He still worked with his dad on their dairy farm. In high school, Doug and I joked that if we combined our dairies, we'd have the biggest farm in the state. He'd been gangly and awkward in high school, but he wasn't now. He'd grown into his body and was a very handsome man.

"Face-painting booth isn't open yet, but you could try out the bouncy castle. Sharon and I supervised the guys setting it up," I teased.

"I'll pass. Good to see you two. Dad and I brought over pigs for the greased pig chase." Doug tilted his head toward the crates outside.

"Those races are always a high spot. Thanks," I said.

"Just being neighborly. What brings you here? Thought you were at the university."

"I was. I mean, I am. I came to help with the open house and because my parents are worried about the cows."

"We're all worried. Don't want some disease spreading. We have more than five hundred cows in our herd. Wouldn't want your cows contaminating ours."

I understood what he meant but didn't like the way he'd phrased it.

Before I could answer, Sharon moved forward and patted Doug's arm. "Ben and I were sorry to hear about your mom," she said.

I nodded my sympathy, mentally kicking myself for forgetting to mention it first. "I liked your mom. She always bragged that her husband and four boys treated her like a queen."

Doug looked at his father, who stood next to my dad. "Mom deserved the royal treatment, putting up with our teenage shenanigans. My brothers were always in trouble."

"I remember you visiting the principal a few times," I said.

"I might have." Doug grinned, then his expression changed. "As hard as it was, we were thankful we could bring her home at the end and hold her hand. We know she's at peace, and with God's help, we're beginning to heal."

"I hope they find a cure soon," Sharon said.

"Me too. One of the doctors told us that about half of those diagnosed with cancer will die. I guess he thought it might comfort us, let us know we weren't the only ones facing the death of a family member."

"Seems insensitive to me," I said.

Doug shrugged. "My brother thought so. I had to grab his arm to keep him from punching the guy. That's one of the good memories of Mom's last days. Seeing my brother's fury and the terror on the doctor's face always makes me smile. You know those family stories you tell at reunions and get-togethers? Well, that's one we'll be sharing for years."

"You big, strong Wagner boys could scare anyone," Sharon said. "How's your dad holding up?"

"He has good days and bad, same as all of us. Trying to get an agreement hammered out is a good diversion."

I looked from Doug to his dad and mine, who appeared to be in a serious discussion. "What agreement?"

"We're offering to buy your place." Doug must have noticed my shocked expression, because he quickly followed up with, "It's not a done deal, still in talks. Sorry. I thought you knew."

I felt like I'd been kicked by an angry cow.

Sharon wrinkled her nose. "Liv, how could you not know? Even Ben and I talked about the merging of the two farms, and we don't talk about anything!"

"We made our offer after your parents turned down Ben's offer to buy Friendly Farm," Doug said.

"Ben wanted to buy a dairy?" Sharon's shock was obvious.

Doug looked at me with a concerned expression. "Your dad called us, Liv. We didn't call him."

The hours twirled past, punctuated with laughter, screams, and a few sobs from exhausted youngsters. Sharon commanded the ticket purchases for the bouncy castle and face painting and also managed the sale of food and trinkets. She knew I'd expected the dairy to be handed down to me one day, so she handled everything while I stared at the silos, barns, fields, the garden, and the grazing cows. I don't know how long I sat there before Sharon nudged me from my reverie and told me we needed to close for the greased pig events.

"Oh, I want to catch Dad's lecture. He's been milking cows for thirty years, but he gets nervous when he talks to an audience."

"Go." Sharon waved me away. "I'll pack up the things we didn't sell and take the money box to the house. See you at the pig races."

Each year's open house culminates with the greased pig races. There are three age categories—under eight, nine to nineteen, and over twenty—with each category winner receiving a $200 gift card for a local restaurant. Not only are the pigs greased, but the enclosure is dampened, so contestants end up muddy. We have a long list of entrants every year, and the winners' photographs make the front page of the Eau Claire newspaper.

Today's constant noise level aggravated the headache that had started with the stunning news that my parents might sell our family farm. I decided to get an ibuprofen from the barn's first aid kit before finding Dad.

My eyes took time to adjust after coming from sunlight into the barn's shadowy interior. But even after blinking repeatedly to clear my vision, I still saw Ben Wimble's body propped in the corner, blood staining his Grateful Dead T-shirt. He stared forward, with unseeing eyes.

I don't know how long I gawked at him before I forced myself to move.

"Ben!" I put a hand on his chest and felt no movement. I placed my fingers on his carotid artery. No pulse. I pulled his heels until his body was horizontal and began doing compressions. No response.

The barn door opened, and Doug slipped inside.

"Liv?"

"He's dead. Ben's dead." I looked at my bloody hands as if they belonged to some alien being.

CHAPTER THREE

When I stepped outside the barn, Mom rang the cowbell and mayhem ensued. The released pig squealed and sprinted away from eager pursuers who were encouraged with shrieks and warning screams by onlookers.

Sheriff Lincoln Miller leaned against the enclosure, holding his youngest grandson on his hip. I waved frantically until he handed the little boy off to his daughter and headed my way, smiling broadly.

"Liv, it's been a great day. The face painting was a good addition to the open house. You can see how my little 'granddogs' loved that booth." He nodded to his grandsons, who sported the remains of painted dog faces now tarnished with mustard and ice cream residue.

"Ben Wimble's been murdered." I managed to get the words out.

He shifted his weight from side to side and grimaced. "You sure? We don't get murders around here."

"Ben's body is in the barn. And he's definitely dead. Doug Wagner's with him. I locked the barn." I showed him the key I'd used.

The sheriff gazed at the open house crowd and settled on Noah, who stood by a flatbed trailer with Wren. He motioned for him to join us. "Noah, I need a doc. Know you take care of animals, not people, but you'll have to do. Wren, you best stay here. Okay, Liv, let's go."

As Noah joined us, I whispered to him, "Ben's dead."

Noah started to ask a question, but I shook my head.

The sheriff waved to a gaggle of men, muddy from their efforts to catch a pig in the last race, who were horsing around and spraying one another with the garden hose. "Move along, fellows. The Olsens won't appreciate the mess you're making." The sheriff waited until they circled the hose around the spigot and left before nodding for me to unlock the door.

Lincoln Miller is a farmer first and lawman second. Elected to a part-time job of twenty hours per week, he deals mainly with teenagers staying out too late, stray cows, and some mischievous tomfooleries.

My hands shook as I fought to fit the key into the lock.

The sheriff took the key and opened the door.

I pointed to Ben's body. "There he is."

Linc moved quickly for a man of sixty, waving Doug away from the dead man. He and Noah checked for signs of life, and then Linc became all business. "He's been shot once, through the heart. What time did you find him?"

"Before the last greased pig events started, so less than thirty minutes ago. I had a headache and came in to get some ibuprofen."

"And you?" Linc turned to Doug.

"Came for the pig crates," he said.

Linc took his hat off and swatted it on his leg. "Dealt with enough death during my time in the service. Never expected to find a murder on my doorstep."

I tried to wrap my head around the idea. "And I didn't expect to find a dead man in our barn."

Linc harrumphed. "Ben didn't shoot himself. I'll call the main office in Eau Claire, ask them to get a team down here. I hope you didn't move anything. Can you find some rope, twine, wire, anything to mark off a perimeter?"

I nodded mutely and went past the body to the storage area. I'd have to confess that I'd moved the body to the floor and tried to give Ben chest compressions. Searching for a length of rope, I saw the open cabinet where the pistol had been stored. It was gone.

Careful not to touch anything near the cabinet, I got a long piece of rope and a garden hose and took both to the sheriff, who stood with hands on hips, head inclined toward Noah, who stared at the body.

"I just talked to Ben this morning," Noah said. "He was mad at me, as usual."

Linc eyed the vet. "Thought you two were partners."

"We were, officially, but he made it clear from the start that our partnership was more an eighty-twenty type deal, not a fifty-fifty one. We had the same number of clients, but the quality was different. He worked with the Olsens, but Liv and her mom wanted me to look at their cows for a second opinion. I tried to be casual about it, told him I was curious about the mystery disease, but Ben didn't believe me. He ranted that I wanted to steal his customers."

The sheriff used the rope and hose to make a circular zone around the corpse while continuing to quiz Noah. "Sounds like a bad business deal you got wrangled into."

"It was," Noah agreed. "Wren wanted me to get out, so last month I talked to Ben, and he informed me he'd take me to court if I tried to dissolve the agreement. I didn't approve of him cutting corners on tests or treatments for the farmers, and he accused me of not thinking like a businessman. I told him he was more a crook than a capitalist. Then he said he wouldn't be a vet forever. I think he was stringing me along."

"Maybe he wasn't. Sharon. . ." I hesitated until the sheriff glanced my way and raised his eyebrows. I continued. "Sharon, Ben's wife, told me that Ben said he would soon be rich and hinted it would be from something other than the vet practice. Uh, Linc, I should tell you the barn pistol is gone. We kept it in a locked cabinet."

"You sure it was in there today? Maybe your folks removed it for the open house."

Doug spoke before I could answer. "It was there. June wanted the gun locked in the barn for the open house. Several people saw her secure it in the cabinet."

"Liv, we'll need to know of anyone who might have the combination."

"Easier to make a list of who wouldn't know. Dad sets all our codes to Mom's birthday so he doesn't forget."

"Even I know it," Noah said. "The combination is 0731. Frank mentioned it earlier today when the barn was full of people."

"I'll start with a list of who was here at that time. Liv, do you have a tablet or some paper and a pen here in the barn? I don't want to leave the scene until the lab people get here."

I fetched an old milk production tablet that had several blank pages. "When Mom brought the gun out, Noah and Wren, Dad, and Sharon and Ben were here. That's right, isn't it?" I turned to Noah.

"Dad and I were here too," Doug added. "And Frank announced the combination in front of all of us."

"Dad trusts everyone," I explained.

"Convenient for a killer not to have to bring a weapon," Linc said. "Do you know the make?"

"Smith & Wesson .38. It's registered. Dad will have the paperwork," I said.

"Might save the coroner time when he checks ballistics. Doug, Noah, find Sharon Wimble. I'll tell her the news while you fellows round up the others who were in here this morning."

I wanted to get away from the body, so I asked Linc if I could go to the milking parlor.

Linc nodded. "Don't go far."

"We're dairy farmers. We never go far." As I passed Ben's body, I slowed and studied it as I would a lab sample. His clothing had bits of straw on them, and he had a chocolate smear on his running pants. His shirt had a trace of orchid-pink lipstick, not the bright red his wife Sharon always wore. He was sitting against the wall when I'd found him. Either he was shot in that position, or the force of the bullet knocked him down.

Perhaps his killer surprised him when he was in the barn with a third person. I groaned. I had enough suspects to consider. I didn't need another party in my whodunit stew. In the milking parlor, I donned my barn overalls and boots and grabbed a shovel. In dairy farming, the routines continue, murder or not.

I'd finished filling the feed troughs when Dad arrived.

His face was ashen. "I saw Linc. He said Doug found you in the barn with blood on your hands."

"I was doing CPR," I said.

"On a man with a bullet through his chest?" Dad squinted at me. "Liv, we don't have money for a high-priced lawyer."

"Why would I need a lawyer? I didn't kill Ben!" I stepped back.

"Of course you didn't." Dad looked shocked that I would think he was accusing me.

Doug interrupted our father-daughter conversation. "The sheriff suggested Frank and June say goodbye to the guests. He thinks it's best if visitors are gone before the crime scene officials arrive. He suggests you not mention Ben's death to anyone."

"Thanks, Doug," Dad said. "Tell Linc I appreciate his discretion."

Mom and Dad entered the milking parlor about thirty minutes later and went straight to work.

Mom moved next to me. "Sharon's taking it hard," she said.

"I wish whoever killed him had done it somewhere else," I said, giving Mom a half smile.

She shook her head. "No joking around, Liv. Linc considers you a suspect."

"I can't help what he thinks." I turned away and forced my mind to concentrate on the cow problem. I hoped we'd get a quick answer from the lab at the university. If something in the feed was to blame, we could correct that problem.

Dad whistled the first group into their stations. He took a sample from each cow. The first six were fine.

Dad stopped the line at the third cow on the other side. "Got another one. I'll check the others, then take her out."

Mom placed her hands on her hips. "Ben should have figured out something. That's what we paid him to do."

"Doug said Ben tried to buy the farm," I said.

"He did. Instead of helping us, he gave us a low-ball offer. Guess he thought we were desperate. Then the cows started getting sick," Mom said.

Dad went to the next cow. "Now, June, I can't see Ben deliberately hurting an animal. He is a vet."

"We'll see how the cows do in someone else's care," Mom said.

Dad led the infected cow away.

I didn't want to talk about diseased cows or murdered vets, so I changed the subject. "Mom, how do you think we did today? With the beautiful weather, the crowd was larger than past years, and the bouncy castle and face painting attracted a lot of kids and some adults."

"Face painting was pure profit. One of my quilting friends offered her artistic talent for free."

I recalled Sharon's promotional spiel for face painting. "Sharon was a good salesperson. Anytime a family came near her, she convinced them the children needed to be decorated with artwork.

Your artist friend offered little butterflies or ladybugs on the arms of children who were afraid of getting their faces painted."

Mom nodded. "Sharon's a sweetheart. Sometime you need to tell me why you two fell out. As for today's profit, I don't know. Doug sold entries to the greased-pig contests but missed the event itself because he left to lock the money box in his truck. We had lots of participants in each category. The Wagners always stay to clean up. We'll get the totals from the greased-pig entries then."

"So Doug wasn't there for all the greased-pig excitement?" I asked.

"That's what I said," Mom answered.

Could Doug be a suspect? He knew about the gun and was gone during the time of the murder, but he had no motive that I knew about. Thinking Doug was involved was as absurd as the sheriff thinking I'd killed Ben. But Doug told Linc he'd come in for the pig crates, and I knew he'd left the pig crates outside.

CHAPTER FOUR

I heard a thud when I hung up my overalls. The overalls on the next peg had fallen to the floor, and a gun landed next to them. I knew the gun belonged to our family and was probably the murder weapon. I held it up by the nose for my parents to see.

"This was in the overalls by the door. I'll take it to Linc."

Mom held out her hand. "Give me the gun."

"I'll take it. All our prints will be on it, and maybe they'll find the murderer's prints too," I said.

"The truth will come out." Dad shucked off his overgarments. "Let's go together."

Noah, Wren, Doug, Albert, and Sharon stood to one side, watching Ben's body being moved from the barn to the ambulance headed for a morgue, not a hospital.

When Sharon saw us come in, she ran to my mom and burst into tears. Mom wrapped her arms around my friend and made shushing noises while she patted Sharon's back.

"Found the gun in the milking room." I handed the pistol to Linc, who accepted it reluctantly.

"And you added your fingerprints to it," he said as he bagged the weapon. "Where was it?"

"It fell out of the pocket of some overalls we keep in the milking room."

Linc waved at the crime scene crew. "We'll get out of your way," he said to them. "I'll expect to hear from you Monday." He turned to our group. "Don't leave town without telling me."

I answered for the group. "We won't. Tomorrow's Mother's Day." I regretted my words when I saw the expression on Doug's face. This would be his first year without his mom.

My mom looked over Sharon's shoulder. "Why don't you all come back to the kitchen? We have leftover barbecue sliders and homemade brownies that need eating. We can all use some food, especially Sharon."

Everyone followed Mom's suggestion. Kitchens are called the heart of the house, and ours fit that description. The room was painted a buttery yellow, accented with black and white, the color of Holsteins. Our sturdy round oak table seated eight comfortably, and there was a Lazy Susan turntable in the center. Mom and I moved the receipts, bills, open-house decorations, and miscellaneous items to the formal living room, a place rarely used.

"Sharon, let's get the barbeque heated. Men, iced tea and sodas are in the garage fridge. Wren, plates are in the cabinet above the silverware drawer. Liv, grab the slider buns from the pantry and put out the relish, onions, and sauce." Mom's orders gave everyone something to do.

Soon the business of eating minimized conversation, which centered on the events of the day—without mentioning the murder in the barn. Albert Wagner recounted the excitement of the first greased-pig race when a six-year-old girl hung on long enough to be declared the winner, disappointing her older brothers.

"How were the other competitions?" I asked.

No one said anything, but I persisted. "Nobody knows?"

"Oh, Liv, who cares?" Sharon burst into tears again.

Mom frowned at me. "Liv, would you get the brownies, please?"

As I placed the pans, napkins, and a spatula on the Lazy Susan, the image of the brown smudge on Ben's running pants popped into my mind. I wondered if someone at this table had shared a brownie with him. No one here liked Ben, but did someone at this table dislike him enough to kill him?

If I'd read the sheriff's body language correctly, he'd cast me as the prime suspect—a ridiculous assumption—but I also didn't want to believe Ben's murderer was sharing a meal at our family table.

"June, thanks for dinner. Wren and I should be going." Noah held Wren's chair, then turned to Sharon. "Don't worry about the practice. I'll take care of things."

"I'll stop by on Monday and go through Ben's office. He could be messy. You'll be busy with your clients and his," Sharon said.

"I could box things for you." Noah picked a piece of straw off his sleeve.

"I want to do it." Sharon sniffed.

Mom thanked Wren for her help with the hayrides and walked the couple to the door. Albert and Doug left next, citing their need to get the pigs and the hay wagon back to their place. They'd stayed the entire day, having hired high school neighbors for the milking and chores. I tried to remember if they'd done that for our past open-house days but came up blank.

"Sharon, why don't you spend the night with us?" Mom asked.

"I should go. I need to call people about Ben's death and think about funeral arrangements. Things keep bubbling up. My mind's a jumble of details."

"The funeral home will have a list of things to do, and you can count on me and Liv."

"I can't believe he's gone." Sharon looked like she might give way to weeping again.

I walked with her to the barn area where Ben's car was parked. "Do you have the car keys?"

"I do. Liv, you know I didn't want Ben dead. I was just spouting off, venting to a friend." Sharon's speech seemed as much for herself as for me.

"Tell me what I can do to help." As I reached to open the car door, she turned to block me and shooed me from the car.

"Please forget anything I said earlier. If the sheriff knew of that conversation, he might consider me a suspect."

My friend looked so anxious that the words popped out of my mouth. "Sharon, would you like me to spend the night with you? If you're making calls to family and friends, you might want company."

She sucked in a breath. "I would, but the house is a mess. Give me thirty minutes to tidy up." She got in the car and gunned the engine as she headed down our lane.

Mom and Dad sat at the kitchen table. But this time, instead of food, they had cash lined up by denomination, the receipt forms from the card reader, invoices, and the farm-visit booking sheets.

"How'd we do?" I tried for an upbeat tone.

"Not good," Mom said. "Probably less than a thousand, and I didn't deduct anything for the food or crafts I made. Guess we broke even."

"How about the bookings? They've always boosted our summer income."

"We started with five, but I expect cancellations when they hear about the murder in our barn. News will be all over the county within the week."

"'The sun'll come out tomorrow,'" I sang in my best *Annie* impersonation.

"It will, but I don't know if things will be any different. I'm going to bed." Mom rose slowly.

"I'm spending the night with Sharon. I thought she could use some support making calls about Ben's death."

Mom touched my cheek. "That's the right thing to do." She looked like an old woman as she trudged down the hall.

Dad watched until she closed the bedroom door. "Losing this farm will kill your mom, but I don't know if I can do anything to stop it. How long are you staying at Sharon's?"

"Just tonight. I expect her relatives or Ben's will come when they find out. I'll definitely be here to cook dinner for Mom tomorrow."

Dad smiled. "You can help, but your mother doesn't give up kitchen control, even on Mother's Day. Tell Sharon she's welcome anytime. You girls were inseparable in school. And don't come over for morning milking."

"I won't, and I'll be here before noon, with or without Sharon."

I hoped my professor might phone Sunday, even though it was Mother's Day, and I knew my brothers would call. Mom and Dad should update them on farm finances, the herd infection, and share the grim news about the murder in the barn.

Sharon opened the door wearing sweats and an oversized T-shirt. She'd removed her makeup and brushed out her hair. The change made her look younger, not older, and she seemed more in control. She showed me to the guest room so I could drop my overnight bag and then led me to the kitchen.

"I started a list. The police have Ben's phone. I'm sure he has contacts on it that I don't have. I'll ask the office secretary to notify his clients and work colleagues. Noah probably expects to buy out Ben's share of the business. He's been wanting to go on his own, but I'm not going to do anything rash."

"Wise people say not to make any major decisions for a year after a spouse's death." I looked at her notification list. "Have you started your calls?"

"Not yet. I'll start with my sister. She'll be easiest. What do you think of this?" She took a piece of paper from her sweatpants pocket and read, "I have bad news. Ben was killed this afternoon, and the police are investigating his death. I don't know when we'll be able to bury him. I'll call or email later with more information and the funeral arrangements, but I wanted you to know right away."

"Sounds fine," I said.

She studied her script. "If people quiz me, I'll say I can't talk because I have more calls to make. If I say Ben was murdered, they'll want details."

"Sounds perfect," I said.

My friend lifted her chin, tapped the contact icon on the phone, and then turned to me. "Would you please check in Ben's desk for his client list? Maybe you'll find something to shed light on who might want him dead. His study is to the right of the entry."

I considered the assignment a stroke of luck. If Ben Wimble offered to buy our family farm, he must have known my parents were vulnerable. I entered his study and turned on the light, eager to search for clues. To my surprise, the space looked ready for a home magazine's photo shoot—a stark contrast to the other rooms, and very different from what Sharon led me to believe. On display were antique medical items, definitely conversation starters for visitors to this sanctum, and two rows of books. I perused the titles—all medical texts, not a single frivolous novel.

Seated in the swivel desk chair, I pulled out the center drawer. Nothing but pens, pencils, scissors, note packets, and a calculator. The folders in the right drawer were arranged alphabetically. I pulled four: Accounts, Bird flu, Clients, and Investments. The client file might have names of persons Sharon should call. The accounts and investments might help Sharon understand what was going on with their finances. And the bird flu file piqued my interest as it was the only medical file in the drawer. I placed those on the desk and checked the left drawers. Inside one was a locked cash box, and in the next was a medical storage box, also locked.

Sharon tapped on the doorframe. "My sister Miranda is coming out tomorrow. She's six years older and acted like an adult when she was ten. She'll take charge."

"Do you want her to?"

"Maybe," Sharon said. "I should get back to the phone. Don't want to call anyone after ten at night."

I slid the file folders together. "I found the contact information for Ben's clients. Want to see it?"

"No, just keep looking and let me know if you find anything else."

I held up the other folders.

She nodded and looked back at her call list. "I'm glad you found the investments and accounts folders. We should take a closer look at those, since I didn't even know Ben made an offer on your farm." Sharon left to continue her phone calls

Would the files confirm her fears?

CHAPTER FIVE

Sunday morning, Sharon hurried me out the door saying she wanted to clean the house before her neat-freak sister arrived. I reminded her about the folders I'd found, and she told me to take them with me and she'd look at them after the funeral.

At home, I slid Ben's folders into my nightstand drawer and then joined my parents in the kitchen. "Any new cow cases today?"

"Not yet." Dad knocked on the kitchen table for luck, then glanced at my clothes. "Need to leave for church in twenty minutes, Liv."

Mom, wearing her Sunday best, looked from me to my father. "We could skip today. The place will be filled with wagging tongues."

"That's why we need to go," Dad said. "We have nothing to hide, and not going to church would make us look like we're guilty of something."

"I'll get dressed." I ignored the files calling for my attention and pulled on a skirt and summer-weight sweater.

Wisconsin's weather presents a pleasant face for May. Some days might be breezier or cooler than I prefer, but it's my favorite month. Attendance at the small community church serving the farms scattered throughout the area was less than I expected, but I still overheard a few whispered comments about Ben Wimble's murder at our open house.

As we left the sanctuary, Albert thanked Mom for the sliders and brownies the night before. "I'm a sucker for chocolate. I bought two dozen brownies at the open house. I shared some, but the majority went right here." He patted his slightly rounded stomach.

"I'll make you a pan next week. You never charge us for the pigs or your hay wagon," Mom said.

"No need, but I'd never refuse anything from your kitchen, June." Albert turned to my dad. "Frank, let me know when you want to talk business. This Ben thing may cause you more problems. I don't believe Liv did it, despite what folks are saying."

My temper flared, and I felt my face getting red. "I'm standing right here, and I didn't shoot Ben Wimble."

"Liv! Apologize. You may be a grown woman, but I won't tolerate bad manners from a child of mine." Dad's voice was low and firm.

When I was growing up, my father frequently reminded me about speaking before my brain was engaged. He was right. I'd been rude to our neighbor.

"I apologize, Albert. I'm upset about the cow sickness, that the farm might be sold, and Ben's murder in our barn. I'm sorry for taking my frustrations out on you. You and your family are great friends and neighbors."

Albert patted my shoulder. "I understand, Liv. I flew off the handle at lots of well-meaning people when my wife was sick. Shucks, I owe apologies to half the people in the county. I know you didn't mean what you said."

Doug motioned to his father from across the parking lot, and Albert said his goodbyes.

"Easier than I thought," said Mom. "I'm glad we came, and the preacher's sermon about 'take no thought for tomorrow' hit home."

"Would you ladies like to go out for a Mother's Day lunch?" Dad asked.

Mom shook her head. "No. I expect our boys to call, and I started the slow cooker. Pot roast should be ready when we get home."

"Mom, I told you I'd cook today."

"Slow cooker meals are no trouble." Mom laced her fingers through Dad's as they walked to the parking lot.

My parents are old-fashioned and rarely hold hands or display any affection in public. My heart ached for them and the worries they faced. I prayed the samples I'd sent to my professor would tell us what was going on with the cows and that the sheriff would soon find the person who murdered Ben.

After a big meal, we got out the laptop for a video chat with my brothers. Mom insisted on the rundown of their lives, their spouses, and the escapades of grandchildren before allowing them to offer their appreciation and love for her on Mother's Day.

After the pleasantries, Dad took over. "Boys, we have some not-so-good news and need your thoughts. Your mom and I are thinking of selling the farm."

If Dad expected gasps and expressions of alarm, they didn't come.

"We'd hoped to pass on the farm to another Olsen," Mom said.

My brothers protested, saying they were happy with their chosen lives and had no desire to return to the dairy farm.

"What about you, Liv?" Tim asked. "I thought you might want to carry on the family tradition."

"Mom and Dad should do what's best for them." My voice caught as I spoke. "Dad, tell them the rest."

Dad fidgeted and then leaned toward the screen. "We've lost some cows, and others are sick. Can't pinpoint the cause."

"And..." I prompted.

"Our vet, Ben Wimble, was murdered in the barn Saturday."

Those revelations reduced my brothers to speechlessness.

Mom twisted her apron and spoke to the laptop screen as if my brothers were in the same room. "Liv was doing chest compressions, so of course her hands were bloody, and now the sheriff suspects her. Ben wasn't a popular person, even with his business partner. . ."

Dad patted Mom's shoulder. "Now, June, we need to trust Linc to do his job."

"Lincoln Miller's the sheriff? Thought he was a full-time farmer," Tim said.

"He's part-time sheriff, but he's a good man. He'll get this straightened out." Dad's optimism seemed to convince my brothers.

"What are you boys doing to honor your wives today?" Mom asked.

My brothers seemed relieved at the subject change and shared their plans before ending the visit.

After we put away the computer, I suggested Mom sit and talk while I clean the kitchen.

"Can't just sit, Liv. If I'm not busy, my mind goes down some rabbit hole of worry."

Protesting would be futile, so we worked together, putting away leftovers and doing the dishes.

"I'll call Dr. Armstrong after we finish. Maybe he'll have the results from the samples we sent him." I placed plates in the cabinet.

Dad looked up from the Sunday paper. "Sure would like some good news. I hate seeing our cows get sicker and sicker. Each one is like family."

Mom dried her hands on her apron. "Boys sounded happy. Liv, a good marriage might be better for you than a dairy farm."

I didn't answer. Mom harped on my single status every time I was home.

Monday turned chaotic before the sun rose. Another cow's milk looked bad, so she was quarantined with the other sick ones, which now numbered twenty.

After milking and chores but before our big breakfast, the sheriff called to say my prints were on the gun and that he'd pick me up for interrogation at county headquarters. Being interrogated by the sheriff sounded more serious than our neighbor Linc asking me questions.

I hoped my supervising professor would call before I was whisked away. Dr. Armstrong had been off campus over the weekend but promised to call as soon as he had results.

While waiting for Linc, I retrieved Ben's files and read through each one, hoping to find a clue or motive to explain why he'd been killed. I started with the accounts file. Of the four bank accounts listed, the two that Ben and Sharon held jointly had much lower balances. Ben paid himself from the veterinary practice each month and distributed the money into the four accounts—joint checking and joint savings and two other accounts with the same designations but listed under his name only. The majority of the monthly withdrawal went to personal accounts rather than the joint ones. Sharon was right to be suspicious. She'd expected to be comfortable once the practice was established, but he'd continued to ask her to be frugal.

The client list seemed cut-and-dried, with names, contact information, and notations about whether Ben or Noah was the attending veterinarian. Apparently, Ben kept paper records as well as digital. Sharon would want to notify Ben's clients of his death.

The bird flu file intrigued me. Ben had articles about the disease and how it might be transferred to dairy cows. In one study, researchers introduced the virus through nasal swabs of four dairy cows. All four were infected, but with different symptoms. One suffered diminished appetite, another a drop in milk production, and the other two produced a thick yellowish milk. The study said that once the disease is introduced into a herd, it can spread through shared milking equipment or feeding troughs. I read the article three times before I noticed it had been emailed from Dr. Armstrong, my supervising professor. I jotted down questions for Noah and for my professor. If bird flu was affecting our cattle, how could we combat it?

I never pegged Ben as a researcher and wondered why he had this file on infecting cattle rather than curing them. I loved animals, especially our dairy cows, and the thought that Ben might intentionally harm them made me see red. When my phone rang, I shouted hello into the mouthpiece.

"Liv, is that you?" Dr. Armstrong asked.

"Yes, sir," I said in a quieter voice. "Do you have news?"

"I do, and it's not good. We used your list of symptoms and did several different tests. What we have now seems unlikely."

"Bird flu?" I asked.

"What makes you think that? Only four or five states have ever reported cases, and Wisconsin isn't one of them."

"Our local vet had a file on it. The symptoms sound like those our cows are presenting. The articles originated from your email," I said.

"I can have the lab do a second round of tests, but that's what it looks like. Liv, when will you be back on campus? You have to present and defend your thesis in order to receive your degree." He'd ignored my statement about the file coming from his office.

"Well, that may be a problem. Our vet died in our barn, and the sheriff's taking me into the station for questioning today."

"What? You're a suspect in his death?"

"I guess I am."

"What happened? Never mind. I'm sure it's a misunderstanding and you'll be released soon. Keep me posted, but I must warn you, if you don't come back to campus before the term ends, you'll have to return for the fall semester. Now, about the cows, how many are showing symptoms?"

"We have twenty quarantined, and we've lost two. Do you have suggestions for limiting the spread? Is there a vaccine?"

"No vaccine. The main thing is to keep the animals isolated."

"Hard for me to concentrate with the possibility of being locked in a jail cell."

"Stay optimistic. You know more than you knew last week. If you want to send additional samples, I'll check them, and I'll send the information about containment."

"Dr. Armstrong, why were you in touch with Ben Wimble?"

The phone went dead. Maybe he hadn't heard my question. Or maybe he had.

"Liv, Noah's here," Mom called from the kitchen.

I slipped Ben's files into my laptop case and hurried down the hall to the kitchen, where my parents and Noah sat drinking coffee.

"Noah, any news?"

"I'm afraid not. I tested for all the usual things and got no results." Noah looked at Dad before continuing. "Your dad and I found another one dead."

I sank into a chair. "Should we isolate the sick cows from all animals—the horses, dogs?"

"You could, but I'm not sure that would help."

"Noah, would you run a test for bird flu?" I asked. "The university lab results point that way."

"Liv, that would be a waste of money we don't have," Mom said. "There's no bird flu in dairy cattle."

Noah shrugged. "Actually, there is, June. We haven't had cases in Wisconsin, but Michigan and Iowa have reported a few. It's rare."

Dad looked at me, then Noah. "Do it, please."

Noah pointed to the clock. "I'll come back this afternoon. I'm supposed to meet Sharon for lunch. She says she wants to talk business."

Mom raised a single eyebrow. "Business? I like Sharon, but her husband isn't even in his grave. You'd think she'd wait before tackling business decisions."

"I'm sure she's at loose ends and doesn't know what to do," I said, but in my heart, I wondered if Sharon knew exactly what she was doing. If I'd been in Sharon's position, I'd want to know about all my husband's holdings before the reading of the will.

When a knock on the door distracted us, I gathered my things and opened the door to face Albert and Doug Wagner instead of the sheriff I'd expected.

Doug stepped back to let me outside. "We came to help load the carcass. Noah told us you lost another one."

Dad, who had followed me, grimaced. "Good news spreads fast. Thanks for coming over."

"You've always helped us when we've needed it," Albert said.

Doug spoke so only I could hear, "Liv, would you like to go to Eau Claire this evening for a movie? Just the two of us, like a date?"

"I'd love to, but I have a date with the sheriff this morning, and I don't know if it's simple questions or if he plans to hold me."

We heard a car door slam.

"That should be Linc," I said.

Sure enough, the sheriff strode up our sidewalk. "Morning, Frank. You've got a full house here." He turned to me. "Liv, you ready to go to headquarters?"

To lighten the mood, I joked, "Should I call a lawyer?"

"Might be a good idea," Linc responded without a trace of a smile.

CHAPTER SIX

As Linc started back to his car, my mind was on the cows and the disease ravaging the herd. "May I take my laptop to do some thesis research?" I called after him.

Linc turned and said, "This isn't a spa visit, it's an official interrogation, but you can bring it. You might have time if I receive a call and need to respond."

I gave each parent a tight embrace and asked them to call me with any updates on the cows. I prayed Noah's test from the state labs might contradict the bird flu diagnosis from the university lab. If that disease had infected our herd, the state would have to take action and our dairy farm would be in desperate straits.

"How many fingerprints were on the gun? Was it a single gunshot? Do you have other suspects?" Linc had allowed me to ride in the front seat, and I barraged him with questions.

He avoided answering my questions in a "just the facts, ma'am" manner. "Liv, I'm not going to answer those questions. I can promise you that I'll work the case methodically, without partiality, as if the people on the scene weren't neighbors."

At the office, Linc asked if he could fingerprint me again. He'd taken prints from all the people in the barn on the day of the murder, but he explained that the office equipment was better than what he had in the field.

"Do you want to wait for an attorney?" he asked.

"I have nothing to hide."

Linc exhaled loudly. "I could ask the judge to appoint a public defender for you. He or she could be here within an hour or so."

To please Linc, I agreed, and he led me to a bare-bones room to wait. The interrogation room was better than I'd envisioned—not that I'd ever imagined being questioned as a murder suspect.

With my laptop open, I ignored my university research and listed people the sheriff might suspect of killing Ben Wimble. I'd be able to give my court-appointed attorney some other people to consider. But lawyers don't investigate, they just represent people in court. I'd need to do my own sleuthing, which wouldn't be easy if I ended up in jail. I tapped on the keys.

Sharon Wimble told me Ben was hiding something from her, possibly something financial.

Noah Reed wanted out of the veterinary partnership. Did he also want Ben out of the way for personal reasons?

Wren Reed believes Ben treated her husband unfairly.

Albert Wagner and Ben Wimble were vying to buy our dairy farm. Would the purchase of our property be a motive for Albert to murder Ben, to remove him as a rival buyer?

Doug Wagner has wanted his own dairy farm since high school. Was Ben standing in the way of the Wagners acquiring our farm? Were father and son acting together or alone? Doug said he'd come to the barn for pig crates—crates that were outside, not inside. Why was he really in the barn?

I decided to add our family names, although I wouldn't share them with the lawyer.

Dad has watched his cows get sick and some die under Ben's care. The cows represent Dad's life work, and he loves each one. My parents have depleted their savings, gone into debt, and are at risk of losing the dairy.

Mom has the same reasons as Dad.

Me? I added my name to the list because Linc obviously thought I was involved and because I should view the suspects from an outsider's point of view.

I didn't want any person on my list to be guilty of murder, so I added a last suspect.

Unknown person, who hated Ben for an unknown reason and took advantage of the open house commotion to kill him in our barn. This was my favorite answer, although it seemed unlikely.

Next, I pulled the files I'd taken from Ben's house out of my laptop bag, planning to scour them for information before I gave them to Linc with a request for copies for myself. Sharon would be going through Ben's clinic files this morning. She must be looking for something, but I didn't know what.

The client file didn't seem to hold any clues, but the accounts file showing separate bank accounts would interest the sheriff. Ben had accumulated enough personal funds to pay for a dairy farm. But the life of a dairy farmer is much less stable than that of a vet, so why would Ben want to become one?

The bird flu file intrigued me, and I pondered every word. Ben had contacted other states about existing cases, treatments used, and containment procedures. I examined each report carefully, hoping the file had the answer to save our herd. His sheet on symptoms listed the signs our cows presented—loss of appetite, low milk production, and thick and discolored milk. In a footnote was information on how a cow could be infected under a controlled research setting. Ben hadn't dated the sheet, so I didn't know if he'd known those facts before or after our herd had been stricken.

The next set of papers stapled together dealt with the prognosis and treatment of bird flu in dairy cattle. As I skimmed the information, I grew hopeful. The death rate for those affected was very low. Although many cows were sick, we'd only lost three cows from our herd of two hundred fifty, technically a small number, but those animals were like family friends. At the time of the study in Ben's file, there was no vaccination available, something Dr. Armstrong had mentioned on the phone.

The protocol included isolation of the cows and sterilization of equipment used in the milking process as well as vehicles transporting anything into or out of the barn area. The guidelines mentioned constant vigilance regarding sanitary practices for anyone in contact with the healthy cows, the cows themselves, and their enclosures. I saw hope. If cautionary action was taken, the disease could be contained. But first, we needed the Wisconsin state lab to confirm that bird flu was the ailment. Since the current lab results were from my grad school in Minnesota, their tests would only be used as supporting documents.

After studying the papers, I felt better about the cow situation, but the facts pointed the finger of guilt more directly toward our family. I was glad Linc insisted on my having a lawyer.

I opened Ben's remaining file, titled *Investments*. This folder held stock information on various companies, which made me wonder if he held a brokerage account too. The listed firms were those dealing with medical apparatus, animal food, dairy equipment, and companies offering animal vaccinations, salves, injectables, and tinctures. Another section included information on milk-processing centers, an island vacation resort, and sales brochures for Wisconsin dairy farms. The only item in the file that spooked me was a handwritten sticky note with the name and number of Dr. Graham Armstrong. I added my mentor's name to the list of people to contact.

Linc opened the door and offered me a cup of coffee. "Is black okay?"

"Perfect. Dairy farmers don't dilute the caffeine," I said.

"Your public defender will be here right after lunch. We'll do the questioning then. Are you comfortable in here?"

I sipped on the strong coffee. "Yes, though I'd like to be helping my parents sort out the herd infection."

Linc leaned against the wall. "Any ideas on that front? I'm not a dairy farmer, but I'd hate to see any type of contagion break out in the county."

"Noah took samples to send to the state lab. They'll tell us what we have to do."

"Everyone's rooting for your folks. The community loves them." Linc gestured to the folders on the table. "What are you working on?"

A nervous giggle escaped my lips. "Files I took from Ben Wimble's home office. They're for you, but I'd like a copy of them." I handed Linc the files and then pointed at my laptop. "I also listed people who might have murdered Ben."

Linc gave me a slow smile. "I've been doing the same. I've ordered you a sandwich, and it should be here soon. I'll get you copies of these files, which you do plan to return to Sharon, right?"

"Right. Thanks for the coffee," I said.

"I'll tell them to bring another cup with your lunch and the file copies." The door clanged shut when he left.

Switching my focus, I pulled up my thesis research. No matter how many times I went through my paper, I found a missing punctuation mark or a statement needing a supporting footnote. I searched for holes in my premise and jotted down questions I might be asked. I wanted to be prepared.

Mom and Wren showed up but weren't allowed to visit, so they sent notes. Mom said she and Dad thought the public defender would be adequate for now, but they would hire a top defense lawyer if necessary.

Wren's message said Noah sent our cow samples to the state lab and requested a rush on the tests. Even though my parents were completely organized at the dairy and in our home, they questioned their computer skills. They'd been more comfortable with Noah filling out the online forms to accompany the samples to the state. I emailed Wren, thanking her and Noah for their help and support.

Already I felt claustrophobic from being in the interrogation room. I could study for hours in an enclosed cubicle, much smaller than my current space, but knowing I could leave when I wanted made a difference.

I took a deep breath after my sandwich was delivered and returned to the suspect list. How could someone I'd known for years commit murder? But the sheriff had the same pool of suspects. I must clear my name and the names of my parents, and I couldn't do that from behind bars.

CHAPTER SEVEN

My court-appointed lawyer was a young man who probably shaved out of habit and not out of need, and I hoped he'd be up to the task.

"Could you give me some sort of timeline for this procedure? I'm scheduled to receive my master's this term and need to go to Minneapolis for a few days."

He shook his head. "I wouldn't push it. Linc's been lenient because he knows your folks." His apple cheeks and bright eyes made me wonder if he'd ever tried a criminal case.

If I honored his advice, I'd give up any hope of finishing my studies this term and lock myself into another year at the university. He explained the procedure, assured me he'd be with me if I had to go to court, and told me to call him night or day. At least he was zealous.

Linc's interrogation was a rehash of what we'd already covered, but this time all my answers were recorded. Reporters waited outside after my release, yelling questions and poking microphones in my face. I willed myself to wear a pleasant countenance. I'd seen newspaper photographs of surly or angry individuals leaving police facilities, and their expressions had biased my opinion about their guilt. I avoided the news hounds and hurried to Dad's car.

"Glad they let you come home," Dad said.

Too drained to talk, I noted familiar items on the way home. The Kaufmans' red mailbox with the miniature weathervane on top, the Bascom place where there was always laundry on the clothesline. The next farm's springer spaniel barked at every passing vehicle, and the Martins' sunflowers tipped their heads toward the west following the sun's course.

Albert and Doug were repairing fencing on their farm next to ours. Doug waved his hammer in greeting as we drove by. I wanted him to be innocent too. I closed my eyes and tried to imagine life without the family farm. If my parents sold the dairy, what would they do? They were only middle-aged, although they appeared older due to the recent stress of sick cows, a murdered vet, and possible loss of their home.

As our car rumbled over the cattle guard, I opened my eyes and drank in the sight of our twin grain silos, the large barn, and the milking house. Our home, protected by a picket fence, had a porch on three sides. I'd used each side to read novels, swing, ponder the shapes of the clouds, and daydream about an uncomplicated life.

Dad activated the garage door opener. I was home—for now. In perhaps a month, I might be in jail and our farmhouse and dairy might belong to another family.

Mom opened the door. "Hungry?"

"Don't have much of an appetite. I'll make myself a peanut butter sandwich. Then I'll call Dr. Armstrong, see if he's analyzed the second samples."

Dad glanced at the bottom of my jeans. "Are you wearing one of those ankle things so the police can track you?"

"No. Linc only asked questions. Thanks to your good standing in the community, he believes I won't flee. He hasn't charged me. . .yet."

Dad nodded. "Good thing my reputation counts for something. I'm going to check on the cows. Noah said he'd come out rather than call when he gets the results. I keep listening for his Jeep."

"When does he expect results?"

"State people promised him they'd prioritize the tests. If it is bird flu, well. . ." Dad's voice trailed off as if he couldn't bear to speak about the future. "I'm off to the barn."

"I'll start some beans for supper." Mom clanged pans, opened and shut the fridge, and then sighed. "Your dad's not well, Liv, and this murder business isn't doing him one bit of good, especially with you caught in the middle of it."

I unscrewed the top of the peanut butter and slathered some on Mom's homemade bread. "What's wrong with Dad?"

"He's worried himself sick. He thought your being home would help, but things have gone downhill fast since you returned."

I topped the peanut butter with banana slices and then wrapped my arms around my mom. "I wish I hadn't been the one to find Ben, but I was, and I'm sorry about the cow sickness."

Tears spilled down Mom's cheeks, and she brushed them away with her hand. "I'm scared."

I pointed to a ladder-back kitchen chair, suggesting she sit, and pulled out another for myself. "What are you afraid of?"

"Our future? We've been married nearly forty years, but in the past year, your dad's become more distant. He's weighed down by burdens." Mom stood and turned up the gospel music channel on the radio, letting me know she wanted no more conversation.

I touched her arm. "I think I'll go to the Wagner farm this afternoon. I'll come back to help with milking."

"You don't need to. Dad and I can do it. The fewer people in contact with the cows, the better," Mom said.

The kitchen I associated with laughter and fun seemed shrouded with despair and fear.

Doug answered on the first ring. "Liv, saw you heading home. Did Linc clear you?"

"No. I'm probably number one on his list. Want some help repairing that fence line? My parents don't want me working with the cows."

"Sure. Dad just left, so I'm by myself."

"I'll get to enjoy sunshine and birdsongs. Seems like I was in that interrogation room forever." I paused and then said, "Doug, there were newspeople waiting when Linc let me go."

"They just needed a picture of a pretty girl," Doug teased. "I want to finish this fence section, then help with the milking, but after that I'm free if you're still up for a movie tonight?"

"I think I'll take a rain check, if that's okay with you. We're calling my brothers tonight. See you soon."

Doug and I had created well-worn paths between our respective farms over the years. We are the same age, both the youngest of three, and we both love the dairy business. We were Jack and Jill in an elementary costume contest, and he pulled my first tooth because I was afraid to wiggle it but trusted him to do the work. I pinned a flower on his lapel for a seventh-grade dance, an event where we sat and sipped punch after one embarrassing try at dancing. We remained confidants throughout high school, and although we dated other people, we always drifted back together until graduation. I left for Minneapolis, and Doug lived and worked at home while pursuing his business degree at the University of Wisconsin-Eau Claire. I've dated several men over the years but compared all of them to Doug and decided they didn't meet my standards.

When I approached, I heard him whistling "Sloop John B," an oldie we both liked, as he worked on stretching and attaching the barbed wire fencing. I began singing the song's lament of *I want to go home, please let me go home*, but he never paused in his labor. When I waved my hand in front of him, he stepped back and removed his earbuds.

"Glad Linc let you go home."

I laughed. "Me too. Let's talk later. I need something physical to do."

"Which job do you want?"

"I'll hammer. I don't have the strength to pull the wire off the roll."

He nodded, and we began our fence-building ballet. That was our way. We seemed to read each other's thoughts and could work on any project smoothly and seamlessly. We were always in sync—except on the dance floor. We never mastered that skill. I'd been able to dance with others, to follow their lead, but not with Doug. I wondered if I subconsciously wanted to assert my equality by refusing to let him control the movement and tempo. Doug wanted to take care of me, but I valued my independence.

After an hour, Doug pointed to a tree. "My cooler is under that bur oak. Water, apples, and cheese are your reward."

"I deserve one."

He held my hand as we walked to the leaf-shaded area. "You never liked fencing. Why are you here?"

My offer hadn't fooled him, so I asked the question that bothered me. "Why did you come into the barn on the day of Ben's murder?"

"For the pig crates." He didn't meet my eyes.

"We both know those were outside the barn. I didn't contradict you in front of Linc, but I want the truth."

"I was standing by the greased pig enclosure when I saw you go into the barn. You were in there for a while. I came to check on you."

"Did you see anyone go in before I did?"

Doug grinned. "I wasn't interested in the going and coming of others, just you."

"Why did you follow me?" I persisted.

"To steal time alone with a beautiful woman?" He took a bite of cheese. "The truth is that you looked mad enough to spit nails when you heard we might buy your farm. I wanted a chance to explain." He paused then said, "I've seen your temper, but I was shocked to see you with Ben's blood on your hands. At least you washed your hands before you went for the sheriff."

"What did you do while I was gone?"

"Are you quizzing me?" Doug emptied his water bottle.

"Are you hiding something? Did you look for the gun? Did you move anything?"

"No. Did you? Ben was lying flat on his back. Either he was asleep and the killer stood over him, or he fell backward when he was shot. But he didn't have a bump on the back of his head. What do you think, Liv?" He fiddled with his empty bottle and avoided my eyes.

"Oh Doug, I did it."

Silence. Doug spoke tenderly. "Then you need the best defense lawyer in Wisconsin, Liv."

"No! I didn't kill him! I mean, I moved him so I could try CPR."

"Why? You knew he was dead."

"I hoped I was wrong."

Doug wrapped his arms around me. "I won't let anything happen to you."

"Don't make promises you can't keep."

After another hour of work, Doug offered to drive me home, but I elected to walk.

I couldn't eliminate Doug as a suspect. He didn't say he hadn't been in the barn earlier, only that he'd entered after me. And when I'd asked him about looking for the gun, he'd evaded answering. I didn't want Doug to be the murderer, and I didn't know of any motive he might have, but he could have had opportunity and the means—access to the gun.

On my walk home, I considered his last statement. How could he say he wouldn't let anything happen to me?

CHAPTER EIGHT

As I jogged toward home from fence building with Doug, Noah passed me, honked, and waved. If he had bad news, I wanted to be with my parents. I crossed the cattle guard as Noah got out of the car. He arched his back and twisted his neck to the right and left like a fighter ready to go into the ring.

I slowed my pace. "Noah, wait."

He leaned against his Jeep. "Saw you running. I should get back in the habit. I always feel better after doing a couple of miles. Oh, before I forget, Wren suggested you and your mom meet her for lunch sometime. She can scoot out on days the doctor doesn't have a surgery scheduled."

"Did you get the reports?" I gestured toward the house.

He pursed his lips. "Not good news."

"An official diagnosis is good news because you know the truth." I held the screen door for him. "Mom, Dad, Noah's here."

They stood stoically under the archway separating the family room from our country kitchen. Mom's hands were fisted at her sides, and Dad swatted his arm with the local newspaper.

"Should we sit in the kitchen?" I asked.

Mom placed a lemon pie and a milk jug on the table, and I got plates, napkins, forks, and glasses. Dad smiled as Mom busied herself with slicing the pie. Only Noah took a serving.

"Sit with us, June. No one's going to starve."

Noah pulled a file from his bag. "I don't beat around the bush. The state lab confirmed bird flu. It's rare for it to spread to dairy animals."

Dad reached for Mom's hand.

"What are the recommendations?" I asked.

Noah read from the paper. "Containment is the priority. The herd will remain isolated until all test negative. No milk can be sold from any of the cows. Anyone in contact with the animals must wear protective equipment—masks, gloves, goggles, and face shields." He looked up. "They suggest influenza testing for anyone who has been near the cows in the past month."

I pictured the crowds of people milling around our farm on Saturday. "What about those who attended the open house?"

"I told them about that. The state is issuing a press release urging all who attended to be inoculated." Noah tucked into his slice of pie.

Dad rubbed his chin. "Sounds like the kiss of death."

"I'm so sorry, Frank."

"It's not your fault, Noah. It's two-pronged trouble. The news story will damage our farm's reputation, and shutting down our dairy could bankrupt us."

Noah sipped his milk, then said, "The state is sending a team to care for the animals. They'll keep them separated, do the milking and testing updates."

"So we're out of business until the state says we're clear," Mom said.

"I'm afraid so. This strain can be deadly."

"Are they going to kill our cows?" Dad asked.

"The goal is to save as many as possible by keeping the healthy and sick separate. The sick can recover." Noah finished his milk and patted his mouth with a black-and-white cloth napkin with dancing cows on the fabric.

"And we can't sell the milk of the healthy ones?" Dad asked.

"No. All milk is to be discarded until the whole herd is cleared. I'll leave you the report."

My phone played "Ode to Joy," indicating a call, and I slipped out to the front porch. "Dr. Armstrong. What's the news?"

"The second tests were the same. Your cows do have bird flu. Would you ask your parents if I could come down and do field testing? This could be a great journal article, and I'm short on publications this year."

"It wouldn't be up to my parents. The state is sending a team to monitor the herd. They'd be in charge."

"I think they'll welcome me. What's a good hotel?"

"You could stay here," I said.

"Thanks, but I prefer a hotel. I'm coming for Ben's funeral and don't want to risk being quarantined. Sharon emailed me the date and time."

"You knew Ben?" I asked, hoping he'd explain the correspondence I'd seen in Ben's files.

"Ben and Sharon. She's a charming and beautiful woman. I never could understand why she married a guy like Ben."

"I'll text some hotel names." I clicked off.

When I returned to the kitchen, Noah was standing by the table. "Frank, June, promise me you'll get the basic flu inoculations. Would you like me to call the medical crew?"

Dad hunched forward. "It'd be nice if you notified Linc. He can tell the law enforcement people and the medical bunch."

Noah bobbed his head. "Glad to. Again, I'm so sorry."

"It's not your fault," Dad said again. "We'll call Sharon and the Wagners. I need to talk with Albert anyway. June and I would rather sell to a friend than some stranger."

Dad called Tim and Frank Jr. Neither acted surprised by the state intervention, and both encouraged selling the farm. I was angry with my big brothers, who viewed the situation as a business deal instead of a personal, life-altering event. Neither asked where my parents planned to go or what they might do to support themselves. They advised selling quickly before more cows died and additional debt accumulated.

Too mad to say anything, I picked at my cuticles as they talked about interest rates, options, negotiation points, buildings and equipment to be included. My parents seemed to shrink with each new point my brothers presented.

When the call ended, Mom said, "The Wagners are coming over tonight. We don't think they'll take advantage, but they're practical folks and will naturally want the best deal they can get."

"When did you ask the Wagners over?" Doug hadn't mentioned it when I canceled our date for tonight. Neither of my parents answered, so I started wiping the counters and table.

After a few minutes, Mom placed her arm around Dad's shoulder. "This isn't your fault."

"I feel like it is. Four generations of Olsens on this land, and I'm the one to lose it."

"We've got each other," Mom said.

"Don't consider myself much of a bargain."

"I do. I've never wanted to go through this life with anyone else, and our lives aren't over."

Dad stroked Mom's cheek. "Our dairy farming life is."

Mom took Dad's hand in hers. "I blame Ben Wimble. Our cows didn't have any problems until we turned down his offer to buy the dairy. I know that man had something to do with this bird flu thing."

"I don't like to think ill of folks, but the thought has crossed my mind." Dad looked up and seemed surprised to see me. "Liv, what do we have to serve the Wagners?"

I lifted the foil on the sheet cake pan. "Plenty of oatmeal cake, and there's the lemon pie."

"I wonder if they'll want to see our deeds and equipment ownership papers. The originals are at the bank, but I keep copies here. Liv, I want you to sit in on the discussion."

I shrugged my shoulders, feigning nonchalance when my heart was breaking. "I probably know less than you do about the legal matters, but I'm happy to listen. If you and Albert come to a basic agreement, a real estate agent or a lawyer will guide you through the details."

Both Albert and Doug looked sheepish and miserable as they settled in at our kitchen table a little after eight that night. Both accepted Mom's offer of cake to forestall the impending conversation. I inquired about Doug's fencing project, and we chatted about the weather, the rain cycle, and the price of milk.

"June, your oatmeal cake is as good as your brownies." Albert lifted another bite to his mouth.

His comment reminded me of the brown mark on Ben's pants. "You're a brownie fan, aren't you?"

"I love chocolate," Albert said.

"Did you happen to give Ben a brownie at our open house?"

"I might have." He peered at me. "Why are you asking?"

"Ben's pants were stained with something that looked like chocolate icing."

"Did our sheriff say it was icing?" Albert ate the last bite of his cake.

"Not to me," I admitted.

I guess Ben could have purchased a brownie. It might not have been one of Albert's. I might be conjuring connections where there were none, but Dad did say Albert offered to buy Friendly Farm as soon as he'd heard of Ben's overture.

"Let's get on with it." Dad shoved his plate aside.

I gathered the dishes before Mom had a chance. "Want anything else?"

Albert asked for water, so I got glasses of iced water for everyone.

"Never thought I'd ever sell," Dad began.

"Never thought I'd be buying," Albert said. "Frank, are you and June sure about this?"

"It's no secret that we're in over our heads financially. It's pretty embarrassing." Dad did the talking while Mom fingered the edge of the tablecloth. "You looking to offer on the whole place?"

"What do you and June want to sell?" Albert countered.

"The dairy, outbuildings, and our house are all tied together. The farm implements and cows are owned separately."

"This expanding isn't a new idea for us. You know the dairy business. Those mega farmers are driving us small owners out of the market. If Doug and I add your place to ours, we might make it. Otherwise, we'll probably be selling in the next five years."

Mom nodded. "What if we combined our farms, formed a partnership?"

Dad's eyes brightened at Mom's suggestion. "Our experience and expertise should be considered in any bargain."

I'd not thought of that. I eyed Albert, then Doug.

Albert took a long drink of his water and then said, "We're not thinking about a partnership."

Doug spoke for the first time. "We thought Dad would continue running our place, and I'd take over yours."

"You planning to live in our house?" Dad sounded surprised, as if he'd not considered another family living in our house.

Albert leaned forward. "Just throwing out ideas. Frank, do you think we should hire an intermediary? We've been friends and neighbors for years. I don't want a business deal to ruin our relationship."

Dad reached for Mom's hand. "Albert, this isn't a financial transaction for us, it's a death. We're giving up on the work of generations. I feel like a traitor to my parents, grandparents, and great-grandparents."

Albert extended his hand. "I'd feel the same, Frank. Take all the time you need."

Doug leaned close to me and whispered, "I'm afraid the state coming in will make things worse. They're super slow in making decisions, and without milk production, a dairy farm bleeds money."

I winced at Doug's term and pictured the blood on Ben Wimble's chest. I knew Ben was at the center of the catastrophe my parents faced. Had he set something in motion that would spell the end of Friendly Farm and our way of life?

CHAPTER NINE

Like most funerals in small communities, Ben's service drew a large crowd. A week after our open house, we stood as family members marched, heads down, to the designated sanctuary pews. I drew in a sharp breath when I saw Sharon enter clutching the arm of Dr. Armstrong. He'd told me he planned to attend, but for him to escort the widow shocked me.

I heard little of the eulogy or the minister's message to the family. Neither the church nor graveside service featured personal tributes. On behalf of Sharon, the pastor invited mourners to the Wimble home for food and to share memories of the deceased.

When I'd stopped by Sharon's earlier in the day with our food contribution, I'd met her older sister, Miranda, who directed the placement of casseroles, flowers, and cards. She'd welcomed my offer to help at the reception and given me a house key. I slipped away after the service ended to heat casseroles and make coffee and tea.

At the Wimble house, people milled in the front yard, waiting for the family to arrive from the graveside. Even though Dr. Armstrong escorted Sharon into the church, he didn't join the family members. Instead, he followed me into the kitchen.

"Let me help." He reached for the tea pitchers I carried.

"Thanks. They go on the end of that table. The larger pitcher is sweetened, and the smaller is unsweetened. You'll see the labels. We should put ice in glasses and pour a few of each so there's not a bottleneck at that spot."

"I have a suite at one of the hotels you suggested." He followed me back to the kitchen.

"When did you get in?" I grabbed potholders and took casseroles out of the oven.

"A couple of days ago."

"I was startled to see you escorting Sharon. I didn't know you were close."

Dr. Armstrong shrugged. "I told you I knew her and Ben. She asked me to walk with her because other family members had spouses or siblings."

"Might start rumors." I glanced away from the oven to check his reaction.

"I expect people to see the gesture as a friend helping a friend."

"I thought you wanted to check our herd. The state people arrived as soon as they confirmed the outbreak." I slid two more casseroles into the oven and set the timer. I didn't want to offend him, as his opinion swayed whether or not I received my master's degree.

"Sharon needed me, and I've seen plenty of sick cows."

"Cows with bird flu? I suspected the disease because of information you sent Ben. I found it in Ben's office."

"We weren't that close. The Wimbles were in Minneapolis for a conference in January. We sat together in some sessions and shared meals. We talked about lots of things."

"Sharon attended a conference on dairy animals? That doesn't sound like her."

Dr. Armstrong laughed. "I didn't say she liked it. Ben wanted to attend every session, which left Sharon at loose ends. I acted as her tour guide."

The image of Sharon leaning close to Dr. Armstrong as they walked into the church flashed through my mind. Before I could quiz him further, the family arrived and people flooded in to greet them. They filled plates and stood in clots, chatting about the service and speculating on who killed the deceased. Conversations quieted when I neared, and some neighbors even avoided eye contact with me.

My parents stood by themselves, apparently being treated with the same wariness. I needed to solve Ben's murder even though it might be too late to save our farm. When Noah and Wren joined my parents, I relinquished my serving duties to capable Miranda and approached them.

"I can't believe my supervising professor escorted Sharon at the funeral," I said. "Noah, do you know Dr. Armstrong?"

"I met him once, but he and Ben spoke often. Ben said they were working on a project together. He was quite smug about it."

"You must be overwhelmed, since you're taking care of your clients and Ben's," I said.

Wren answered for her husband. "We're not sure how much Ben was doing. Noah's schedule isn't much busier than it was before."

"Really?" I looked at Noah.

He tilted his head. "I don't think Ben did as much talking to farmers as I do. You have to bond with clients. If the animal's owner doesn't understand why a treatment is recommended, they won't do it. Their animals are like family."

"That's the way I feel about our ladies," Dad said. He leaned toward Noah. "Any idea about how much longer the state people will be crawling around our place, poking their noses into everything?"

Again, Wren spoke for her husband. "Noah says about thirty days. The situation is stable, but they don't want to risk a reinfection by putting the herd back together."

Mom took Dad's empty plate and put it with hers on the hearth. "I'm ready for this to be over."

Wren cleared her throat. "Frank, June, are you selling to the Wagners?"

I'm sure Wren was only asking what the whole community wanted to know, but the comment seemed meddlesome. In the past week, I'd seen my lifelong neighbors in a different light. They all expressed sympathy. Everyone knew how tenuous a dairy farmer's existence was, but it was as if they were relieved that it was our family, not theirs, that suffered this plight.

"Wren, maybe we could discuss things over lunch next week. Mom and I have literally nothing to do since the state took over the farm."

"Sure, Tuesday or Wednesday would work. Do you want to meet at my office?"

"Tuesday," Mom said, and then added, "Sharon's finally eating something. I thought she did very well at the service. She wasn't overly emotional."

I turned to Noah. "Sharon had me go through Ben's desk at their house."

"She went through his files at work. I offered to go through them with her, but she refused. Closed the door and came out with only a few papers. The sheriff took the computer before she arrived. She's pushing me to buy her out."

Wren reached for Noah's hand. "Let her push, Noah. We have to make certain the practice wasn't involved in anything shady."

My ears perked up. Maybe they knew whatever it was Sharon was afraid of. "Shady? Do you think Ben was involved in something illegal?"

Wren leaned closer to Noah. "We're not sure, but we're not buying Ben's half on a handshake. We'll get a lawyer involved. There are some things. . ."

Noah placed an arm around Wren's shoulder. "The Olsens don't need to know about our personal business."

Dad stuffed his hands into his suit pockets. "Seems everyone knows about ours. Can't say I recommend it. Don't ever get in debt, Noah. People I thought were friends cross the street to avoid a conversation. Guess they're afraid I might ask them for a buck or two."

I caught the look between Wren and Noah. Had they intended to ask for payment on our vet bill? Maybe I needed to talk to my brothers about pooling our money to help our parents through this rough patch.

Noah finished his tea. "Your warning about debt is too late, Mr. Olsen. Wren and I are struggling too. We both had student loans, then we bought into Ben's practice. Buying Sharon's half now would be a burden. Her 'friend' is encouraging her to sell immediately." Noah threw air quotes around the word *friend*, and I knew he meant Dr. Armstrong.

"Sharon hinted she'd find another buyer if we don't act quickly," Wren added.

"We should go." Noah took Wren's hand.

Wren gave us a finger roll wave. "See you gals on Tuesday. Text me when you arrive."

"I never thought a doctor would have money worries," Dad said. "June, Liv, you ready?"

I nodded. "I'll say goodbye to the family for us and meet you at the car."

The path to Sharon was blocked by her sister. "Liv, will you talk to her? She's ignoring the people who came to pay their respects."

I looked over to where Dr. Armstrong was monopolizing Sharon's attention. "Have you talked to her?" I asked.

"Of course. Sharon says she needs his support. But why would she? She has a houseful of relatives and neighbors to support her. You're her friend; maybe she'll listen to you."

"We were friends, but we drifted apart." I didn't want to get caught in this sisterly squabble.

"But you stayed the night with her after Ben was killed," Miranda protested.

"I did. She'd helped with our open house, then I found Ben's body. I didn't want her to be alone."

Miranda persisted. "What do you know about that man?"

"He's a professor at U of M. In fact, he's my supervising professor. I'm working toward an advanced degree in animal nutrition."

"Then try and talk some sense into *him*, since she won't listen." Miranda tilted her head in Dr. Armstrong's direction, grabbed some plates, and headed to the kitchen.

Sharon did not present the picture of a grieving widow. Her attire was black, but she hadn't shed any tears.

I touched her arm. "Sharon, we need to get back to the farm. Mom and Dad wanted me to tell you it was a lovely service. Call me if you need help or company."

Sharon gazed at Dr. Armstrong. "I won't need either yet. Graham is helping me tick off the items to be done. The funeral home gave me a long to-do list."

I turned to Dr. Armstrong. "Do you plan on stopping by our farm before you leave?"

"If I have time. Liv, I'm sorry you missed getting your degree. You'll have to register for the fall, and you'll have to select a new advisor. I won't be at the university next term."

"But you're the only professor with an emphasis in animal nutrition," I protested.

"Sorry, but I'm taking a sabbatical."

I hugged my friend good-bye and turned to look for Miranda. Instead, I saw Linc. He lifted his chin, indicating I should join him.

He wasted no time. "Who's the man with Sharon?"

"Dr. Graham Armstrong, a professor at U of M. I understand he and the Wimbles became friends at some convention."

"Appear to be close friends," Linc said. "I found those files from Ben's home office useful."

"I thought the bank arrangements were weird. I hope you learned more than I did."

"I might have," Linc said.

"What was it?"

"Liv, stop trying to be a detective."

"I'm trying to get off your suspect list."

Linc grinned. "Can't take you off yet."

CHAPTER TEN

On the ride home, Mom twisted her body so she could see me in the back seat. "What did Sharon's sister say to you? She seemed upset."

"Miranda thought Sharon should visit guests other than Dr. Armstrong."

"I thought the same thing myself." Mom turned to face the front.

"That professor of yours ever coming out to see us?" Dad asked.

"He wouldn't give me a straight answer," I said. "He did inform me that I'd need to return in the fall to complete my degree."

"I expected him to make an allowance," Dad said.

"I did too. I may not finish, just get a job—if I'm not serving a life sentence in prison."

"Don't joke about that," Mom ordered.

At home, my parents changed and headed outside, eager to see the "ladies" and check on their conditions. They had to dress in protective clothing to go into the barn area to see the animals, although they weren't allowed to tend to them. Having state employees handle animal contact for thirty days cost dearly. The fee for monitoring and testing was done with another loan, adding more debt to my parents' shoulders.

I grabbed Ben's home files to see if I could find what Linc considered a clue. I'd studied Accounts and Bird Flu thoroughly, so I started on Clients and Investments.

The client list was a roster, nothing more. The Wagners had been clients of Ben's, not Noah's, but so were Mom and Dad. Professional contacts followed the client list and contained state agencies, other vets, laboratories, and various suppliers, but one number jumped out at me. The number of the consultant for disease information was Dr. Armstrong's. But his field was nutrition, not disease. However, Ben's records appeared meticulous, so I doubted it was a mistake.

I checked Ben's calendar for the conference dates in Minneapolis. There it was, at the beginning of the year, which corresponded with the time Dr. Armstrong said he'd met Ben and Sharon. I looked at the weeks after that and saw that Dr. Armstrong and Ben had been meeting either in person or virtually twice a month through the middle of May, right before the open house.

I searched my memory and recalled Ben made his offer in March. After my parents refused him, the cow sickness started and the debts piled up.

This was not a path I wanted to pursue. If my parents thought Ben was responsible for infecting their beloved cows... I couldn't let myself imagine that scenario, so I went to a reliable source, the internet, to find out why a person might commit murder. A writer's website provided several motives. I discounted those that didn't apply in Ben's case.

I grabbed a legal pad and listed primary motives and the names of individuals who might have wanted Ben dead.

A fight turns deadly: Albert, Doug, Noah, Wren, Sharon.

Jealousy: Noah, Wren, maybe Sharon. I was thinking mostly about the clinic practice, but added Sharon's name since she was feeling insecure in her marriage. Then I penciled in Dr. Armstrong because he'd said he didn't understand why Sharon married Ben and he'd been there to support her.

The victim was abusive, and a business partner or family member is sick of the situation: Noah, Sharon, Wren. I listed Dr. Armstrong too, because he might have been in business with Ben.

Money—life insurance, inheritance, or gain from the victim: Noah, Sharon, Wren.

Eliminating a rival in love, business, or politics: Dr. Armstrong, Albert, Doug, Noah.

Revenge: Noah, Wren, Sharon.

My only conclusion was that I was not a detective. Noah and Wren mentioned debt problems. Owing people weighed heavily on my parents, and it might be more devastating to a young couple. My sleuthing was pathetic because, like my parents, I look for the best in people. I paired names to motives on paper, but in my heart, I couldn't see any of the suspects committing murder.

Tuesday morning, I was antsy waiting for the clock to move its hands so we could depart for our Eau Claire lunch with Wren. She'd seemed eager to share her disdain for Ben Wimble. I wanted to ask if he'd ever behaved inappropriately toward her, because his T-shirt had a smear of orchid-pink lipstick, Wren's signature color. I was grasping at straws, which reminded me that Ben had straw on his clothing, as did Noah and Wren. Wren had supervised the hayrides, so her clothing legitimately had bits of straw, but Ben? Noah? Maybe Wren could explain about the lipstick.

Wren chatted away from the time she got in the car until we parked. Even on a Tuesday, the restaurant line snaked down the sidewalk, so I edged inside to place our name on the list. Tilly's

Sandwich Shop was a gold mine. Customers didn't mind waiting, because Tilly made everything from scratch and charged fair prices.

Tilly started the business as a young widow forced to support her family. At first, locals came to encourage her, but her great food earned repeat business. Word-of-mouth kept the tables full. Her daughters were both in college now, and Tilly joked that with the cost of tuition and books, she'd be working for several more years. The truth was that Tilly, like Mom, loved to work, and both loved the work they did.

When our name was called, we were seated at the same booth where we'd met before a murder flipped our lives upside down. We all opted for the Tuesday special: a Reuben sandwich with a side of potato salad.

After taking our orders, the server turned to Mom. "Mrs. Olsen, Tilly saw you come in and asked if she could talk to you. I'll get those drinks and be right back."

Mom sucked in her breath. "I wonder what Tilly wants."

"Don't wonder, ask. Do it now, or you'll end up with indigestion," I said.

"You're right." Mom went to the combination hostess/cashier station where Tilly visited with entering and exiting customers.

This was my chance to quiz Wren about Ben. I began slowly and tentatively, "Wren, did Ben Wimble ever. . ."

"Yes!" Wren answered before I finished my sentence. "With Noah and Ben being partners, I couldn't avoid being around him. He'd put his arm on my shoulders or my waist, kiss me on the cheek, or hold my hand longer than necessary when shaking hands at church. I felt like I was playing dodgeball when we were with him."

"Did Noah know?" I probed.

"He knew of Ben's reputation. I never complained to my husband. I tried to handle Ben's 'overtures' discreetly."

"I experienced the same thing when he and Sharon were dating, and wanted to believe he was just being nice to her friends. Guess marriage didn't change his habits. Did Ben try anything the day of the open house?" I nodded to her. "That lipstick shade you use looks like the one that was on his T-shirt the day he died."

Wren pulled a tube of lipstick from her purse and handed it to me. "It is. The lab people matched the T-shirt smear to my shade. Linc asked me to come in for questioning tomorrow. I'm nervous."

"You know he interrogated me. It felt cold and formal, but he let me go home," I said.

"Noah's going with me."

"Did Linc ask Noah to come?"

"No, but we're going together anyway. We'll tell him the truth. We should have done it earlier, but we were afraid it would look bad."

Mom and Tilly were engrossed in conversation, so I encouraged Wren to continue. "What would look bad?"

"I went into the barn for a bottle of water. Ben was there, alone. He opened the cooler holding the water bottles and handed me one. As I turned to leave, he grabbed my shoulder and said I should pay him a finder's fee for the drink. He tried to kiss me, but I pulled away. He got a lipstick smear on his shirt, no kiss. Then Noah showed up. He was furious."

"Did he think you and Ben were having a rendezvous?" I asked.

"Heavens, no. Noah knew how I felt about Ben. He'd seen Ben reach for me and was ready to fight. Then Ben started laughing and told Noah to back off. He said, 'Noah, you know I like women. Nothing personal, partner. Besides, we're tied together for the next ten years.'"

I shook my head. "Ten years is a long time."

"We were both angry, but Noah grabbed my hand and led me away from that horrible man. Ben was alive when we left. I realize we're each other's alibis, but it's the truth."

She looked so earnest I wanted to believe her, but I remembered the list of reasons someone could be provoked to murder. She and Noah fit all six categories.

The server arrived with our sandwich plates, followed by Mom and Tilly.

Tilly nodded to the Reubens. "I tweaked an old family recipe. The Reubens are always a hit." She touched Mom's shoulder before leaving. "June, the offer is serious."

Ignoring the delicious-smelling Reuben, I demanded Mom explain Tilly's statement.

Mom grinned. "Tilly wants to start a second business and wants me to manage it. Until it opens, she wants me to make desserts for this café. I can't wait to tell your dad."

"When would you start?" Wren asked.

"I didn't give her an answer yet," Mom said.

I took a big bite of the Reuben. My mom has a drawer full of blue ribbons from baking contests. Her pies, cakes, and cookies earn her lots of praise and prizes. She always says she doesn't know which she likes better, dairying or baking.

Mom patted her mouth with a napkin. "Love this sandwich. I don't make them at home. Tilly says she'd welcome my help ASAP because she's doing all the baking now. With us not being able to work with the cows, I could start right away. The restaurant she's opening is near the mall."

"Did you tell her yes?" I asked.

"I told her I'd talk to your dad, but Liv, this seems like God opening a window. Debts mount every day the state people are at the farm. This is my chance to do something more than worry."

All three of our phones buzzed at the same time. The text from Noah read "Taking Frank to hospital. Possible heart attack. Meet you there."

CHAPTER ELEVEN

After dropping Wren at her office, I drove to the hospital with my mom. My tires squealed when I stopped in the emergency lane. I let Mom out and then plowed the rows, looking for a parking spot. I spied a large sedan backing out and quickly snagged the space.

I was out of breath when I reached the admission desk. "Frank Olsen," I gasped.

"He's being evaluated. The family waiting area is on the second floor."

Dad has high blood pressure, but he'd never had heart problems. I pushed the elevator call button repeatedly. If Dad was still being evaluated, chances were we'd be twiddling our thumbs for the next hour or so, but I wanted to be there when the doctor came out.

I spotted Noah standing by Mom's chair. Despite the waiting room being jam-packed, only whispered voices broke the quiet. Even children were subdued, drawing on paper or gaming on their devices.

"What happened?" I asked Noah.

"I'm not sure," he said. "I had an appointment at the Wagners, so I stopped by your place to check on things. I went to the house to let your folks know I would be stopping by the barn. I heard what sounded like someone in distress, so I went inside. Your dad was hunched over, struggling to breathe and clutching his chest. I checked his airway and called the doctor. I rubbed his back, and his breathing slowed to normal, but his pulse was elevated and he complained of body aches. By then, Dr. Maxwell was on the line, and she said she'd meet us at the hospital."

"Have you talked to her since you got here?"

"Not yet. I haven't been here long. The police may be trying to catch you. I just sent that text."

Mom nodded. "Liv might have broken the speed limit. I'm surprised they took him right in. Hospitals want you to fill out a ream of paperwork before you're allowed past the front door."

"He had his insurance card in his wallet, and the receptionist made a copy of it before the nurse took him back. He didn't object when they offered him a wheelchair." Noah rubbed the back of his neck. "Oh, I called the Wagners to tell them I'd be late and asked them to latch your gate at the road."

"It's a blessing you showed up when you did. Thank you." Mom patted his hand.

"I should check on Albert's horse, but I can stay if you want."

"Go," Mom said. "There's nothing more you can do. I'll make you and Wren a casserole to repay your kindness."

"No need for that, just let me know what the doctor says." Noah turned to leave. "June, I suggested they test him for bird flu. If that's what it is, you want to identify it quickly."

"I never thought of that." Mom fished in her purse for a tissue.

"I'll walk you to the elevator." I fell in step beside Noah. "Was Dad okay when you brought him in, or were you trying to protect my mom?"

"Because of his recent stress, I thought the shortness of breath and chest pain might have been a panic attack. But when he complained about the body aches, the possibility of bird flu came to mind. The people who did the intake evaluation didn't think it was heart related."

The metal door whooshed open, and Doug stepped out but pressed his arm against the side of the opening so Noah could enter the elevator.

When the doors shut, Doug opened his arms, and I grabbed him around the waist and hugged him. "What are you doing here?"

"Thought you might need a shoulder to lean on," he said. "Know anything?"

"No." I left my head on his chest, comforted by the strong arms holding me.

"Our family spent hours in waiting rooms when my mom was sick. Sometimes looking at a different face helps."

"We were having lunch with Wren at Tilly's. The Reuben sandwiches were great. Mom and Tilly were chatting about. . ." I stopped talking, and my hand found his as if it had a life of its own. "Doug, I'm so scared."

"I know." He kissed my hand and led me to where Mom sat twisting her wedding band back and forth on her finger.

Mom's eyes widened when she saw us. "Doug?"

"June, consider me your handy helper. I can fetch coffee, sandwiches, aspirin, tissues. I can check on your animals, feed the chickens, bring you books and magazines, or just sit quietly."

Mom smiled. "Good to have your company."

"Olsen family." The sound reverberated in the room.

As Mom stood, Doug slipped into her chair. "I'll save the seat for you."

My heart pounded as Mom and I approached the desk where Dr. Maxwell, a stocky, white-coated woman with graying hair, waited.

"How's Frank?" Mom asked.

"Let's go to a cubicle where we can have some privacy." She led us to a small room with a table and four chairs and closed the door behind us.

"Is he okay?" Mom's voice trembled.

"He's resting. June, it's not his heart. He does have a virus, and we're testing for flu. I understand your cows have bird flu, and it can be transmitted to humans in a number of ways, including being sprayed with an infected cow's milk. We don't want the virus spreading, so I'd like him to stay here in isolation. Are either of you experiencing fever, chills, headaches, coughing?"

Mom and I murmured "no" to each symptom.

"We'll get you tested since you're here. And I recommend getting a regular flu shot. Since Noah brought Frank in, he should get tested too."

"Can I see him?" Mom asked.

"You can peek into his room, but don't go inside. Even the mist from speaking to each other could spread the disease. After the nurse tests you, you should go home and wait for the results. Please don't go shopping in a busy mall." Dr. Maxwell offered a slight smile.

"How serious is Dad's condition?" I asked.

"We're taking precautions," Dr. Maxwell said.

"That doesn't answer my question," I said.

"Bird flu can be serious, but he's getting treatment. We have antivirals to treat a basic flu, and that might help."

I remembered resting my head on Doug's chest. "A neighbor is with us. Should he be tested too?"

"Yes, it's better to be safe." Dr. Maxwell flagged a nurse, gave instructions, and said good-bye.

I motioned for Doug to join us in the small room where we waited until the nurse came to give us masks and administer the tests. When she finished, the nurse pointed to the exit.

Mom shook her head. "Dr. Maxwell said I could see my husband. I know we can't go in. I just want to see him."

"Follow me." The nurse led the three of us to the end of the corridor and then went inside the room and raised the blinds.

I expected Dad to have IV connections, but I didn't expect him to look so small and listless. He lay unmoving, eyes closed, with an oxygen mask covering his mouth and nose.

Mom grabbed my hand and Doug's to create a circle. "Let's pray."

At home, Mom acted like a sleepwalker, wandering aimlessly and refusing to go to bed or sit.

"Do you want me to start something for supper?" I asked her.

"No. I don't feel like eating, and there should be plenty of leftovers for you." Mom continued her pacing.

"Why don't I get your recipe box? If Tilly wants you to bake for her, you could give her a list of your specialties." I retrieved the green box stuffed with slips of paper and index cards.

"We might as well do something other than worry. I'll make a pot of coffee. Did you see how pale your dad looked?" Mom filled the carafe with water and then emptied it into the coffee maker.

I was as anxious and nervous as Mom. The ugly thought that Ben had willfully infected our herd in an attempt to force my parents to sell was hideous enough, but if Dad didn't make it, I'd consider Ben a murderer.

We both jumped when the house phone rang. An unfamiliar number popped up.

"Friendly Farm," I answered.

"Is Frank there? This is the vet monitoring your herd's health."

"This is Liv. My dad's out, but my mom is here. I'll put you on speaker."

"I have good news and bad."

"What's the bad?" I asked.

"Another cow died this morning. The good news is that four of the ones in quarantine gave good milk."

"Which cow died?" Mom asked.

"Let me check." Papers rustled, and then he said, "Number 364, name's listed as—"

"Mary Martha," Mom said.

"Right. We're doing daily tests, none of the other cows are testing positive, and it looks like the ones we culled are recovering." He sounded cheerful.

"Except for Mary Martha," Mom said. "That's four who've died. What are you doing with the separated cows that are giving good milk?"

"We're moving them to another area. You know, this has been a great opportunity to study how bird flu affects a herd. We'll use our experience to help other farmers. Frank stopped in every day to check on the cows. He's a good dairy man. Wish I could have shared the good news with him."

"I do too," Mom said. "He'll be away for a while, but please call us with any reports."

"Happy to." The man ended the call without asking where Dad was or why he was gone.

"Do you remember Mary Martha, Liv?" Mom asked. "Flies always flocked to her. We sprayed her more than the other ladies, but her tail was always swishing, trying to get them off. She had a sweet personality."

I poured coffee. "The news sounds positive. Maybe the worst is over with the herd."

"It's too late." Mom pulled recipes from the box and started a list of desserts on a yellow pad. "We're selling the farm. Your dad and I looked at every option. We'll sell, pay our debts, and start fresh."

Even though Mom wanted the subject closed, I wasn't ready to give up.

"Mom, I know Ben wanted to buy the farm in March. When did the Wagners offer to buy?"

"Liv, your dad and I have made our decision. You should concentrate on finding who wanted Ben dead so you don't end up in prison for something you didn't do."

Was I behaving like a puppy chasing its tail and ignoring everything around me? I'd become so invested in the farm and the possibility of losing it that I'd lost sight of the fact a man had been murdered.

A pickup truck bounced down our long driveway, leaving plumes of dust in its wake. I peeked out the front window. "It's Albert."

"You talk to him," Mom said. "I'm going to rest."

I opened the door and watched Albert get out, followed by Doug, who wore a mask. When they got to the porch, Albert said, "Doug and I came to do the chores, and since tomorrow's garbage day, we'll take the bins to the road when we leave."

"That's nice of you, but I can manage."

"Many hands make light work," Doug said.

"Glad it wasn't Frank's heart." Albert picked up a hoe that leaned against the porch.

"If it hadn't been for your ailing horse, things could have been different. Dad was lucky Noah found him."

"How's your mom?" Doug asked.

"Tired. She's resting." I smiled to reassure him.

"How about you, Liv?"

"I'm fine. Doctors love to do tests," I added. "My guess is they'll call it a virus."

Albert nodded. "If it's a virus, you'll have to rest and drink lots of water. That's what the medical people always say."

"And we get to pay for their sage advice," I quipped.

"I've been thinking of hanging out my doctor's shingle. I could tell people that and make more than I earn as a dairy farmer," Doug said.

"It wouldn't suit you. You're a dairy man through and through." I winked at Doug, who looked very attractive in a light blue shirt that matched his eyes.

"Liv. . ." Albert swatted his cap on his leg.

I waited. Albert had something to say but was taking as long as a baseball pitcher's windup.

"Liv, I don't want your mom and dad worrying. We'll work something out based on their time frame."

"You still want our farm, don't you?"

"I do. Truth is, I'd rather have you as neighbors than own your land and dairy, but I'm in a position to help them and myself. I'm not going to take advantage of them. Doug and I will deal fair."

"My parents are resigned to selling, but I keep looking for another option."

Doug gave me an understanding glance. "You love the dairy business as much as I do, Liv."

"I do. Guess milk's our life's blood."

Albert took a couple of swipes at the ground with the hoe. "Ben's murder made a right muddle of things. Do you know anything more?"

"I know the sheriff's still following up leads. Has he called you in yet?"

"Yep. Me and Doug, separate days. Linc's the closed-mouth type, but I think he knows something. He didn't seem baffled by anything we said." Albert shook his head. "I guess we should quit jawing and get to work." He headed toward the garden with the hoe.

"I'll go with you to gather eggs." I grabbed a basket and bumped Doug's shoulder with mine as we cut through the yard to the henhouse. "I've always been able to count on you, Doug."

"I'm a nice guy," he said.

"And modest." I grinned up at him.

An hour later, the Wagners were ready to leave. After he started the truck, Albert leaned out the window. "Liv, if you or your mom needs anything, just whistle. I hope Frank gets better soon. Keep in touch."

I waved goodbye and went into the kitchen. I could handle the chores, but it felt right to have Doug beside me this afternoon.

My mind returned to the murder of Ben. Albert thought Linc had figured something out. I hoped he was right.

CHAPTER TWELVE

The next morning, I tiptoed through the house because Mom is a light sleeper—well, she was when my brothers and I were teenagers. Since the state people were taking care of the dairy, she was sleeping a little later. Both the state crew occupying our barn and Dr. Armstrong said there was no vaccine for bird flu in dairy cattle. They should know, but I wanted to look for myself, so I booted up my laptop. I found several farm and veterinary journals with brief mentions of the disease. But *The Bovine Journal* cited several recent articles concerning bird flu. Dr. Graham Armstong's name appeared as a contributor. I marked his articles. My professor's field was nutrition, and those articles populated first, but in a second tier was his paper detailing how a bird flu vaccine for dairy animals might be tested.

The company backing the project sounded familiar. Bovinics, a company listed in Ben's investment folder. The hair on the nape of my neck bristled. This was the missing connection. I'd assumed Dr. Armstrong was romantically interested in Sharon Wimble when he might have been more interested in Ben's vet business. My fingers flew over the keyboard as one lead led to another. After I pieced things together, I'd call Linc. I needed to work with the sheriff rather than on my own, and this discovery could be a motive for murder.

The phone interrupted my thoughts.

"Hi, Liv, this is Dr. Maxwell. Is your mom available?"

"She's sleeping right now, Dr. Maxwell. Do you have our test results?"

"Your tests were negative, Liv, but we should retest you in a week. You know the rules. Limited contact with others, handwashing, and mask wearing." Dr. Maxwell continued, "Your mother does have the virus. Because of her age and history of bronchitis, I'd like her in the hospital for the next couple of days. I've alerted the staff to expect her later today."

"I'll let her know. How's my dad?"

"That's the other reason I'm calling. Unfortunately, your dad has developed pneumonia. For now, we've moved him to the ICU on the fifth floor. A respiratory specialist is treating him. You can call the nurses' station there for updates."

"He's never had problems with his lungs," I said.

"His overall health is good, but his body needs rest to recover."

"I'll bring my mother very soon." I put on the mask I'd been given at the hospital.

Mom was sitting up when I entered the bedroom. Her racking cough prompted me to grab the thermometer, a bottle of aspirin, and a glass of water.

"I put an extra quilt over me when I came in because I was cold. Now I'm burning up," Mom said.

"Let's get your temperature before you drink this water." I held the button and swiped the instrument across her forehead—103 degrees. I handed her the glass of water, which she downed.

"My shirt's sweaty. I'm going to change." Mom wobbled as she stood.

"Take my hand. The doctor called. You have the virus too. She wants you in the hospital for a couple of days."

Mom leaned heavily on me. "I don't want to go. That's just more money out the window. Can't I rest at home?"

"Dr. Maxwell didn't offer that option. You should look on the bright side—no cooking or cleaning for a while."

"I prefer my own cooking to anyone else's," Mom said.

I shared the other news. "Dad developed pneumonia. He's in the ICU."

"ICU? Pneumonia?"

"He's receiving breathing treatments. Dr. Maxwell commented on his basic good health and said he needs rest. Want me to pack for you?" I went to their closet and pulled out an overnight bag.

"Your father likes hospitals even less than I do. When our friends have been in the hospital, he won't visit. I have to be the one to go," Mom said. "Bless his heart, he must be miserable."

"The nurses will make sure he rests. It's good he's in the hospital. You know we couldn't keep him from working if he were here."

"Your dad is not one to sit on his hands," Mom said. "Should we call the boys and catch them up on everything?"

"I'll do that tonight while you're being pampered in the hospital."

"Guess I'll just need my toothbrush and the essentials. I heard they don't even let you bring your meds now, and I doubt they'll let me wear my own nightgown. They'll probably stick me in one of those gowns that flaps open in the back."

"That's hospital chic. Everyone's wearing that style." I touched her forehead with my wrist. "You feel cooler to me."

"It got too hot under that extra quilt. I'm fine. You can get the car. I won't be long. You'll need to return in time for . . ." Mom let the words go unsaid.

I didn't need to be home for milking today or tomorrow.

After admitting Mom, which required filling out the identical information at least three times, the head nurse requested I limit my phone inquiries for updates to once a shift. She assured me someone would call if the condition of either parent changed and shooed me off.

I jumped when a horn honked, and the car's driver raised a fist and glared at me. I shook the cobwebs from my mind. Instead of getting influenza, I might get run over in a hospital parking lot.

My first call after I got home was to Linc. He was out for the day, so I left a message that I had important information and would call tomorrow. Then I sent a text to my brothers, asking if they could do a three-way call at six my time. That would make it midafternoon for one brother and after dinner for the other. Having siblings on opposite coasts made the timing of phone visits among the three of us challenging. I checked with the overseer in our barn, who assured me things were stable and they anticipated turning the farm back to us in a couple of weeks. He didn't mention they'd also hand us a hefty bill for their services.

I scribbled bullet points on a lined tablet for the conversation with my brothers:

- *Cows have bird flu, 4 dead, no new cases, continue quarantine/testing for two weeks.*
- *Dad has virus, my guess bird flu, which morphed into pneumonia, ICU, doctors optimistic.*
- *Mom has same, she's in hospital too, case not as severe—yet.*
- *I tested negative.*
- *Mom and Dad definitely selling to Wagners. Timing not firm.*
- *Tilly offered Mom a job baking in her sandwich shop with possibility of Mom managing a second restaurant Tilly plans to open in Eau Claire.*

- *On Ben's murder, I'm still a suspect, but now I have a theory of who the actual killer might be.*

With those items on paper, I opened my computer and pulled up the Bovinics website, a startup company claiming to be pursuing new medicines for cattle. According to the files I'd found in his home office, Ben followed this company daily. I played a hunch and called Martin Evermeyer, the head of the Bovinics research department.

He answered on the first ring, "Evermeyer here."

"I'm one of Dr. Graham Armstrong's research assistants—"

He interrupted me. "Let me put you on speaker. Does Graham have good news? Is our vaccine working on the infected cows?"

I sat up a bit straighter, wondering how to respond. I went out on a limb and tested my intuition. "There's a problem. Did you hear that the vet for that herd was murdered?"

"Graham mentioned Wimble's death, but not that it was murder."

"Well, he was murdered, and because of it, Dr. Armstrong has limited access to the herd. Do your records show how many cows Wimble infected? Did he do so by nasal swabbing?"

"What? Who are you?" Evermeyer shouted. "If you really work with Graham, tell him to call me directly." He hung up before I could get in another word.

I rested my head in my hands. Dr. Evermeyer knew both Ben and Dr. Armstrong. Ben had introduced the disease to our cows with the plan to use Friendly Farm as his personal laboratory. If a new vaccine could be developed that prevented the disease or a medicine that reversed the effects of bird flu, that would mean a huge payout for the company and its investors.

Ben would get money on his investment in the fledgling company, even if he had to wade through years of additional field trials. Now his offer to buy Friendly Farm made sense. He'd wanted to test the new product on his own animals. But when my parents refused his handsome offer, he went forward on his own and introduced the disease to our cows.

What didn't make sense was Dr. Armstrong's role. With the state techs swooping in, I didn't think he'd had a chance to use a trial vaccine to prevent the disease's spread, but the animals were recovering. Had he managed to get to the herd undetected?

I drew three circles and labeled one of them *Ben*, another *Dr. Armstrong*, and the third *Sharon*. Sharon's connection seemed sketchy. Did she have a romantic connection with Graham Armstrong? Was their outward affection a ruse to make people think there was a romantic relationship? Was Sharon aware of the business deal between her husband and the professor? I recounted my time with Sharon on the day of the murder, her reaction to her husband's death, and her behavior the night I'd spent at her house. Was Sharon a pawn, or a player?

I pulled out the suspect list I'd made while waiting for my court-appointed lawyer. Maybe Graham Armstrong was the unknown person. But if he killed Ben, how did he get on the property without being seen, and how did he get the gun? My assumptions all came with more questions.

I wanted to talk with Linc. I'd explain what I'd learned about each suspect, which might help his investigation.

My phone rang. The caller ID showed the hospital number, and my heart raced.

"Liv Olsen," I said.

"Hi, Liv, this is Dr. Maxwell. I promised to notify you of changes, and your dad's condition has deteriorated. You may want to come. You'll have to wear a mask and gloves, but we've found personal visits can rally a patient and convince them to fight."

A knot formed in my stomach. "I'll be right there. How's Mom?"

"She's fine, complaining about the food. I see that as a healthy sign."

"Could Mom see Dad too?" I stuffed the notepad with the items to discuss with my brothers in my bag along with a pen.

"We'll talk about your mom visiting your dad after you get here," Dr. Maxwell said.

I called our pastor and relayed what Dr. Maxwell had said about Dad, and our minister promised to activate the prayer chain. Knowing others would be lifting Dad up was comforting, and I joined my prayers with theirs as I drove to the hospital.

CHAPTER THIRTEEN

Dr. Maxwell pushed Mom's wheelchair into Dad's room where I sat, gloved, gowned, and masked.

I reached for Mom's hand across Dad's bed. "Mom, the doctor says you're complaining about the cuisine."

Dr. Maxwell smiled. "If she behaves, she might get to go home tomorrow. Has your dad responded?"

"He squeezed my hand, but he hasn't opened his eyes," I said.

"That's a good sign. Keep talking to him." Dr. Maxwell turned to Mom. "I'll send a nurse later to take you to your room before they get busy with the shift change."

"I could take her," I offered.

Dr. Maxwell studied Dad's chart, and added notes. "I'll ask one of the staff. I want June in her room for her next delicious meal."

"I wouldn't mind missing lunch," Mom said.

After the doctor left, I resumed my bedside conversation. "Dad, did you hear that? Mom is going home tomorrow, and she'll be lost there without you."

Mom reached for his hand. "Liv's right. I might go a little crazy without you. I might drink tea instead of coffee for breakfast and eat sweet rolls instead of eggs and sausage. I might sit with my feet up all day reading a book."

"Or we might binge-watch silly romantic movies. Dad, we need you to keep us in line," I said.

The beeping of machines and the intermittent sound of the blood pressure machine provided a backdrop for the movements of nurses and people speaking in hushed tones. The ICU felt different from the regular hospital wing. Here, a sacred quiet reigned.

Mom stroked his arm. "Frank, get well so you can come home. I miss you. I can count on two hands the number of nights we've spent apart since we got married."

Mom reminded Dad about the milestones of their lives. I felt like an interloper, but one who wanted to record each word. She reminded him of the grief they'd shared when she had miscarried on her first pregnancy. That was a detail of their lives they'd not shared—at least not with me. She talked about when they thought they would lose the farm before Y2K, when the whole country seemed to prepare for a catastrophe that passed without much notice. She spoke to him of their future, perhaps a life without the dairy, but a different situation they could embrace and love. Then she stopped the monologue.

I bowed my head. "God, surround Your servant with Your love, and, if it be Your will, heal his body."

"Amen," Mom added.

Dad's eyes fluttered, and he turned his head toward Mom. "Cows?"

"Frank, you're awake!" Mom kissed his forehead through her mask.

"Dad, you gave us a scare." I leaned closer to him. "The cows are recovering."

Mom kissed his hand. "Rest easy."

"Several quarantined cows are giving good milk again, no contamination. The protocol is working. But we did—"

Mom held up a warning hand, not wanting me to mention the death of Mary Martha. "The state people said we'll get some monetary reimbursement for the milk disposal and toward the PPE clothing, even for vet costs."

"I like. . .that. . .man. . .working. . .with. . .our. . .cows." Dad struggled to get the words out. "You need. . .to know. . ."

He was talking. I wanted to jump up, shout, and dance.

Dad managed a few more words before drifting off.

Mom patted Dad's hand. "I like that man caring for our cows too."

As if the conversation had taxed all his strength, Dad began to snore softly.

Mom laughed. "Doesn't he look peaceful? He does that all the time. I'll be talking away, and he'll fall asleep and start snoring. Guess I'm not much of a conversationalist."

Mom and I sat in contented silence, each holding one of Dad's hands and watching him sleep. His face showed no pain or tenseness, an encouraging sign.

Mom whispered, "Liv, call Linc, see if he's figured out who did it. The burden of Ben's murder happening at our place is too weighty on your dad."

"Linc's out of town, but I'll talk to him tomorrow," I promised.

"Talk to Linc, but don't hire on as a deputy," Mom said.

"Being a deputy might be my only career option." I wondered what path Dad would encourage me to follow. Finishing my master's degree seemed a waste without the family dairy farm.

When a nurse woke Dad to take his vitals, he answered her questions about how he was feeling. "Mr. Olsen, you're doing much better. Guess it's these two pretty ladies who are responsible. Would you like something to eat or drink?"

"Water," Dad said.

"How about some Jello or pudding or broth?"

"Broth, please."

"I'll put in the order." She cocked her head toward the door as she left, indicating that I should join her at the nurses' station.

I followed her out. "Is anything wrong?" I asked.

"No. He's much better than when I came on shift. We weren't able to get any response this morning. Guess love really is the best medicine. I'll text the doctor. Why don't you go home after he eats? Patients usually nap after their meal."

"But Dr. Maxwell told us to come in," I said.

"And we made an exception for your visit. In the ICU, we limit visitors and the time they stay. I'll call if the situation changes." The nurse entered notes on the computer.

"May I come back tonight? You said our visit helped Dad."

"Dr. Maxwell's the boss." She patted my shoulder.

Even eating the small serving of broth exhausted Dad, so Mom and I left. I pushed Mom's wheelchair to the nurses' station with a joyful heart and offered prayers of gratitude with every revolution of the wheels.

Before I left the hospital, Linc called. "You left a message saying you had information."

"I did. I mean, I do. But Mom and Dad are in the hospital, and the doctor wants me to isolate at home."

"I'll come to your place about two, wearing a mask."

"I'll put the coffee on," I said.

"Don't need to. I keep my travel mug filled with caffeine." Linc sounded upbeat, but then, he always did.

With both parents in the hospital and our farm about to go under, I was ready to share my discoveries with Linc and let him figure out "whodunit." At home, the printer whirred as I prepared a copy of my notes for him. I re-created the conversation with Dr. Evermeyer of Bovinics as I remembered it. Linc wouldn't like that I tricked the Bovinics researcher, but I hadn't said anything that wasn't true. After I'd stated I was one of Dr. Graham Armstrong's research assistants, Evermeyer took over the conversation. He asked if their vaccine was working on the infected cows.

When I mentioned that the vet for the herd had been murdered, Evermeyer knew the name of the vet—saying "Graham mentioned Wimble's death." He'd used Dr. Armstrong's first name, so I assumed he knew him as a friend rather than a colleague.

A knock sounded on the front door, and I heard Linc call, "Liv?"

"I'm in the office," I called back. "Meet you at the kitchen table." I confirmed each stack had the same sheets before entering our sunny kitchen, which basked in the afternoon's sunshine.

Linc raised his eyebrows when I placed my sheets in front of him. "What's this?"

"A lead. Wish it was more."

Linc skimmed his set, then read them more carefully. "Thanks."

I leaned forward. "I've ruled out a lot of people, and I've come to the conclusion Dr. Armstrong and Dr. Wimble were working together."

"I see." Linc pulled out his pen and notepad.

"The state people monitoring our cows believe the herd was deliberately infected."

"Did they tell you that?"

"The head man told my dad that they think the disease might have been introduced through nasal swabs laced with a virus sample. I can't imagine anyone being so cruel."

"Liv, sticking yourself in the middle of this investigation could be dangerous." Linc's demeanor made me wonder if he knew who murdered Ben.

"In my opinion, their plan got out of hand. I believe Wimble only wanted a few cows to get the virus. Then he could offer a trial vaccine. If it was successful, they could ask the CDC for funding and more testing."

Linc sighed. "Am I going to have to lock you up to keep you safe?"

My laugh was muffled by my mask. "Please don't. I just wanted to share my theory that Ben tried to buy our farm so he would own the infected cattle. When my parents refused, he gave some cows the virus anyway. Being our vet, he could be here daily and keep an eye on the herd. I don't think he anticipated how virulent the strain was."

Linc let the silence grow too long for my liking, and when he did speak, it wasn't about murder, bird flu infections, or guilty suspects. "What does the doctor say about your parents?"

"Well, Mom may get to come home tomorrow, and Dad has rallied. But back to the other thing, I believe Ben and Dr. Armstrong were in this together and that Graham Armstrong killed Ben, but I can't prove the connection."

"You take care of your parents. I'll take care of the murder inquiry. I mean it, Liv." I noticed the severe frown line between his eyes.

"Linc, have you ruled out any suspects?"

"Liv, I'm not discussing this investigation with you." His brittle tone edged on anger.

"I've done nothing but research for the past two years. Guess I got into the habit of chasing details."

"Break the habit." He left our house, holding the papers I'd prepared for him.

I locked the door behind him, something we never did at Friendly Farm, even at night.

At the table, I studied my scribbling again. "Where does Sharon fit into all of this?" I said aloud.

If Linc wouldn't talk to me, I'd talk to myself. I don't think Sharon expected her husband to die, but now she was very chummy with Graham Armstrong.

CHAPTER FOURTEEN

Despite Linc's warning that I could be in danger, I called Sharon the next morning. She'd been my best friend growing up, and I wanted to trust her.

"Liv, how are you?"

"Lonely, missing a friend. Mom and Dad are in the hospital with what the doctor thinks is a virus they might have gotten from the cows with bird flu." I heard a gasp, and it didn't sound like Sharon's. "Are you by yourself?"

"No, Graham, uh, Dr. Armstrong is with me. I'm so sorry. How are they?"

"Improving, but the doctor insists I isolate at home, which doesn't suit my personality. I need someone to talk to, even if it's just over the phone."

"Why don't I come over? We can sit on opposite sides of your porch. It's a beautiful day, and I can bring my own drink, so your possibly contaminated hands won't be anywhere near mine."

"And Dr. Armstrong?" Despite working with him for two years, he'd never encouraged me to use his first name.

"He's working," she said. "I could use a girlfriend session too. See you soon."

While I waited, I texted my brothers with updates, then wrote down the day's to-do list. My habitual list making was a blessing and a curse. The task organized my thoughts, but I sometimes took it too far by listing more things than I could ever accomplish in a single day.

Sharon sat in the passenger seat, and Dr. Armstrong served as her chauffeur. I grimaced, not happy he was here.

"Graham wants to check on the cows. He may have discovered something." Sharon gave him a peck on the cheek before he headed to the dairy area.

I was a bit nervous about Dr. Armstrong visiting our cows, but I trusted the state crew wouldn't let him near them.

"You brought your drink." I held up my glass of iced tea to toast her soda can and took the swing on the left side of the porch.

She sat in the rocker on the right and leaned forward. "Liv, Graham and I are getting married."

My mouth fell open like I was a cartoon character. "What? Your husband just died. What in the world are you thinking?"

"He was a good friend before Ben's death, and he's been a rock since that awful day. Before you ask, we were not having an affair." Sharon held up her left hand. There was a gold ring with a small turquoise stone on the third finger.

"When's the date?"

"Soon. The stone's nontraditional, like Graham. He's taking a sabbatical in Brunei or the United Arab Emirates, so we'll marry before the end of summer."

"Unusual choices," I said.

"Please be happy for me, Liv. My life with Ben was not what I expected. Graham says Ben invested heavily and lost most of our money. He's offered to marry me and pay off Ben's debts."

I shivered despite the warm June weather. The financials I'd seen showed Ben's assets to be considerable. "Sharon, you didn't kill Ben, did you?"

"No. You and I were together until you left to go to the barn." Sharon admired her engagement ring.

Taking advantage of her distraction, I clicked my phone's note-taking option so I could record her words.

"Could Dr. Armstrong—Graham—have killed Ben?"

"Graham is a wonderful man."

"Who gave you an engagement ring."

"He says he loves me," Sharon said.

"People in love can do strange things," I said. "Sharon, didn't you look at the bank accounts yourself? From what I saw, you and Ben didn't have any debts."

"Graham wouldn't lie to me. Maybe he knows something you don't."

"Possibly. As your friend, I'm asking you not to rush into a second marriage. You have the rest of your life in front of you."

"I just want to put Ben's accident behind me."

"An accident? Sharon, he was shot." I was pleased my phone was recording her words.

"Yes. It was an accident. Ben was the one who got the gun from the cabinet."

"How do you know Ben had the gun?"

"Graham told me."

"How could he know? Was he at the farm on open-house day?"

"Yes. Graham came with us, but he didn't want you or your family to know. He wanted to get blood and milk samples from your infected animals. Ben was supposed to do it, but he bungled the job. Graham told me he wanted to help because of his fondness for you and your family."

I knew then that he was lying to her. Dr. Armstrong hadn't shown any curiosity about my home life until this semester. When he'd questioned me, I happily chattered on about the number of cows we had and the procedures we followed. I thought we'd finally bonded. Now I saw his curiosity for what it was. My professor saw our farm as a laboratory to initiate a bird flu infection with Ben Wimble as his flunky.

"Dr. Armstrong didn't need to come today. The state team has things well in hand." I had an uneasy feeling.

"Graham wanted to check their progress, but you've been on his mind too. He said you were angry about not receiving your degree this term. But Liv, you can't blame Graham for that. You're the one who didn't get the work in on time."

"As a murder suspect, I was ordered not to leave the county. So, yes, I did think it was unreasonable for him not to allow an extension for me."

Sharon wagged her finger like a teacher to a complaining student. "Liv, I know you. You procrastinated on projects when we were in school together. Then you had to scramble to get the work done. Face it, you haven't changed."

I refused to address her comment about my work ethic and instead encouraged her to talk about the important issue. "Explain how Ben was accidentally shot."

"Graham told me he was upset when he saw the condition of the cows. He said he accused Ben of not caring for your cows properly. Graham said Ben went crazy, got the gun, and shouted that Graham and I were having an affair—which we weren't. Graham tried to take the gun from him, but it went off."

"Why didn't he tell the sheriff?" I asked. "And why did he hide the gun in the overalls in the milking parlor?"

"The sheriff might have arrested him, and he wanted to continue working on a cure for your cows. And no one knew he was at the open house. He needed time to solve the problem for your family. You should appreciate what he was trying to do."

"And did he explain hiding the gun?"

"To give himself more time. He didn't expect it to be found."

"So he came to our farm to help us?" I tried to hide the skepticism from my tone.

"He came to the open house with Ben and me. As I told you, he was not happy with the way Ben had treated your cows. And your farm was so crowded, he had no trouble blending in with the others. But after the accident, he went to our car and waited."

"Really? He had a long wait. You ate dinner with us," I reminded her.

"Yes. Your mom was so sweet, and then you offered to spend the night with me. Ben's death was such a shock that I'd completely forgotten about Graham."

"Until you saw him in your car?" I prompted.

"Yes. I tell you, it scared the dickens out of me when I saw him in the back seat. I panicked because I had to delay you. You remember I told you to give me thirty minutes or so to tidy up before you came over? That was so Graham could leave or hide. He insisted I not tell anyone that he'd been to Friendly Farm that day."

I had another question, but Sharon wasn't finished.

"Liv, Graham was so sweet that night. He wrote the message I used to tell family and friends about Ben's death. You remember how perfect it was, don't you?"

"I thought you'd done it."

"No, Graham did."

The phone buzzed, and I sighed with relief when Linc's name popped up. I accepted the call, which ended my recording of Sharon's narration. "Hello, I'm just having a glass of tea with Sharon Wimble." I smiled at Sharon, hoping she'd think the person on the other end was someone other than the sheriff.

Linc's voice sounded angry. "I told you to stay out of this. Is Graham Armstrong with her?"

"Yes," I said cheerfully. "She has interesting news." I turned to Sharon and mouthed, "Can I tell?"

"May as well, word will be out soon." Sharon smiled and twisted the ring on her finger.

"She and Dr. Armstrong are getting married, and they're planning to live overseas, maybe the United Arab Emirates or in Brunei."

"Those are places without extradition treaties, and marriage will prevent her testifying against him. Try to stay alive until I can get there." I heard his car accelerate before he ended the call.

I spoke as if continuing the conversation, "That's wonderful news. Thanks for the update."

"Was that about your parents?" Sharon asked.

I evaded answering her question by telling her something I knew. "Mom's getting out of the hospital today. I think I'll call Doug and see if he wants to go with me when I pick her up."

"He can't go. You're isolating." Sharon's face lit up, and I knew, without turning my head, that Dr. Armstrong was near the porch. "Good news, Graham. Liv's mom is coming home."

"Then she had a speedy recovery. Liv, I understand we have a common acquaintance, Dr. Evermeyer of Bovinics."

"I wouldn't say he's an acquaintance," I hedged—and prayed that Linc would be there soon.

"You did call him, didn't you? He told me it was one of my assistants, and I don't know who else it could have been. I've admired your tenacious investigation of topics, but you must not interfere with *my* research." Dr. Armstrong glared at me. "Dr. Evermeyer is upset about your deception. I told him you'd apologize in person. Shall we go?"

"Where is Dr. Evermeyer's research facility?"

"The trip won't take long."

I knew if I left with Dr. Armstrong, I might never return. I stammered excuses. "I—I thought if I helped you with your project, maybe you'd approve my thesis and give me an extension so I could receive my master's." My voice jumped around, reflecting the jitters I felt inside. "And I might be contagious, and I'm—I'm supposed to pick up my mom from the hospital."

"If you want that degree, you'll have to return for fall term."

"When you'll be in Brunei or the United Arab Emirates. Sharon told me about the upcoming marriage. Congratulations." I remembered Linc's words about no testimony and no extradition.

"Your well wishes are accepted. Sharon, why don't you drive us back to your house? I'll get my car and take Liv to see Dr. Evermeyer."

"Graham, what if she is contagious? I don't want you to get sick," Sharon said.

"I'm willing to risk it. Go start the car, sweetie." Dr. Armstrong bounded up on the porch and grabbed my arm, twisting it behind me.

I winced in pain as he forced me down the steps. "It would serve you right if you caught the virus my mom and dad have," I hissed.

He ignored my comments and forced me into the back seat, sliding in next to me. "I'll sit with Liv," he said to Sharon. "I don't want you exposed to any of her germs."

"May I call the hospital? I should tell them I'll be delayed in picking up my mom." Surely Sharon would insist I be allowed to pick up Mom.

"Sharon can do it for you. Now let's pay that visit to Dr. Evermeyer."

If Sharon realized that her future husband had strong-armed me into the car, she didn't show it. Instead, she followed his instructions and headed down our long driveway. I sat up straight when I saw that our access to the highway was blocked by Doug's pickup. My high school sweetheart stood next to his truck, waving a gas can. The vision was startling, because cautious Doug Wagner would never run out of gas.

Sharon put the car in park, and the welcome sound of Linc's siren filled the air.

Our Fourth of July get-togethers always include freezers of ice cream cranked in an old-fashioned bucket with ice and salt between the wooden sides and the metal cylinder. My brothers and their families flew in for the festivities. Friendly Farm would be ours until late September, when the Wagners would assume ownership. Radio music provided a background for the warm day, and the scent of money, aka manure and alfalfa, added to the ambiance of what I considered home.

Contrary to my expectations, my parents seemed euphoric about the future. They placed a bid on an Eau Claire house, close to the restaurant Mom would operate for Tilly and a short distance from the Wisconsin regional dairy offices. The man who'd facilitated work with our herd recommended Dad for a position, and he accepted. Dad claimed he looked forward to a job with set hours that didn't start at three a.m. and didn't involve worrying about sick cows or the cost of feed.

Only two months had elapsed since Dad had knocked on my apartment door and asked me to return home. In that short span, my life and the lives of others had changed irrevocably.

I watched my brothers and their wives giving child-rearing tips to Noah and Wren, whose faces glowed with the knowledge they'd have a son in the near future.

Sharon arrived wearing an island print and oversized sunglasses. "Like my outfit?"

"I do, but it doesn't have much of a Wisconsin vibe." I gave her a bear hug.

My friend had been devastated when Graham was charged with involuntary manslaughter, tampering with evidence, and attempted kidnapping. Because he'd planned to flee the country, he was denied bail and was stuck in jail awaiting trial. Sharon faced the fact that Graham didn't love her, and the two of us became even closer as she worked through the loss of a husband and the deception of a man she'd trusted. She grieved for both.

Sharon pushed the sunglasses on top of her head for better eye contact. "Liv, I'm going to live on a Caribbean island for a while. You know I've never liked Wisconsin winters." Her voice sounded cautious but determined.

"Could be a new start. Nervous?"

"Yes, but after what I've been through, I think I can handle anything." Sharon certainly didn't lack for money. She'd sold the house, the Wimble half of the veterinary business, and collected Ben's life insurance money plus the funds Ben had squirreled away. She was a wealthy woman, and today she looked the part.

"Maybe I'll go with you," I said.

"You know dairy farmers can't leave home." Sharon nodded to Doug, who hefted an ice cream freezer from his truck bed. "I'll go say hello to your brothers." She gave me a quick kiss on the cheek.

Doug carried the ice cream freezer my way and grinned. "You look good today. Not as dramatic as Sharon, but perfect for my taste. I made Mom's peach ice cream recipe. Want to help crank?"

"It's the least I can do after you saved my life." We headed for the tree-shaded area by the picnic table.

"Told you I'd never let you come to harm," Doug said.

"When you said that, I was afraid you might be the murderer and that you would have confessed if I'd been convicted."

"Liv, I've loved you since we were in elementary school, and I would have gone to prison to make sure you didn't. Fortunately, we have a good sheriff. He made saving you easier by telling me to block your driveway so the real killer couldn't escape."

I placed my left hand, which sported a sparkling diamond ring, in his. "I'm glad we're going to build our own home. Your suggestion to make Mom and Dad's house into a B&B is a great idea. We can continue the popular summer farm vacations and have our own place for us and our children."

Doug released my hand. "I'm not ready to talk about children, but I am ready to marry you, now or after you finish your master's degree."

"We'll have to master dancing before we marry. There's the tradition of the bridal couple's first dance, and we've never been good at it."

"Come with me." Doug left the ice cream freezer, took my hand, and led me to the center of the lawn. "Shall we try?"

I melted into his arms, and we swayed to the radio's music with the grace of a professional dance duo, perfectly in sync.

Linda Baten Johnson enjoys research as much as writing and she learns new information for each book topic. *The Dark Side of the Moo* gave her a chance to interview dairy farmers who love their career even though they get up between three and four a.m. Linda prefers the urban life and currently lives in Frisco, Texas, where she writes, serves as a museum docent, works in the library bookshop, volunteers for various organizations, and conducts Grandkid Camps in the summer. Her squeaky-clean romances, cozy romances, and historical fiction for young readers are available in print, e-book, and audio format. Please visit her website: https://lindabatenjohnson.com.

FOWL DEED

BY TERESA IVES LILLY

DEDICATION

I'd like to thank Rebecca Germany for allowing me to work with Barbour Books, Cythia Hickey for including me in the collections, and Linda Baten Johnson for always being willing to join in on a writing adventure.

CHAPTER ONE

You may wonder how I found myself sitting on my bottom in the middle of a one-hundred-square-foot chicken coop with broken eggs all over me. I was wondering the same thing. It's not a habit I'd like to take up. However, having decided to open an egg farm to provide the locals with a steady flow of eggs has put me in several peculiar positions lately. The kind which seem to end up with me sprawled on the ground with eggs dripping down my front. That's also why I always wear an egg apron now.

What is an egg apron you ask? That too is a very good question. A few months ago, I realized that the only way I was going to be able to afford the upkeep on our family homestead was to somehow make it pay for itself. I had to do that in order to provide the funds to move my father, after his third fall and second hip surgery, into the White Pine Nursing Home, named after the famous white pine trees that are native to Maine.

My job at the time, working as a server in the local café, didn't provide enough money. Thankfully, with the help of my dearest friends, ideas began to form, and I now own the Rein Homestead Egg Farm and Gift Store, which is slowly becoming one of the highlights for those visiting the small town of Hopeville.

Converting the large front living room of our two-story Victorian house into a small store caused an immediate sensation in town, and business was off the ground and running.

We are located on the main highway that runs into town, so anyone coming or going has to pass by us. Many people stop for eggs, gifts, or even a fresh glass of sweet tea, which I serve cold on our wraparound porch. Business is beginning to grow, but I know it'll take a lot more time before I'm completely out of debt. That's why I've agreed to host the once-a-month weekend Market Days here, which runs from April through October. The vendors will get more exposure to travelers because the site where it was being held isn't on the main drag like the Homestead. I'll get twenty-five dollars per vendor, and that will help my financial situation a lot.

About twenty (hopefully more as time goes on) vendors will set up tables and tents once a month on the property, drawing even larger crowds to my gift shop. I sell many fun items, such as hand towels, candles, figurines, paintings, and yes, egg aprons. (You thought I'd forgotten what I was talking about, didn't you?)

Speaking of the aprons. Picture, if you will, an apron—tied at your neck and waist—with small pockets sewn all over the front of it. Each one the perfect size for just one egg. I have a website as well and sell these aprons there. *1pc, Polyester Apron, Colorful Rooster Hen Farm Egg Pattern Family Pastoral Style Apron, Waterproof & Oil-Proof, Halter Apron for Egg Collecting, Gardening, Cooking, Baking, Flower Arranging, and Painting.* This is what I now wear when collecting eggs from my forty chickens each day.

Forty chickens? you ask. Yes! I was surprised too. Before going into the business, I'd imagined one chicken would produce twelve eggs a day, so I reasoned that if I had ten chickens, I would have dozens of eggs to sell every day. But nooooo. It turns out, one chicken only produces one egg a day. Grrr. Therefore, if I wanted a few dozen a day, which I sell in half-dozens to stretch them out and make more people happy, I had to expand my coop to house forty chickens. It actually comes out to only about six half dozens, and I've got quite a few locals wishing for more. On the occasional day when one of the hens goes crazy and lays two eggs, I can splurge for my own breakfast.

I have an egg honesty box set up close to the road, where I place the half cartons. It's first come, first served, but everyone knows they should never take more than one. Of course, there is that one man. . .Jeff Barr. Oh, don't get me started on him. As I was saying, the honesty box, which looks like a small chicken coop but is actually an insulated box to keep the eggs cool, is set up close to the road. Customers deposit their payment in a locked metal box unless they want to come inside and shop.

The truth is, selling eggs doesn't pay the bills, but you can't very well have a chicken-themed gift store unless you sell eggs. It's also a draw to have a real chicken coop for certain customers to see. If I could charge admission for chicken coop tours, I would make a bundle. Everyone wants to see the chickens, and most of these inquisitive people have questions and comments that range from silly to outrageous.

"Can you make one of the chickens lay an egg right now so we can see it?"

"I've heard if you give them cod liver oil, the eggs come out shiny."

"Is it true that long eggs produce roosters and short ones produce chickens?"

That's just a few of the crazy things I've been asked. Luckily, my Southern Belles don't mind the people and love to put on a show for them, strutting and clucking and sometimes giving an all-out show by squawking.

Southern Belles, you ask? Yes, I've named all my chickens good, old-fashioned Southern Belle names like Annabelle, Charlotte, Scarlet, Georgina, Isabelle, Maribelle, Maisie, Dixie. . . Well, you get the idea. But even if I don't always remember which is which, they all seem to love me, and they flock around me whenever it's time for me to feed them or collect eggs.

There in itself is the problem. Imagine trying to shoo forty chickens away while collecting their eggs. It's a feat meant for a person who can walk a balance beam and juggle at the same time. I can do neither.

That is how I ended up on my bottom in the chicken coop with broken eggs running down my egg apron. Unfortunately, this occurred just at the moment a car pulled into the driveway.

Whose car, you ask? That is the best question of the day, and for me, the most frustrating part of all of this, because it's a nice white Tahoe, owned by a local artist who also happens to be the best-looking man I've ever seen. His name is Rene Dempsy. He's an artist (did I mention single bachelor?) and paints portraits of my chickens to sell in my shop. He portrays them in their coops, in fields, and on the porch. I sell them for a small commission, and they are snatched up quickly. He also does some lovely paintings of old homes in the area and just recently decided to create printed greeting cards for me to sell as well.

He's only lived in the area for a few years, but I never met him when I was a server. I think that's why he treats me with more respect than any of the other local men I know. He's polite and friendly. I wish he'd be a bit more friendly, if you catch my meaning. However, he's never tried to bring up anything except business with me. I've mentioned things like I attend church alone, that there's a community picnic coming up soon and I wasn't sure about attending alone. . . You get the idea. He hasn't ever gotten the idea.

So, there I sat, feeling like a fool, while he parked his car and got out. I hoped he hadn't noticed me wallowing in the chicken coop muck as he opened the trunk and pulled out a box that I assumed was filled with paintings and cards.

I hopped up and hurried out of the coop, which is behind the Homestead in an area that can't be seen very well from the front of the store. I wanted to sneak into the house before he could see me, but that meant walking right past where he stood on the porch, the box at his feet. I tried to shuffle by him quickly, but it was not to be.

"Good afternoon, Miss Rein." His velvet tones stopped me midstep. I hated to turn around but had no choice. Slowly, I faced him.

"Mr. Dempsy, I have asked you to call me April. My name is April Rein." I tilted my head with a smile, hoping he hadn't noticed the eggs, but his eyes were glued on my apron.

I shrugged, grimacing.

An endearing smile flitted across his face. He probably wanted to laugh, but he's too much of a gentleman. "All right then, April. I'll call you by your first name if you do the same. My name is Rene."

Rene is pronounced with a long *e* sound, and it's an unusual name that sounds so romantic being that it's French. I gave a little nod, hoping he couldn't read my thoughts. I could feel a warmth blush my cheeks.

"Having a tough time with the Southern Belles this morning?" he asked. I tried to cover the broken eggs smeared across my chest, but to no avail. I'm not the type prone to tears or swooning, but I felt a bit faint. I wanted to fade away, but knew I had to face the truth.

"They've been especially wicked today. I'm not sure what, but something is bothering them." I stopped speaking, realizing that telling him my issues with my brood of chickens was not a very attractive conversation. I lifted my chin, deciding not to be concerned. It wasn't such a big deal. When I worked at the café in town, spilling eggs, coffee, and other various food items down my apron front was par for the course. Still, he'd never seen me there, so this was a new sight for him.

"I'm sorry, April." His gentle words brought a lot of healing to my soul. "My mother used to raise chickens, and I know it can be very trying. I'll stop by and give them a talking-to before I leave."

His words surprised me, and I gulped. I knew from local gossip that his mother had passed away a year ago, and I hated to have him associating her with my misadventure. "No use crying over broken eggs." I headed for the door.

"Do you want to inventory the paintings and cards now, or should I come back later?" When I turned, I could see the hesitance in his eyes. He was being kind. One thing I like about Rene is the lack of mockery in his tone. No matter what, he doesn't seem to ever be laughing at me.

The men in town were always laughing at me when I spilled things at the café. It was humiliating. They'd even nicknamed me "Trip." I didn't miss that.

Rene is different. I can't imagine him ever being rude, mocking, or condescending. It made me like him all the more.

"Bring them in now. I can't wait to see the cards. I think they'll be a bigger seller than the paintings, especially online."

I'd only recently discovered I could sell items using the Facebook page I'd created for the Homestead, and our following had doubled since I'd added one of Rene's paintings. There were even requests for them, but Rene preferred to paint what he liked, not work off of requests.

We moved across the porch. He stepped ahead of me and held the front door open while holding the box in his other hand. I ducked my head as I passed, smelling his manly aftershave, which was woodsy and dreamy.

When I reached the counter, I slipped the offending apron off, careful not to break any other eggs in the pockets, knowing I would deal with them after Rene left. I took a quick peek into a mirror hanging near the counter and brushed back my hair, glad there was no egg on my face.

"Here are the cards." Rene held up a pack and handed it to me. The top card featured a painting of chickens on the Homestead's porch. I could tell right away they were going to be some of my bestselling items.

"Rene, these are so beautiful," I gushed. I picked up another pack and found he'd used other settings as well. They were just as nice.

"How much do you think I should sell them for? There are six in a set."

"Hmm, I'd say fifteen for each set." I hoped I wasn't insulting him by underpricing, but I know my buyers. He nodded.

"Sounds good to me." He pulled a few paintings from the box. These he hung on the empty spaces on the walls around the shop. I couldn't keep my eyes from following him. Even from the back, he's gorgeous. Muscular, with dirty blond hair that waves just perfectly. . .

I was so absorbed, I didn't notice him turn around, but after a few moments of silence, I shook my head and met his eyes. I could tell he knew I'd been staring at him. Again, no mockery, but my cheeks flushed anyway.

"I hear you're going to host the first Market Days here this weekend." Rene, the gentleman, introduced a new subject to smooth over the awkwardness of the moment.

"Yep, twenty vendors." I looked at him anxiously. "Are you wanting a spot?"

"No. I can hardly keep up with the things I'm making for your shop." His grin made tingles run through my body. "I'll bring more over on Saturday, if that's okay and won't cause you any inconvenience."

I exhaled slowly. If he were to start selling items outside the shop, he'd make all the profit. I needed the money from his paintings. Although business was doing well, if I didn't catch up soon, I risked losing the Homestead because of back taxes that needed to be paid.

"Yes, that'll be fine. I can take double what you bring me now," I said. "Your paintings are a favorite."

His smile was contagious. "That's good to know. An artist gets a certain amount of joy from his work, but knowing others like it really is pleasing." He stepped back and looked around. "I haven't brought everything I have in stock. Some of my paintings don't have any chickens in them, so I wasn't sure…" His voice dropped.

"Any kind of a country scene is okay with me. It doesn't always have to be chickens."

He shrugged. "Okay. Maybe I can add a few chickens to some of my rural settings. Then they'll fit, and I'll feel better about bringing them in."

"Have you considered making prints so you can sell more than one of each painting?"

He cocked his head. "That's something I could consider. I'm using small prints for the cards, of course, but I've never done that with my paintings. I suppose if you keep selling them like you are, I'll need to at least think about it. I'm used to painting eight or nine canvases a year, and you've sold four in the last month. It's a good thing I have a stack of them ready to go."

"Wow, I had no idea. I figured you painted one a day or something. I know nothing about painting."

He chuckled. "Even one a week would be tough to do. I could do one a month, maybe. Having them in your store is the first time I've ever tried to sell them."

"How do you support yourself then?" The words popped out before I could stop them. I slapped a hand over my mouth, then shook my head. "You don't have to answer that."

He ran a hand through his hair. "No problem. My grandfather died and left me an inheritance and the log cabin at the lake. I don't have to work now, but I love painting."

Before I further bombarded him with questions about his personal life, I changed the subject.

"How did you hear about Market Days?" I asked, thinking it would help to know which form of advertising was working.

Rene frowned. "Oh, that big mouth, Jeff Barr, was spouting off about it at the bank the other day."

I tilted my head. "What do you mean?"

"He was telling the bank manager that he needed to force you to sell your place. He said you might think you can save it by setting up Market Days on your land, but it wasn't going to help, and he would make sure you sold it to him." He met my eyes and said, "I'm sorry."

Jeff Barr moved into the area a few years ago and, since arriving, had done nothing but cause trouble. He did well as a real estate agent, but his personal skills were lacking. Yet I knew two women in town who swooned over the man, which seemed incomprehensible to me.

I clenched my hands. "That man..." I started to complain but felt a nudge in my spirit. It wasn't going to help me to badmouth Jeff Barr. God was his judge, and if God wanted me to keep my place, He would work it out. I would do the best I could and leave the consequences to the Lord.

But Rene must have known what I was feeling. "If anyone has the right to say something bad about that man, it's you."

I shook my head. "That's not what God wants from me." I wasn't sure how Rene would receive this statement. He didn't attend my church, so I had no idea if he was even a Christian. He just smiled at me.

"You're stronger than me then," he stated.

Our conversation was interrupted when the bell over the front door jingled. I looked up and smiled. "Welcome to the Rein Homestead."

A woman stepped in. She smiled and began to move around the store. I looked through the front window and noticed that her license plate was from out of state.

"Gotta go," Rene whispered. He picked up his empty box. "Got chickens to paint." He chuckled and walked out the door. I felt a bit let down. We'd been having such a nice conversation. I'd hoped it would lead to. . .something more.

Shaking that feeling off, I tried to focus on the customer, but my mind kept slipping back to what Rene had told me about Jeff Barr. He was only a real estate agent and didn't have any power to get the bank manager to make me sell the property, but he was known to be underhanded. There could be ways for him to hurt the business. I determined to keep my eyes and ears open when it came to the odious man.

I lifted up a prayer.

"Lord, please help me find ways to make money, keep this land, and be able to take care of Daddy as well. I praise Your name and thank You for all You've already done for me."

CHAPTER TWO

When the woman finished shopping, the counter boasted one pack of Rene's cards, an egg apron, two kitchen towels, and a jar of honey from Carol Anne, a local beekeeper who raised just enough bees to make a few jars of honey to sell. Carol Anne and her friends were known as the Sewing Bees and sold quilts as well.

As I rang up the items, the woman asked, "Is there a bed and breakfast around the area?"

I shook my head. Our town is barely on the map. Most people don't even stop unless they're visiting family. "No ma'am, there isn't."

She frowned. "That's too bad. I think this area is delightful. I'm from Harbor Inn." She cleared her throat. "I'd love to stay overnight, drive around, see some of the lake and all the area has to offer, but if there's no place to stay, I won't be able to do that."

"I have access to the lake on the back of my property. You can stroll over that way if you want." I pointed out the side window.

She met my eyes. "Thanks, I'd like that, but if there isn't somewhere to stay, I won't have time." She walked toward the window. "My, that's a big coop. How many chickens do you have?"

"Forty. And four roosters," I added. I don't always talk about the roosters. Unlike my Southern Belles, my roosters are not

Southern Gentlemen, and I avoid thinking about them. I mean, four roosters crowing every morning is not very pleasant. I'm just glad they don't do it for very long.

She turned back. "Oh, I really want to explore the area. There's no Airbnb around either?"

I had only recently heard of Airbnb, basically like a bed and breakfast, but no breakfast served. "No, sorry."

"What about here? I mean, it looks just like the pictures of the perfect bed and breakfast. Surely you have rooms in the house."

I cocked my head. I did have four bedrooms upstairs, all ready to go for guests. Not for any reason, except that's how they always were when I was growing up. I stay in the main bedroom downstairs that's situated off the kitchen in the back.

"How much does an Airbnb usually charge for a night's stay?" I questioned.

"Well, it's according to how big the place is, what they offer, the draw of the area, and how many others are trying to stay the night. I've seen a small room in a house go for about thirty dollars a night..." Her voice faded.

Thirty dollars wasn't much. It didn't even seem worth the effort of washing the sheets for that. I sighed, and she said, "But for a place like yours, I'd recommend fifty dollars a night for a room with a double bed. Seventy-five for a queen, and maybe a hundred for a king." She smiled, a bit of hopefulness in her eyes.

Now that sounded interesting. I decided I'd look into the whole Airbnb thing soon. I'd heard that a person could easily sign up online.

"If you decorate the rooms to match the theme here—you know, chickens and roosters—you can advertise it as a chicken farm. You'd be bound to get customers. There are plenty of women's groups that love to go on overnight visits to quaint little places."

The woman had truly sparked my interest. The rooms were already lovely, but I could easily add a few chicken pictures and rooster paintings to them. I remembered my aunt was in a Red Hat Society group, and they would probably like to come stay.

"I'm willing to pay one hundred dollars right now if you'll let me stay the night. I'd love to settle in, take an afternoon nap, then have the rest of the day to explore the area."

I gulped. Was this really something I could do to make more money? I didn't have time to cook, but cleaning the rooms and making beds wouldn't take much work. "There's a good place for breakfast in town called Bacon on Main. One, because the owner's last name is Bacon and it's on Main Street, and two, because she serves the best bacon around."

Her eyes were wide and lit up. "That sounds good. I write articles for a travel magazine. I'm known for finding little out-of-the-ordinary places. My readers will often fit them into their upcoming travels. I think they'd love to hear about your chicken-themed store, and if it's an Airbnb, that's even better."

I was sold. "That's great. Let me take you upstairs and show you around." I suggested she go out and move her car to the side of the house. A few minutes later she returned with a small suitcase.

Feeling nervous, I found myself behaving like a tour guide. "Now, this house has been in my family for years. I've kept it as rustic as I can, but I've made several modern adjustments, such as internet, special lighting on the stairs, and other small things. I think you'll be comfortable." I was babbling a bit, but it was just my excitement. "There aren't any locks on the doors yet."

She smiled. "I think I can trust you. Are you married? Will there be a man walking around at night?"

I shook my head. "Nope, just me."

"That'll work. If you want to open as an Airbnb, put a small refrigerator and microwave in each room."

That made sense. I added it to my to-do list in my mind along with locks on the doors.

I showed her the four bedrooms. The one with a blue quilt with a sunflower pattern was her favorite. I'd pulled some of the yellow out in the curtains and rug. I closed my eyes and tried to imagine adding one of Rene's paintings to the room and a few other things to give it the feel of chickens.

"You think if I sign up on Airbnb, I'll get customers?" I asked.

She was moving around the room, and I could see the appreciation in her eyes for some of the fine things. "Yes. Post good photos with your listing and mention that you do tours of the farm, and you'll get a lot of interest. You can charge an extra fee for the tours."

I shook my head in awe. This sounded almost too good to be true, but then I remembered the prayer I'd spoken. Had God really worked so fast? I didn't question it. I would accept all good things as from the Lord and, so far, this seemed like a very good thing.

"I'm Stacy Monson." She shook my hand. "I've been to Airbnbs where I can use the living room, play the piano, cook in the kitchen. . ." I think she saw my smile disappear at that. "Some people might want to do their own cooking, especially if they don't drive in the dark," she said. That wasn't great in my mind. I love cooking my own dinner and don't like to share the space, nor did I want to have people wandering around the living room in the evenings.

She must have read my mind. "It's not a requirement. If you advertise that restaurant you mentioned and provide microwaves and refrigerators, people can bring their own goodies. As long as they can get to a grocery store and a restaurant or two, most of them won't mind not having access to the kitchen."

I sucked in a breath, realizing that I'd been holding it—a bad habit of mine. I was already sold on the idea of the Airbnb and didn't want denying guests access to the kitchen and living room to be the only thing making it impossible, but sharing my personal space seemed too much to ask.

"If you really think it would be okay," I murmured.

She nodded. "Yep. That's the beauty of Airbnbs. You do what you want, and if someone doesn't like it, they don't have to choose to stay here."

My mind was whirling with ideas. New ways to raise money to pay the bills for the Homestead and some of Daddy's medical bills. I was just glad Daddy's social security was enough to pay for the retirement center. With an Airbnb, Market Days, and the gift shop, I was sure I could eventually pay off the back taxes on the property.

Excitement was shooting through me, and I wanted to get to my computer and look up the Airbnb website. This was too good an opportunity to miss. Stacy offered to photograph the bedrooms, the chicken coop, and the store for me. She needed the photos for an article anyway and thought it would be fine for me to use them on an Airbnb listing as well.

I realized I needed to get back to the shop. I could be missing customers as I stood talking to Stacy. She genuinely seemed pleased with the room, so I left her to rest.

The store was empty, so I walked out to the chicken coop, trying to see it through the eyes of an Airbnb guest. One of the four roosters was scratching at the dirt, generally ignoring me. But the Southern Belles all began clucking at me at once.

"Shh, ladies. Please be quiet," I scolded them. I didn't want them waking Stacy if she'd fallen asleep.

I turned back to the store and looked down the driveway, where someone was just driving away from the egg honesty box. I gave a wave and stepped inside. I moved toward the new paintings Rene had left and stood looking at them. They were good, really good, but should I buy them myself to hang in the guest rooms, or just purchase some cheaper things off the internet?

I wanted the place to look good, but was it reasonable? Would I really get enough customers to make a purchase of his paintings worthwhile?

I'd pray about it and, in the meantime, get set up on Airbnb. Of course, I had Market Days to consider, and then there was the issue with Jeff Barr and his pressure on me and the bank. I would have to do something about him—and soon.

To my surprise, setting up the Airbnb online later that evening was very easy. Stacy forwarded me some photos to get started with. Then all I had to do was get Gordon Bane, the local handyman, to put locks on the guest room doors. I called, and he promised to come by the next day. I made a list of things to have him work on, then turned my mind back to the upcoming weekend. The Airbnb could take a long time to catch on, and in the meantime, I had Market Days to consider.

I decided to walk the property and mark the rental spots with spray paint. That would ensure each vendor kept to their own space. I'd been told there had been a bit of arguing at the last location because of lack of definite lines and vendors not paying for double spots. I didn't want any ruckus.

As I painted, I heard another car pull in. I looked up, and my heart dropped. No one else in the whole world could possibly own a beige Cadillac that coughed and sputtered like that except Jeff Barr. How old it was I couldn't tell, but I wouldn't be surprised to see it dead alongside the road one day. In fact, for a moment I almost hoped his car would die, but then I quickly brushed away the thought, asking God to forgive me and to help me have a good attitude about the man.

Even so, I found myself clenching my fists as he pulled up the driveway too fast. He came to a stop with a screeching of tires.

The chickens started their high-pitched screams, letting me know they were frightened.

I set the can of paint down and walked slowly toward the store. He would be inside, waiting, and I was in no hurry to see him. Then I remembered that there was a chance Stacy might come into the store. I didn't want him to hear anything about me turning the Homestead's rooms into Airbnb rooms. If he did, he would be sure to find some way to cause problems for me.

CHAPTER THREE

As I stepped into the store, brushing back a lock of hair, Jeff Barr turned toward me. "'Bout time you showed up. Is this any way to treat your customers?"

I barely acknowledged him and took my time. Once behind the counter, I looked up and gave him a big smile. "Hello, Mr. Barr. Is there anything I can get for you today?"

I think my smile confused him. He glared at me. "Uhm, yeah . . .I mean, no." He stepped closer to the counter. "I've come to tell you I'm looking into the laws about you holding Market Days on the main highway. I don't think it's legal."

My anger surged, but I kept smiling. "That's interesting. I spoke with the mayor last week when he picked up a half dozen eggs. He told me everyone in town was glad to hear I was taking over Market Days. He assured me this was the best location for it and that all the legal papers concerning it were in order. He's hoping to pull more visitors into town. He plans to set up a booth himself and hand out flyers about other points of interest in town—like our historic jailhouse, the art museum. . ." My voice faded. There wasn't much point in going on.

I watched the vengeful look on his face droop into a frown. I'd outsmarted him, but I wondered how long I could continue to put him off. If he kept digging things up, he might find a way to close the Homestead down. I made a mental note to call the mayor and make sure opening an Airbnb was okay.

I decided that a direct approach was best. "Mr. Barr, why, exactly, do you want my business to fail?"

He huffed, showing that he was taken aback. "I represent some investors. They're looking to build a luxury apartment complex along this stretch of highway. Your land sits in the middle of the plan. I've assured them I can get the land on both sides of the road, but they won't proceed until I do. You have the best access to the lake."

This was news to me. Not only did I not want to sell my property, I surely didn't want a luxury apartment complex to go up so near town. A few more visitors from Market Days was one thing, but several hundred people living on the outskirts of town would change the dynamics of everything. The traffic alone would be unbearable.

"There are a lot of people who want to live in the country but don't want the responsibility of home ownership. We are close enough for them to drive into the city for work. It's the perfect distance." He stopped talking rather abruptly. I assumed he realized he'd given up too much information.

"Thank you for letting me know. I'll keep it in mind and fight even harder to make sure you can't go through with it. No one in town wants a luxury apartment complex out here. If push comes to shove, I'll fight you in the town meetings. I'm sure I could get plenty of people to sign a petition against it."

"Well, there isn't anything they can do about it, and you owe taxes on this place," he said. "I doubt you'll be able to pay anytime soon, so it's only a matter of weeks—a month or so—and I'll be able to get the bank to foreclose on you. My investors will swoop in and purchase the property from them." His voice dripped with arrogance.

"Is there anything I can do for you right now, Mr. Barr, as a customer?" I could barely speak through my gritted teeth.

"My aunt asked me to buy her an egg apron." He glanced around, a blank look on his face. "I have no idea what that is."

I could barely contain my surprise. How could this man, who was trying to steal my home and store from me, actually come in to shop? I considered sending him on his way with a flea in his ear but then realized the profit on an egg apron was worth dealing with him further. I believed God wanted me to open this store, so why should I worry about Jeff Barr's plans to close me down? As long as he was a customer, I would deal with him.

I reached behind the counter and pulled out my most expensive egg apron, the one in a Blue Willow pattern. I'd almost kept it for myself because it was so lovely. "Here you go." I handed it to Mr. Barr and watched the horror cross his face when he looked at the price. He scanned the area as if hoping a cheaper one would magically appear, but the other ones hanging didn't have price tags showing, so he had no indication that they were any less expensive.

"I'm sure your aunt will love it." I pressed, reminding him of why he was there.

He nodded. "You have no idea what she's like. If she sent me for an apron, I better have it in the mail to her today."

A bead of sweat slipped down his face. "All right, I'll take it." I placed the apron in a bag, added the tax on the cash register and told him the total. He grudgingly handed over his credit card.

I have to say, I did feel guilty. I would never have treated my other customers like that. I would have offered options and allowed them to pick their favorite item. I grimaced at my own shallowness. The man made me crazy, but I was going to have to pull up my big-girl pants and start acting like a mature Christian when it came to him.

As I handed him the bag, I smiled. "Thank you, Mr. Barr. It was a pleasure doing business with you." My words were as fake as a mannequin in a store window, and he knew it. He grabbed the bag and began to stomp out of the store, but then he stopped and turned back. "You don't happen to sell fresh butter, do you?"

I blinked. "Butter?"

"Yes, you know, freshly made, right from the cow."

I almost laughed. The man was incredible. He was trying to ruin my business and take my land, and yet here he was buying an apron and asking for butter.

He shrugged. "I can't abide margarine, and most of the butter in the stores these days isn't real."

I shook my head. "This is a chicken farm, Mr. Barr, not a dairy farm." I crossed my arms over my chest.

He ran a hand around his collar. "Well, a farm is a farm to me. Should get you a dairy cow and sell some butter." He exited, allowing the screen door to slam behind him.

I could barely contain my anger, and yet I started laughing almost hysterically. The man was crazy. Wanting to close me down but suggesting I buy a cow.

I watched as he made his way to his old Cadillac and drove out of the driveway. It was only then that I took in some air and realized I had been holding my breath as I watched him. A small sound behind me broke the silence. I turned to find Stacy standing in the corner.

"Oh, hi." I smiled, trying to put away the thought of Jeff Barr. "All settled in?"

She hesitated for a moment. "Yes, it's perfect. I'm going to go drive around." She moved toward the door. "Who was that man?" she asked.

I humphed. "Jeff Barr, a real estate agent."

She stared at me. "A real estate agent?" The sound crackled from her lips as if she didn't believe what I'd said.

I nodded, wondering why she seemed so interested.

She gave a weak smile. "He didn't look like a very pleasant person." I wanted to agree, but that bordered on gossip, so I just stood there.

She turned and headed out the door, but I thought the brightness she'd displayed earlier had somehow gone out of her.

Later that day I leaned the 4-tine hand cultivator rake against the chicken coop. I use it to scratch lines in the dirt because I like to feed my Southern Belles in lines. Why, I don't know. There are blisters on my hand from using the rake, but I choose not to wear gloves because they make the rake slip around in my hands.

The chickens scurried over to peck at their food. I stood by, watching, but frowned. Their feathers seemed to be falling out, and there were small bald patches on some of them. They looked terrible. When had that started? I hurried back to the shop, pulled out my phone, and dialed the local vet. The receptionist handed the phone right to Doc Harding.

"Hello, April. How are the Southern Belles?"

I love that he also calls them that. "Looking a bit ragged, I'm afraid. A few have lost feathers. I'm afraid they might be dying or something."

The doctor laughed. "You know, when God made all the beautiful creatures in the world, he took more time on the Southern Belles. He gave them the ability to shed old feathers and grow new ones. It's called molting."

Relief rushed through me. I hadn't read about that yet.

"Might not put out as many eggs as usual either. Pamper the ladies, and they'll be okay. I'll stop by tomorrow and check to make sure."

I thanked him, and we hung up. It's really nice to live in a small community where veterinarians still make house calls. I'm not about to load forty chickens into my car and take them to see the vet.

I looked up chicken molting on the internet and could tell right away it was what my Belles were going through. The new emerging feathers looked like bean sprouts shooting up from the ground, which meant all was fine.

Doc had said there was sure to be a drop in their laying, which wasn't going to make my customers happy. I decided to send a post to the town's official website and let people know. I jotted the words on paper: *Southern Belles molting. Egg production down. Selling in sets of four instead of six.*

I wasn't happy to have to reduce the count, but it was better than disappointing buyers completely. I read further and realized there was little I could do about them molting until it was over.

Poor Southern Belles!

When the day was finally over and Stacy had returned, I walked to the end of the drive and pulled the metal fence across it. If I ever get enough money to pay off the taxes, my next project will be to get an electric gate. I can't expect Airbnb guests to open and close the gate themselves, and I'm not comfortable leaving it open all night long.

The moon was bright and lit my way to secure the coop for the night. I don't have issues with wild animals, but there's always the chance a fox or skunk could come slinking in.

I stopped on the front porch and looked out over my property. With an earnest prayer, I asked God to help me pay off the taxes. So far, He'd sent Stacy to give me the idea for an Airbnb and the mayor's offer to host Market Days. Remembering Romans 1:17, I whispered, "The just shall live by faith." I knew I could put my faith in Him.

CHAPTER FOUR

Saturday morning, Market Days opened at eight. I was nervous we wouldn't have enough customers to cover what the vendors had paid for their spots. I needn't have worried. By ten, there were already at least fifty customers milling from booth to booth. Several of the vendors gave me a thumbs-up when I passed by, which gave me a sense of relief.

One of my favorite booths was owned by my good friend Tamara Spencer. She sold organic drinks made from fresh greens, carrots, ginger, and more. She regularly sold out. As I walked by her booth, I noticed her usual cheerfulness had waned. Her crowd had thinned, so I stepped up. "Anything wrong, Tamara?"

Her eyes met mine, and I could see the light in them was dim. "No," she said, her eyes glancing away from me. I moved closer.

"Tamara, I can tell something's not right. I won't press, but I'm here if you need to talk."

Her shoulders dropped. "Sorry, I do need to tell someone, just to get it off my chest." I looked at her lovely eyes brimming with tears.

I leaned on her counter. "I'm listening."

"You know the farmland I own just down the road? Well, I thought I owned it, but Jeff Barr looked into it, and he claims I don't have a clear title. Seems the couple I bought it from didn't have a clear title either."

My teeth were already grinding together. "Why did Jeff Barr feel he had to look into your land?"

"Something about wanting the land for a development." A tear slipped down her cheek.

I nodded. "He wants my land because I've got access to the lake in back of the acreage."

Tamara's eyes opened wide. "He wants all the land on this stretch of road then. I don't have the funds to fight him."

"He wants the bank to foreclose on me because I'm behind on taxes. It cost a lot to get my father established at the retirement center. I'm still working on his medical bills, and I had to put in quite a bit to get the store up and running." My words came out in a long sigh. I could feel anger boiling inside. Jeff Barr was ruining what otherwise should have been a great day.

Tamara nodded. "I see. So, chances are I'll lose my land. If it wasn't for Jeff, neither of us would be having problems. No one ever questioned my rights to the property before, and I'm sure the bank would never pressure you. They know your daddy." Her gaze shifted, and she seemed lost in thought for a moment. I could see her gripping her fists. I'd never seen Tamara so angry.

"I've got to do something. . ."

I wanted to ease the moment, so I reached for her hand. "Let's agree to pray about it," I suggested.

Her lips quivered into a small smile. "I'm not sure God really cares about this."

I frowned. I'd been talking to Tamara about God for a while, and she wasn't completely convinced He was as powerful, loving, and kind as I tried to tell her. She'd never openly seemed to reject Him before though.

"If anyone can do anything about it, God can," I encouraged. She took my hand reluctantly. We bowed our heads, and I prayed. When I lifted my head, feeling happy for the moment, I saw the beige Cadillac pull into the yard. Tamara must have felt me tense, because her eyes moved in that direction and settled on the vehicle.

"Grrr." She actually growled. "What a way to ruin a perfectly good moment." She laughed, which broke the tension. "I could just. . .grr."

"We won't let him bug us." I squeezed her hand. "If I see him coming this way, I'll try to head him off so you won't have to deal with him today."

"Thanks." Tamara turned back to her booth. There were several people gathered in line, so she continued pouring her famous green drinks. I preferred her mango drinks.

I decided to stroll around again, but from the corner of my eye I watched as Jeff got out of his car and began to walk in Tamara's direction. The last thing I wanted to see was him giving her a hard time during Market Days, so I sidestepped and headed over to ward him off.

In a few moments, I realized I wasn't going to have to stop him. He'd been approached by Katie Jane, one of the Sewing Bee ladies. I followed as they moved toward the chicken coop, which I wasn't happy to see. I didn't want anyone bothering the Southern Belles.

I was about to approach them when I noticed that Katie Jane seemed to flit around him like a bee dancing around a daisy. Her cheeks were flushed, and I could hear her laughter, but it ended abruptly.

It was well known around town that two ladies from the Sewing Bee's group, Katie Jane and Sadie Rose, were at least half in love with the odious man. As I said, how anyone could be attracted to Jeff Barr was beyond my comprehension, but to each their own.

I rounded the corner of the house in time to hear Jeff's words directed at Katie Jane. "Look, I never promised you anything. You need to get over it." She stood still, her eyes big in shock and her shoulders slumped. She turned and hurried away, leaving Jeff alone at the chicken coop. As she rushed by, I fell in step with her.

"Katie Jane, is everything okay?" I asked, noting her eyes brimming with tears. She stopped and stared at me but then suddenly swiped at her tears and straightened to her full height. "Of course."

"Is there a problem with Jeff?"

At his name, she snapped her head up. "Jeff? What problem could I possibly have with him? He's a lovely man." Her voice trembled.

"Oh, I thought I overheard—" It was obvious Katie Jane didn't want to talk about it, so I decided to clamp my mouth shut. She had to be embarrassed. Here she was, a woman in her late forties, maybe early fifties, fawning over a man like Jeff Barr. To be scorned by him was probably more than she could bear. He wasn't much of a catch as far as I was concerned.

"Excuse me." She pushed by me, rushed down the driveway, and slid behind the Sewing Bees booth. The ladies sold quilts, potholders, and potato warmers. They also sold honey harvested from Carol Anne's beehives.

Three ladies actually made up the Sewing Bee's group, but I'd never heard anything about Carol Anne having a crush on Jeff. She was always so stiff and stern, I couldn't imagine her falling in love with anyone. I noticed that Carol Anne and Sadie Rose moved aside and ignored Katie Jane when she rushed into the booth. I cocked my head in wonder. These women had been best friends since childhood. Could it be that Jeff Barr had come between them? I understood Sadie Rose being upset with Katie Jane over him, but not Carol Anne.

I looked around. Tamara wasn't behind her table, so maybe she'd seen Jeff heading her way and had run out to escape him.

I strolled down the aisle of tables, sampling fresh almonds, salsa, and iced tea. I bought something at a few booths, even though I knew I shouldn't, but I couldn't refrain. I wanted to thank everyone for putting their faith in me by participating in Market Days.

When I passed the Sewing Bee's booth again, there was a young girl, about seventeen with lovely blond hair, standing behind the counter.

"Where are the Sewing Bees?" I asked, surprised they were all missing.

She shrugged. "I don't know about all of them. Katie Jane asked me to step in for her so she could go to the ladies' room. Sadie Rose and Carol Anne weren't here when I took over."

I noted two sets of red gloves on the table. The ladies always wore velvet gloves when handling the quilts, to keep them from getting stained. I glanced around but didn't see Jeff anywhere in the area. I hadn't seen him since he was talking to Katie Jane. I did see Stacy Monson though. She'd just walked away from the Sewing Bee's area and was taking photos at different booths. If she continued in the direction she was headed, I assumed she'd end up taking photos of the chickens. I shook my head. I didn't imagine her readers would care much about my little coop and the Southern Belles.

I was excited that she'd decided to stay a few days, and it looked like she'd be staying at least one more night. She'd paid up front too! This Airbnb idea seemed more and more promising.

At one point in the next half hour, I heard a ruckus. The Southern Belles were squawking. From where I was standing, I couldn't see if anyone was near the coop. There shouldn't have been, because I'd placed cones in front of that area to keep people from approaching them. That was why I was a bit upset that Jeff and Katie Jane had been back there talking. I was concerned about a group of young boys I'd seen earlier, wondering if they'd found their way to the coop. I headed that way but was glad to hear the chickens quiet down, so I stopped in front of Tamara's booth, which was closest to the coop. Tamara had just slipped into the booth.

"Hey. How's sales?" I asked. She'd been standing with her back to me and spun around when she heard my voice. I could see her slipping off a pair of gloves she usually wore when making drinks. I wondered why she had them on when she hadn't been in her booth. There was a pile of kale near her.

"Pretty good." She twirled a piece of her hair absently. Her eyes looked a bit haunted. I moved closer. For a moment, the entire Market Days was quiet. The Belles were silent now as well. There was an eeriness about it.

I looked at Tamara. Her cheeks were red, and her hands were shaking. "Did Jeff bother you?" I wasn't sure where he'd gone after being so rude to Katie Jane. Maybe I hadn't been able to keep him away from Tamara after all.

She nodded slowly. "Mmhmm. Yep." She bit her lower lip and looked away. It was a strange reaction.

"Did he. . .say anything else?"

She shook her head. "He started to." She took a deep, jagged breath.

"What did you say?"

Her shoulders dropped. "Nothing, really. I'm so tired of it all. . ."

I nodded in understanding, expecting her to tell me more, but a friendly voice behind me caused Tamara to grow quiet. I turned. My eyes met those of Rene Dempsy. His face was sweaty, and he had a streak of dirt across his cheek. He was stuffing some work gloves into his pants pockets.

"Hi, April. Pretty good crowd." His hand moved slowly, indicating all the booths set up. I was pleased with the turnout. Rene must have felt the seriousness of the conversation he'd interrupted, because he looked at Tamara and then back at me. "Everything okay here?"

"It's Jeff Barr," I growled. "I'm not the only one he's been trying to force into selling their land."

Rene's eyes opened wide, and he looked closer at Tamara. "Yours too?"

She nodded. "But I don't think it's going to be a problem."

Rene tilted his head and laughed. "Yeah, I wouldn't worry about him anymore."

I looked at Rene in surprise, wondering what he could possibly mean. We all needed to worry about Jeff Barr, because he could ruin everything.

"He isn't worth the effort," Rene said to Tamara. "Don't let him spoil your day."

I stood there, watching this interaction. I didn't think they were attracted to one another, but it was as if they shared some kind of secret. Did they know something I didn't?

Rene finally turned to me. "I've been asking around. Everyone's making more money this weekend than ever before. I think having Market Days here was a good idea." He smiled, which—as usual—caused my stomach to tighten.

"I'm glad," I said. "Maybe more people will sign up next month and it will help pay my late taxes."

"I thought I saw a person carrying out one of my paintings?"

I nodded. "Your cards are all gone. They were a big seller."

"That's great. They're much easier to produce than new paintings."

I moved closer to him. "What's with the dirt on your face?" I reached up and wiped at his cheek, then realized how intimate that must seem to onlookers. I immediately dropped my hand.

"Umm, nothing." He swiped at his face. "I dropped a pencil by the chicken coop, trying to get some sketches for my next set of cards. I got dirt on myself when I was searching for it."

That was probably what had caused the Southern Belles to do all that squawking earlier. They must have seen the handsome artist and decided to shake their tail feathers. Yes, chickens actually shake their tail feathers when they're happy. I imagined they were showing off for Rene. When he was near, I was tempted to shake my tail feathers too.

He stepped back, and I noted his clothes were dusty. He must have rolled under the chicken coop to find that pencil. I wondered why he'd been wearing gloves.

I glanced around. The crowd had thinned, and several vendors were beginning to pack up. I was sure it had been a success for everyone but was glad the day was coming to an end.

Just then, Sadie Rose waved, beckoning me to her side. Torn between wanting to stay and talk with Rene and being polite to the older woman, I excused myself, leaving Tamara and Rene together. Tamara is a friend, and Rene. . .well. . .I admit, I'm attracted to him, but the way they'd been acting earlier, I didn't want to leave them together.

As I moved toward Sadie Rose, I lifted a little prayer. "God, you know my heart and my desire. If anything is supposed to come of my feelings for Rene, I put it in Your hands. If Your plan for his life is Tamara, give me the grace to accept it."

Sadie Rose seemed flustered as I drew near. "What's up?" I asked.

She glanced around and lowered her voice. "Do you know who that woman is?" she asked.

I frowned. "What woman?"

"The one who's asking everyone if they know Jeff Barr. I've never seen her before, but she's been taking photos and asking about him." Her voice indicated she was highly irritated.

The only person I'd seen with a camera was Stacy, my Airbnb guest. She'd seen Jeff at my shop and hadn't seemed to know him. But then I remembered she'd asked who he was and then had acted a bit surprised when I said he was a real estate agent.

"If you're talking about Stacy Monson, she really likes the area, so maybe she's looking to buy and wants to consult with him."

Sadie Rose let out a breath in a soft sigh. "Oh, okay. I mean, it's already an issue with Katie Jane."

I frowned. "What's an issue?"

"Katie Jane seems to believe that Jeff wants to marry her. Or at least that he should want to marry her. I'm afraid he may have inadvertently led her on a bit." Her cheeks reddened slightly.

"And you?" I asked innocently.

"I thought. . ." She scanned the area, and her voice lowered. "I made sure he wasn't going to have anything to do with Katie Jane ever again."

My eyes widened. I hated seeing these best friends torn apart because of him when I doubted he had feelings for either of them. I think he liked the attention, and the ladies tended to vie for his attention by giving him baked goods and dinners at their houses.

I felt like banging my head against the wall. Surely these women couldn't both think Jeff Barr was in love with them? Even if he did let them believe that. The man was. . .well, he made me think of something slimy.

"April, we might have a thief here as well," Sadie Rose added.

I blinked. "Thief?"

"Yes, someone took a pair of gloves we use to handle the quilts. They were on the table where we always keep them, and now they're gone. Of course, they're *my* gloves."

"I'm sorry. I'll look around for them. Maybe they got dropped somewhere." I didn't think the gloves were worth stealing. Sadie Rose gave a small snort as if dismissing my offer of help. I wasn't sure what else to say, so I decided I'd talk to Stacy later, maybe give her a heads-up on the type of real estate agent Jeff Barr was. Then again, just because I was mad he was trying to get me to sell my land didn't mean he wouldn't be a good agent for Stacy. He was known for finding deals for his clients that no one else could accomplish.

I watched Sadie Rose return to her booth. All three women were there now, working together to pack up. I did note that they weren't smiling or laughing or talking to one another as they usually did. I walked away and visited with other booth owners. Later I saw that all three Sewing Bees were done putting their supplies into their van. Within the hour, the yard was barren. Not a car left in sight, not even Stacy's.

The last person to pull out of the driveway was Rene. I waved, but he didn't turn his head toward me, which I thought was weird. He was always very polite. He drove away quickly, and I wondered why he was in such a hurry.

I moved to the porch and sat on a rocker, resting my eyes and allowing the quiet to fill my soul. The day had been a success. There wasn't much garbage on the ground, so cleanup should be easy. The money I'd made from the day was going to be taken to the bank on Monday and then put toward the taxes owed.

I wasn't sure exactly what the amount was, but I hoped if I showed good faith and started paying on a monthly basis after every Market Day, the bank would be happy. It was a small town, and a few outstanding tax payments had never caused anyone to lose their land before.

I could hear the Southern Belles beginning to get fussy. I needed to give them their afternoon feed. I prefer a twice-a-day feeding schedule over pouring out large piles in the morning and allowing them to gorge themselves all day. I always make the girls work for their food by spreading it out in a larger area. Because of Market Days, I was very late feeding them. Poor things!

I stood up and slapped my thighs to wake myself up a little, then headed toward the coop. As I drew closer, I blinked a few times. There was something lying beside the coop, but I was unable to make it out. As I got closer, I thought it looked like a man who was sleeping, which made no sense unless he was drunk.

I didn't allow the sale of alcohol at Market Days, so I couldn't imagine anyone drunk enough to pass out. I hesitated, a sense of dread beginning to overtake me. Step by slow step, I moved toward the man, noting the 4-tine hand cultivator rake had fallen over and was lying on his stomach.

As I reached the corner of the coop, my hand flew to my mouth and stifled a gasp. Not only was the man lying there with the rake on top of him, but from what I could tell, he wasn't breathing. I blinked and wiped at my eyes, trying to change what I was seeing, but nothing helped. It was Jeff Barr, lying dead next to my chicken coop.

CHAPTER FIVE

I'm not sure if I was screaming or if the chickens started squawking, but there was suddenly enough noise to wake the dead. I glanced at the body again, but Jeff didn't wake up. He didn't move. One of his hands was across his chest, and the other lay sprawled on the ground.

"Oh no," I repeated over and over. How could this have happened? I didn't like the man, not one iota, but I never wished for him to die—and from the looks of things, he'd been murdered.

My hands were shaking. I reached out to remove the rake, then good sense set in. I'd watched enough detective shows to know I shouldn't touch the weapon or the body. I stepped back quickly, looking around. I couldn't make out any specific footprints, but I also knew I shouldn't disturb the dirt, just in case there were some.

The chickens' meal would have to wait. I jogged a few yards away from the coop and pulled out my phone. Everything in me wanted to call Rene. I wanted a man to comfort me, but we weren't a couple, and he might think it was weird, so instead I dialed 911 and gave the details to the dispatcher when she answered.

I knew the dispatcher by name. Gretchen Tombow. She was pretty good at keeping emergency issues quiet, but when I told her who I was and that Jeff Barr was lying in my yard, dead, she gasped.

"Are you sure?" Her voice sounded a bit shaky.

"Yes. I mean, I didn't touch him, but I can see his chest isn't moving. I don't want to disturb anything."

The line was silent for a few seconds. "Okay, April. I've contacted the correct authorities. It won't take long. There will be an ambulance and fire truck and the police. It's gonna get pretty crazy there. I suggest you wait at the house."

Her voice was calm and soothing. I felt like I did when I was a child and Mom would put me to bed and give me a cup of warm milk. I could almost feel myself begin to relax. That's one of the reasons why Gretchen is perfect for the job. She's been known to even talk someone out of suicide before.

My teeth were chattering, but I was able to spurt out, "Thanks. Should I stay on the line?"

"No, you can hang up. You'll hear the sirens in just a few minutes, unless you want me to stay on the line with you."

I shook my head, then realized she couldn't see me. "No, I'm okay, I guess. I'll sit down and wait." I ended the call and trudged to the porch. I hadn't noticed, but while I was at the chicken coop finding a dead body, Stacy had pulled up. She wasn't in the vehicle, so I assumed she'd gone to her room, clearly oblivious to the fact that there was a man lying dead within a hundred yards of the house.

I could have called out, asked her to help me, but all I could think to do was sit and wait, eyes peeled on the driveway. In just a few minutes, I heard sirens.

Three police cars, one fire truck, an ambulance, and ten local volunteers' cars showed up. The police quickly placed a yellow line far from the crime scene to keep onlookers back. When approached, I didn't really say anything, just pointed to the chicken coop. I hoped they would all come traipsing back, laughing, telling me I'd been seeing things, that Jeff Barr's body was not lying dead beside my Southern Belles—but that was not to be.

I was glad there were no reporters.

It was about twenty minutes before one of the officers finally approached me. "Miss Rein?" He was young, maybe new to the force, barely out of the academy. He looked pale.

I glanced up. "Yes."

"I was told to come and get your initial statement." He pulled out a notepad and pen and looked at me intently. I saw him take a few gasps of air. I felt sorry for him but felt even sorrier for me. Jeff Barr's death on my property wasn't going to look good for my new business, especially since it had happened during Market Days.

"First, is Jeff Barr really dead?" I asked.

"Yes. It looks like he was hit on the head with the rake. Hard enough to kill him. Can you tell me about the day and the events that led up to you finding. . ." He gulped. "The body?"

I nodded. "Today was Market Days, and when it was over, I decided to feed my chickens. When I got there, I saw a man lying beside the coop. I thought he was passed out, but then I realized he was dead."

"Did you know the, um, the deceased?"

I nodded again. "Yes, his name is Jeff Barr." I didn't want to give too much information because, from my viewpoint, if anyone guessed the way I felt about the man, it would look bad for me. Not that I would ever kill anyone, but I suppose in a way I had the motive to do it. Without Jeff Barr's pressure, I wouldn't have to worry about the bank taking my land. The thought crept into my mind, and I began shaking again. What if the police decided to pin it all on me?

He gave me a nod. "Did you know Jeff Barr well?"

I shrugged, noncommittal. "He's a local real estate agent." I snapped my mouth closed. Even that seemed like too much information.

The young man wrote something in his notepad. He scratched the back of his head with his pen. "Kinda strange he was killed here, by your chicken coop. Any idea why?" His eyes, now looking intelligent, bored into mine.

"No. He was at Market Days." Again, I wanted to slap a hand over my mouth. Less said, the better.

He turned and faced me squarely. "Now, Miss Rein, I work in the bank part-time as a security guard, and last week I happened to overhear Mr. Barr speaking to the bank manager. You were mentioned—and also your *property*." He emphasized the final word.

I gulped. Now what was I supposed to say? I remembered what they do on crime shows, so I looked up and smiled. "Officer, I'm not sure what you're implying. I think I've answered all the questions I'm willing to answer without my lawyer."

His shoulders sagged. He tilted his head and gave me what could only be considered a naughty schoolboy's smile. "Sorry. I did hear that conversation, but I don't imagine it has anything to do with what happened here today. As a matter of fact, your property wasn't the only one Mr. Barr was talking to the bank manager about. Seems he was trying to press the man into forcing several landowners to sell."

I was sure the officer should not have been sharing this information with me, but I stood quietly, nodding my head in an encouraging way, hoping he would tell me more. I already realized that I was going to be a prime suspect in Jeff Barr's death. I had motive, means, and opportunity, which in a good mystery meant I could possibly be the murderer. If I didn't know myself so well, I'd wonder if I did it.

He believed I wasn't going to talk anymore, so he tucked his notebook in his pocket then informed me that I might be called to come downtown the next day to make an official statement. I released my breath, which I think I'd been holding almost the whole time.

Lord, this is a bad situation. The police could suspect me of killing Jeff. I'm going to need Your help. I lowered my head and continued praying silently. It was clear I was going to have to "help" the police come up with names of others who might have killed Jeff so I wouldn't be their only suspect.

I hurried inside the shop and grabbed a small notepad and a pencil. I narrowed my eyes, trying to think, but something moved across the room. My eyes widened, then I relaxed when I saw Stacy looking out a window.

I wasn't happy to have her see all this. It was terrible that it happened at my Airbnb, especially during my first guest's stay, but at this point I couldn't do anything about it. I stood behind the counter and started a list. Every name I put on it made me cringe. Not one of them could I imagine killing the man.

First, I wrote Katie Jane's name. I'd overheard Jeff tell her he wasn't going to marry her. Could that have made her mad enough to kill him? Second, I wrote down Sadie Rose's name. She told me she'd done something to keep him from ever marrying Katie Jane. Could that have meant murder? Then, sadly I added Rene's name. He was pretty angry with Jeff, and he'd been covered in dirt earlier, which might indicate he'd had a struggle with him near the coop. And he'd told Tamara she shouldn't worry about Jeff anymore. But would he kill someone? Finally, I wrote Tamara's name on the paper. Jeff was threatening to get her land away from her, and she had disappeared from her booth for a while earlier in the day. I shook my head and thought about crossing out her name. I couldn't see Tamara ever hurting anyone, but maybe she'd done it out of fear.

I reread the list and hated that I'd included any of them, even though I didn't know anyone else to include. I was going to do some snooping around and hope that in the meantime the police would find a better suspect.

As I was setting down my pen, Stacy came into the store from the other part of the house. She looked drained of all color.

"Hi." I smiled, not sure if I should ask her what was wrong.

"What's going on out there?"

"There was a man killed by the chicken coop." I stated it rather bluntly, but how else could I tell her about something like that?

She stepped back as if she'd been slapped. "Killed?"

"Yes, remember the man I told you is a real estate agent in town, Jeff Barr?" She nodded. "I found him lying by the chicken coop, dead. He'd been hit in the head with the rake."

"That's disconcerting." Her voice dropped, and she picked up a small glass figurine of a chicken and stared at it for a long time.

"Did you know Jeff?"

Her head shot up. "Why would you ask that? I'm not from here."

I realized she had evaded the question. "Someone said you'd been asking about him at Market Days."

She placed her hands on her hips. "Who said that?"

I wasn't about to share that information with her. "Well, they actually said a woman who was taking photos at Market Days was asking questions about Jeff Barr."

"And you assumed it was me?" Her voice had reached a higher pitch.

I nodded.

She put the chicken down and headed toward the front door. "Maybe I better just check out now," she called back over her shoulder. "I don't like to be accused of murder." The door slammed behind her, making me jump. I stood still, wondering what had caused such erratic behavior in the woman. I hadn't accused her of murder at all.

I looked at my list again and wrote out another name. *Stacy*, with a set of three question marks after it. Why would she have killed Jeff Barr? By all accounts, they were complete strangers. Of course, he'd only lived in town for a few years. He'd just showed up one day, opened a real estate office on a side street off Main, and eased himself into everyone's lives.

Because I believed that Stacy was the one asking about him, I had to consider her a suspect.

Since moving here, Jeff had never missed an event in town, be it a cook-off, a holiday fair, or a craft show. He seemed to know everyone, and he'd proved that when he wanted to acquire someone's land to sell it to an investor, he wasn't afraid to dig deep to find things he could use against them.

I glanced out the window and watched as Stacy got in her car and drove away. I wondered if she would come back. She needed to get her suitcase, so I assumed she would return. Was there a chance that she really had known Jeff before? And if so, how could I find out that information?

I tapped my lower lip with my pencil. Should I add Carol Anne to the list? As far as I knew, Jeff hadn't been spending time with her, at least not like he had with Sadie Rose and Katie Jane. I hadn't paid much attention to Carol Anne's whereabouts during Market Days, but it was a line of questioning I could follow up on. She had been missing from their booth, and she did give Katie Jane the cold shoulder earlier.

My mind was in turmoil. Why was I even considering asking anyone any questions? Surely the police would interrogate the right people. They would find the murderer. I actually laughed out loud, thinking how silly I was to imagine the police would think I'd killed Jeff Barr.

I walked over to the window. The ambulance was pulling out of the driveway. I assumed Jeff's body was inside. The fire engine was already gone, and the police cars were lined up to leave.

I moved to the door and stepped out onto the front porch. I needed to feed the Southern Belles and hoped the police hadn't caused them too much trauma. They were already molting. Something like this could cause them to lose all their feathers.

The last police car pulled out of the driveway, and I made my way to the coop. This time I hesitated, looking at the spot where Jeff's body had lain. I searched for the 4-tine rake, but it was gone. Obviously it was the murder weapon, and the police had taken it. It looked like they'd cleaned up any blood from the scene. There wasn't even a yellow caution tape up, which surprised me. I was worried they would have blocked off the area, and what would I have done about the Southern Belles then?

I grabbed the feed bag and began spreading the contents out in long lines, having to improvise without the rake. The Southern Belles were more than ready and ran up and began pecking at their food. Within minutes, they were all quiet and happily eating. I scooted closer to the area where Jeff had been killed and searched the ground. I didn't see anything that would give a clue. There were no footprints of any kind, which wasn't good. I'd hoped the killer had left a very obvious print and the whole thing would be cleared up in a day.

I shook my head. That was not to be.

"Well, girls, can any of you tell me who killed Jeff Barr?" Not a single one of them looked up at me. Obviously their dinner was more important than their owner's dilemma.

I finished feeding them then quickly headed back to the house. In there, I felt at peace. I was home. The only thing missing was my parents. My mom had passed a while back, and having just recently moved Dad into the retirement center made the house seem lonely.

Dad was fine. He loved the activities and the food at the center. He had grown weary of taking care of the property. He tried to talk me into selling it, but I just wasn't able to. I want to live here, maybe get married someday and raise a family of my own. When

I'm tired of it all, my kids can move me into the retirement center, but for now, this is home.

I headed to the small office, which is actually a den, and began the bookkeeping that was required after Market Days. All in all, the event had been a success, between the vendors and the influx of shoppers. Still, there was this murder to consider. Was it going to kill off my business too?

CHAPTER SIX

The hens began to squawk much too early the next day, but they weren't the only thing that woke me. My phone, which I keep beside my bed, began to ring earlier than any reasonable human should have to be awake. I rolled over, grabbed the phone, swiped the screen, and held it to my ear. My voice had its morning crackle. "Hello?"

"Ms. Rein? This is Officer Brinkle."

I sat up straight. "Yes?"

"We'd like you to come to the station as soon as possible."

I held the phone out and stared at it. What could it mean? Had they figured out who had killed Jeff Barr already? I pressed it to my ear again. "It's Sunday," I stated.

"Mm, yes. Well, we do have a murder on our hands. I'm sure even God wants us to solve this case as soon as possible."

I felt silly. "Okay. I've got to feed the chickens, then I'll drive on over. Is there any news you can share with me?" I asked hopefully.

"No." The officer's voice was evasive. "Just come as soon as you can."

I hung up and sat for a few minutes, praying. That was my normal morning routine, but this morning, the need for prayer was very pressing. I hated that Jeff Barr had been murdered, but the fact also relieved me of pressure, as much as I hated to admit it. I still planned to pay off the back taxes, but for the time, I could catch my breath. I wondered if Tamara felt the same way this morning.

A quick stop at the chicken coop assured me the Southern Belles were all fine. They really were looking bad though. I could only hope the molting was almost over and soon they'd grow back their lovely feathers.

I headed for the car and shot out of the driveway. Usually, I'd hold off eating on a Sunday morning and join a few others after church, but today my plan was to stop at Bacon on Main and grab a coffee to go, maybe a donut. I hoped the officer at the police station wouldn't mind me taking that much time to get there.

I pulled into a parking spot, slipped out of the car, and took a peek in the window. Rene was sitting at a booth. How, you may ask, did I know he was going to be there? Did I plan this, hoping he would notice me, call me over, ask me to join him?

I pressed my hand to my forehead, trying to make my thoughts stop. Right now, the last thing I needed to be thinking about was Rene in that way. Sure, he's good looking, nice, and well, exactly what I'm looking for in a man—as long as he's a Christian. But with this murder hanging over my head, it just wasn't the right time. He did appear at Market Days, from the direction of the chicken coop, covered in dirt. Could he and Jeff have had an altercation that ended in murder?

I opened the door and stepped in, trying to avoid eye contact with him. I walked straight up to the counter and ordered a coffee, two creams, one sugar, to go. I skipped the donut. When the server handed me the cup, I turned and headed for the door, but Rene had seen me.

"In a hurry, April?" His voice drew me in, and I stopped.

"The police called this morning and told me to come to the station as soon as possible."

His eyebrows rose. "Why?"

"Because of Jeff Barr." I wasn't sure if Rene or anyone else besides the police knew about the murder yet. It was a small town, though, and I expected word had gotten around.

Rene frowned. "Yes, if you're wondering, I know about the murder. Nothing stays quiet for long in this place. But why do the police need you to come to the station?"

I shrugged, realizing I'd put on one of my oldest sweatshirts, which made me look like an old frump.

He patted the table. "Come sit down and tell me about it. I'm sure they can wait a little longer."

I couldn't help myself. My mind screamed *no* but my feet moved, and before I knew it, I was ensconced in the booth across from him. Rene always carries a sketchbook with him, and I could see he'd been working on a pencil drawing of the oldest general store in town. It has a lot of history. If he could turn that into cards, those would sell.

"Why do the police want to see you? Didn't they take your statement yesterday?"

"I'm not sure, but so much of the day was just a blur. I can't believe someone was killed on my property." I looked in his eyes. He didn't blink. Was that suspicious? Or not?

"I'm worried this will ruin business." I lowered my voice. "I don't have to worry anymore about Jeff getting the bank to take away the property, but I need the shop and Market Days to pay the bills."

He took a sip of orange juice. Rene is not a coffee man. I wondered about that. Can anyone trust a man who doesn't drink coffee?

"Hmm, I doubt his death will hurt your business. From all the chatter I've heard today, no one really liked him and there seem to be plenty of people who were at odds with him."

"What about you?" I blurted out.

He tilted his head and gave me a steady stare. "What about me? I had no reason to kill the man, except I didn't like the way he was going to the bank manager and trying to hurt you." His eyes met mine and I felt like I was floating into them. "I don't want anyone hurting you, April." His voice was filled with a tenderness I wasn't used to.

I gulped. Was he telling me he liked me?

I smiled shakily, wondering why I hadn't taken more time to brush my hair and put on a decent outfit that morning. "Thanks, that means a lot to me. But someone killed him—and on my property. I saw you covered in dirt, just about or right after the time he was murdered."

Rene frowned and sat up straight. "And you think I killed him?" he said incredulously.

I shook my head. "No, not at all, I mean, not really, no... Well, I did wonder." Better to be truthful up front. This was an issue that was going to come up in my statement to the police. I lifted my eyes and looked directly at him, hoping to gauge his reaction.

He sat quietly for a few moments, his hand suspended in midair over his orange juice as if he were going to pick it up. Finally, he set his hand on the table. "April, trying to see things through your eyes, I can understand your thoughts. You don't know me well enough to assure yourself there is no way I would kill anyone, plus you saw me covered in dirt coming from near the chicken coop. But I can promise you, I would never kill him or anyone. I'm a Christian, and I hope that speaks for itself."

I felt a smile flit across my face. He was a Christian, which on top of his looks and his kind ways, made him the perfect man. Now, if only we could put this murder behind us and try to develop a relationship!

"Do you think I killed him?" I asked.

He shook his head. "Of course not."

I breathed a sigh. "Good. I may have had reason to dislike Jeff, but I'm also a Christian, and murder isn't the way I deal with things. A bit of prayer is the extent of my show of force."

Rene reached across the table and laid his hand over mine. He smiled, and I smiled. There was nothing more to say. Neither of us had killed Jeff Barr, and we were both Christians. In my mind, the matter was settled, but is claiming to be a Christian really all it takes to be cleared of a murder?

I gently wriggled my hand out of his, which seemed to break the almost trance-like state we were both in. I stood up. "I better go. I'm sure the officer who called didn't expect me to stop for coffee on my way in." I eased out of the booth, dreading what lay ahead of me.

Rene stood and tossed a ten-dollar bill onto the table. "Hold on, I'm coming with you."

"What?"

"I don't want you to be alone. Do you have a lawyer?"

I shook my head. "I don't think I'll need one."

Rene laughed. "April, a man who was trying to get the bank to force you to sell your land was killed on your property. Of course you need a lawyer."

Hearing that spoken out loud felt like a slap, but I had to accept the truth.

"I better get one, then." I bit my bottom lip, wondering how to even go about that.

Rene took my arm. "I happen to know a great lawyer. I'll call him on the way. You drive."

I didn't want to appear surprised or overly pleased, but I was glad to have him along. Going to the police station isn't something anyone looks forward to. We didn't have far to go.

"This interview could take a long time, Rene," I said.

"I've got all day. I don't want you to face this on your own. They may not let me in the interview room, but I'll be in the hallway waiting for you."

It isn't a very big town, and the police station was just down the street. I drove around the main square twice while Rene got on the phone with someone named Clive. When he hung up, he nodded at me.

"Okay, April. Clive said to go ahead and get started but not to talk about anything you don't feel comfortable talking about. He'll be over in about fifteen minutes."

I parked the car, and we got out and walked toward the station. I hoped Clive didn't end up being too expensive. With all my other bills, I just couldn't afford it.

Rene was reading my mind. "Clive's a great guy, and he gives big discounts on his services. He doesn't need the money, because his parents were wealthy and he inherited it all. He does a lot of pro bono work just to keep active when he's not flying in his private airplane."

I blinked. "Why haven't I ever heard of this guy before?"

"He lives pretty far outside of town and keeps to himself."

"How do you know him?" I asked.

Rene shrugged his shoulders. "Oh, I've known him for years. I'll tell you more about him over dinner one night this week." He gave me a self-assured grin.

I glanced up at him. Was he asking me on a date? To find out, I poked him gently in the side and said, "Oh really, am I cooking this dinner? I'm not a very good cook, but I can order in great hot wings."

He smiled at me. "I'm not a spicy kind of guy. . ."

I didn't want to contradict him, but in my eyes, he was very spicy.

"To be safe, I'll take you out. A nice Italian restaurant with some plain old spaghetti will suit me." He tilted his head and gave me a wink.

At this point, we were at the front door of the police station, and joking time was over. Rene took my hand, and we made our way to the front desk.

"I'm April Rein," I told the woman behind the desk.

She gave me a cursory scan and said something I never imagined hearing in my lifetime. "You don't look like a murderer."

CHAPTER SEVEN

I wasn't sure what to say. Being called a murderer at a police station didn't fill me with any assurance. Did she know something I didn't? Had they found some evidence that pointed to only me?

Sweat formed on my forehead. The woman told me to sit on the hard bench across the hallway and wait until I was called. I sat, feeling like I was in elementary school and had been sent to the principal's office.

Rene stepped outside to wait for the lawyer. It seemed as if I waited forever, but in reality, it was only a few minutes before the officer from the day before came and got me, telling me to follow him.

To get grilled shot through my mind. When we reached the interrogation room, I sat in a chair across from the one he took.

"I thought I was asked to come and give a statement. So far, I've been treated like a suspect." I glared at him.

"Well..." He paused. "The only evidence we have points to you."

I gulped. "What evidence?"

He ran a hand through his hair slowly, as if debating on telling me more, then leaned forward. "The 4-tine rake, which is the murder weapon, has your fingerprints on it and no one else's."

"I use that rake every day. Of course my prints are on it."

He sat back, "Yes, but why not anyone else's? It's not like a murderer carries around a pair of gloves at Market Days, just in case he's planning to kill someone."

Gloves? Rene had worn gloves; Tamara had worn gloves; Carol Anne and Katie Jane had worn gloves. Sadie Rose's gloves had been stolen. Could someone have picked them up, knowing they were going to kill Jeff Barr? Or did Sadie Rose wear them, kill him, and then throw the gloves away? Perhaps that was why she'd mentioned the missing gloves.

I told the officer about all the gloves I'd seen that day, and he wrote everything down. "That's very interesting," he said. But he didn't sound interested at all. I wondered if he'd even share that information with anyone above him.

I felt as if I were being strangled, and it was getting harder to breathe. "I didn't kill Mr. Barr, and if I'd done it with my own rake, you'd think I would've been smart enough to either get rid of it or wipe my fingerprints off of it." I met his eyes, firm in my thoughts.

He nodded. "That makes sense." He tapped his pen on the table.

I sat quiet for a few minutes, then snapped at him, "What about footprints?"

He shook his head. "Nothing specific. Besides, footprints are not a very reliable way to find a suspect these days."

My shoulders dropped. I'd already guessed they hadn't found any, since the police hadn't sectioned the area off with yellow tape.

My hands were shaking, and I felt sick. "Am I under arrest?"

"No, but don't leave town." I almost laughed when he said those words. It sounded as if they had come right out of a TV show.

I nodded. He began to ask me more questions and the interview seemed to go on for ages, and still no lawyer had shown up.

"Can you let me know if you find out anything else?"

He grimaced. "No. I shouldn't have even told you everything I did."

I put a finger to my mouth. "I won't tell, but I may stop by from time to time and bring you a donut. We can talk." I gave him a wink, hoping he realized it meant I'd come by for more information and *not* that I was flirting with him.

He stood up, slightly flustered, then opened the door. Rene, who must have been standing right by it, nearly stumbled into the room. When he got his footing, he turned to the officer and said, "I insist you stop questioning Miss Rein until her lawyer gets here."

The officer chuckled and left the room.

As he righted himself, I smiled at Rene.

"Too late?" he asked innocently, giving me the most adorable shoulder shrug I've ever seen. "Clive called back and said he was held up."

"It's okay. Right now, they aren't charging me with anything." I hiccupped, taking in a deep breath. Rene must have realized I was on the verge of tears, because his face shone with sympathy. I walked into his open arms. The hug was comforting, but I still wondered about him. Was he innocent? And did he really believe I was innocent?

My emotions were all jumbled up. It was too much to think about this early. I'd missed the first service at church and didn't feel like going to the second one. A good cry in bed was what I needed, but I was obliged to drive Rene. . .where? Home? To Bacon on Main?

"Earth to April." Rene snapped his fingers in front of my eyes. I blinked and stepped back from his arms.

"Sorry, I'm just so tired. I'm going to spend the rest of the day in bed." My cheeks instantly heated. I didn't want him to think I was lazy.

"Sounds like a good idea." He shrugged it off. "Clive is headed this way, so I'll wait for him. He can drive me home. Maybe I'll do some snooping. Never know what I might overhear."

A part of me wanted to stay and do some snooping too, but more than likely Rene would find out more alone. Remembering how he'd overheard Jeff talking to the bank manager, I decided to put my trust in him.

"Won't they wonder what you're doing here?" I asked.

"I come here to use the public printer. They have legal-sized paper in theirs." He nodded toward the front hallway, and sure enough, there was a printer.

"I would have gone to the library for that."

He nodded. "This is the printer from the library. They're remodeling their office space and have moved several things to storage, but people still need to use the copier, so the librarian asked, and here it is."

"All right then, I'm heading home."

Rene placed a hand under my chin and lifted my head. "Call me if you need anything. I want to be there for you."

I wanted to beg him to come home with me, stay all day, comfort me, but the truth was, if I was going to have a relationship with him, we needed to have this murder cleared up. And the best way to do that right now was for him to do some snooping and for me to get some rest. I would begin my own campaign of information gathering tomorrow.

"Thank you, Rene. You're a true friend." I stepped back, and his hand dropped to his side, but he whispered, "I'd like to be more than that."

I gave a small nod. "That would be nice, once this situation is behind us." I turned and slipped out of the room and out of the building. There was nothing more Rene could do for me at the moment. My heart was beating fast over his statement, but there was no way we could form any kind of lasting relationship with this murder hovering over my head.

As I drove home, I felt tears of frustration and exhaustion slipping down my cheeks. I was feeling fearful at the moment, thinking I could be accused of Jeff Barr's murder.

Lord, I've put my trust in You. I need You to intercede in my life. My prayer was silent but full of hopefulness. Only God could fix this situation, but I planned to start asking a lot of questions tomorrow and maybe, just maybe, I could give God a hand.

I don't open shop or fill the egg honesty box on Sundays, so there wasn't much traffic when I reached home. Bed beckoned, but the Southern Belles needed me. I would feed them, collect the eggs before they spoiled, and clean up the coop. If I opened the store, everyone in Hopeville would be stopping by with questions about the murder. In small towns, the draw to the grotesque is powerful.

My real shoppers would know I needed space, and they would give me time. It wasn't like the town couldn't survive without my few eggs and chicken-themed kitchen supplies.

Stacy's car wasn't there, although I knew she came back the night before. I wondered if she'd left town this morning. She never said how long she'd be staying, but with this murder on the property, she was sure to feel uncomfortable sticking around. I couldn't blame her. The hopes of an income from an Airbnb began to fade.

Unless this murder was cleared up and it was proven that there was no connection to me or the Homestead, I couldn't even try to run an Airbnb. I had listed my rooms on the website and had received notice that it was up and running. I'd forgotten about it with all the bustle of Market Days.

I made my way to the computer, logged into the account, and felt my eyes open wide. I couldn't believe what I was seeing. Every weekend for the following month was already filled with guests. A couple was scheduled to come in on the upcoming Friday and leave on Sunday, the following week a single woman was scheduled just for Saturday, the third week two women were scheduled. They'd left a note asking if I had other rooms because their group would love to stay in the same place. The fourth weekend a single man wanted to stay Friday and leave Saturday.

I gulped. If I accepted all these bookings, what would happen once the people arrived and found out about Jeff Barr's unsolved murder? My hand hovered over the mouse, and then I finally clicked on the accept button over and over.

Now that the Airbnb was booked solid for the next few weeks, I was going to help the police clear my name. I moved back to the counter and picked up a pen. I began to make notes on everything I knew about Jeff Barr and the people I'd seen yesterday who could have killed him.

It didn't really make sense that an outsider would have come all the way to town, on a Saturday, and risk being seen by so many people just to kill the man. I wrote the word *stranger* on the other side of the paper. The only name that I knew of that could go on that side was Stacy's.

It did cross my mind to wonder again why Stacy had been asking around about Jeff. I knew it must have been her, because she was the only one taking photos that day.

I hoped she'd return for the evening. I wasn't too sure how I felt about staying alone since the murder. But for now, I had to take care of my girls.

"Afternoon, Southern Belles," I called out as I drew near the coop. I glanced hurriedly around, a bit concerned that I might see another dead body on the ground. Then I stopped myself and stomped my foot. "Get ahold of yourself!" I ordered. It was plain silly to think I might find someone else murdered on the property. I had to shake off those thoughts.

Then I remembered that in most mystery books I'd ever read, there was usually a second murder. I bit my lower lip and moved toward the coop. I was glad to see the chickens happily scuttling around and no body in sight.

"My you ladies are looking better. In just one day." I was pleased to see small feathers popping up, covering the splotches where they'd molted. Their excitement at seeing me was announced by clucking.

When I finished collecting the eggs and feeding the chickens, I carried the eggs to the house and laid them out on a big worktable I keep on one end of the front porch. I ran inside and filled a bucket with cool water and brought it out to give each egg a good cleaning.

As I was placing the washed and dried eggs into cartons, I heard a car. For a second, my heart stopped. Was it the police? Was it Rene? I turned quickly and saw it was Stacy pulling in. I was glad to know she hadn't left town for good.

When she slid out of the vehicle, she had her camera ready. "Stop right there and let me take your picture. My readers will love to see how you take care of those eggs."

Even though I looked terrible, I allowed her to take a few shots. I was sure she would edit them later and decide not to use any of them. I explained how I collected, washed, and boxed the eggs, and she jotted a few notes in her pad. Finally, she sat on a porch rocker.

"I'm glad you decided to stay," I said, recalling how she'd stormed away the day before.

She smiled. "I get heated up pretty fast, but it's all bluster."

I should have apologized, but I didn't know if she was the one who killed Jeff or not.

"You left early this morning," she said.

I nodded. "Called into the police station."

Her hand flew to her mouth. "Oh, really?"

"Yes. Currently I'm their primary suspect."

"Seriously?"

I nodded. "The only fingerprints on the rake are mine." I sighed and sat on the second rocker. It felt good to relax.

She stared at me for a minute, like she was sizing me up. "You couldn't hurt a flea."

I smiled, not sure if I was insulted or relieved by her comment. "I'm not too sure about a flea, but I surely wouldn't kill a man on my own property where I would be the main suspect. Everyone knows Jeff Barr was trying to talk the bank into taking my land. He wanted to sell it to some big investors."

She cringed. "Did they say if his death was. . .instant. . . painless?"

"No. I didn't even think to ask that." The realization hit me hard. I disliked Jeff Barr so much that I didn't even care if he'd died painfully or not. Something wasn't right in my heart. I was going to have to do some real soul searching and ask God's forgiveness about that. I glanced back at Stacy just in time to see her swipe a tear off her cheek.

I sat up. "Stacy, you did know him, didn't you?" My words came out quickly and in a demanding tone. She hadn't been able to hide her feelings fast enough.

She slouched even more in the chair, and her head moved slowly up and down. "He. . .he and I dated about five years ago. I thought. . . I hoped he was going to ask me to marry him, but when I brought it up, he laughed and told me we had lots of time for that serious stuff."

I shook my head. How many women in the world believed that Jeff Barr wanted to marry them? I couldn't understand what they all saw in the unappealing man.

"We didn't have any more good times though. A few days later, I showed up at his apartment, and he was gone. Moved out, no note, no goodbye letter." She sniffed.

"Are you still angry?" I asked. Stacy now seemed a likely suspect.

She laughed. "Not at all. At first, for a week or two, I was sad and confused, but the landlord at his apartment called me and told me that Jeff had left some things behind and suggested I might want to take a look. I went over, and the new renter was there. He just happened to be a very handsome man who found me attractive, and before I could say, 'Smile for the camera,' he and I were dating."

"Really? That's sort of romantic."

"Yes, and I owe it all to Jeff. Dylan and I have been dating ever since, and see…" She held out her left hand, where she sported a very nice diamond ring. "He asked me three weeks ago."

Her story was almost too good to be true. I sighed. "Then why were you searching Market Days for Jeff?"

"I wanted to show him my ring, sort of rub it in his face." She gave me a wink. "I never thought I'd see him again, and when I found out he was here, that little bit of 'get even' took over."

"What did he say when you showed it to him?" I asked.

She shook her head. "I never found him. I saw him near the chicken coop, but his back was to me. I could tell he was angry about something, and he was yelling at someone."

I sat up straight. "Who?"

"I wish I knew, but his body was blocking my line of sight. I assume whoever it was is the person who killed him."

"Do you think you can tell the police about that?"

"Sure, I've got nothing to hide." Once more a tear slipped out of her eye. "Oh, I'm silly to cry when Dylan is such a better man. When you realize someone you cared for…thought you loved… is dead, well, you just can't help yourself."

Stacy looked so much younger than Jeff. But maybe she went for older men. She wasn't as old as Sadie Rose, Carol Anne, and Katie Jane. Maybe after dating Stacy, Jeff had decided to form relationships with older women, thinking they wouldn't press him to marry them. If that was the case though, he was surely wrong. Those women had been looking for beaus as long as I could remember.

Stacy was watching me. "Do you believe me?" she asked.

"Yes. But I'm still the main suspect, and now that I have to cross you off my list of potential suspects, I don't know where to go from here to prove my innocence."

"Shouldn't you let the police figure it out?" She twisted her diamond back and forth on her hand. "I'll tell them what I saw. That should clear you."

I shrugged. "Not really, because you didn't see who it was. In their eyes, it could have been me."

Stacy smiled. "I'd hate to think it was you. This place is so wonderful, and you are too."

"Thanks," I answered, pleased with the compliment. "By the way, I've got four bookings on the Airbnb website for next month."

She clapped her hands together. "That's great. I was going to ask, do you think Dylan and I can have our wedding here?"

My jaw dropped. "Here? Like here in town, or here on my property?"

"Here, on your property. I saw an area down by the lake that would be perfect. Just think, you could host weddings here. You know that's big money. I'm willing to pay you five thousand dollars."

I almost jumped out of my chair. "Five thousand?" I gulped. "Do I have to cater it too?"

"Nope. I'll have a caterer from the city, and I'll provide the flowers and the chairs, and well, everything. The five thousand is basically just to rent the lakefront for the day."

My mind was whirling with excitement. "What if it rains?"

She shrugged. "I was snooping around the other day. You have that big barn at the back of the property. It's rustic, but I think it could be converted easily enough." Her smile widened, and she looked at me expectantly.

I almost laughed. "I don't have the finances for that—or the time." The barn was sturdy enough, but my daddy had used it for storage over the years. It needed a lot of cleaning up.

She pressed her lips together then said, "What about a partnership? Not for the Homestead or Airbnb but for a wedding venue? I've always wanted to be a wedding planner. I would take care of everything that has to do with the wedding venue, and you'd get 50 percent of the profits."

I gulped. "But what about your job at the magazine?"

She gave an airy wave. "I'll finish this article, do a follow-up article about this property as a wedding venue, then I'll quit. It's not my favorite job, and I've always wanted to live in the country. But come to think of it, I can write a column about life in the country just using the local area. My editor will love it, and I can keep my income while we work on the venue."

"What about Dylan?"

Her smile grew bigger. "He'll love it. He's not really a city boy and works remotely, so he can live anywhere. I'll just need to find a real estate agent."

My mind flickered. Jeff Barr was the main real estate agent in town. He'd taken over when he moved here, and no one else had a chance against him. I wondered if there was anyone in town who wanted his job.

Stacy turned to head out of the room. "Let me talk to Dylan, and we can make some plans. Mind if I stay a few more days?"

I nodded absently. I was excited about the idea of adding a wedding venue to the Homestead and the Airbnb. With that, there would be no more financial problems for me, but I did have to wonder if Stacy had sidetracked me so I wouldn't ask any more questions about whether she killed Jeff Barr or not.

CHAPTER EIGHT

Monday morning, I was awakened by my phone ringing. Hope that it was Rene flashed through me, but it was Tamara.

"Hey, April."

"Hello."

"So, a few of us local growers want to form a co-op. We thought you would join us." Her voice was a bit bubbly for so early in the morning, in my opinion.

I sighed. A week ago, this might have been very interesting to me, but now my plate was full with trying to solve a murder, opening an Airbnb, partnering up on a wedding venue, and still trying to run my chicken-themed shop. If I wasn't careful, I'd be forgetting to take care of my Southern Belles altogether.

"I don't know, Tamara. I'm pretty busy, and besides, I'm already maxed out on how many eggs I sell a week. I don't need any more business." I sat up straight, thinking about all I had to do for the day.

"Oh, come on, April. It'll be fun. We're meeting at Bacon on Main and eating while we talk. You have to eat breakfast."

That won me over. I was in no mood to get out the pots and pans and cook my own breakfast. So I agreed to be there in a few minutes. "But I'm not making any promises about joining. I really am busy. I have so much to tell you though."

"Great, I want to hear everything."

Tamara must have been relieved now that Jeff Barr was gone and she had time to get her land paid for. However, was she really as happy as her voice sounded, or was she covering up her true feelings after killing Jeff? I shook my head. Tamara just wasn't the type. I expected she would be dark and brooding if she'd done the foul deed. Of course, she hadn't been in her booth at the time I assumed he was murdered, and she was wearing gloves, and she did tell me she wasn't going to worry about him anymore. . .

"Well, Lord. Sitting here thinking about Jeff Barr's murder won't help me find the murderer. Give me favor today as I question a few more people," I prayed.

I rushed around the bedroom and bathroom, throwing myself together for the day. Within minutes, I was headed out the door and driving to the restaurant. The Southern Belles weren't going to be very happy with me, feeding them late again, but I wanted to get Tamara by herself and ask her some questions.

As I drove toward town, I found myself thinking about Rene. I needed to remind him to bring in more cards and another painting. At that moment, my phone rang and caller ID showed it was him. I answered, and his voice came over the speaker in my car.

"Good morning, April. Did I wake you?"

I laughed. "No, that was already taken care of by Tamara. She wants me to join a local food co-op."

"That's a great idea!" His voice was also too enthusiastic for so early in the morning.

"Maybe, but I don't have enough eggs to offer any to a co-op. I'm just going for the breakfast." I giggled at how silly that sounded.

"Breakfast? At Bacon on Main?"

"Yep."

"I'm on my way there. How about we have breakfast together?"

My heart skipped a beat. Breakfast with one of the best-looking men I'd ever seen wouldn't be half bad, and bumping into him at the restaurant was becoming a habit.

But I had promised Tamara.

"I'll have to give the co-op at least a few minutes of my time," I murmured, already wishing I'd never agreed to join Tamara. But then, I wouldn't even be on my way to the restaurant and I wouldn't be able to see Rene at all.

"Okay, see you there." He ended the call.

I parked in the closest spot I could, which was actually pretty far away because so many others had filled the front spots. The restaurant was very popular for breakfast, even on weekdays.

As I entered, I was surprised at the size of the crowd at the co-op meeting. It looked like half the vendors from Market Days was there—or at least all those who sold any food products. It was obvious a lot of people in our little town wanted a chance to make more money.

At the time, the restaurant was barely big enough for the crowd, although the owner, Janice Bacon, has recently added a second room and revamped the inside. The theme of the new room, of course, is pigs. The black-and-white flooring is bright and new, and the Formica tables with four red or white chairs at each are lovely. The booths along the front with window views are black-and-white-checkered faux leather—a bit cheap looking, but still in keeping with the ambience of the rest of the room.

On one wall is a large diagram of a pig with the cuts of meat labeled. It stands out almost like a sore thumb, but the other walls are decorated with much cuter pictures of pigs in fields or in barns. So many pigs, it almost makes a person feel bad ordering bacon at all. I mean, just think of those sweet little pigs and then think of bacon. See what I mean?

Janice was working as a server, wearing a small half apron. She moved around the room with a coffeepot in one hand and an order pad in the other. She loves to talk and can easily get caught up in long conversations. Sometimes she actually sits down at a table to converse. She knows everyone in town by name and keeps an eye on strangers. That thought gave me hope. There had been a lot of strangers at Market Days. I didn't know everyone. Someone else might have had a grudge against Jeff Barr. That could explain things. . .

I shook my head to clear it, stepped farther into the diner, and watched as Janice moved from table to table, smiling at one person, laughing with another. I know that orders can get piled up if she gets too carried away, but the main thing I love most about Bacon on Main is that when the diner gets busy, the locals are helpful. They get up and serve coffee—and even go so far as to carry plates to the tables and dirty dishes to the kitchen.

Tamara stood and waved me over. I passed by the table where Rene had sat the morning before. He hadn't arrived yet, which made me feel better about joining Tamara, but I knew I'd be watching the door carefully.

When I reached her side, I gave her a hug. She felt a bit stiff. She leaned back and looked directly into my eyes. "How are you?" she asked. I knew she meant, considering the murder of Jeff Barr on my property.

I shrugged. "I'm okay, but so far the police don't have anyone else as a suspect. Only me. My fingerprints were on the weapon."

Tamara cringed. The gray shadows under her eyes made me think she hadn't been sleeping well.

"I suggested to the police that the killer might have worn gloves."

Tamara's eyes opened wider.

"Are you saying that someone who wore gloves that day killed Jeff Barr? Are you saying it could have been me?" Her voice rose. "I mean, a lot of people had gloves on that day. Besides me, I mean."

"Yes, that's true, but you weren't in your booth when he died. You had gloves on, which you took off right after his murder, and you told Rene you weren't going to worry about Mr. Barr anymore." I tried to give my words a friendly tone, but I could tell she knew I was questioning her.

She plopped back into her chair, and I took the one next to her. "Wow, you've done your homework," she said. "From what you're saying, I could easily be a suspect."

I felt awful, basically accusing her.

She smiled. "Don't worry. I'm not *really* upset. Everything you just said is true, and I guess I need to figure out exactly what I was doing when Jeff was killed." She thought for a moment. "Ah, I know. I had my gloves on because I'd run to the van to get a few bunches of kale. I didn't want to contaminate them. You saw me when I got back to the booth."

I nodded. I remembered the kale piled on the counter. "Did anyone else see you?"

"Yes. I actually spoke with Mark Jenson. He's the one who's leading this co-op."

I felt relieved. I didn't think Tamara was capable of making up a story in such a short time. Of course, it didn't help me prove my innocence.

"And as to me saying I wasn't going to worry about him anymore, I decided not to even think about him anymore. Now, about this co-op?" Tamara changed the subject abruptly and looked at me expectantly.

I shook my head. "No, Tamara. I'm really not interested, except to offer the co-op the ability to set up on my property once a month for free. Like I said, the Southern Belles don't produce enough eggs for a co-op and I don't want to expand in that way. But I *have* decided to open my house as an Airbnb, and with some help, I'm going to start allowing the land to be used as a wedding venue."

Her jaw dropped. "Wow, when did all this happen?"

I shrugged. "Well, you know the woman who was taking the photos at Market Days?"

"Yes, I saw her."

"Her name is Stacy, and she's the one who suggested the Airbnb. Now she's thinking of going into business with me on the wedding venue idea."

Tamara's expression didn't change. "That's great. With all that money, you should be able to pay off the back taxes. You lucked out. I've still got to get a clear title."

Someone in the group must have told a joke, because suddenly everyone but Tamara and me burst out laughing.

The restaurant door opened, and Rene stepped in. He looked around until his eyes met mine. The smile that spread across his face warmed my insides. He nodded, and I nodded back.

Tamara's head tilted. "What's that all about?"

"Uhm, Rene offered to have breakfast with me," I murmured. I didn't want to make her think anything was going on when even I didn't know. "Listen, Tamara, I'm not going to join the co-op, so if it's okay, I'll just slip away." I stood up.

"You go, girl." Tamara grabbed my hand and gave it a hard press. "But I want to hear all about this new development later on. And you can tell me about Stacy then. Plus, I want to know everything you find out about the murder." Her voice dropped as she spoke the last words.

I bobbed my head and moved quickly across the diner and slid into a booth across from Rene.

"Hi." I smiled.

"Hi." He smiled. It felt awkward, which was strange because we'd talked many times about his paintings. But now, we both knew something was different.

CHAPTER NINE

Breakfast was nice. We talked about general things: his paintings, my shop, the Airbnb, and potential wedding venue. He seemed happy for me. I didn't want to discuss Jeff Barr anymore that day, and I think he purposely avoided the subject.

When the meal was over, he walked me to my car. Before I got in, he took my hand in his. "April, I think you can tell I like you. I just want to know if I could pursue dating you?"

I felt my cheeks heat up and knew they were pink. "I would like that, Rene," I answered.

"Great!" His smile took up his whole face. "How about dinner Friday night?"

I gulped. I hadn't dated in a long time, but I was ready. "Yes... that is, if I'm not in jail for Jeff Barr's murder," I joked.

Rene frowned. "Don't even say that." He looked me straight in the eyes. That sobered the mood instantly. This was not a joking matter.

"Sorry," I murmured.

"I'll pick you up at six."

I didn't ask where he planned to take me. This town only offered a local pizza house, Bacon on Main, and a coffee shop.

There was no fine dining without driving to another city, and I'd been ordered not to leave town.

When he stepped away from the car, I pulled out of the parking spot. From what I could tell so far, it didn't seem that Tamara, Rene, or Stacy had killed Jeff. I hoped not. I mean, I'm not a real detective, and I could have been on the wrong track completely. Perhaps I should have just left the whole thing alone. But somehow I felt that finding the answer was up to me. My only other suspects were Katie Jane and Sadie Rose.

Katie Jane and Sadie Rose lived in the same apartment building along with about thirty other residents. Carol Ann lived on two acres of land adjacent to them, where she had a small farmhouse and her beehives. From time to time another person would join their sewing group, but no one else had lasted as long as those three.

They'd been friends for so many years, but Jeff Barr had come between them, and I hated to see how they reacted to one another since he'd entered the picture. I wondered just how they were feeling now that he was dead. I wanted to talk to each of them, but it was too early to visit, so I decided to go home. I could plan a visit after I fed the chickens.

Right before I reached my house, I saw a car pulling out of my driveway that looked very much like Sadie Rose's car, but it sped by me so fast, I couldn't tell for sure and I didn't see who was driving.

Now, one thing about chickens that I haven't mentioned is they are usually content in their coops, but every once in a while, one will escape—and then you never know exactly what to expect. When I pulled into the driveway, my eyes were immediately drawn to the cluster of chickens on my front porch. I glanced at the coop and saw that the door was standing wide open.

I screeched my brakes, hoping I didn't inadvertently hit one of the Southern Belles. I turned off the car, jumped out, and began running toward the flock, which only terrified them, and they began running in all directions.

"Shoo!" I screamed. I knew I wasn't handling this as I should have. In fact, I looked like a chicken with its head chopped off, running here and there, trying to shoo them or scoop them up. I literally had to pull one out from under the coop. It took a good half hour before I decided to get their food and scatter it as usual. Within minutes, all the Southern Belles were placidly inside the coop eating.

When I closed the door, I took a ragged breath. Tears pressed at my eyelids, but this was not something to cry over. I reached for my 4-tine rake, then remembered. It had been taken as evidence. I stepped closer to the coop and rested my head on it.

"I wish you ladies could talk and tell me who killed Jeff Barr."

At that, one of my favorites, and the sassiest of them all, squawked at me. I looked down. She was standing at the very edge of the coop, trying to peck through the mesh at something sticking out from under the edge of the cage.

That something sparkled. I reached down and picked up a silver charm bracelet. There was only one charm on it, a bee. There were swish marks in the dirt, as if someone had been running their hand under the building.

I assumed it was Sadie Rose's bracelet, since it was her car that had just squealed out of my driveway. She could have been searching for it and given up before she found it. The Southern Belles must have seen the sparkle and pecked at it enough to pull it out.

I moved across the yard and up the porch steps. This could change everything.

I heard the car pull in, the footsteps on the porch, and the squeak of the front door, but I wasn't able to lift my eyes to see who it was. They were glued on the bracelet, which I had carried in and laid on the counter in the shop.

I knew that a bee charm was worn by the three Sewing Bees, Sadie Rose, Carol Anne, and Katie Jane, and I was pretty sure there could only be one reason this one had been lying under the edge of the coop: One of the three bees had lost it in a struggle with Jeff Barr.

Still, it was almost impossible to imagine any one of those ladies having the strength to lift the rake and. . .well, you know. I'm not even sure any of them felt strongly enough about Jeff for their passion to turn to murder. Sadie Rose and Katie Jane made it clear to everyone how they felt about the man, but I think they both knew he wasn't anything more than a flirt. I'd never heard Carol Anne mention Jeff, and she didn't strike me as being as silly as the other two women. She didn't seem the type to fall for the man's flattery.

I shook my head. Sadie Rose or Katie Jane had to have been by the coop recently and lost their bracelet. Unless one of them had been there with Jeff, neither had reason to be near the coop. Chickens were not a favorite of any of the Sewing Bees.

Stacy stopped at the counter. "What's got your attention?" She glanced at what I was looking at.

"A bracelet."

She cocked her head. "It's nice. I love the bee, but maybe you should sell chicken charms instead of bees."

I looked up at her and blinked. "What?"

She nodded at the bracelet. "I assume you're planning to carry bracelets and charms in the store."

I straightened and pushed the bracelet into the top drawer. "No, it's just something I found. But now that you mention it, chicken charms would be a really cute idea."

Stacy stared at me a moment then blinked. "Uh, April, are you aware that you have a streak of dirt across your cheek?"

I reached up and swiped at my cheek. "Those chickens! The coop was somehow opened today, and they were all over the yard. I've been running around trying to get them back into the coop."

Stacy giggled. "That must have been quite a show."

I smiled, knowing she was right. "I guess I'll go take a quick shower."

Stacy headed toward her room. I followed behind, heading for mine. As we passed the opened rolltop desk in the living room, Stacy picked something up from on top of it. She turned quickly, holding my very sharp letter opener. I hadn't stopped fast enough, so it ended up pressed against my stomach.

I stepped back with a gasp. My eyes swept up to meet hers, which were wide with what, I couldn't tell. Was it mania, or fear?

CHAPTER TEN

Stacy, what—what are you doing?" The room was silent, and I could hear my heart beating.

She blinked then looked down at her hand. "Goodness. I was just walking by your desk and noticed this beauty. Are you aware it's a rare antique letter opener?" She tilted her head slightly and gave a strange smile. Her words were short and clipped.

I couldn't speak for a minute, then stuttered, "Y–yes. It belonged to my father's father."

Stacy inspected it closer. "What's wrong?" she asked. Then she seemed to understand the situation. "You didn't seriously think. . . ?"

I nodded. "Yes. No. I mean, we did just have a murder here."

She threw back her head and laughed. "That's the funniest thing I've heard in a long time. Keep in mind, April, there are rumors going around that you killed Jeff Barr. But I'm still staying in your Airbnb, so I must not think you're the murderer."

I felt a hot flash of embarrassment. I needed to be careful not to jump to conclusions so quickly. "I'm sorry."

She set the opener down, moved closer, and gave me a hug.

"Let's agree to believe that neither of us is the killer," she whispered in my ear.

"Yes." I said, and she dropped her arms and moved back. It was awkward, but I believed her hug was sincere. I was sure Stacy had not killed Jeff Barr, and I hoped she believed me too.

Stacy went on to her room, and I stood alone. At first I felt myself trembling, but after a few minutes, I relaxed. I needed to get my head together. Freaking out over someone holding a letter opener was crazy.

Lord, help me to keep this thing straight in my head and to find the real killer before the police give up and arrest me.

Besides, now that I'd found the bracelet, which could have been dropped at the coop if one of the Sewing Bees killed Jeff Barr, I doubted even more that Stacy was involved. I decided to shower later and did an about-face and returned to the counter. I slid the bracelet into a small plastic bag I kept in the drawer and slipped the bag into my purse. I planned to take it to the police station. I was sure they would check it for fingerprints before they tried to contact any of the ladies who owned that type of bracelet. In the meantime, I still had some investigating to do on my own.

Just then, I heard a yell. I looked down the hall but didn't see anyone. Then I realized that Stacy was calling out to me from her room. My heart leaped into my throat, and I rushed through the living room to the room she was occupying. Stacy was standing beside her bed, pointing a shaking finger at the pillow.

My eyes lowered. Smack dab in the middle of the pillow was a perfect oval egg. Obviously, one of my Southern Belles had been in the room and had laid her egg right on Stacy's bed. I looked around and saw that the window was open.

I burst out laughing. Stacy's face was pale. She obviously wasn't very pleased to find an egg on her bed. I explained that one of the Belles must have gotten in through her open window after someone let them out of the coop.

"There's no more chickens in the room, right?" Stacy asked, her voice shaky.

Where exactly she thought a chicken could be hiding in the room, I didn't know. "Nope, all have been accounted for and put away." I moved across the room and picked up the egg. "This will make a nice breakfast," I said.

"Please, no." Stacy flopped onto a chair.

I smiled. "Okay." I knew she wouldn't have any idea what egg I cooked for breakfast. But I wasn't providing her meals anyway, so it didn't matter. I reached over to close the window. "No more chickens," I stated firmly, trying to reassure her.

Stacy was really shaken, and her gaze kept darting around the room. She glanced at me. "I'm afraid of chickens. I was okay taking photos of them from a distance, but up close and personal is not okay with me."

"I get it," I said as soothingly as I knew how. "They're gone, I promise." I moved out of the room and closed her door. If her reaction to an egg on her bed was any indicator of things, there was no way Stacy would ever have gone close enough to the coop to be Jeff Barr's killer.

After I dressed in a fresh pair of jeans and a gray T-shirt that boasted a brood of six chickens and the phrase *Just a girl who loves chickens* on it, I stared at myself in the mirror and gave my head a shake. This was considered one of my best shirts, which didn't say much for my wardrobe.

Over the last year, dealing with trying to save my property, I'd allowed my clothes to wear out, and every time I needed something new, I grabbed a shirt from the shop. If I was going to start dating Rene, I needed to make some changes in that category—and soon.

I looked up. "First, Lord, I need You to help the police find the real killer so that won't be hanging over me." Then I remembered

Psalm 46, which says that God is our refuge and strength and an ever-present help in trouble. Right now, I was in trouble, and I needed His help more than anything.

The day was busy, and I didn't have time to run over to see either Katie Jane or Sadie Rose. Several times I pulled the small bag from my purse to assure myself the bracelet was still there.

Trying to imagine Sadie Rose killing Jeff Barr was just crazy. The woman is only in her fifties, but she dresses like an eighty-year-old, gingham skirt and all. Why he would have shown her any interest at all didn't make sense, unless it was for her pot roast. Everyone in town knows she makes the best pot roast in the world.

There's always a lot of talk at Bacon on Main about what secret ingredients she uses. She's been approached several times to sell her recipe, but she's always refused. It's rumored she'd made a pot roast every week for the last three years for Jeff, which I'm sure made her think she was winning him over, but my mind just couldn't wrap itself around the thought.

However, I was sure it had been Sadie Rose's car leaving the Homestead, which meant she'd let the chickens out of the coop while searching for her bracelet.

That night, I lay in bed, the bright moon glistening through my window lulling me to sleep. I tried to envision Sadie Rose or Katie Jane lifting that 4-tine rake, but stopped myself, knowing I'd just give myself nightmares if I dwelt on that scenario.

The next morning I decided to speak to Sadie Rose first thing. It was earlier than I usually awoke, but the need to know the truth was pressing on me. Dressed and in the car by seven allowed me to see the sun rising in all God's glorious brilliance as I drove toward town. It made me praise God once again for all the beauty He placed in our world.

On my way, I pulled out my phone and called Tamara. I wanted to let someone know where I was going and what I thought. I mean, stopping by the apartment of someone I believed to be a killer probably wasn't the smartest thing, but I didn't know what else to do. The police weren't going to investigate Sadie Rose because I found a bracelet by my chicken coop. I needed more proof.

When I finished explaining my thoughts to a very sleepy Tamara, I could tell she didn't like my plan. "April, I don't think you should get involved in this."

"I want to feel her out, and I can't go to the police and tell them what I suspect. I told them my thoughts the other day, and they barely took any interest. I need more proof." As I spoke, I steered my car into the apartment complex parking lot. I promised Tamara I would call her back as soon as I spoke to Sadie Rose. The last thing Tamara said was, "I'm sure there's nothing to this. Can you really imagine Sadie Rose as a killer? Why don't you just drop it and leave it to the police?"

I let that run through my mind. Of course I couldn't see Sadie Rose as the killer, but I also couldn't imagine Rene or Katie Jane or even Stacy as a killer. Still, someone killed Jeff Barr, that was for sure and certain.

The apartment complex is beautiful, with many different types of trees scattered throughout the property. The gardens are well tended, with an abundance of roses, daisies, tulips, and more. It could be a place I might consider moving to if I ever need to downsize. I love my home and don't want to give it up for many years. My father stayed until he just wasn't physically able to stay there anymore.

After parking in an allotted slot for guests, I walked to the entrance and went in. I slipped by the empty reception desk and made my way down the hall to Sadie Rose's door.

On most of the residents' doors were colorful spring wreaths, but on Sadie Rose's door there was a small quilt with a lovely pattern of sunflowers and bees. She's the one who started the Sewing Bees, and she takes it very seriously, often wearing a bee-pattern vest or apron, and any gift she gives is sure to boast a bee of some type.

I knocked a few times then waited. I could hear someone moving around inside. When the door opened, Sadie Rose stood there in a house robe and a head full of tiny curlers.

She blinked. "April? What are you doing here?" She opened the door farther and ushered me into her room.

"I—I wanted to ask why you were at my property yesterday."

She tilted her head, a look of confusion on her face. "Yesterday? Why, April, I haven't been out of the apartment since I got home from Market Days. I'm starting to get a cold, and I've stayed home trying to ward it off." She sat down on the couch. "Now, sit and tell me what all this is about."

I chose an armchair across from her. I mean, sitting next to someone I thought might be a murderer definitely wasn't a smart choice. I looked around the room, making sure my way to escape was clear.

"Go ahead, dear, tell me why you're here." She followed her words with a yawn.

I took a deep breath. "Yesterday, I saw your car coming out of my driveway. Then, when I got to my house, I found that all my chickens had been let out of their coop."

Sadie Rose sniffled, and she wrung her hands. "I had a terrible night, tossing and turning thinking about. . .about poor Jeff." Tears started to flow down her cheeks. Suddenly, she looked up at me and asked, "Why would I want to release your chickens?"

There was no way anyone could fake those tears. The woman was truly distressed about the man's death. I decided to try another tactic.

"What did you mean when you told me you'd made sure Jeff Barr would have nothing to do with Katie Jane anymore?" I leaned in as if this were a good piece of gossip I was waiting to hear about.

Sadie Rose gave a funny giggle. "Oh, I was so tired of her taking him meals that he seemed to like more than mine. He often compared them. So I told him that she uses margarine instead of real butter."

Because I knew of his preference for butter, I laughed.

"Please don't tell her. Now that the man is dead, well. . .she and I can get back to being real friends. Something like that could ruin things." She glanced at me with pleading eyes.

"Not a problem. Your secret is safe with me."

Although these were reasonable answers, I still wasn't completely convinced of her innocence, so I asked, "Do you and the other Sewing Bees have matching bracelets?"

She looked through me, as if I wasn't there, but I think that was just her own sorrow she was feeling immersed in. She nodded slowly. "Yes, we all have one. It binds us together."

"Any chance you can show me yours?" I asked in a quiet voice, hoping not to arouse suspicion. "I've been thinking of buying some charms for the shop, and maybe I could get an idea from yours." This wasn't a lie, because I really was thinking about adding charms and charm bracelets to the shop's inventory.

"Is that what you came over so early to see? You could have called me, and I would have gladly stopped by later today to show you my bracelet." She rose slowly and moved from the room. As I've mentioned, of the three Sewing Bees, she's the one I couldn't imagine could kill anyone. She dresses, walks, and acts much older than her age.

She tottered off to her bedroom and returned a few minutes later. She held out her hand, and there lay the exact same bracelet as the one in my purse. My jaw dropped, and I looked up at her. "But what about your car?"

She looked bewildered. "What does my car have to do with my bracelet?"

I gulped, not sure I should tell her about the bracelet at all. That might be something to keep secret. I could feel her curious stare on me.

Finally, I stood up. "Listen, Sadie Rose, I'm sorry I got you up so early. I'm a bit turned around myself. Can I get back to you about this?" I gave her a smile that I used as a child when I wanted to get my own way.

She frowned. "All right, but now that I'm up, I'll be wondering all day what you're on about. And I don't know why you think you saw my car at your place." She went to a small table near the door, picked up her purse, and rummaged through it.

"Goodness, the key is gone." She looked at me in surprise. "Now where could it be?"

I shrugged. I imagined someone had stolen it, used the car to come to my place and search the coop, but I wasn't about to say that out loud.

"Who was here visiting you last?" I asked.

"Well, it's been a very boring week. Saturday night, after Market Days, the Sewing Bees met here. We knew we had to put some finishing touches on our latest quilt, but with Jeff's death, it wasn't a very pleasant gathering. Katie Jane thought he wanted to marry her, and I thought he wanted to marry me."

I moved closer and patted her shoulder. "What about Carol Anne?" I asked.

"She's never even spoken his name, as far as I can remember. When he first moved to town, I recall he tried to warm up to her, like he did to Katie Jane and me, but Carol Anne wanted nothing to do with him. Whenever we talk about him, she just rolls her eyes."

Sadie Rose moved to the window. "I can usually see my car from here." She leaned closer to the glass. "I don't see it. Could it really have been stolen?"

I took her by the arm and walked her back to the couch and pressed her to sit down. "Yes, I think so. I'll call the police and tell them. Maybe they can figure this out."

Sadie Rose nodded, then stiffened. "I don't know why anyone would steal my car."

"It's baffling. You stay here, and I'll call the police when I leave. I'll inform the person at the front desk so they'll be prepared for an officer to come see you." I moved to the door. She still had fresh tears on her cheeks.

"I'm sorry for your loss." I spoke the words with heartfelt meaning. I didn't like Jeff Barr, but I knew Sadie Rose had been in love with him. She was feeling a lot of grief. It didn't mean she wasn't the one who killed him, but from my viewpoint, she had her own bracelet, her car key was missing, and she was genuinely saddened by the man's death. There wasn't an ounce of anger in her about him. For now, I was putting her on the *didn't kill Jeff Barr* list in my head.

CHAPTER ELEVEN

I decided to run down the hall and visit Katie Jane. She lived at the opposite end of the building. It was still early. *The early bird gets the worm*, I reasoned, thinking how glad I was my chickens didn't eat worms. I can't stand those wigglers. I feed my ladies the best feed I can afford.

I knocked on Katie Jane's door. She opened it immediately, her eyes wide with surprise.

"April?"

"Hi, Katie Jane. I'd like to ask you a few questions."

She smiled and stepped to the side. "Come in. I was about to eat breakfast. My, you're out early."

I moved into the apartment. Like Sadie Rose's, it was pleasantly decorated, but not so much with bees. It looked to me like Katie Jane was more of a Texas bluebonnet sort of person.

"What a lovely place," I gushed. "I love bluebonnets."

Katie Jane sat at her small kitchen table and offered me the other seat. "What are your questions?"

I decided to use the same story about the bracelet I used on Sadie Rose. "I'm thinking about carrying charms and charm bracelets in the store. I've always admired the bracelet you Sewing

Bees wear, and I wanted to get a closer look at yours, you know, check the quality and the brand."

Her eyes brightened. "Oh, that's a wonderful idea. We Sewing Bees love our bracelets." She lowered her voice. "Even when we don't love one another."

I nodded to show her I understood.

"Do you have yours?"

Katie Jane stood. "Yes, I take it off at night when I'm sleeping. I keep it in the box beside my bed." She left the room and came back a few minutes later with the bracelet in her hand.

I felt my heart drop. How could this be? The only people with that bracelet were the Sewing Bees, and I'd already determined that Carol Anne wouldn't have had any reason to kill Jeff Barr.

I took the bracelet and inspected it, turning it over and over. "This is really nice."

"Yes, I got them for the Sewing Bees. I can give you the information about where I bought them, but if you want to sell them, you'd have to find a company that would wholesale." She took the bracelet back and put it on before taking her seat again.

"Yes, I'll look into that. Did you know that Sadie Rose's car was stolen yesterday?" I waited to see her reaction.

Her head lifted quickly. "Stolen? Who says so?"

I thought that was a strange question. "Well, I saw someone driving it away from my place yesterday, and it wasn't Sadie Rose. She's been home sick. And, well, her key is missing."

Katie Jane shook her head. "How do you know her key is missing?"

"She looked in her purse, and it wasn't there."

"That explains things. Sadie Rose keeps her key in the small bowl next to the door when she's home, but sometimes she forgets where it is. If it's in the bowl, I can pick it up whenever I want. I don't have a car, but Sadie Rose allows me to drive hers."

I sat staring at her, trying to make sense of it all. Both women had their charm bracelets, and either of them could have driven Sadie Rose's car, but it didn't seem likely, since neither was missing her bracelet.

"I didn't drive to your homestead yesterday," Katie Jane said.

I shook my head a few times to clear my thoughts. "Maybe her car wasn't stolen after all. Could Carol Anne have borrowed it?"

"She doesn't need to borrow a car. She has a truck, the one we use to carry all our Sewing Bee supplies in when we set up for Market Days. Why would she take Sadie Rose's car?"

I shrugged. At this point I had to assume the missing bracelet belonged to Carol Anne. She also could have taken the key and the car and driven to my place, hoping no one would recognize her.

Half the morning was over, and I needed to get back to open the shop. I would have to find a way to meet up with Carol Anne later. It was frustrating, and I wondered how the police could stand all the time it took, interviewing people, making conclusions, and finding out they were wrong.

I decided to bring up one more thing. "Katie Jane, I overheard Jeff tell you he wouldn't marry you."

Her head shot up, and I could see tears swimming in her eyes.

She clenched her fists in her lap. "That man, that man. He made me believe so many times that he loved my cooking and couldn't do without me. But all he couldn't do without was my food. I pressed him about marriage and. . .well, you saw the reaction. It was very hurtful and shameful, having my so-called lover rejecting me in public like that." A tear slipped down her cheek.

"I'm sure that was awful. You must have been very angry," I pressed.

"Yes. . .no, not really. I was hurt."

"What did you do?"

"I straight up told him I wouldn't be making him any more food. I said he should know that all those wonderful meals I served him had been made with margarine, not butter. The man is obsessed with fresh butter."

I held back my laughter, remembering his behavior in my store. I believed her story and could see she felt that was all the revenge she would ever need.

I thanked Katie Jane and headed out of the apartment. I stopped at the front again, but there was still no one there, so I jotted on the notepad, *Police coming to see Sadie Rose about stolen car*. Then I headed to the parking lot. To my surprise, Sadie Rose's car was now in the parking lot, so whoever had taken it had brought it back. I figured I could cross Katie Jane off the list, since I was with her during the time the car showed up again. I looked in the driver's side window and saw the key fob on the front seat.

The thought of dusting the car for fingerprints went through my mind, but whoever had done this thing had been careful so far, so I doubted there would be any. Besides, that would only prove who stole the car and set my chickens loose. It wouldn't tell me who killed Jeff.

My phone rang. It was Tamara.

"Well, what happened?" She sounded worried.

"Nothing. We determined that someone stole Sadie Rose's key and took her car. She showed me her bracelet, so I don't see how it could have been her, unless she has an extra one."

"Listen, April. You should drop this whole thing. Let the police do their job."

I huffed a bit, miffed that Tamara wasn't even offering to join me in this endeavor. I mean, Jeff had been threatening her as well. I thought she'd want to help. "I can't. They suspect me, and I don't think they've done much else about it."

Tamara sighed. "They won't be able to prove anything about you, so I think you should just stop this investigation."

It wasn't like Tamara not to back me on anything I wanted to do.

"The police want to close this case. If no one else fills the bill, it will be me. I'm thinking of dropping the bracelet off at the station later. I've got to open my shop so I can pay my bills."

Tamara didn't say anything else, so we ended the conversation and I drove back home. I hurried out to feed the Southern Belles and collect eggs. Then I opened the store. After half an hour, Rene pulled up and came in carrying a laundry basket filled with his cards and small paintings. "Time to restock, I hope," he said with a smile.

"Great," I nearly shouted, then tried to calm down. I couldn't act so excited every time I saw him, even if my heart did skip a few beats.

"I came by earlier, but you weren't here." His words were more a question than a statement.

"Yes, I. . .uhm. . .went to see Sadie Rose and Katie Jane."

He met my eyes and set the basket down. "And why was that?"

I bit my lip. "To question them."

Rene shook his head. "April, you shouldn't be—you do know there's a murderer running around, right? You asking questions could cause that person to turn their eye on you." He moved closer to me and took my hand. "I don't want you to get hurt."

"Can you see Sadie Rose or Katie Jane hurting me?" I actually laughed.

"No, but you think one of them may have killed Jeff Barr. If they could do that, they could hurt you." He lifted my hand to his lips and kissed the back of it.

I felt chills run up my arm but pulled away and turned my head so he wouldn't see the flush on my cheeks. "I'm pretty sure neither of them is the murderer, but. . ."

"Yes?"

I reached over the counter to my purse and pulled out the small bag with the bracelet. I showed it to Rene and told him all about finding it.

After I finished, he whistled and leaned back against the counter. "That only leaves Carol Anne, but there's never been any talk about her and Jeff Barr."

I shrugged. "I know, that's what makes this all seem so impossible." I turned and looked in the basket he had carried in. There was a magnificent painting of my house. I held it up and inspected it. "Oh, Rene, this is gorgeous. I would hate to sell it."

"Then don't. Let me give it to you." He moved closer.

I took a deep breath as the hint of manly cologne filled my senses. "Oh, thank you so much." I lifted my face, and he pressed his lips on my forehead. A gentle kiss to be sure.

"Dear April, please give up this questioning of suspects. I'm worried for you."

I wanted to promise, but I also knew I had to find a viable suspect for the police or I could end up in jail. Then there would be no relationship between Rene and me.

"I promise to be careful," I said.

He frowned.

Just then a customer came in, so Rene picked up his basket. While I waited on the young woman, he set his cards out on the counter then hung his paintings on blank spaces left from the sales of his other paintings. We didn't get a chance to talk anymore before he had to leave. Right before he exited, he turned and said, "See you Friday night."

I was glad to know he still wanted to see me, even knowing I couldn't agree to comply with his wish that I would stop investigating. I gave him a nod and a wave, then turned back to my customer who had just asked if she could see the chickens.

"Yes, I'd be happy to show them to you. I call them the Southern Belles. You mustn't worry when you see them, because they've just finished molting and haven't grown some of their feathers back. It's all perfectly normal."

CHAPTER TWELVE

I spoke to Tamara that night on the phone, and she agreed to come over the next day so we could discuss the case. I was anxious to speak to Carol Anne too, but Tamara convinced me to wait until she and I had gone over things together.

I puttered around the kitchen in the morning, even offered to cook some eggs for Stacy, but she still hadn't completely recovered from the egg-on-her-pillow episode, so she opted for breakfast at Bacon on Main.

I opened the shop at ten, set the eggs out in the egg honesty box, and also checked the Airbnb app. There were a few questions about future bookings that I would answer later. I decided to look for charms and bracelets wholesale first.

It was a quiet morning, so I had the windows open and could hear the soft call of birds. Suddenly, I heard the Southern Belles. At first, they were just clucking more than usual, then quickly, it escalated to squawking. I moved to the window and looked out, even though I knew I wouldn't be able to see anything.

I grabbed my phone, slipped out the door, and hurried to the chicken coop, scanning the area. Ahead, at the place where I'd seen Jeff's body, I was shocked to see someone bent over, staring under the coop.

As I drew closer, I slowed and took small but hesitant steps. It didn't take me long to figure out who it was. When the person straightened up, I sucked in a breath.

"Carol Anne, what are you doing?"

She glared at me and wiped her skirt. "I would think that's obvious. I'm looking for something."

"I can see that, but what could be under my chicken coop?"

She huffed. "If you must know, I lost my Sewing Bee charm bracelet."

I tilted my head innocently. "And why, or how, would it have ended up under my chicken coop?"

I didn't expect her reaction, but she stomped her foot and burst out crying. She was taking in huge gulps of air and stuttering. "I was t–talking to Jeff Barr. He got angry and g–grabbed my arm. I tried to pull away, but h–he wouldn't let go. Somehow, in the struggle, my bracelet must have broken and fallen off."

Something in the back of my mind reminded me that the woman could be a murderer, but her anguish was so genuine, I rushed up to her, took her by the arm, and started to lead her away from the coop.

"Come along, don't worry about your bracelet. I have it in the shop."

She stumbled slightly beside me. When we got inside, I took her past the shop and had her sit on my couch. I got a glass of water and a cool washcloth. I handed her the glass and applied the cloth to the back of her neck.

"Now calm down and tell me all about it." I sat in a chair across from her. "What were you talking to Jeff about that made him angry?"

She looked at me, and I felt as if she was sizing me up. "Well, no one in the whole town knew this, or ever will, but Jeff and I were partners."

That was a strange thing to call a dating relationship. "Partners?"

She nodded. "Yes. I invested in many of the properties he bought and sold."

Understanding dawned on me. "Oh, I see." I was feeling confused. Jeff Barr did well at all his investments, so I didn't see how being his business partner would give Carol Anne reason to kill him.

"I was unhappy with what he was doing recently." She looked at me shyly. "I know he was trying to get the bank to foreclose on you, and then when I found out about Tamara and how she didn't have clear title to her land and he was going to reveal that. . . Well, I just couldn't stand by quietly."

I hoped beyond hope that she wasn't going to tell me she killed him. I didn't want Carol Anne to be the killer.

"So I asked him to meet me by the chicken coop. I figured the chickens would make enough noise to cover our conversation. I told him I was pulling out as his partner." She glanced up at me, her eyes begging me to believe her. "He was very angry, grabbed me, and broke my charm bracelet."

I squirmed in my seat. "Carol Anne, did you kill him?"

Her eyes opened wide. "Of course not. I had more to gain from him alive, if he would give up pressuring the people I knew into giving up their land. I have to admit, though, I did push at him, very hard, with all my might, and he fell down. I think his wallet fell out of his pocket, because when I walked away, he was scrounging around in the dirt."

She sat up straight and took a deep breath. "I've needed to tell someone all of that. I've been worried sick, because if the police find my bracelet, they'll assume I killed him."

"Were you the one who took Sadie Rose's car?"

She slumped back. "Yes. I didn't want anyone to know I was here. She always leaves her key in that basket, so easy for anyone to take. I got there early enough that I knew she'd still be in bed, and I slipped in."

"Wasn't the door locked?"

"We all have keys to each other's places. That way someone can come to the rescue if one of us gets locked out of their house for some reason. So I was able to open the door and grab the car key. Oh, I wish I'd just come right out and told all this to the police."

The same wish reverberated in my soul. But as I didn't want to be found guilty by the police, I could understand Carol Anne not wanting to either.

"Do you believe me?" Her voice quivered.

I nodded. "Yes, and in my mind, that clears all three of the people I suspected. I'm almost positive Rene didn't do it, and Stacy had no good reason."

Carol Anne sat up. "Who does that leave?"

I shook my head. "I just don't want to believe it, but that only leaves—"

"Tamara!" Carol Anne shouted the name, and I nodded, but then realized Carol Anne had also gasped and was pointing over my shoulder.

I turned slowly to find Tamara standing there. Her usual pleasant smile was nowhere to be found. Instead, there was a dark and menacing-looking woman, holding a gun pointed straight at me.

CHAPTER THIRTEEN

Tamara, what are you doing?" The words barely squeaked out.

"What does it look like? I only wish Carol Anne wasn't here."

Carol Anne spoke. "I can leave."

Tamara turned the gun on her. "Not now you can't. You've seen me and know I'm the one who killed him." Her voice was flat.

Carol Anne slipped farther down in her chair.

"Tamara, I'm sure there's an explanation," I said. "It was an accident, right?"

She laughed. "Accident, I wish. No, April, I killed him. After Carol Anne walked away, leaving Jeff crawling around on the ground searching for his wallet, I saw my opportunity to stop him."

My mouth opened and closed, but no words came out.

"You were right about my gloves. I had met up with Mark Jenson at the truck and was putting kale into bags to take back to the booth. I saw Carol Anne and Jeff slipping behind the chicken coop. I rushed over to see what was going on, figuring she was another one of the crazy women in love with him, but I overheard her trying to convince him to leave you and me alone about our land. The man was relentless. He wouldn't agree and kept laughing at her. After their struggle, my blood was boiling. I picked up your rake and, well, bashed him."

"Oh, Tamara, I'm sorry you felt pushed to do that, but I'm sure the judge will understand and go easy on you."

She didn't seem to be listening.

"Then you had to get involved, sneaking around, asking questions. I knew you'd finally come to the conclusion that everyone else was innocent. Then you'd finally start suspecting me again."

What could I say? That was exactly what had happened.

"So now I have to kill you."

I was shaking but trying to keep myself from reacting to her words. Instead, I was praying inside, *Lord, help me. Help us.*

"I think I'll take you out to the chicken coop and do it there. Both of you. I'd hate to make a mess in the house." She waved the gun, indicating for us to stand, but as we did, a car pulled into the driveway.

Tamara turned to look, and in that split second, I rushed forward, passing my rolltop desk and grabbing the sharp letter opener. Before she knew what was going on, I barreled into her, and the gun fell from her hand. I pressed her against the desk and held up the letter opener to show her I meant business.

The door opened, and Rene stepped in, calling out that he'd brought another painting. Carol Anne started shrieking, and I called out for him to come help. In a flash he was there, standing beside me, holding the gun and watching over Tamara so I could call the police.

I was surprised Tamara didn't put up a fight. Instead, she fell to the floor and curled into a fetal position. I suspected she had some kind of mental breakdown.

The police arrived within minutes, and after I explained the whole thing—leaving out the part about finding Carol Anne's bracelet—they arrested Tamara. My heart was broken.

A few minutes later, I handed Carol Anne her bracelet. We both knew it was something neither of us would tell anyone about. She gave me a big hug before leaving.

"I hope the information about me being partners with Jeff Barr won't get around. We Sewing Bees need to heal our relationship, and that wouldn't help. I never told the other ladies about it."

I promised they wouldn't hear it from me.

When she was gone, I turned to Rene. His face was pale.

"April, I told you this whole thing was dangerous."

I nodded. "Yes, I'm stubborn and didn't want to believe it. I'm just glad you showed up when you did. I had Tamara against the desk, but I'm not sure what I would have done then."

Rene opened his arms, and I ran over and allowed him to envelop me in a hug. It was warm and comforting. "Do you still want to take me out on Friday night?" I asked hesitantly.

He squeezed me even harder. "Yes, and every Friday after that. In fact, I plan to come see you every day and keep a closer eye on everything you do. I have a feeling you'll find yourself mixed up in all sorts of situations."

I snuggled closer, feeling the strength from him flow into me. If I could avoid ever being accused of murder again, I think everything between Rene and me would be wonderful.

Just then, I heard a demanding squawk.

I turned and saw one of the Southern Belles sitting on a pillow on the couch.

"How did you get in here, you naughty bird?" I waved my hands. She jumped down and ran to the front door, which the police had left open.

I shook my head, aggravated. "Chickens!" I said.

Rene was leaning over and looking at one perfectly oval white egg on the pillow. He glanced up at me with a big smile and said, "Breakfast!"

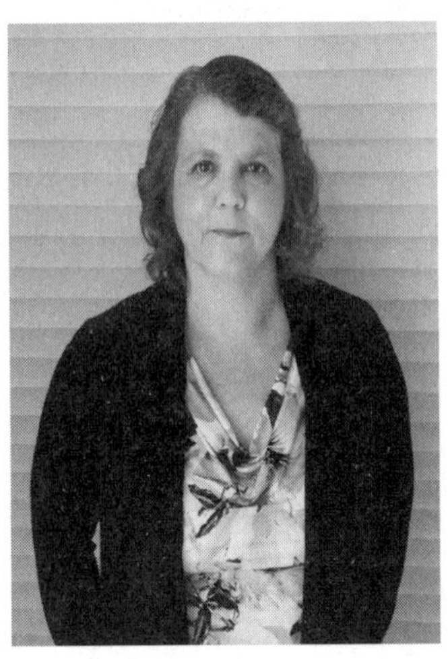

Teresa Ives Lilly has been writing for over forty years. Her writing has appeared in magazines, and her books are published by Barbour Books, and Lovely Christian Romance. She gives all the glory to God for allowing her dream of being a published author to come true.

Teresalilly.wordpress.com

SEARCHING FOR SUNSHINE

BY JANICE THOMPSON

DEDICATION

In memory of my father, Billy Hanna,
and his favorite horse, Sunny's Halo.

Together, you taught us the beauty of a race well run.

CHAPTER ONE

"You can take the girl out of the country. . ." I pressed the accelerator as I changed lanes on the busy interstate. "But you will *never* convince her that big-city traffic is a great alternative to quiet country back roads."

Especially when that girl happened to be pulling a sixteen-foot horse trailer behind her older-model Ford F150, the one with 189,000 miles on it.

A quick glance in the rearview mirror convinced me that the trailer, though wobbling a bit, was hanging in there.

I ushered up a quick prayer for Cosmic Sunshine, my favorite mare, who was secured inside one of the padded stalls. Hopefully she was hanging in there too. A niggling of guilt came over me as I pondered how hard this trip from Jefferson to Magnolia might be on her.

Just as quickly, I pushed those worries away. I gave the trailer another glance as I eased over one lane into the flow of traffic heading south on Highway 69. Then I did my best to focus on the road, the wide, smooth asphalt making that a bit easier now.

To the right of the highway, a smattering of bluebonnets caught my eye, tucked in and among Indian paintbrushes, alive with vibrant color. I love Texas in the springtime. And it did my heart good to see that our wildflowers did not discriminate. They seemed as happy to reside alongside a busy city highway as they did in the expansive fields on our family's farm up in Jefferson.

I glanced upward, happy for the bright, cloudless sky. The storm I'd faced in Lufkin, just ninety miles back, had threatened to ruin the trip, but the worst was behind me now. I hoped.

I managed to make the transition from Highway 69 to the toll road with little effort and breathed a sigh of relief when I saw the traffic was light. My mind drifted back to our family farm and the precarious state we were in. Short of a miracle, Kingston Farms would not survive another year. We would find ourselves at the mercy of the bank.

But God.

And our friends. They had rallied to send me on this trip to Magnolia, where my precious Cosmic Sunshine would have the opportunity of a lifetime.

A short while later, my phone rang and I put the call on speaker. I didn't even have to look down at the screen to know who was calling.

"Hey, Mama."

"Hey, Jessie. How's it going?"

"Had a little trouble getting the trailer across that bumpy section on 2208 just outside of town. And there was a bad storm in Lufkin. But I'm on the toll road now, headed west to Magnolia. Clear skies overhead, so all is well."

"Sunshine hanging in there?"

I glanced in the rearview mirror and noticed the horse's muzzle peeking out of the trailer's drop-down window.

"She is. I checked on her when I stopped to eat that sandwich you packed. A little anxious maybe, but otherwise great."

"I've been praying all day—for a safe, successful visit."

"And for a lovely outcome one year from now."

"Amen to that." Mama paused. "How are you feeling about all of this, Jessie?"

"Excited. Nervous. It's a lot. We've invested so much in this venture."

"What's life without a little gamble?" Mama asked.

Funny words, coming from my conservative mother.

"I'd feel better if I happened to be gambling with my own money," I countered as I approached my exit. "The fact that our friends raised more than twenty thousand dollars for Sunshine to make this trip. . ." My words faded off as I pressed back the lump in my throat.

"They love you, honey. And the folks at the farm in Magnolia will too. This is a marvelous opportunity—for Sunshine and for us."

"Right." But Cosmic Sunshine was more than just another thoroughbred horse. She traced her roots back to Man o' War, a line that included names like the famous Seabiscuit. And with a family lineage like that, my girl deserved an ongoing legacy. Like the Wind would give her that opportunity.

A former Breeder's Cup winner, Like the Wind hailed from a superstar—the great Bold Ruler, whose line had produced one of the most memorable names of all time: Secretariat.

"It's the opportunity of a lifetime to merge her line with a Breeder's Cup winner." A delightful shiver ran down my spine as I pondered the possibilities. My girl, my Cosmic Sunshine, might one day produce an offspring from Like the Wind. If we made it to Magnolia in one piece.

I continued the chat with my mother as I turned north, and she kept me preoccupied all the way. Eventually, I took the exit ramp down to Farm Road 1488 and came to a stop at the light. My nerves kicked in as I saw a couple of potholes in the road ahead.

"I need to let you go, Mama. I'm just a few minutes away, so I'm going to pull off and get gas and check on Sunshine one last time. I want to make sure she looks her best when we arrive."

"Good idea." Mama paused. "Oh, before I go—Calliope called to say she's got her guest room ready for you. I'm so glad the two of you are going to have a chance to catch up."

"Me too." I put on my signal and eased the truck over one lane. With all the money we were spending on stud fees, I needed to save every penny I could. Staying with my cousin was a good option. I couldn't wait to see her.

I ended the call and headed west, my senses coming alive again as I took in the beautiful countryside. The two-lane country road narrowed as I came into the small town of Magnolia. I always breathed a little easier on two-lane country roads.

I passed a grocery store on my left and a Mexican restaurant on my right. Las Fuentes. Then I came to a four-way stop at Highway 1774 and checked the GPS. Just three more miles to the west, then a turn south.

Lickety Split Farm awaited. If all went well, I could be there by five thirty.

After the light turned green, I eased forward. I rolled down the window to take it all in—the bluebonnets, the scenery, the sound of the road humming underneath my tires. The warm Texas breeze danced across my cheeks, and the luscious scent of the wildflowers wafted my way. The creak of the trailer hitch caught my attention, and I prayed it would hold. Behind it, the trailer rattled and moaned, as if in pain. Poor old thing.

Worries about my family's financial state swept over me like the rain back in Lufkin.

So much was riding on this trip, but I, Jessie Lyn Kingston, would save the day.

Those sagging fences? They would be replaced.

That leaky barn roof? Repaired.

Those overgrown pastures? Cleared and usable once again.

Cosmic Sunshine was our best shot at turning all of it around.

No, God was our best shot. And He'd already proven Himself faithful, hadn't He?

My phone dinged, and I glanced down to see my cousin's note: YOU GETTING CLOSE?

I tapped the brakes to stop at a light and responded with YEP. JUST CROSSED OVER 1774.

MEET YOU AT THE FARM.

I breathed a sigh of relief, knowing Calliope would join me. She lived here. She knew the ropes. And, as a skilled vet tech, she knew a thing or two about animals.

A couple minutes later, I pulled into a large gas station, one with a spacious parking lot.

Easing the trailer over to the edge of the lot, I finally breathed a sigh of relief. The moment I turned off the truck, my phone rang. I glanced down, and my breath caught in my throat when I saw the name on the screen. *Asher Brooks.* I knew better than to answer.

Once upon a time I thought I might be interested in the handsome twenty-nine-year-old neighbor in Jefferson. The past couple of years had proved me wrong on a dozen levels, and not just because of his ever-present pressure to buy Cosmic Sunshine back. No matter how desperate I got, that would never happen.

Before I could think it through, a text caused my phone to beep. I glanced down to read "You really did it?"

I shoved the phone away, determined not to let Asher get to me.

Clearly, he thought it was a mistake, bringing Sunshine here. But she was my horse now, and I would do what was best—for her legacy and for my family's. Right now, saving our farm was paramount. And my sweet Sunshine was going to help me do that by providing an offspring so lightning fast, so impressive, that we could get a remarkable price for it. No matter what Asher thought.

And besides, I'd already heard through the rumor mill that Asher was headed to some sort of auction this weekend to buy a top-ranked stallion. Maybe he would leave me alone once he got his own breeding business up and running.

I climbed out and nodded at an older man coming out of the store. He nodded back and called out, "It's a warm one today!"

I hadn't even noticed, to be honest. But I responded with a cheerful "Yup, sure is!" then turned my attention to the trailer.

I could see Sunshine peering out of the drop-down window, and she whinnied as I drew near. I opened the smaller side door of the trailer for quick access to her head, then gave her a pat.

"We'll be there in just a few minutes, girl." I patted her again. "Then you can stretch your legs."

"Who've we got here?"

I turned and noticed the man had slipped up on me.

"Oh, this is Cosmic Sunshine."

"She's a beaut." He reached over to pat her muzzle, and she let out a whinny.

"She's been very patient with me," I explained. "We've had a long day, but we're almost to our destination."

"Oh?" He gave me an inquisitive look. "Where you headed?"

"Lickety Split Farm. Ever heard of it?"

A smile as bright as the cloudless skies overhead lit the man's face. He extended his hand. "Liam Hayes. Owner of Lickety Split Farm. And whom do I have the pleasure of talking to?"

Oh, wow.

"Jessie Kingston."

"Kingston. That's a familiar name."

I used my hand to shield the glare from the sun. "What are the chances I'd meet you here? That's crazy." Providential, even.

He gestured back to the store and then reached down to open the paper bag in his hand. "Pretty good chances, I'd say, since you happened to stop at my favorite hangout. Bob's has the best taquitos in town, and I had to have one." He pulled out a paper wrapper and unwound it to show off a taquito inside. "My wife says I spend way too much time here, but how can I help myself? You can't find a good taquito just anywhere, now can you?"

I'd never given much thought to taquitos, but nodded anyway.

"You headed to see my boy? Colton?" Mr. Hayes asked.

"Yes, I'm bringing Sunshine to breed with—"

"Like the Wind." Mr. Hayes took a bite of his taquito and swiped at his mouth with the back of his hand. "You'll never see a finer stud. He's from Bold Ruler's line. Did you know?"

"Oh, yes. Trust me, a lot of research has gone into this. I've come all the way from Jefferson."

"Jefferson, Texas." A broad smile lit his face. "I once met a girl from Marshall, just a hop, skip, and a jump away from Jefferson. Married her, in fact." A faraway look came over him, then he snapped back to attention. "Tell you what, we're only a couple miles away from the farm. Follow me. I'll lead you there."

"Sure. Sounds good."

I took a couple of steps toward my truck but found myself distracted by an oversized white pickup entering the parking lot. It was pulling a small stock trailer with a Livestock in Tow bumper sticker on it. He came dangerously close to hitting my trailer, which caused me to gasp. He didn't seem to notice us, but Mr. Hayes' gaze was glued to the guy as he whizzed by and stopped at one of the gas pumps nearby.

A man in jeans and a light gray T-shirt exited the truck moments later, cell phone pressed to his ear. Whoever was on the other end of the line was getting an earful. The angry man yanked the handle of the pump from its resting place.

Mr. Hayes muttered something under his breath, then walked to his truck and got inside.

I gave the young man a closer look as I climbed back inside my truck. Broad shoulders. Handsome. I would even go so far as to say ruggedly handsome. Dark, messy hair. Brooding expression. Tight expression while clenching the gas pump. Seemed tense.

Mr. Hayes pulled his bright red Dodge Ram—the limited Tungsten edition—onto 1488, and I eased my way out behind him, carefully navigating as he made yet another turn to the right onto a smaller road. And what a road it was! The narrow country lane rose and dipped, then curved tight around a bend, the trees much thicker than before. Their overhead branches cast dappled shadows onto the road, which made the whole thing feel a bit surreal.

We turned a corner, and the farm came into full view. I gasped at the sheer magnitude of the place. The rolling fields framed a pond where horses roamed underneath a canopy of pecan trees. And oaks. Magnificent oaks that spread along the driveway up to the house. Wow.

"We're not in Kansas anymore, Toto," I whispered.

I swallowed hard and remembered my mama's words: "Rich folks don't sweat, sweetheart. They glisten with entitlement."

But Mr. Hayes didn't seem entitled at all. Nope. Nibbling on a taquito, he looked like a friendly older fellow, happy to show me the way to his digs.

And wow, what digs!

Even from the road I could make out the fabulous barn. And that house! My stars. The Texas-themed stone-and-wood monstrosity caught my eye at once, the grandeur hard to miss.

No, we definitely weren't in Kansas—er, Jefferson—anymore. But we were here for a reason—a good reason. A *God* reason.

I followed Mr. Hayes up the lengthy circular driveway, past the field where the horses grazed, and we came to a stop in front of the house. In that moment, I suddenly felt small. Out of place.

Just as quickly, I ushered up a prayer that God would lead the way. Hadn't He done so already? At every step. From the initial idea to the crowd-sourcing from our community, He had made His will known. We were to bring Cosmic Sunshine to Like the Wind, and they would produce a foal so exquisite, so fast, that even a south Texas hurricane couldn't outrun it.

CHAPTER TWO

Okay, so the farm was amazing, in a distracting sort of way. But something else—er, *someone* else—caused an even bigger distraction. Headed my way, sandy hair tousled from the wind, the handsomest fella I'd ever seen.

I did my best not to gasp aloud as I clapped eyes on the tall, rugged cowboy in the well-worn jeans and blue button-down shirt. He flashed a warm smile as he approached with a confident stride. I rolled down my window, distracted by the smattering of freckles on the end of his nose and those beautiful blue eyes.

"Hey, you Jessie?" A warm smile tipped up the edges of his lips.

Pretty sure I was Jessie. But in the moment I couldn't think to say so. So I offered a lame nod.

"Colton. We spoke on the phone."

I gathered my wits and climbed out of the truck. He extended his hand and I took it, my gaze traveling up to those eyes once again. Heavens.

To my right, the older Mr. Hayes got a call on his cell phone. I could tell from the tightened expression on his face that something was amiss. He took the call and then walked away, leaving me alone with the handsome son.

I cleared my throat as I realized I was still holding Colton's hand.

Pulling it away, I reminded myself why I'd come. All business. No distractions. Everything depended on it.

Colton's gaze shifted to the trailer. "This Sunshine?"

Before I could say yay or nay, he was at the slide, his hand on her muzzle.

"Hey, girl. You're a beaut."

Just what his dad had said. They knew their horses. Clearly.

"She needs to stretch her legs," I said. "Okay to unload her?"

He nodded. "Of course."

I walked around to the back, opened the door, and stepped inside the trailer.

Colton jumped into gear to help, and before long we had Sunshine outside the confines of the trailer. She rewarded us by emptying her bladder.

Not that Colton seemed to notice or care. He was too busy looking her over, eyes wide.

"Wow, she's something else." He rested his hand on her muzzle again, and she nestled into him, a contented girl. "The white diamond on her forehead reminds me of Secretariat."

"I've always said that too."

Sunshine kicked up the gravel under her feet.

"Let's take her to the field and let her run off this energy." Colton took hold of her lead and led her through the gate to the turnout area, where he released her. She took off like thunder.

"And. . .there she goes." I laughed as my girl raced to the far side of the field, her mane lifted by the breeze.

"Fast on her feet, just like Like the Wind." Colton gave her an admiring look as she bolted around the field. "I can't even imagine what their offspring will be like."

I could, and I told him so. On and on I went, dreaming aloud about that precious babe and ending with the words, "We've already named the foal, by the way."

"Wait." A look of surprise registered in his eyes. "You've named a foal that won't be here for a year?"

"Yep."

"Well, don't keep me in suspense."

"Shine Like the Wind."

"Well, now." He flashed a grin. "Can't argue with that, can I?"

"Nope. And it'll work, filly or colt."

"Colt." He laughed. "In case you're wondering why they called me Colton. Born on a horse farm. Guess my parents couldn't resist."

"Oh, funny. I hadn't put that together."

"Trust me, you don't want to know all the jokes I've been the brunt of over the years."

"I'll bet." Poor guy.

We turned our attention to Sunshine, who ran with such grace, such freedom, that we could barely speak while watching her. She always had that effect on me, but clearly Colton was smitten with her too.

Moments later he leaned against the fence, ready to fill me in on the plan of action for the breeding. I was surprised he didn't bring up the finances. I did have a rather large cashier's check in my purse to give him. Should I mention that?

I was sparked with curiosity as I listened to him carry on about the plan for how and when the breeding would take place. Early tomorrow morning, strategically timed with Sunshine's heat cycle, and complete with an ultrasound. All very clinical. Scientific.

Which, frankly, I was counting on. We only had a window of a few days to get this done, after all. Otherwise, we would have to wait until her next cycle. I couldn't risk that.

"Sorry." He laughed after rambling on at length. "I haven't let you get a word in edgewise."

"It's okay. I'm good."

Was I though?

I found myself struggling a little bit to balance my nerves with the excitement that bubbled up inside of me as he spoke. The stakes were high here. Very high. If Sunshine really produced a runner, it would change everything for Kingston Farms. But I couldn't let the pressure of all of that interfere with the ongoing conversation.

Which appeared to be mostly one-sided.

I really needed to learn to speak up. So when he hit on questions about Sunshine's temperament, I was happy to oblige.

"She's stubborn as a mule at times but by far the most loving horse I've ever owned."

"Was she born to one of your mares?" he asked.

"Nope." I shifted my gaze back to the field and watched as my girl did that funny little sprint I'd grown to love. "She belonged to an elderly neighbor. He passed away owing my dad a tremendous amount of money."

"Awkward." Colton turned his attention to Sunshine.

"Yeah, definitely." I paused as I thought about just how tricky things had gotten between our families. "Anyway, after Mr. Brooks passed a year and a half ago, my dad was willing to let it all go. You know? But apparently there was a stipulation in the will that his family cover the debt. So an arrangement was made to transfer Cosmic Sunshine to us."

"Well, that's a blessing."

"Yes." Only, Asher Brooks certainly wouldn't call it a blessing. He had struggled to pass his father's most valuable horse to us. "She's definitely the horse of my heart." I glanced her way as she barreled across the field, kicking up dust every step of the way. "I can't explain it, but I feel differently about her than any other horse I've ever known."

"Exactly how I feel about Like the Wind. He's only been with us a couple years, but I feel like he's been part of my life forever."

We both sighed in unison, two horse lovers who understood the height, breadth, and depth of a special relationship with heaven-sent horses.

Before we could say anything else, a screech of tires stirred up dust in the driveway. I turned to discover a small Toyota Tundra in varying shades of Aggie maroon moving toward us.

The vehicle shrieked to a halt. The driver's side door swung open, and out stepped a colorful creature—all decked out in an ensemble that defied logic.

Calliope.

She galloped my way—galloped being the only descriptor that made sense to her movement—and flung herself into my arms.

"Hey, you! Long time, no see!"

I returned the hug, happy for a familiar face.

Colton looked on, clearly amused—if not a little perplexed—by my cousin's over-the-top appearance. Maybe it was the streak of purple running through her sloppily braided dark curls. Maybe it was the overalls, only half fastened over the brightest embroidered Mexican blouse I'd ever seen. Or maybe—just maybe—it had more to do with the colorful sneakers and socks.

This girl would not go unnoticed.

And she didn't. She carried on, a mile a minute, greeting me with such enthusiasm that I felt my cheeks grow warm. Colton didn't seem to mind. In fact, judging from the twinkle in his eyes, he was getting a kick out of this.

From the barn, another young man approached, this one with dark hair, his skin as golden as the setting sun overhead. He ambled our way, amusement on his face, and stopped short when he saw her.

"Calliope Atkinson."

"The one and only." She squinted in his direction. "Whoa. Brody?"

"Yep." He kicked the toe of his boot into the dirt and then looked up, a half smile sharing his excitement at seeing her.

"How do you two know each other?" Colton asked.

"A&M." These words came from Brody, who couldn't seem to take his eyes off my beautiful, eclectic cousin.

"We were in a couple classes together," Calliope explained. "Graduated the same year."

Brody took several steps in her direction. Seconds later, the two of them were caught up in a conversation so spirited, Colton and I couldn't avoid being drawn in.

"Remember that night we went to IHOP on all-you-can-eat pancake night?" Brody asked.

"You mean that time we ended up staying awake all night studying?" She laughed. "Only to figure out your truck had a flat when it came time to leave the restaurant?"

"I can't believe they didn't kick us out. You were so loud."

"Me?" She feigned an innocent look.

"Yeah, you." Brody couldn't seem to take his eyes off of her. "I heard you were working in town. Dr. Anderson?"

"Yep." A grin lit her beautiful face. "And you?"

"Work here with the horses. I've been here six months or so." He turned his attention to Sunshine, who had slowed her pace on the near side of the field.

"Couldn't have asked for a better helper." Colton slapped Brody on the back.

"An answer to prayer, especially after all we've been through." These words came from Colton's father, who shoved his phone into his pocket as he approached. "Sorry. I had to take that call." He shot a glance Colton's way. "That was Katy."

"Oh?" Colton looked concerned at this news.

"Yeah." Mr. Hayes released a slow breath. "I saw Jake gassing up at Bob's as I left."

Colton's jaw flinched. "What's he doing back in town?"

Mr. Hayes shrugged. "No idea, but he's got Katy rattled."

Okay, so the guy in the white truck was Jake. Whoever that was. And he went with Katy—whoever that was. Had I somehow stumbled into this family's personal business?

And then, just like that, Mr. Hayes offered a smile so warm and inviting it almost caused me to forget all of that. "You folks getting acquainted?"

"Yes, sir." I looked back and forth between father and son, noticing the resemblance between them. They both had the same sandy hair. And twinkling blue eyes. And welcoming smile.

Off in the distance a woman approached. She had the same brusque stride I recognized from most of the gals in our neck of the woods—a confident woman. But this one was a bit more high-end in appearance, with a contemporary hairdo, fancy jeans, ruffled white blouse, and boots that must've cost a small fortune. Sequin inlay. I'd seen that style before but rarely up close.

Colton made the introduction as he gestured her way. "Meet my mama."

"Rose Hayes." Instead of extending her hand, the lovely woman swept me into her arms and gave me a hug that made me feel more than welcome. "We've been waiting for you. Jessie, right?"

"And her cousin, Calliope," Colton interjected.

"I know you." Rose Hayes crossed her arms and gave my cousin an inquisitive look. "But *how* do I know you?"

Calliope paused, then said, "Chiweenie."

"Chiweenie?" I asked.

Calliope nodded. "Mrs. Hayes brings her chiweenie, Taquito, to Dr. Anderson."

"Oh my stars, yes!" Mrs. Hayes threw her arms around Calliope's neck. "You're that sweet gal who saved my Taquito that time he ate all those cherries!"

"Cherry pits are toxic to dogs," Calliope explained. "You wouldn't even believe what we had to do to save him."

Which led her into an intense conversation with Brody about exactly what they had to do to save him. Before long, Mr. and Mrs. Hayes had both joined in the very animated conversation about the day my cousin saved their dog's life.

Which left me with only one question, which I directed at their handsome son.

"What in the world is a chiweenie?"

"Half Chihuahua, half wiener dog," he explained. "Basically, a science experiment gone horribly wrong."

"Oh my." I could only imagine. "What does he look like?"

"An over-stuffed sausage with trust issues and an oddly shaped head."

I tried to imagine it but could not.

"I'm pretty sure Taquito was born with a warning label tacked to his backside," Colton added. "But someone pulled it off before they passed him to us. We should sue."

"Now, Son, don't you be bad-mouthing my boy." Mrs. Hayes gave him a warning look. "Or we might just give Taquito your spot in the family will."

"Figured you already had," Colton responded and then laughed.

"That dog is definitely like a child to her." Mr. Hayes opened the gate and stepped inside to whistle at Sunshine, who responded by taking a few slow steps in his direction. I watched as my sweet girl responded just as I'd hoped, with grace and gentleness.

"You've got to meet Taquito, honey." Mrs. Hayes' words interrupted my thoughts. "Then you can decide for yourself."

"I'll stick with the taquitos from the corner store, thank you very much." With the cluck of his tongue Mr. Hayes coaxed Sunshine to the gate.

A smile formed crinkles on his wife's weathered face as she turned to face me. "Once y'all get this beautiful horse settled in her stall, you want to come in for a spell? I made some homemade peanut butter cookies, and I've got a fresh pitcher of sweet tea."

I had to admit, that sounded mighty good. Peanut butter cookies were my weakness.

Well, one of them.

My gaze shifted back to Colton's gorgeous blue eyes.

"You can tell us all about your place in Jefferson." Mr. Hayes opened the gate and pointed Sunshine toward the barn. "I haven't been in that neck of the woods in years."

"Jefferson?" Mrs. Hayes' eyes lit up. "You're from Jefferson, honey?"

"I am. Kingston Farms."

Her smile broadened. "I grew up in Marshall, not far at all from Jefferson."

"We're in Marshall all the time. In fact, my uncle just took on a pastorate at a little white church called Calvary. Do you know it?"

"Know it?" She laughed. "Liam and I got married in that church." She slipped her arm around my shoulders. "I'd say this is all a little providential. Now you can't turn me down. You've got to come inside for a visit and get me caught up on everything I've missed since we moved away."

"When was that?" I asked.

"1999."

Looked like we had a lot of catching up to do. Still, this wasn't supposed to be a social visit. Right? I was here on business. I definitely hadn't planned to stick around, just get Sunshine settled and then head over to Calliope's place.

"I really need to clean out the trailer first," I explained.

"I've got it." These words came from Brody, who took long strides toward the trailer.

"Oh, I can't let you do that," I argued. "I—"

"Need some help?" Calliope's eyelashes batted like a horse sprinting toward the finish line.

"You're offering to help me clean out a messy horse trailer?" Brody looked her way with a half-smile. "Sure, if that's what you want."

Judging from the expression on her face, it was *exactly* what she wanted.

I would have offered to join them, but a squeal of tires caught our attention from the road. We all glanced that way as a large white truck peeled by, the attached stock trailer leaving a trail of dust from the gravel.

I did a double-take. It was the guy from the gas station, the one Mr. Hayes was so concerned about.

Colton's eyes narrowed to slits as he took in the vehicle. His jaw flinched, and I watched as he glanced his father's way with concern in his eyes. Unspoken words traveled between them.

For a moment, no one said anything. Well, until Calliope popped off about what a hot day it was, completely oblivious to the problem at hand.

As the truck disappeared from view, Colton snapped back to attention. "Dad and I will get Sunshine settled in one of our premiere stalls. Jessie, you go on into the house with Mama and have some cookies. She won't rest until you do."

"You sure?" Sunshine looked happy nibbling on grass.

"Yeah. We'll make sure she's comfortable. You can swing by and say your goodbyes before you leave."

Surely that wouldn't take long. A couple of cookies. A little conversation. And then Calliope and I would be on our way.

CHAPTER THREE

I hated to interrupt whatever Calliope had going on with Brody, and I also didn't want to appear rude, so I accepted Mrs. Hayes' invitation to head inside and eat peanut butter cookies.

I wondered what Mama would think if she saw this well-to-do woman leading the way into the massive house with its rustic stone and wood exterior. And those heavy wooden shutters. Wow! My favorite part of the home was the Mexican tiled roof. We didn't see much of those up in Jefferson.

If I'd thought the outside of the house was spectacular, nothing could have prepared me for the inside. Mrs. Hayes swung wide the front door and gestured for me to follow her. I did my best not to gasp aloud as I took it all in, my gaze traveling up, up, up to the over-the-top wrought iron light fixture in the expansive entryway with its octagon-tiled floor. Terra cotta. Wow.

I'd seen a few houses like this in magazines, of course. That heavy Texas decor. Lots of stone. Oversized leather furniture. Expansive windows overlooking the most gorgeous property, including a swimming pool out back. And just beyond that, another pond and green pastures that took my breath away.

I didn't have time to think about it for more than a second because a shrill yapping noise sounded at my feet, causing quite the jolt. Next thing I knew, a stocky, short-haired creature with pointy ears was biting at my leather boots, yapping like mad.

"Now, Taquito, you be nice to her." Mrs. Hayes reached down to scoop the chubby pup into her arms. "What have I told you about eating our guests?"

He settled at once, though I did notice the side-eye he was giving me. The low growl from the back of his throat caused a shiver to run down my spine. This was a pit bull trapped in a sausage casing.

Just as quickly, he reached up and gave his owner a lick on the cheek.

Mrs. Hayes cuddled him close. "My sweet baby boy." Her lips curled up in a smile, and she planted kisses on his forehead. "I won't let him bother you."

I flashed the canine a weak smile but must've failed his vibe check, because he lunged my way as if ready to consume me for dinner.

At this point I was in need of the ladies' room, and said so. I was directed to a bathroom to my left.

Turned out, even the guest bathroom was magnificent. Who had faucets like that? Wow.

Moments later, as I dried my hands, I stared at my reflection in the oval mirror that hung above the sink. I looked road weary. Not the best first impression, but there wasn't much I could do about it now. I reached into my purse and grabbed my lipstick.

Outside the door of the bathroom, I heard the *yap-yap-yap* of little Taquito. Moments later, the yapping quieted and I braved the door handle.

"I put him in the laundry room," Mrs. Hayes explained. "It'll be quieter that way."

And safer, hopefully.

"Come with me, honey."

Mrs. Hayes never stopped talking as she led the way through the living room and into the massive kitchen, where she poured a large glass of iced tea and passed it my way. Moments later she set a tray of cookies in front of me. Then we settled at a spacious table in the breakfast room, which connected to a kitchen with cabinets so high even the angels couldn't reach them.

I found myself so captivated by the easy conversation with her that I almost forgot to be nervous. Almost. And the first bite of a peanut butter cookie made me feel right at home. They tasted just like my mama's.

"You said your last name is Kingston?" Her brow wrinkled. "That right?"

"Yes, ma'am." I nodded as I reached for the oversized coffee mug.

"Call me Rose, honey." She paused. "Your mama's name wouldn't happen to be Eliza, would it?"

"No." I shook my head. "Eliza is my daddy's sister. Do you know her?"

"Liam and I both did. We went to college together at East Texas Baptist University years ago."

"That's my alma mater!"

"Fun! Well, let's just say that I had to pretty much steal Liam away from Eliza Kingston my sophomore year." Rose seemed to lose herself to her thoughts. "I'm not sure she ever quite forgave me."

"Oh my." I laughed. "Well, I'm sure you'll be happy to hear that she married one of the sweetest men in Marion County. We all love Uncle Toby."

"Toby?" Rose's eyes widened. "Toby Atkinson?"

"Yep. He's a real card."

"He always was." She cleared her throat and shifted her gaze to the laundry room door. Inside, Taquito carried on like we were under some kind of attack.

I had a feeling there was more to the story about my uncle, but before I could ask, Rose pushed her chair back. "Want to help me, honey?"

"Sure." I wasn't sure what sort of help she needed, but I knew my way around a kitchen.

"The guys will be in here expecting a full-on taco bar at six thirty, but don't worry. I've got this down to a science." She paused, and then her eyes lit up. "You and Calliope should stay for dinner."

"I could run that by her."

About fifteen minutes later she and Brody appeared, along with Colton and his father. My cousin and Brody were hot and heavy in a conversation about a professor who had been particularly hard on them.

Only Colton acknowledged me as he entered the room. He flashed a smile my way, taking a few steps in my direction.

"How's my girl?" I asked.

"Acted like she was starving to death. But don't worry, we fed her. She'll be comfortable in her stall. There's plenty of room in there to decompress from the long day she's had."

"Thank you."

"Sure." He brushed by me on his way to the sink. "I introduced her to Like the Wind on her way in. She passed right by him, and I'm pretty sure it was—"

"Love at first sight." These words came from Mr. Hayes, who gave his wife a kiss on the cheek.

"I'm not sure if it was love, exactly, but he was definitely interested in her," Colton said. "Sunshine seemed more interested in eating."

"Nothing new there," I said. "The girl can hold her food."

This girl could too. And the scent of the taco meat simmering on the stove was drawing me in like a preacher to a potluck.

Colton reached to turn on the faucet. "Are you coming back in the morning?"

"If that's okay." I'd never done this before, so I didn't really know the protocol.

"Sure. Lots of mare owners like to be present, but I understand if you don't. It's all pretty clinical. But you'll see that we do everything we can to eliminate stress so she's as calm as possible." Colton added a couple of squirts of hand soap to his hands and ran them under the stream of water.

I wasn't worried about that part. I'd been raised on a farm, after all. But I needed to be there. I knew my dad would prefer I stick close, from start to finish. I knew how delicate this process was and how much money had gone into it.

Money!

I glanced Colton's way, eyes wide as it hit me. I still needed to give him the check.

Only, he didn't seem concerned about it. As he scrubbed his hands, he carried on about how beautiful Sunshine was.

"Now that your hands are clean, you and Jessie can help me out by warming up those tortillas," Rose said.

His eyebrows elevated. "You're putting the guests to work?"

"These gals aren't going anywhere," his mother said. "I've invited them to dinner."

"I accept!" These words came from Calliope, who managed to divert her attention from Brody to Rose. "How can I help?"

"Chop up these tomatoes." Rose gestured to three large tomatoes on a nearby cutting board. "And that lettuce too."

"Sure thing."

Calliope walked over to the sink and started lathering up like she was prepping for surgery.

Moments later, Brody let out an unexpected groan and we all glanced his way.

"Sorry. I just realized I left the water running."

"Water?" Colton gave him a concerned look.

"Yeah, I was filling the trough and got distracted." His gaze shifted to Calliope, whose cheeks flushed pink. I'll be right back, y'all." Seconds later, he disappeared out the kitchen door.

"That's not like Brody at all," Rose said. "He's usually very focused."

Calliope cleared her throat and then dried her hands and went to town chopping up lettuce and tomatoes while Colton and I grated cheese and warmed tortillas. The simmering taco meat still held me spellbound, but it was now vying for my attention alongside the salsa, which bubbled in a big pot on the stove.

"You haven't lived till you've tasted my mama's homemade salsa," Colton said. "She makes it from scratch with the tomatoes and peppers from her garden."

"Best in all of Magnolia," Mr. Hayes boasted. "And we have a lot of great salsa in Magnolia."

Before I could say, "No thank you," he dunked a tortilla chip in the vibrant salsa and passed it my way. I took a nibble, more concerned about the physical heat than the peppers.

I should have been more concerned about the peppers.

Seconds later I went into a choking fit that made me look like a northerner.

Rose passed a glass of water my way, along with an apology about the spice. I brushed it off, not wanting to hurt her feelings, then offered to help set the table.

"No need for that," she explained. "I line up all the taco fixin's on the counter, and folks make their way down the line. I've got flour tortillas, crispy taco shells, chips, guacamole, sour cream, and everything else you could imagine. Just follow our lead."

And boy howdy, did I ever follow their lead. I loaded up my plate with reckless abandon. Mama's PB&J sandwich had worn off hours ago, and my empty stomach felt like a feed trough at a county fair.

After filling our plates, we all took our seats. Mr. Hayes bowed his head to pray, and I watched as the guys removed their cowboy hats in sync. I couldn't help but notice how he interjected a line about Katy's safety. I really needed to find out who Katy was.

When the beautiful prayer ended, we dove right in. Well, the guys did. I did my best not to behave in an unladylike fashion. They already thought my horse was a little piggy. I wouldn't give them any ammunition to think the same about me.

Okay, so I gave them plenty of ammunition. I ate every bite of food on my plate right down to the last crumb.

At this point Brody came rushing back in, apologies flowing, and filled his plate. "Sorry about that. I guess the latch didn't catch on the barn door earlier. It was standing wide open when I got out there."

"How's my girl?" I asked.

"Didn't make it that far," he explained. "I was too preoccupied with the mess I'd made. The trough was overflowing. Would've turned the whole area into a pond if I'd left it overnight, so I'm glad I remembered." He lifted his hands. "Washed up outside, so I'm good to go."

A full conversation ensued, and then Rose insisted we all go back for second helpings. She found no argument from me. I loaded up my plate with more chips and queso and a small scoop of that salsa. By now, I was acclimating to the heat and found myself enjoying it.

As we continued to eat, the conversation flowed so easily—and everyone around me ate with such gusto—that I settled right in, no longer caring what anyone thought about my food consumption.

Eventually, I crossed the line from satisfied to post-Thanksgiving regret. I tugged at the button on my jeans and pondered my life choices.

I looked back and forth at the others—now fully engaged in a story about something that happened to Colton at the rodeo a few years ago—and realized I'd only known these people about two hours at most.

I glanced at the clock on the wall and almost did a double take. Was it really almost eight thirty? A quick look out the large kitchen window clued me in to the fact that the sun had now fully disappeared from view.

I shot a glance Calliope's way and gestured to the clock. She gasped. "Oh, no! I hate to bust up this party, but I've got to swing by the clinic to check on one of our overnight patients before I go home. Peanut needs meds before nine o'clock."

"Peanut?" Rose asked.

"Cutest little pup." She pulled up a picture on her phone, which resulted in oohing and aahing from Rose and me.

"Are you coming back with Jessie in the morning?" Brody asked.

Calliope tucked her phone into her pocket. "No, I've got to be at work at seven, and it's going to be a long day. We've got a couple of surgeries in the morning. But y'all know where to find me if you need me."

He gave her the sweetest smile ever. "It's been great catching up, Calliope."

"I agree." She threw her arms around his neck and gave him a hug.

I thanked Rose profusely then pushed back my chair and rose. Calliope followed suit.

Rose wrapped up some cookies and handed them to me. "You gals take these home. We'll never eat all of them."

"Are you sure?" I asked.

"Yup. I'll probably bake something else tomorrow. It's what I do."

"When she's not decorating, she's baking," Mr. Hayes interjected. "You should taste her blackberry cobbler. Best in the county."

"I love blackberry cobbler." I paused, then turned to my cousin. "Hey, do I still have a minute to say goodbye to Sunshine?"

Calliope nodded. "Sure. If we hurry. The clinic is about ten minutes away, so I think we'll be okay."

Colton rose and offered to go with us.

We said goodbye to his parents, and Colton and Brody walked us out to the barn. Under the mantle of the Texas sky, the stars shone bright and clear.

My gaze shifted upward, and I sighed. Under the cover of that brilliant night sky, this place felt just like home.

"It's really pretty here at night," I observed.

"Yeah, we're blessed, that's for sure." Colton led the way to the barn and opened the massive door. Then he navigated the row of stalls, pausing to introduce me to Like the Wind. The moment I laid eyes on the gorgeous stud horse, my heart skipped a beat.

This was why I had come all this way—to meet this majestic animal, the one who would sire an offspring so gallant, so fast on its feet, that the world would sit up and take notice.

I reached out to stroke his muzzle, and he nestled against me.

Right away, a lump rose in my throat as I realized how this fabulous stallion was about to be forever linked to my family. "Oh, Colton, he's magnificent."

"We think so."

"We're going to have the sweetest little baby ever!" I couldn't help but giggle.

From off in the distance, I heard the sound of other horses stirring in their stalls. This only served to make me want to see Sunshine even more. I could sense her destiny, even from here.

"I guess we'd better get a move on. Let me go see my girl, and then we'll hit the road."

“Sure thing.” Colton pointed us toward the back of the barn, but when he reached the stall at the end of the line, he stopped cold.

“What is it, Colt?” Brody took a couple of steps in his direction.

He didn’t even have to say the words. I could see it for myself.

Sunshine’s stall was empty. My girl was gone.

CHAPTER FOUR

For a moment I thought I was having one of those weird out-of-body experiences. Yes, surely I would wake up to discover my girl, my Sunshine, was right here in front of me.

Only, she wasn't.

And judging from the look on Colton's face, he knew we were in real trouble.

"Brody?" Colton shot a glance his way. "Please tell me you moved her to a different stall when you came out earlier."

The color seemed to wash out of Brody's face as he shook his head. "I told you. I came out to turn off the water, and when I got here, I closed the barn door but didn't come inside the stall area."

"Then we go look for her," Colton responded.

"In the dark?" I didn't know the lay of the land, and they clearly didn't know how fast Sunshine was.

"She's probably down by the pond," Brody said. "That's where they usually end up."

"*Usually* end up?" Was this the norm, mares slipping out of the high-end barn and cavorting at the pond?

I couldn't stop the trembling that took hold of my body as fear kicked in. If I lost Sunshine, all bets were off. Kingston Farms was lost. My eyes burned with the sting of tears.

"I know you two have got to leave." Colton shot a glance Calliope's way. "We'll text you when we find her."

"Over my dead body." My words came out with a definite tremble. I wasn't going anywhere until I clapped eyes on my girl.

"I'm so sorry, Jessie, but I've got to get to the clinic by nine." Calliope gave my hand a squeeze. "I'll give the dog his meds, and then I'll come right back to get you."

"Are you sure?" I asked.

"Yes. I'll rest easier if I know he's had his meds. And that will give y'all time to search." She took several quick steps toward her truck and moments later tore out of the driveway.

Colton walked to the far side of the barn and flipped a switch. The whole area in front of us lit up like Christmas. He then called his father, who met us out on the lit field moments later.

After a quick recap of what had happened, we all flew into action.

I went straight back to the stall to look over every square inch. I didn't see anything until I was at the giving-up point. Then I happened upon a scrap of folded paper by the gate. I reached down to pick it up and saw *#0258* written on it.

The logo at the top was partially torn, but I made out an *L* and an *F*.

Colton stepped into the spot next to me and looked at the paper. "What is that?"

"No idea. Just a scrap of paper with some numbers scribbled on it."

"Number 0258." He shrugged. "No clue, but I'll ask Brody."

Only, Brody knew nothing about it. So I shoved it into my pocket, and we kept searching.

Minutes later I was in a golf cart driven by Colton. Brody and Mr. Hayes followed behind us in a separate cart. We made our way from field to field, the headlights illuminating the path in front of us.

Colton did all the talking. I was praying. Hard. My girl had to be here. Surely.

We covered a lot of ground over the next several minutes. On we went—over potholes, through thick grasses, beyond groves of trees, past the cattle, and then around again. All with no luck. No sign of Sunshine. I did my best not to give up hope, but after some time, I couldn't help but let a couple of silent tears escape.

After half an hour or so, we finally gave up and headed to the barn, hoping she had miraculously reappeared. I could read the tension on Colton's face as we neared the area lit by overhead lights.

Colton stopped the cart near the entrance of the barn as Rose headed our way, phone in hand. "I called the sheriff's office."

"Good." Mr. Hayes exited his cart, and Brody pulled it into the barn.

Colton eased our cart forward into the open spot next to Brody, then came around to my side and offered me his hand.

I took it and climbed out, trembling.

Rose took one look at me and slipped her arm around my shoulders. "Come back in the house, honey. It's getting chilly out here."

I wanted to stay put, wanted to remain calm and focused, but with her arm safely wrapping me, all I could do was cry. A wave of sobs rose up inside of me. She rested her hand on my back. After I finally calmed down a bit, I looked her way.

"Sunshine isn't just my prized mare," I explained. "She's my family's future."

These folks had no idea what we were up against. If we'd lost Sunshine, we'd lost everything.

No. I drew in a deep breath. Not everything. None of this had taken God by surprise. He watched over it all and surely knew right where my girl was.

"I don't know the whole story," Rose said. "But I know who does, and I'm going to ask Him to bring that sweet horse back where she belongs."

In spite of those comforting words, I was tearful all the way from the barn to the kitchen door. Once inside, Taquito tried his usual yapping routine, but Rose scooped him up and told him to shush. Then she ushered me to the plush leather sofa in the living room and insisted on making me a cup of hot chamomile tea with honey.

Which I accepted minutes later.

My nerves felt raw, but I didn't have time to worry about how I came across to the Hayes family right now. Our family's financial worries would be magnified a thousand times over if I didn't find Sunshine.

I needed to call my parents, and the sooner the better.

As I reached for my phone, Colton, Brody, and Mr. Hayes entered the front door, talking on top of each other. Seconds later the doorbell rang and Calliope entered the room.

"Well?" She looked back and forth between us.

I shook my head. "We've searched everywhere," I said. "She's gone."

"Or hiding." These words came from Mr. Hayes. "Wouldn't be the first time one of the animals went into hiding mode."

Rose gestured for Calliope to sit next to me on the sofa, then poured her a cup of tea from the pitcher on the coffee table. "The sheriff should be here soon."

Colton paced the room. "I know I closed that barn door. You guys saw me." He looked back and forth between Brody and Calliope.

"I'll be honest—I was a little distracted," my cousin said.

No doubt.

"I saw you close it," Brody said. "But like I said, when I went out to turn off the water, it was wide open. Figured it hadn't latched, so I closed it again."

Before we could delve any deeper into this topic, the doorbell rang. Colton went to answer it and returned to the living room with a broad-shouldered deputy behind him who looked to be in his early forties. I could hear Taquito yapping all the way from the laundry room but chose to ignore him.

"Hey, y'all." The deputy offered a curt nod. "Heard one of your horses went missing?"

"My horse." I raised my hand.

"And you are?"

"Jessie Kingston from Jefferson."

He extended his hand and I shook it. "Wade McAllister. Montgomery County Sheriff's Office. Nice to meet you."

I pulled my hand away. "I brought my mare to breed with—"

"Like the Wind." He gave Colton a nod. "Am I right?"

Colton and I nodded back in tandem.

"I'm a good guesser." Deputy McAllister looked my way again. "And you made it here with no problems?"

"Yes. We unloaded her a little after five thirty, let her run in the field, then the guys—and Calliope—put her into her stall a few minutes after six."

"What's a Calliope?"

My cousin cleared her throat and raised her hand. "I'm a Calliope."

His dark eyebrows arched as he took in her appearance. "You were there, with the guys?"

"Yes, sir." She offered a weak smile. "I helped with her feed. And then we all came back in the house for tacos."

"At six thirty," I added.

His lips curled up in a smile. "I thought I smelled something delicious when I walked in."

"You hungry, Wade?" Rose asked as she reentered the room. "I've got plenty of leftovers."

"I would never turn down your tacos, Ms. Rose." He flashed a crooked grin, one that put me at ease right away.

And that answered my internal question about whether or not this particular deputy knew the family.

Rose disappeared back into the kitchen, and Deputy McAllister settled into one of the leather armchairs across from us. Mr. Hayes took the other one. Colton, I noticed, refused to sit. Instead, he paced, clearly worked up.

"Let's start at the beginning." The deputy reached into his pocket and pulled out a notepad. "So, no one else was here but you folks?"

"Jake came by earlier," Mr. Hayes responded.

"Jake?" Deputy McAllister's brows arched as he flipped open the notepad. "What's he doing back in these parts?"

"We had the same question," Colton said. "It's got to be more than a coincidence that he showed up like he did."

"Katy said he's been hired as a livestock handler for the auction at the pavilion this weekend," Mr. Hayes said. "You got to admit, he's a great wrangler."

"Yeah." Colton nodded. "He's always had a way with the horses. He certainly knows his way around skittish animals, so I guess that's right up his alley."

"Interesting." The deputy scribbled something in his notepad. "Anything else?"

"We saw him at the gas station around five thirty, and then he turned up in front of our place a little before six," Mr. Hayes explained.

"Didn't pull in?"

"Nope. He must have slowed at the end of the driveway, because we heard him peel out of here." Creases formed between Mr. Hayes' eyes.

"Would he have a particular reason to take an interest in this mare?" The deputy looked up from his notepad.

I couldn't think of any and said so.

"Wait." Calliope raised her hand. "You lost me. Who's Jake?"

"Jake Owens. My older sister's ex-husband." Colton's jaw flinched. "Not a good guy. They just went through a nasty divorce a while back, and he's made threats against her."

"Against all of us," Mr. Hayes interjected. "I think he needs to be questioned."

I had to ask the obvious question. "Wouldn't we have seen him? Heard him? That stock trailer was noisy, remember?"

"Maybe." Colton shrugged and then turned his attention to the officer. "But y'all know Jake."

"Yes, we all know Jake." Deputy McAllister's expression tightened. "If he's behind this—"

"And I feel sure he is—" Mr. Hayes interrupted.

"Then he figured out a way to get onto the property, nab the horse, and take off again with no one knowing."

Calliope leaned my way and whispered, "Kind of glad I don't know who Jake is."

"We were always close to him," Colton said, "but apparently he wasn't who he said he was."

Rose entered the room with a plate in hand, which she set on the coffee table in front of the deputy. "Katy didn't breathe a word about the abuse until she filed for divorce. By then, he was so riddled with bitterness against the family that he made threats against all of us."

"What sort of threats?" Deputy McAllister eyed the plate.

"The usual stuff," she responded. "'You'll be sorry.' Stuff like that."

"This is all my fault." Colton paced the room, visibly upset. He looked my way, and in that moment I felt genuinely sorry for him. This young man carried the weight of his family's business in much the same way I did.

"Colton, don't be silly," Rose interjected. "You run the breeding business like a pro."

"Have you checked the security cameras?" Deputy McAllister asked.

A wave of relief passed over me. They had security cameras. Good.

Only, apparently the cameras were turned off.

"That makes no sense at all." Colton stared at the app on his phone, clearly stunned at this revelation. "They're never turned off."

"Unless there's a power outage," his mother reminded him. "Which we had this afternoon around three when that wind storm came through. Remember? It blew out the power for a good half hour."

"Oh, right." He chewed on his lip and messed with his phone. "Let me turn it back on." He messed with it a little longer and then groaned. "It's not accepting my password." Colton shot a glance at his dad. "Did you change it recently?"

"Nope. I don't mess with technology. You know that. That's your thing."

Colton looked at Brody, who put his hands up and said, "I tend the animals, not computers. You know me better than that."

"Who else has the password?" Mr. Hayes rose from his armchair and took several steps toward Colton. "Does Jake?"

"He did, at one time. And he certainly knows the layout of the land." Colton shot a glance my way. "Jake worked for us for years, before Brody came along. He knows every square inch of this place."

Gracious. This wasn't looking good.

"What else?" Deputy McAllister asked.

"He knows our routines," Mr. Hayes said. "He saw a mare owner here with a trailer and knew that mare would be placed in the barn. That's how we've always done it."

And yet you went ahead and put Sunshine in the barn, knowing he might do this? I wanted to ask, but didn't. Instead, I took a couple of slow, deep breaths. I wanted to give the Hayes family the benefit of the doubt, especially when I saw the concern in all of their eyes.

"So he knows the land, he knows the routine." The deputy scribbled something into his notes. "Still doesn't explain how he got the horse off the property without being seen."

"He's strong, and he's crafty." These words came from Rose. "He could've guided her out to the road—or even the grove out back—and then loaded her up."

"Well, I'll have my guys keep an eye out for his truck." The deputy closed his notepad and tucked it into his shirt pocket then glanced at Mr. Hayes. "Can you think of anyone else who might have reason to do this?"

"The only other person I can think of is Garrett Stone."

"Garrett Stone?" Rose seemed perplexed by the mention of this name. "What makes you say that, Liam?"

"He's had a grudge against me for as long as I can remember."

"Stone Line Thoroughbreds?" The officer's brow knitted. "That Garrett Stone?"

"Yes." Mr. Hayes' jaw tightened. "Let's just say he's not happy that we've done so well with our business and he hasn't. I tried to help him out a year or so ago—told him about that computer program that Colton created for marketing, stuff like that—but he wasn't interested."

"You think he would sabotage you to prove some kind of point?" the deputy asked.

Mr. Hayes shrugged. "Never would've thought it of him until now, but the idea is floating around in my brain. We've got that big auction coming up on Saturday, and he knows we're both vying to get the same stallion. Southbound Fury. Do you know him?"

"No." The deputy shook his head. "But it sounds like you might have a jealous competitor on your hands."

"And a dangerous ex-son-in-law," Brody said.

I wasn't so sure about the Jake angle. Cosmic Sunshine was fast. And clearly unfamiliar with her surroundings. It was just as likely she'd weaseled her way out of the barn and was running for her freedom.

Which meant that I should probably take off in search of her, outside the confines of this beautiful home and these people who had welcomed me as one of their own.

CHAPTER FIVE

Before I could make this suggestion, the deputy grabbed his radio and broadcast an alert for officers to be on the lookout for Sunshine. When he asked for her full description, I pulled out my phone to show him photos of her, which caused a lump to rise in my throat all over again.

The idea that Sunshine was lost out there broke my heart, but the deputy promised he would do everything in his power to find her. When he headed out moments later, we decided to leave as well, but not before I threw my arms around Rose's neck and thanked her profusely for her kindness.

The guys helped me disconnect the trailer from my truck, insisting it made more sense to leave it there. Afterwards, Calliope and I hit the road, headed toward her house. I barely remembered the drive. I spent much of it on the phone with my parents, who were equally distressed by the news.

Mama—being Mama—stopped right then and there and prayed with me, both for Sunshine's swift return and for my heart, which, she rightly sensed, was broken in two. My father was more concerned about Sunshine.

"I hope she's not out there roaming the streets or something. She could be hit by a car. . .or worse."

I wasn't sure what was worse than being hit by a car, but I got his point.

Up ahead, Calliope slowed her truck to a halt at the light and then turned right. I followed closely behind her, a bit unsure of where we were heading.

"You just stay strong, honey," Mama said. "And don't you dare take any guilt on yourself, you hear me? None of this is your fault. Do you hear me?"

I heard her. Loud and clear. But that still didn't ease my guilt.

By the time we wrapped up the call, I was pulling into the driveway of my cousin's tiny cottage home, not far from the center of town. I grabbed my suitcase and followed along behind Calliope as she led the way inside and guided me to the guest bedroom, which I found to be both old-fashioned and charming in its own way. The bed was one of those vintage iron frames, and the quilt on top—pastel florals—reminded me of something our grandmother would have had in her house back in the day.

A second glance at it, and I realized it actually *was* a quilt that had once been in our grandmother's house in Jefferson. Wow. A tiny lamp on the bedside table looked familiar too.

"Was that Granny Kingston's?" I pointed at the lamp.

"Yes. She passed it to Mama, who gave it to me when I moved here. I've always loved the stained-glass shade."

"I love the colors it puts off in the room."

Under better circumstances I would have carried on about how darling the room was, but I couldn't think straight. My head, my heart. . .everything was in a whirl. I still hoped someone would wake me and say, "It was all a bad dream."

Only, it wasn't.

Calliope sat on the end of my bed and patted the spot next to her. "You should sleep in tomorrow."

I sat. "I can't even imagine sleeping. . .at all."

"I pray that will change." She rested her hand on my arm. "And Jessie, remember. . .God knows where Sunshine is."

"Hopefully He'll show the rest of us."

"I know He will. Until then, we pray."

I had been, for sure. And wouldn't stop until my girl was returned to me.

I dressed for bed but not before pulling the slip of paper out of my pocket. Why hadn't I remembered to show it to the deputy?

I looked at it more closely under the light of the bedside lamp. What was that letter before the L? A *B*, maybe? I couldn't tell. But the *#0258* was intriguing.

The next several hours were spent tossing and turning. And praying. And checking my messages, just in case the police had any news. Not that I expected them to text me, but in my addled state, checking my phone was the only thing I could do.

I must've dozed off at some point, because when I awoke, the sun was peeking through the gingham curtains and the clock said 8:31 a.m.

I checked my phone once again to see if anyone had called or texted. There were half a dozen texts from my parents. And, strangely, one from Asher Brooks that read "We need to talk. Soon." Ugh. He would flip if he heard Sunshine had gone missing.

I reached for the business card Deputy McAllister had given me and placed a call to him right away. Unfortunately, there was no news about my beautiful Sunshine.

"We're still looking for her," he said. "I've got all my guys on it, trust me."

I took a quick shower and dressed for the day. Then I headed to the kitchen, where I found some store-bought blueberry muffins in a basket on the island, along with a note that read *Help yourself!*

I took one, though I certainly didn't feel like eating it just yet.

Calliope had also left the address of the vet where she worked, with a note encouraging me to stop by.

I would. Maybe. But first, I had to talk to Colton. In person. Maybe in the daylight we could search his property once again. Sunshine had a habit of sneaking into tucked-away spaces. She particularly loved hanging out under the trees in heavily wooded areas. Maybe she was just playing an elaborate game of hide-and-seek.

I got into my truck, feeling a little turned around myself. The GPS on my phone would have to guide me back to the Hayes' property. I certainly couldn't find it on my own.

As I approached the intersection at 1774 and 1488, I noticed a Whataburger on the corner and decided to drive through for some sweet tea. After placing the order, I inched forward, my heart still twisted in knots. I attempted to pray, but the only words that came to my mind were *God, help!*

I replayed every event from the night before in my mind. Driving up to the farm for the first time. Meeting the Hayes family. Watching Sunshine stretch her legs in the field. Passing her off to Brody and Colton as I followed Rose into the house. Meeting Taquito. Sharing the most delicious and enjoyable dinner with some of the kindest people I'd ever met. And then. . .

A sigh wriggled out as I remembered the exact moment when we discovered the empty stall. Now my heart felt almost as empty.

A horn honked behind me, and I startled to attention. I inched my way forward in the line of cars, and my breath caught in my throat as I noticed a familiar Chevy Silverado pulling out of the parking lot on the 1488 side. Silver.

I squinted and tried to make out the details. Only one person I knew had the Redline Edition of the Silverado with those red and black accents. But surely Asher Brooks wasn't here, in Magnolia. There had to be more than one person with that same sporty truck.

I watched as the Silverado headed west. I only caught a brief glimpse of the driver—and from such a distance couldn't see much but the profile of what appeared to be a man. Before I could give it any further thought, I was at the window paying for my sweet tea, which Whataburger served up in a Styrofoam cup so large it defied sensibility.

After paying for it, I hefted it into the car, took a sip, and wedged it into the drink carrier. Then I pulled out onto 1488 and turned west, picking up speed once I got past the lights to 1774. I kept going as fast as I dared until I reached Bob's gas station, the one with the infamous taquitos. Which I suddenly had a hankering for.

Until I saw that same sporty Silverado in the parking lot.

My breath caught in my throat, and I tightened my grip on the steering wheel as I watched Asher get out of his truck and walk toward the door. None of this made sense. Why would he land here, in Magnolia?

I tapped my brakes and slowed down to try to get a better look, my drink nearly tipping over in the cupholder. I managed to grab it, my gaze shifting between the road, the cup, and the man who now captivated my attention.

"Why are you here, Asher Brooks? Are you following me?"

The very idea sent a wave of unease wriggling down to my stomach.

Behind me, a car honked its horn, and I realized I'd slowed almost to a stop in the middle of the road. So I picked up speed and passed the station, my thoughts tumbling.

I drove another quarter mile or so and then pulled into a large lot. I parked my truck alongside a black Ford F250 with a custom-built aluminum trailer attached, one with slatted windows and polished steel bars.

It was rare to find a trailer this fancy, and even more unique to see one with swanky black paneling. Whoever owned that truck had money—and lots of it. I squinted to read the sign on the side, but the glare from the sun made it impossible.

I reached for my phone, anxious to go back through my messages from Asher, just to see if I'd somehow missed something.

I read the message he'd sent yesterday: "You really did it?"

And the one from this morning: "We need to talk."

Okay, then. We would talk. I would call him. Right now.

Or maybe not. I nearly came out of my skin when someone tapped on my driver's side window. I let out a scream and then realized Colton Hayes was standing next to my truck.

I took a second to gather my wits about me and then rolled down the window.

"Sorry." He gave me a sheepish look. "Didn't mean to scare you."

"Well, you did. Are you following me?"

"Uh, no. I'm here to shop."

"Ah." I did my best to calm my racing heart. "Have you heard anything about Sunshine?"

"No." He shook his head. "You?"

"No."

He gave me an inquisitive look. "Inquiring minds want to know what you're doing at the feedstore."

"Oh. . ." Was I at a feedstore? My gaze traveled to the large sign that read MAGNOLIA WEED & FEED.

"I just needed a place to pull over. Something happened. I saw someone—"

"Was it Jake? We've been looking for him all morning. He showed up at my sister's place late last night, and she threatened to call the cops on him, but he ended up leaving."

"No, but I'm glad she's safe."

"She said he didn't mention anything about Sunshine. Or any of us, for that matter. He just showed up—drunk, I should add—and gave her a hard time about the divorce. He's not doing so well on his own."

"So are we ruling him out as a suspect then?" I asked.

"It's too early to know anything for sure." Colton shrugged. "But she said he was flashing around money, and he's usually broke."

"Weird."

"Exactly." He gave me an imploring look. "I need to go inside to pick up some supplies. Come with?"

Minutes later, I was pushing a basket and Colton was tossing bags of feed inside, along with a variety of other items he needed for his animals. Before long the basket was full to overflowing. . . and heavy. He offered to take the wheel, but I refused to let him.

When we got to the register, I noticed a burly man who looked to be in his early fifties checking out. He was preoccupied with his phone and didn't notice us, but I could tell his presence made Colton nervous.

After paying for his items, the man happened to glance our way. As he did, his already-hardened expression tightened even more. His piercing hazel eyes narrowed with a calculated and penetrating glare.

"Hayes."

"Mr. Stone." Colton's words were short. He hefted his items from the basket onto the counter, and the clerk began the process of ringing him up.

The man glared at Colton, shoulders squared. "Why did you sic the cops on me?"

"Sic the cops on you?" Colton continued to empty his items onto the counter.

"Yeah, they showed up at my door this morning asking a bunch of questions about some horse disappearing from your property. Wanted my input." The older man's expression tightened. "Any clue why they would do that?"

"It's my horse," I explained. "Cosmic Sunshine. I brought her down from Jefferson to breed with—"

"Let me guess. Like the Wind."

The man's sour expression gave me the shivers.

"Yes. But after we—they—got her settled in her stall, she disappeared."

"And somehow my name is the first one you think of?" The older man rolled his eyes. "Look, I get that we're not the best of friends, Colt. And I know we haven't always seen eye to eye. But I'm no thief. Besides, I wasn't even in town last night. So point your finger at someone else."

I could tell from the look on the clerk's face that he felt awkward at somehow finding himself in the middle of this feud. I felt the same way, but what could we do?

CHAPTER SIX

Turned out, we didn't have to do anything. A few seconds later, Mr. Stone grabbed his bags and stormed out.

I could read the relief on Colton's face.

"You okay?" I asked.

"Yeah." He pulled out his debit card to pay for the purchases. "But don't let him fool you. Garrett Stone is a bully. And he's ruthless. You don't even want to know what he's put our family through these past couple years. He's undermined our business, tried to undercut us with prices on all sorts of things. There's been a kind of rivalry between the Stone family and the Hayeses for as long as I can remember."

"He seemed pretty adamant that he had nothing to do with this."

"Yeah, but trust me when I say he usually gets what he wants."

We walked out to the parking lot, and Colton unloaded the basket's goodies into the back of his truck. Only then did I notice that the huge black F250 with the fancy trailer was gone.

"You never did say who you saw earlier." Colton gave me an inquisitive look.

"Oh, right." I released a slow breath. "It was someone from home."

"Home?" His eyes narrowed. "From Jefferson?"

"Yeah. Remember I told you the story of the man who died owing my dad money?"

"The original owner of Sunshine."

"Right." I paused. "His son, Asher. That's who I saw."

Colton crossed his arms and leaned back against his truck. "Any chance he has business here or something?"

"I've known Asher since we were kids. I've never heard him talk about any connections to Magnolia."

Worry flickered across Colton's face. "Does he have some sort of beef with you?"

"He wasn't keen on me bringing Sunshine here to breed her."

"Why is that?"

"He's hoping to start up a breeding program too. He's got a nice stallion he was probably hoping we would breed Sunshine with. And he thinks I'm being reckless with other people's money."

"Wait. . .hold up." Colton put his hand up. "Other people's money?"

"Yeah." I released a slow sigh. Might as well tell the whole tale. "Our farm is in dire straits right now. But we live in a community filled with people who care about each other. So, a friend from church set up a fundraiser, and before we knew it, we had the money to cover your stud fee." Which reminded me, I still had the cashier's check in my purse.

Only now I didn't have a mare.

"Jessie, you should have told me."

I gave him an inquisitive look. "Why? What would you have done? You don't—didn't—know me."

"But now I do. And I feel even worse than I did that you went to all that trouble, came all this way, and—"

"Now Sunshine is missing."

"But this guy Asher isn't missing. He turned up in Magnolia." Colton squared his shoulders as if ready to dive into action. "I say we go find him. Then you can ask him what he's doing here."

"No offense, but I'm not really in the mood to confront anyone right now. I'm too overwhelmed."

"He doesn't know me."

"Meaning?" I gave him an inquisitive look.

"I could strike up a conversation with him. Ask if he's new in town. Make easy conversation."

"Ah." Maybe. "But he could be anywhere by now."

Colton nodded. "Point taken." He paused. "I was thinking about driving out to the roads behind our property to search for Sunshine. Want to come with? We can keep an eye out for this Asher guy along the way. You leave your truck here, and we'll ride together in mine."

I gave that gorgeous Dodge Ram a closer look. I'd always wanted to ride in the newer model.

"I also need to stop off at my sister's place, to drop something off for my mom. That okay with you?"

"Um, sure."

But I didn't want to leave my truck out there in plain sight, in case Asher happened to drive by. I said so, and Colton suggested I pull around the back of the store and park behind the dumpster.

We were on our way a few minutes later, once again on 1488, this time headed east. Colton slowed his pace as we drove past the gas station, then took the second entrance and ground to a halt in the very spot where I'd first met his father yesterday.

Was that really just yesterday? My thoughts shifted back to that moment when I'd reached through the slide to comfort Sunshine. A lump rose in my throat.

"Any sign of him?" Colton asked. He glanced my way, then his gaze shot to the parking lot, as if expecting Asher to materialize in front of us.

A shiver ran down my spine, and I scoped the whole parking lot but saw no sign of Asher's truck. "No. He drives a Silverado, and it's long gone. I was afraid of that."

"Silverado, huh?" Colton quirked a brow. "We're Dodge Ram folks in these parts."

"Noticed that. It's a nice truck." I rested my hand on the dashboard and then shifted my gaze to the oversized screen that showed our current location.

He pulled out of the parking lot moments later, and we turned off on the side road leading past his family's property. The luxurious Ram hugged the narrow backroad as it twisted and curved beneath us.

My gaze shifted to the trees overhead as he led us down the road that started to feel more like a roller coaster. The branches arched over the road, forming a tunnel of sorts, with sunlight peeking through the leaves. Splashes and splatters of light danced on my hands resting on my lap. Texas never ceases to impress, even outside of Jefferson. Especially in the spring.

"Oh, look! More bluebonnets." I pointed to the field on the right. Exquisite wouldn't begin to describe it.

"Want a picture?" Colton slowed his pace and pulled onto the shoulder near a grove of trees. "This is one of the areas I was telling you about. Once or twice we've had a horse—or cow—escape through our back fence into this area by the road."

I wouldn't offer a comment. We'd lost a cow or two over the years, only to discover them in a neighbor's field. They really were Houdinis.

Maybe Sunshine was too. Maybe she'd panicked, being closed in that unfamiliar stall, and bolted.

I ushered up a quick prayer that we would find her there.

We got out of the truck, and Colton led the way into the thick grove. I managed to snag a couple of pictures of the bluebonnets along the way. Then, just as quickly, the trees opened up into the most beautiful pasture I'd ever seen. My breath caught in my throat as the sheer magnificence of the place caught me off-guard.

"Oh, Colton. It's gorgeous. And those flowers!"

"Bluebonnets. Obviously. But Indian paintbrushes too. And black-eyed Susans."

"It's remarkable, like one of those images you use for your computer wallpaper."

"Only prettier." He pointed at a spot to our left. "I always thought it would be nice to build a house on that patch right there. It's great in the early morning when the sun first comes up."

I could only imagine waking up with a view like that.

We made our way along the edge of the fence, and I saw the back side of his family home in the distance.

"Oh, I get it. We were here last night, right? But on the other side of the fence."

"Yeah, and there wasn't much to see in the dark. But sometimes. . ." He pointed at the cattle grazing a couple hundred yards away. "Sometimes they manage to get out."

A thorough look-see convinced us Sunshine was nowhere in the area, but we did find a section of downed fence pickets.

"She could have gotten out." He yanked the fence post upright, but it fell over again. "I guess it's possible."

He suggested we return to his truck and move on to the next spot, about a half mile down the road.

That stop proved fruitless. And so did the one after that.

"Do you mind if I go ahead and make that stop at my sister's place?" Colton asked after a while. "Mama wants me to drop off something."

"Don't mind a bit."

"We can keep looking as we drive—for Sunshine and for. . ." He paused. "What was his name again?"

"Asher Brooks."

"Asher Brooks."

A truck approached from the opposite direction, and my heart shifted to my throat as I saw the silver paint. Only, it turned out to be a Mazda, not a Silverado.

The truck sailed on by, and we kept going.

About five minutes later Colton pulled into the driveway of a little wooden house—more of a cottage, really. He came to a stop then looked my way.

"This is it. Want to come in?"

"You don't think it would be an imposition?"

"My sister is the friendliest person you'll ever meet. She loves having company."

"Okay. Sure." I opened my door, but before my feet landed on the pavement below, Colton was at my door, holding it open.

He closed it behind me, then led the way to the teal front door of the adorable little cottage. Only then did I notice the Walmart bag hanging from his forearm.

After a couple of knocks, the door swung open and the loveliest young woman greeted us with a toddler on one hip and a little girl who appeared to be about four clinging tightly to her other leg.

"Uncle Colt!" The tiny blond imp in the fairy costume flung herself into Colton's arms.

He grabbed her, almost dropping the Walmart bag in the process. I managed to snag it.

"Well, someone's glad to see you!" Katy laughed, then shot a glance my way. "To what do I owe the honor?"

"Mama wanted me to bring you something. Not sure what's in the bag."

"Pajamas. She told me all about them, thanks." Katy took it from him and returned her gaze to me. "Who do we have here?"

"I'm Jessie."

"Oh, yes! Mama told me all about you. You're not the one with the purple hair, so you must be the one from Jefferson."

"Yes."

Her smile faded. "The one whose mare went missing?"

"Sadly, yes."

"Come in. I just made a fresh loaf of sourdough, and I've got coffee in every flavor you can imagine, including Texas pecan, my personal favorite. You can tell me all about it."

The luscious aroma of freshly baked bread wafted through the air as we stepped through the living room, which was cluttered with toys.

"Don't mind the mess." Katy sighed. "It's not like I don't try, but these two keep me on my toes."

I could only imagine. I padded along behind her into an adorable kitchen, which was quite the contrast to the one in the house where the rest of her family lived.

Before I could say "Yes, please!" Katy had sliced big chunks of sourdough and served them up with soft butter and homemade dewberry preserves. She had a cup of hot coffee ready for me a couple minutes later, the aroma so powerful, so beautiful, that I couldn't wait to give it a try. So I did. Heavens. A girl could get used to this.

We settled in at the little breakfast table, and the kids played at our feet while we ate and drank that amazing coffee.

We somehow managed to avoid the primary topic of conversation until she had put the little one down for a nap and the four-year-old—Carley—was playing in the living room with her dolls.

"You saw Jake?" Katy shifted her gaze to Colton. "He came by your house?"

"Didn't come in, but he came by last night before sunset. Stirred up dust and kept driving."

"Well, he didn't keep driving when he came by here. He was pounding on my door at eight thirty last night, drunk as a skunk. He woke Hunter up, and probably half the neighborhood too."

"Ugh."

I did the mental calculations in my head. The best I could figure, Sunshine had gone missing between six thirty and eight thirty, the two hours when we had been wrapped up in conversation in the kitchen. So Jake's eight-thirty arrival at Katy's place didn't rule him out. Right?

"Jake has his problems." She released an exaggerated sigh. "I'll be the first to admit it. But I can't picture him stealing one of the animals."

Colton's expression tightened, and I could read the concern in his eyes. "He's threatened Dad, Katy. You know that. I wouldn't put anything past him."

"Look, he's a terrible husband—and a jerk—but he's not a thief."

I could tell from the expression on Colton's face that he wasn't so sure.

CHAPTER SEVEN

I heard Jake's working the auction this weekend," Colton said. "That right?"

"Yeah," Katy said. "They've hired him to do some wrangling."

"He's the best. Can't argue that."

"Mama said Garrett Stone came up in conversation. Has he been making trouble again?"

"Just the usual stuff. We're getting more business off Like the Wind than he is off his stallion Set Sail."

"Yeah." Katy ran her index finger around the rim of her coffee cup. "Mama told me you're running circles around him in the horse breeding business and he's not happy about it."

"Set Sail ran in the Preakness but didn't place. Not the same thing as a Breeder's Cup winner."

I felt a little awkward at this point, like I'd somehow horned in on their private conversation. I took a sip of my coffee and shifted my gaze to Carley as she played with her dolls.

"Oh, I know you've got the better horse." Katy put her hands up. "I'm not implying otherwise. Just saying he's probably a little jealous that you've done so well with the business while he's struggling."

"Didn't look like he was struggling to me." I couldn't help but interject my thoughts. "We ran into him at the feedstore."

"True," Colton agreed. "But he did seem genuinely upset that I suspected him of anything. Said he's not a horse thief. And I've got it on good authority that he plans to bid on Southbound Fury at the auction tomorrow."

"That's the one you're interested in?" Katy asked.

"Yes."

"How did Garrett know you suspected him?"

"Apparently Wade went by his place this morning. Just ran a few questions by him."

"He seemed really worked up," I chimed in. "I mean, I don't know the man, but he was clearly upset."

We were silent for a moment. I took a nibble of my bread and savored the delicious chewy texture. With that butter and jam, it was as good as any dessert I'd ever had—and that was really saying something.

"So, y'all were at home when it happened?" Katy asked after a moment.

"Yes, we were eating tacos," Colton explained.

"I miss taco-bar night."

"Come any time, Katy," he said.

She shrugged. "I've got little ones, and they're in bed by eight at the latest. Which is another reason I was so upset at Jake for coming by so late. Like I said, he woke Hunter up."

"Don't blame you there," I said.

She glanced my way. "You think there's any chance your mare just got out and is running free?"

"We've been out looking," I explained. "But there's no sign of her."

Colton nodded. "We've searched the grove and the other spots where Friendship escaped last summer. Remember that?"

"Of course I remember it. It's not every day I get a call saying my cow is in the middle of the road blocking traffic and refusing to move."

"You have a cow named Friendship?" I bit back the laugh that threatened to escape.

"I got her years ago when I was in FFA," she explained.

"I was in FFA too!"

"Good for you." She nodded, and I could tell she really meant it. "Friendship came to me when I was feeling kind of down in the dumps. You know how it is during those weird middle-teen years. I spent a lot of time with her, and we bonded."

Colton looked my way. "She was supposed to be raising the cow to be sold at auction, but when the time came—"

"Let me guess." I knew this story well, having lived through it myself.

"Yeah, I couldn't let her go." Katy sighed. "I fell in love with that cow. It was love at first moo."

Okay, that made me laugh.

But I also got it. Deep in my core. So I told her so. "I understand. That's how I feel about Cosmic Sunshine."

Katy offered a warm smile. "That's a spectacular name, by the way. How did you come up with it?"

"Oh, her former owner did. She was out of Southern Sunshine."

"And her daddy?"

"Cosmic Flare." I paused. "She used to belong to my neighbor. It's kind of a long story."

"A neighbor who mysteriously turned up in Magnolia this morning," Colton said. "We've been on the prowl, looking for him."

"Your neighbor is here?" Katy's eyes widened. "In Magnolia?"

"Yeah." I took a sip of my coffee. "It's weird. I had no idea he was coming."

"But the horse belongs to you, right?"

"Yes." I set the cup down. "We got Sunshine as part of a debt settlement when our elderly neighbor passed away."

"Pardon the obvious question, but how did he follow you here if he's deceased?" Her eyes sparkled with mischief.

I couldn't help but laugh. "Oh, it's his *son* who followed me here, sorry. Asher Brooks."

Katy's eyes widened. "Sounds kind of creepy."

"Does he know where you're staying?" Colton asked.

"I don't think so. He hasn't seen Calliope for years."

"Calliope." Katy gave me a thoughtful look. "That must be the one with purple hair."

"Yes. She's a vet tech. Apparently, she saved Taquito's life once. Cherry pits."

"Oh, boy. You would have to go and mention Taquito." Katy put her hands together as if praying for protection. "That dog is a menace to society."

I didn't want to say anything derogatory about her mother's dog, so I let Colton do all the talking. A short while later, he glanced at his phone. "Man, it's later than I thought. We'd better get a move on. I want to take a quick drive through town to see if there are any traces of Asher."

"The neighbor. The one who's still alive."

"Yes."

"Keep an eye out for Jake too." Her demeanor changed as she mentioned her ex-husband's name. "He promised to steer clear of your place. But, like I said, he's working the auction this weekend. There's nothing we can do about that. The man has a right to work wherever he wants."

Colton glanced at his phone and startled to attention. "Sorry, change of plan. I've really got to get home. Looks like Brody is sick."

"Brody? Sick?" Katy laughed. "Well, that's a first. That guy works longer hours than anyone I know."

"And I've never known him to call in sick before," Colton added. "Must really be bad."

Only, he didn't sound bad last night, did he? In fact, he didn't look sick. . .at all. Strange that he'd come down with something so quickly.

We left Katy's place a few minutes later, and Colton took me back to the feedstore to get my truck. We passed the livestock pavilion on the way to town, and he pointed it out.

"I've got to be at the auction tomorrow afternoon. If you're still here, would you like to come with?"

"Let me think about it. Okay?"

"Sure."

Colton dropped me off at the feedstore, and I thanked him for the time he'd spent searching for Sunshine.

"My pleasure."

And I got the feeling, from the twinkle in his eyes, that he meant it.

As I walked toward my truck, my phone rang. Calliope.

"Any word about Sunshine?" she asked.

"Nope."

"Want to come by and pick me up? I've got an hour for lunch, and there's a cute little diner just up the street from the vet's office. I thought we could sneak away for a little while and get reacquainted. Yesterday was kind of a bust."

That was one way of putting it.

Turned out, "picking her up" entailed meeting every single employee in her office. And a couple of dogs to boot. Oh, and a cat with diabetes. Who hissed at me.

One little pup seemed to garner my cousin's undivided attention. Calliope opened a kennel and pulled out a tiny mixed-breed pup, a mass of wild, wiry hair. "This is Peanut. He's a rescue. He's the one I had to give meds to last night."

"Oh?" I figured all the animals at a vet came from loving homes, so that surprised me.

"Yeah, we work with a local shelter, so we see a lot of rescues. He came to us suffering from malnutrition and in need of fluids. It's been a long road, but he's better now, thank goodness."

"He looks great to me." A testament to my cousin's love and care, no doubt.

"He's needing a home, poor fella." Her gaze shifted to me. "You in the market for a dog? I think he would get along great on the farm."

"Um, no." Right now, the only animal on my heart was Sunshine. Until I got her back, I couldn't focus on anything else.

Calliope released an exaggerated sigh. She returned the pup to his kennel, and we both climbed into my truck and headed out to the Magnolia Diner, the cutest little place, with red-and-white checked curtains and an overabundance of fifties decor, including red leather booths with linoleum tables.

The place was full to the brim with customers chatting it up and eating all sorts of dreamy-looking items—chicken-fried steak, burgers, salads, and so on. In spite of Katy's delicious sourdough bread offering, my stomach rumbled as I took it all in.

Across the room, a jukebox played a lively fifties song. My mama would've loved this place. It reminded me of a restaurant in the heart of Jefferson where we often had lunch. I pulled out my phone and snapped a couple of pictures to send her later.

Calliope and I settled in with our menus, and before long she asked the obvious question. "So, you said there's been no news on Sunshine. . .at all?"

"Nothing. We've been searching for her all morning, but no luck."

"We?"

"I've been with Colton. There are some places behind his property where the animals sometimes sneak out. He took me there. Man, did we see some beautiful scenery."

"Mm hmm." She quirked a brow and gave me a playful look.

"Calliope. Really?"

"You've got to admit, he's super cute." She paused and reached for a menu. "Speaking of cute, any sign of Brody today?"

"No. But Colton got a text from him just a little while ago. He called in sick today."

Calliope's brow furrowed. "That stinks. I hope he's okay."

"It's weird, don't you think?" I glanced down at the menu, my gaze landing on a picture of a Texas-sized burger. "He seemed perfectly fine to me when we saw him last night. No signs of illness at all."

"Maybe it came on quick?"

"Clearly."

If, indeed, it happened to be true. Maybe he was just avoiding us. Maybe. . .

"What looks good to you?" Calliope's words interrupted my thoughts. She pointed at her menu, all smiles. "I usually get the chicken-fried steak. It's fantastic."

I glanced over the menu and settled on a chicken-finger salad with ranch dressing. When the server—the sweetest older woman named Doris—came by, we placed our orders. We complimented her on her cute fifties ensemble: a red-and-white checkered uniform, complete with white ruffled apron. She did a little spin to show it off and then pulled out some cat-eye glasses and perched them on her nose.

"These are just for my favorite customers." She gave us a wink and headed off to turn in our orders.

Before long, she returned with our drinks and we engaged her in conversation once again. After she left, Calliope and I sipped our Dr Peppers and made small talk while we waited for our food to arrive.

"Nice try, asking the server if she wanted a puppy." I swirled my straw around in my drink.

Calliope's smile faded, and she offered a forced pout. "Poor little Peanut. He really needs a good home. But don't worry, I know someone else I can ask."

"Who?"

"Mrs. Hayes!" Calliope's eyes sparkled with excitement. "Taquito could use a friend."

"Taquito would *eat* a friend."

"Sometimes dogs do better in twos. Might be the best thing for him."

Or the worst. Besides, I had a feeling Rose was a one-dog kind of gal. And it was clear Taquito wasn't going to give up any of his current territory—to humans or dogs, I suspected. More likely he would file a restraining order against any new canine that tried to horn in on his space.

Thinking about Rose caused me to replay the events of the prior evening. Before long, I had lost myself to my thoughts. By the time I snapped back to attention, Calliope was chatting it up with someone at the table across from us—a friend from her church who was overly animated and particularly enthused about the upcoming auction.

Eventually my cousin turned back my way. "Sorry about that. Everyone's so excited about the big auction tomorrow. They've got a derby runner in the mix. Southbound Fury. So lots of folks are hoping to bid on him."

"Including Colton," I said. "And—from what I heard—Garrett Stone too."

"Yeah, Lickety Split is one of the bigger breeding outfits in town, but certainly not the only one. Magnolia's developed quite the reputation. Folks come from all over the state for our auctions."

"Colton invited me, but I really hope this is all behind me by then and I'm on my way home."

"I have to be there really early tomorrow morning. Dr. Anderson has asked me to go with him for the vet checks. Do you mind? He needs my help, and I always love those big events."

"Of course I don't mind. You do whatever you need to do, Calliope. I'll be fine."

"If you are still here, you should definitely come. You can see all the horses up for auction before the event begins."

I knew how horse auctions worked. I'd been to plenty. But it might be fun to see another derby runner.

The bell above the door jangled, and Doris called out, "Welcome to Magnolia Diner. Be with you in a sec!"

My gaze shifted to the man in the doorway. The sun beamed through the window, disrupting my view. Only when he took a few steps in our direction could I make him out.

Garrett Stone. The same man whose name had just rolled off my lips. Crazy.

Doris grabbed a menu and called out, "This way, Garrett," then led him to a booth beyond ours. As he passed by, he gave me an inquisitive look, as if trying to figure out where he'd seen me before.

I shifted my gaze to the sugar packets on the table and tried to avoid any confrontation. I certainly didn't want a scene in a small-town diner. I most certainly did not want to end up on Mama's prayer list for some random run-in in Magnolia, Texas. Wouldn't that be something?

CHAPTER EIGHT

"You okay over there?" Calliope asked.

"Yeah." I could feel Mr. Stone's eyes bearing down on me from the booth behind us, and I lowered my voice to respond. "I'm fine."

Still, it seemed a bit strange that he'd turned up here. Was he tracking me?

Before long Doris and Garrett were in a loud conversation about the weather. Laughter peeled out, and I got the sense they were chumming it up. That helped me relax a little.

Until I happened to see a white Silverado drive by in the parking lot. Then my heart rate kicked into overdrive.

"Did you see that?" I pointed at the window as the truck disappeared from view.

"See what?" Calliope yanked around to follow my pointing finger. "Something happen?"

I shook my head, determined not to let my imagination get the better of me.

Before I could say anything else, Doris showed up with our food.

"One chicken-fried steak and one chicken-finger salad. Bon appetite, y'all!" She plopped the plates down on the table with a smile. "If you need me, just holler. I'll be right over here, visiting with Garrett." As she walked away, Doris started singing "Jailhouse Rock" out loud along with the jukebox.

I took a bite of the salad and practically swooned. The fried chicken *was* fantastic. And the ranch dressing tasted homemade. I couldn't get over the tomatoes. They were huge, ripe, and delicious. Just my kind of salad.

Calliope and I shifted into an easy conversation about her job, and she shared one story after another. I didn't mind. I needed the distraction. Every now and again I gazed at the window to make sure Asher wasn't about to make a surprise appearance, but my cousin didn't seem to notice. She had already shifted gears and was carrying on about how tickled she was to meet up with Brody again.

"I'm sure he'll be at the auction tomorrow," she said. "I mean, if Colton is going to be there, he'll have his best hired hand with him, I would think."

"Likely."

"Might be fun to see him again." A little smile tipped up the edges of her lips.

I dabbed my mouth with my napkin, then set it back down. "So, you and Brody—"

She laughed. "There's no me and Brody, girl. Yesterday was the first time we'd clapped eyes on each other in almost three years. But I have to admit, it was mighty nice to see him again. I've thought about him quite a few times since we graduated."

"How well did you know him in school?"

"Really well." She smiled. "We hung out with the same people."

"He seems like a great guy."

"He is."

I cleared my throat and then took another sip of my drink. "I hate to even let my imagination go there, but I'm a little worried about something that happened last night. I mean, he did slip out to the barn just before Sunshine went missing."

"Jessie!" Calliope nearly dropped her fork as she stared at me. "There's no way Brody has anything to do with Sunshine's disappearance."

I poked the lettuce in my salad around with my fork, caught off-guard by her stern response. "You know him better than I do, but he was the last one to see her. We can't ignore that."

"No." She gave me a stern look. "Brody, Colton, and I were *all* together in the barn when they tucked Sunshine in for the night. Brody said he never went back to her stall when he left the house to turn off the water."

"I know that's what he said."

"But?"

"I'm just saying, it's kind of weird that she was there one minute, gone the next, and Brody was the only one who was anywhere near her while the rest of us were in the house eating tacos."

"Those were some really good tacos. Mrs. Hayes is a great cook."

"Yes." But that was clearly not my point. "Brody is the only one we know of who was near her around the time she went missing."

She set down her fork and leaned back against the booth. "You're serious right now."

"I am. But I guess we'll never know, because the security cameras were turned off."

"Right." She dabbed at her lips with a napkin.

"And the password was changed. That would have to be someone who was familiar with the family's security company. Right?"

Creases formed between Calliope's eyes as she pushed her plate away. "I get what you're implying, and if we were talking about anyone other than Brody, I might give this theory some credence. But if you knew him. . ." Her words drifted off. "He wasn't just a fellow student, he was that guy who pushed the rest of us to work at the local animal shelter. He had more empathy than anyone else. He took in goats, for Pete's sake. In his student housing apartment."

"He rescued goats. . .in his apartment?"

"Well, until he got caught and they made him rehome them. But, yes. He was that compassionate soul who always cared more about the animals than the—"

"People?"

"Jessie." She shook her head. "Really?"

"I'm just saying. Maybe he has some kind of secret beef against the Hayes family that we don't know about. Stranger things have happened."

Judging from the tight expression on my cousin's face, she wasn't buying my theory. So I changed the topic to share about Katy and the kids. And that delicious sourdough.

Calliope seemed to perk up at this news. "Yeah, we have whole sourdough clans here. It's a thing. Stick around, and we'll show you our ways. You might just be able to weasel some starter out of Katy. Folks are overly generous here."

"Sounds just like home."

"It *is* home." She reached across the table to rest her hand on mine. "And speaking of which, I think you would love it here, Jessie. Would you ever consider living somewhere other than Jefferson? I could sure use a roommate."

Her question caught me off-guard. Other than my four years away at college at ETBU, I'd never experienced life outside of Jefferson. And even then, my school was only half an hour away from home.

"You don't mind being so far from your parents?" I asked. "Because your mama goes on and on about how much she misses you."

"I've always been the sort to spread my wings," Calliope said. "It felt like a natural transition to go from home to A&M to this great job in Magnolia. God arranged it all so seamlessly. Hey, speaking of Jefferson, the weirdest thing happened this morning."

"What's that?" I lifted my fork with a piece of fried chicken dangling from the tines.

"A guy showed up at our reception desk around ten o'clock. He reminded me so much of someone we used to know back in Jefferson."

"What? Who?"

"You remember that guy who lived next to you when we were kids? Asher something-or-other. The one whose mother always wanted you for a daughter-in-law?"

"Brooks."

"Yes. Asher Brooks." She crossed her arms and leaned back in her seat. "It's been years since I've seen him—probably at least seven or eight—but when I went out to the front desk earlier to check on something, there was a guy standing there, asking our receptionist questions. And he reminded me for all of the world of Asher Brooks."

My hands trembled as I rested them on my knees. "Okay, that's crazy. I saw him this morning too. He was pulling out of Whataburger when I drove through to get a sweet tea."

"Whataburger has great sweet tea."

"I know. But I couldn't figure out why Asher was here in Magnolia. I saw him again at Bob's."

"Bob's has great taquitos."

"So I've been told. But it's really throwing me off that he's come all this way. It's got to be more than a coincidence, you know?"

"How so?"

"Because Cosmic Sunshine used to belong to his family," I explained. "It was Asher's dad who owed my father money. When he passed, we got the horse in lieu of a payment from the family trust."

"Oh, right." Her nose wrinkled. "I knew there was something about a neighbor who owed your dad money, but never knew the details. But that still doesn't explain why he's here."

"He's not happy that I brought Sunshine to be bred."

"Why?"

"Because he's trying to start up a breeding business in Jefferson. He's got a couple of stallions he would prefer I choose for Sunshine. But I have my heart set on Like the Wind."

"I doubt seriously any ordinary stallion would compare to a derby winner."

"He's got a great stallion—Noble Echo—out of the Nearco line, but he hasn't won any big races. Asher seems to think he could produce a runner if the right mare came along."

"And Sunshine is the right mare?"

"I think that was always the plan." I shrugged. "But his father ruined all of that for him."

And I felt bad about that. I always had. But none of it was my fault.

"Are you thinking he had something to do with Sunshine's disappearance?"

"I have no idea." None of this made any sense to me.

Before I could say anything else, Calliope glanced at her phone and gasped. "Oh no. I've stayed too long." She reached for her purse. "We've got a demon-possessed cat coming in at one fifteen, and Dr. Anderson specifically asked me to be there to help. They call me the cat whisperer."

She whipped out her debit card, but I gestured for her to put it away.

"Let me take care of the lunch tab. You've been so kind to let me stay with you."

"Jessie, there's no need for that." She paused, her card dangling from her fingertips. "And by the way, you're welcome to stay with me, not just overnight but as long as you want. I really meant what I said earlier about the roommate thing."

"Looks like it might be a few extra days if we don't find Sunshine."

"You'll find her. But beyond that, my door is always open to you. That sweet little room you're staying in has your name written on it."

I had to admit, this wonderful little town held some appeal, especially when I factored the Hayes family into the mix.

I flagged Doris down, paid the check, and made sure to leave her a generous tip. A couple minutes later, Calliope and I climbed into my truck and crossed the crowded parking lot. My cousin was busy texting someone while I drove, but I was pretty sure I remembered how to get back to the vet clinic without her input, so I forged ahead.

As I crossed the area in front of the grocery store, a young man stepped out directly in front of me, forcing me to slam on my brakes.

Calliope jolted forward against the seat belt and glanced up from her phone. "What in the world?"

I pointed to the guy in jeans and a dark brown T-shirt. "Crazy guy's so glued to his phone he isn't even looking where he's going." I tapped my horn to send him a message, and he glanced up for a second but then kept walking, his gaze on his phone.

"Brody." Calliope and I both spoke his name in unison as he disappeared into the store.

"I thought he was too sick to work?" I inched my way forward as a car behind me got a little too close for comfort.

Her nose wrinkled. "Weird."

I tried not to make too much of it, especially since Calliope seemed genuinely interested in Brody, but I couldn't stop thinking about how he'd gone back out to the barn last night by himself.

My phone rang just as I pulled into a spot at the vet's office. I didn't recognize the number but answered anyway, hoping to hear Deputy McAllister's voice with good news about my girl.

I was surprised to discover Rose Hayes on the other end of the line. I put the call on speaker so Calliope could hear.

"Hey, sweet girl," Rose said, her words chipper and carefree. "Any word on your Sunshine?"

"No, ma'am. I actually thought this call might be from Deputy McAllister with news."

"Sorry to disappoint. But I'm calling to ask if you and Calliope would like to come back for dinner again tonight. I'm making lasagna and homemade sourdough with a big salad. And when I heard that you like blackberry cobbler, I decided to whip one up. No pressure though."

No pressure? How could I say no to all of that?

I was still overly full from the salad I'd just eaten but didn't want to hurt her feelings.

Calliope nodded as she reached to open her door. "I get off at five," she whispered. "So that's fine with me."

Across the parking lot I saw an older woman exit her sedan with a rambunctious cat in hand, one who was clearly plotting an escape. Calliope leaped from the truck and rushed to help the woman—and the cat—inside.

"Thank you for the invitation." I shifted my attention back to the call. "We would love to."

"Perfect. Is six okay? If you come early, we can visit."

"Sounds great."

When we ended the call, I decided to do the one thing that could genuinely make a difference to my current situation. I would find a quiet spot and spend some time in prayer. I didn't know where Sunshine was, but God certainly did.

I circled around to the area that Colton and I had driven earlier in the day. Before long I found the spot with the bluebonnets and Indian paintbrushes.

I pulled the truck off the road and into the grass and turned off the radio. Then I prayed—as never before—asking the Lord to show me where Sunshine was or to return her to me.

My attention drifted to an opening in the grove, to the field just beyond, to those black-eyed Susans in all their glory. I reflected on what Colton had said to me, about hoping to one day build a house there. I could almost imagine what that would be like.

Once again, I took note of the area where we'd found the fence trampled down. Looked like Colton had already tacked it back up. Good for him.

After spending some dedicated time in prayer, I pulled my truck onto the road once again, ready to peruse the area with a closer eye. Only, I couldn't quite figure out which way to go. As always, I headed to the most scenic spots. Before long I was on a road called Nichols Sawmill.

I came upon a familiar intersection and realized I'd been by this spot earlier with Colton, on our way back to town from his sister's place. Off to my right I saw the entrance to the livestock pavilion. My gaze shifted to the large sign promoting tomorrow's spring sale.

What really got my attention, though, was the sporty Silverado in the parking lot. The one with the horse trailer attached to it.

And that's when I put it together. Asher Brooks had told me himself he was headed to an auction this weekend with the hopes of being the highest bidder on a derby runner.

But he had neglected to mention that the auction was in Magnolia, Texas.

CHAPTER NINE

As I passed the pavilion, I caught a glimpse of a gas station across the street, so I looped around and pulled into the parking lot. Once there, I strategically planted my truck in an obscure place off to the side so as not to be noticed. From my current location, I could see the goings-on at the arena.

Turned out, the parking lot at the pavilion was pretty full and getting more crowded by the moment. It's the practice of many of the owners to arrive with their horses a day ahead of time to get them settled in. There is always a lot of paperwork to sign for these events. Health documents to produce. Ownership records to verify. Bloodlines to check. I knew the drill.

Stall assignments were probably already underway, along with sneak previews for potential buyers. For all I knew, Colton might already be there as well.

The town of Magnolia was taking this auction very seriously. I understood now why Dr. Anderson had requested Calliope's help early the next morning. Vet inspections for these events can be grueling and time consuming.

I squinted to get a better look at the trailer behind the Silverado. A few steps in that direction were my only option if I wanted to see more clearly.

Okay, more like a few hundred feet. I was at the edge of the road before I could make out the print on the side of the trailer: BROOKS LEGACY FARM: BREEDING CHAMPIONS, ONE BLOODLINE AT A TIME.

My breath caught in my throat.

In that moment, I knew what I had to do—dangerous or not. I needed to slip over there and make sure Sunshine wasn't in that trailer. I returned to my truck and grabbed my sunglasses, which I hoped would serve as a sort of disguise should Asher catch a glimpse of me.

I made it across the busy street, then sprinted toward the Silverado, anxious to get this over with.

"Please, God," I prayed.

I stopped at the trailer, just short of the Brooks Legacy Farm sign, and peered inside. . .to find the trailer empty.

My heart felt as heavy as lead as I realized my girl wasn't there.

My sadness shifted to concern as I heard a familiar voice from the opposite side of the trailer.

"I can't leave until I hold up my end of the bargain."

Asher.

Before he could discover me, I turned around and sprinted toward the road and then crossed to the safety of my own vehicle.

I sat, panting in the driver's seat, my heart racing.

By now, my nerves were so shot I could only think to do one thing—get back to the safety of Calliope's house to contemplate my next move.

And get cleaned up and changed for my evening at the Hayes house.

When the trembling in my hands stopped, I hightailed it out of there and headed toward town. Only, somehow I got turned around and found myself in an area I didn't recognize. I reached for my phone to set up my GPS, but it slid off of the passenger seat and onto the floorboard.

I had no choice but to pull over into a driveway up ahead.

The impressive wrought iron gates at the front of the ranch I now faced were very much like the ones at the front of my family's property. But the house off in the distance—a two-story stone monstrosity—was vastly different, and far more impressive, in size and design.

I slipped the truck into park and took a second to note the sign on the front of the gate. Stone Line Thoroughbreds. Oh dear. My gaze shifted to the gate code box to my left. Hopefully the folks inside the big house couldn't see me right now, or they might start talking to me through that box.

I reached down to grab my phone and heard the crunch of gravel as a vehicle pulled into the drive behind me. Oops. Nothing like stopping a homeowner from accessing his own gate.

I rose up, ready to offer an explanation, when I realized the man in the truck behind me was the same fellow I'd already bumped into twice today.

Garrett Stone.

I sucked in a breath and clutched my phone as he approached my window.

When I rolled it down, he took one look at me and his eyes narrowed to slits. "You."

"Yes, sorry. I pulled in to turn around. I'm lost."

"You just happen to be lost at my place?"

"Just happen. Those are the right words." I offered a faint smile. "I'm trying to get back to Calliope's house."

"What's a Calliope?"

"My cousin. The one I was having lunch with at the diner."

"Are you following me?"

"No, sir." I put my hands up. "I promise, this is all just a weird coincidence. I'm truly lost. I need to get back to town to my cousin's place, and I'm turned around."

"They have this little thing called GPS."

"I know." I held up my phone. "But my phone fell onto the floorboard, which is why I had no choice but to stop. I'm sorry I blocked you. I'm leaving now."

Only, with his truck behind me, it would be tricky, especially with that huge horse trailer attached.

The long, sleek one with the shiny black paneling and polished steel bars.

The same one I'd parked next to at the feedstore.

This time I was able to make out the logo on the side of the trailer: STONE LINE THOROUGHBREDS.

"Go left out of the drive—that's north—on Nichols Sawmill. And when you get to 1774, turn left. After that, you're on your own."

"Thanks. Sorry I inconvenienced you."

"You didn't inconvenience me. You confused me. And that's not easy to do."

He climbed into his F250 and backed up as best he could. I managed to get myself turned around. Then I hollered, "Sorry about that!" and waved as I took a left onto Nichols Sawmill.

By the time I located Calliope's house it was three thirty. I wanted nothing more than to rest for an hour or so before getting dressed for dinner, but my phone wouldn't stop beeping. Mama was very anxious. And I fended off a couple of texts from Calliope as well.

Around four fifteen I finally placed a call to Deputy McAllister, who apologized that he had no news.

"We're still looking for her, I promise. We drove out to Garrett Stone's place this morning to ask him some questions."

"Oh, trust me. Colton and I heard all about that."

"Oh?"

I explained what had happened at the feedstore earlier.

"What about Jake?" I asked him. "Katy's ex-husband?"

"He's working up at the pavilion, so I plan to go by there in a bit. We've had kind of a busy day here. Lots of folks converging on Magnolia for that big auction."

"Yeah, I drove by the arena earlier. Speaking of which. . ."

I quickly filled him in about Asher being in town and on what I'd heard him say.

"His end of the bargain?" Deputy McAlister asked. "What does that mean?"

"I have no idea. For all I know he could have been on a phone call. I couldn't see anyone from where I was."

"Gotcha."

He promised to keep an eye out for Asher's Silverado.

When we ended the call, I rested my eyes for a few minutes. But sometime around five I decided to get cleaned up and put on fresh clothes and makeup.

A text came through from Calliope about fifteen minutes later. "Sorry, I'm running late. Can you go on without me? I'll meet you there."

I wrote back: "No problem."

Then I headed to Lickety Split on my own.

I was getting more familiar with the route from town to the Hayes place. I arrived at six straight up, and Rose greeted me at the door holding the yapping Taquito, who wriggled like a greased pig at a county fair.

"All alone?" she asked as she shifted the feisty pup in her arms.

I nodded and took a step backward as Taquito lunged my way. "Calliope got held up at work and said she would meet me here."

"Good." Rose ushered me inside. "I need to speak to you in private, so this is perfect. Just let me put Taquito in my bedroom so he'll leave us alone."

Rose disappeared and then returned moments later. She led me into the kitchen, the spicy aroma of lasagna pulling me in.

"Have a seat, honey." She gestured to the barstools at the island. "We can visit while I work."

Without even asking, she poured me a tall glass of tea and passed it my way.

"You said Calliope is your cousin?"

"Yes."

"Liam and I put it all together last night after you left that Calliope is Eliza's daughter."

"That's right."

Rose's cheeks flamed pink. "I have a little confession to make. There's a bit more to the story I told you last night."

"Oh?"

The timer went off on her stove at that very moment.

"Hang on a second." Rose peeked in the oven, and the smell of oregano and other Italian herbs became even more pronounced than before. She closed the door and reset the timer.

"Your aunt Eliza was dating Liam, like I said. But I was so head over heels in love with him, I couldn't see straight. I hate to even admit this, but I dated Toby—Liam's best friend—just to make Liam jealous."

"Oh my."

"I'm not proud of it. And when my devious plan worked out, Toby was hurt. A lot. And so was your aunt Eliza. She was brokenhearted, in fact."

I paused to let it all soak in. "That's crazy, but how ironic, that she ended up with Toby in the end. They're such an amazing couple. Funny how life turns out."

"Yes, God's plans are far beyond our own. That's for sure. You never know what He's up to, do you?"

"Nope."

The back door opened, and Colton stepped inside. He glanced my way and grinned. "Hey, you're back."

I countered with a nod. "I am."

Rose set a large bowl on the counter and looked back and forth between us. "Like I said, you just never know what the Lord is up to." She gave me a little wink. "Now, you two scrub up. I need help with this salad."

CHAPTER TEN

A short while later Calliope arrived, and we put her to work chopping vegetables.

Mr. Hayes showed up moments later, deeply engaged in a phone call. When he ended it, we settled at the table to share another meal. We loaded up our plates with salad, bread, and gooey, rich lasagna. The food was every bit as good as it looked. Over-the-top delicious, really. I could definitely get used to this.

The blissful moment passed when I remembered Cosmic Sunshine. If my girl didn't turn up, and soon, I wasn't sure what I was going to do. I certainly couldn't head back home without her.

No, I would stay put until she turned up. And she would.

My cousin must've noticed my somber demeanor. I could read the concern in her eyes as she glanced my way.

"Y'all, help me out." Calliope looked back and forth between the Hayes family members. "I'm trying to talk Jessie into becoming my roommate."

"What?" Rose let out a little squeal. "You're thinking of moving here, Jessie?"

"I. . ." I shot a warning glance at my cousin. "No. I mean, it never entered my mind to leave Jefferson."

"Until she fell in love with all of us." Calliope giggled. "Now I'm guessing she's willing to give the idea some thought."

Okay, so I might be tempted—on some small level—but this certainly wasn't the time to entertain that notion.

"At least come and visit more often," Calliope said. "Mi casa es su casa."

Thank goodness the conversation shifted to the upcoming auction. I heard all the details about Southbound Fury, the stallion Colton was interested in acquiring.

"He stands at stud at a farm in Fredericksburg," Colton explained.

"What does he look like?" I asked.

Colton reached for his phone and scrolled to a website with several photos. I gasped when I saw the magnificent stallion.

"Three white socks! I love it."

"And that gorgeous blaze down his face is divine," Calliope interjected. "I love the little crescent-shaped snip above his upper lip."

"He's six years old," Colton explained. "Just over sixteen hands. Great runner."

"How great?" I asked.

"Came in third a few years back at the derby. Fiery at the starting gate, which is actually how he got his name. I've been researching this horse for months. I think he would be a perfect fit for our farm." He then told me about a computer program he had designed to pair up mares with his various stallions.

"Works like a charm," he said. "I can almost tell you from the moment they're born what kind of runners those foals are going to be."

This, of course, just made me miss Sunshine even more.

"I hope you get him." I offered Colton a smile and then dabbed my lips with my napkin.

"Me too."

And the quiet moment that settled between us at that proclamation sealed us as fellow entrepreneurs.

Rose served up big bowls of steaming blackberry cobbler for dessert, topped with Blue Bell Homemade Vanilla ice cream, my personal favorite. Afterward, we shifted to the living room to continue our conversation. Mrs. Hayes went to fetch Taquito, who joined us after a brief trip outside to do his business. I couldn't help but notice the narrow-eyed glare he shot my way. What the Hayes family offered in the way of Southern hospitality, this dog more than made up for with his y'all-can-leave-now look.

Speaking of looks, every now and again I thought I noticed Colton glancing my way with more than a little interest.

Was he interested? Or was he simply feeling bad because my horse had gone missing on his watch?

No, he seemed genuinely interested. Maybe he saw more in me than just an emotional girl with a missing horse and a crazy cousin.

About an hour into the post-dinner chat, I could tell that Calliope was antsy. She shifted her position on the sofa several times, each time glancing at her phone.

"You okay over there, honey?" Rose asked.

"Yeah." Calliope shoved her phone into her purse and stood up. "I'm so sorry, but I have to be up super early. I'm meeting Dr. Anderson at the pavilion at seven to start vetting the incoming animals. We've got to give health certificates before folks start showing up. So I really need my beauty sleep."

Rose insisted we take the leftover lasagna, and Calliope willingly obliged.

We said our goodbyes, and Calliope and I headed out to our vehicles.

I was surprised to see an unfamiliar truck in the circle drive, one I'd never noticed before. The older-model Dodge was blocking my way out.

Before I could consider my plan of action, someone came walking our way from the barn. Brody.

Calliope's mouth fell open. "Brody, what are you doing here? I thought you were sick."

"I am." He rested his hand on his throat. "I have strep throat."

That might account for the odd way he was talking.

"But we saw you earlier," I countered. "Walking into HEB. And you looked perfectly normal."

"Um. . .thanks?" He shrugged. "After I went to the doctor, I went to the pharmacy in HEB to get my meds. He prescribed an antibiotic and steroid for the swelling in my throat. It's miserable. But if you saw me, why didn't you stop and say hi?"

"Good grief. So you really are sick?" Calliope asked.

"Of course. I said that."

"I know, but. . ." She shot an I-told-you-he-was-a-good-guy look my way.

To which I responded, "Did you really have goats in your apartment?"

"Huh?" Now he seemed genuinely perplexed.

"Ignore her." Calliope rolled her eyes. "Jessie has a tendency not to believe the stories people tell her."

"Of all the things you could have told her about me, you went with the goats-in-the-apartment story? Really?"

"I found it very entertaining," I said. "If not slightly improbable."

"I had *a* goat—singular—in my apartment. A small one, I might add. Just a few weeks old. Not much bigger than a schnauzer. Until my landlord found out. At which point the goat went to a farm in Bryan. But I'm still not sure why we're talking about goats."

I wasn't either, honestly.

"Speaking of animals, is there any word on your mare?" he asked. "I'm sorry I've been out of pocket and couldn't help with the search."

"No. The police haven't found her. And we searched several locations this morning with no clues."

"I'm sorry." And the expression on his face told me he meant it.

Which probably meant that I could drop him from my list of suspects, in spite of how things had gone down the night before.

I heard a noise behind us and turned to discover Colton exiting the front door of his house. He took several steps in our direction, confusion etched on his brow as he looked Brody's way. "I thought you were sick?"

"I am. I have strep. But nobody seems to believe me."

Colton took a giant step backward. "What are you doing here?"

"I just stopped by to give Friendship her meds," Brody responded.

"Friendship. . .Katy's cow?" I managed.

"Wait." Calliope looked more than a little perplexed. "Y'all have a cow named *Friendship*?"

To which Colton and I both responded, "Long story," in unison.

"She's got some arthritis issues in her old age," Colton explained. "So we ordered some supplements that are supposed to help." He turned his attention to Brody. "But I could have done that, Brody."

"Nope. You couldn't. I still had the supplements in my truck. Besides, I wanted an update on the missing mare. They just filled me in. No clue who took her?"

"Nope." Colton shook his head. "The deputy's keeping an eye on Garrett Stone. And Asher Brooks too."

"Who's Asher Brooks?" Brody asked.

"A neighbor of mine from Jefferson who showed up in town today," I explained. "Kind of a long story, but he used to own Sunshine."

"Oh, wow. You think he took her?"

"Could be."

"He drives a Silverado," Colton interjected. "So keep your eye out."

"Silverado?" Brody's nose wrinkled. "Who drives a Silverado?"

"Exactly," Colton said.

Brody rubbed the back of his neck. "Sorry, but I've got to head home and crash if I'm going to be in any kind of shape for that auction tomorrow."

"I'll be there." Calliope gave him a nod. "Maybe we'll bump into each other."

I had a feeling they would. On purpose.

But first, I had to get my cousin home to catch some z's.

Brody turned and headed toward his truck, then looked back. "Hey, you didn't mention Jake. I thought he was the one you were worried about."

"Deputy McAllister talked to Jake this afternoon," Colton responded. "He has a receipt from Las Fuentes with a time stamp of 7:29 p.m. Apparently he was having dinner with a friend."

"Weird," Brody said. "I don't know anyone who's still friends with Jake."

"Me either. But he has the receipt."

"They have great queso blanco at Las Fuentes," Brody said.

"Best in town," Colton countered.

Brody reached to open the door of his truck, suddenly looking a little pale and wobbly.

"You okay over there?" Calliope asked. "Need some help?"

With the wave of a hand, he dismissed her offer. "I'm fine. Or I will be. After some sleep. And more meds. Night, y'all."

Brody climbed into his truck and moments later took off out of the driveway. Calliope got into her truck. My vehicle was no longer blocked, which freed me up to leave. But I still had one lingering question, which I posed just as I reached my driver's side door.

"Where is Las Fuentes?"

"Close to HEB. Which is a good fifteen minutes from my sister's place. Katy said he showed up at eight thirty."

"Right."

"So, he wrapped up dinner at 7:29 and was at her place by eight thirty," I said. "That still leaves a few minutes for him to steal Cosmic Sunshine in between."

"You're forgetting the fifteen-minute drive part. I don't think there was enough time for him to steal a horse between dinner at Las Fuentes and the time he showed up at my sister's place, not if we factor in the drive—both to Katy's place and here. You know?"

"If Jake doesn't have her and Brody has nothing to do with this, then who does that leave?" I asked.

"Brody?" Colton's eyes widened. "You thought *Brody* had something to do with this?"

"Look." I kicked at the gravel with the toe of my boot, my emotions soaring into high gear. "I don't know any of you. Not really. So I haven't figured out the good guys and the bad guys just yet. I had to take Brody into consideration because he was the last one to see Sunshine."

"Good gravy. Well, don't send him off to the penitentiary just yet, okay? We need him around here."

"Okay, okay. So Brody's off the list," I said. "And maybe Jake too."

"I still can't believe you thought Brody had anything to do with this."

"I told you, I don't know the players in this story. A little grace, please!" I put my hands up. "So, who does that leave?"

"Garrett Stone and your neighbor. I don't like the idea that he's in town, possibly trailing you."

"Me either."

"If he causes any problems, I hope you know you can call on me."

"I will. I promise."

Colton took another step in my direction and looked at me with such intensity that I found it hard to breathe. My heart rate intensified as he leaned in close. . .

. . .to open my door for me.

I climbed inside, still feeling a little unnerved by the feelings that now flooded over me as he lingered so close we were practically touching.

Excitement? Disappointment? Confusion?

All of the above, likely.

Behind me, Calliope flipped on her headlights, a sign that she was ready to head out.

I closed my door and rolled down the window, ready to put this conversation behind me.

"I've got my eye on Garrett Stone." Colton spoke through the open window. "And Deputy McAllister does too. Stone's got the connections. And he's worked up about tomorrow's auction. I think he's got the financial backing to take the bidding up to some high-dollar amount on Southbound Fury, so I'm ready for a showdown."

"Sounds exciting."

"Yeah." He paused. "But the more important thing right now isn't *that* horse. It's *your* horse."

I was glad he saw it that way. I certainly agreed.

Now, to find Sunshine. And to put this story—and my exhausted cousin—to bed.

CHAPTER ELEVEN

Calliope was up and gone before I even awoke the following morning. I showered, dressed, fixed my hair and makeup, and headed to Whataburger for a couple of breakfast tacos before driving up to the pavilion.

I checked my phone, hoping to hear something new from Deputy McAllister. The pit in my stomach wouldn't leave as I contemplated where Sunshine might be. Somebody out there had my girl. Garrett? Asher? Today, I would figure it out and bring her home.

Home.

I thought of Jefferson, of the home I loved so much.

But just as quickly, I thought of how at home I felt here, in Magnolia.

When I reached the Whataburger parking lot, I grabbed my purse to fish out my debit card but couldn't find it. And that was when it hit me. Yesterday. The diner. I'd paid with my card. I replayed the whole scene over in my head and realized I had very likely left my card there. So I pulled out of Whataburger and headed straight for the Magnolia Diner.

I walked inside and saw Doris waiting on a customer at the counter. A ripple of laughter reverberated between them, and I saw the broad smile on her face as she talked to the elderly man with the Stetson and button-up shirt.

Garrett Stone.

Did he live here, or what?

I took a few steps in their direction, and Doris waved at me. "Hey, you! I'm guessing you came back for a little red debit card."

"Yes. Thank you so much for holding on to it for me."

"Wasn't sure how to track you down, honestly. I thought I knew everyone in town, but Kingston isn't a name I know."

"Kingston?" Garrett looked my way, and his smile faded. "Oh, no. Not *you* again."

I put my hands up. "I promise I'm not following you."

His expression tightened as he swung back around and grabbed his coffee mug, then shifted his attention to Doris. "Give me one to go, will ya, Doris? I've got to hit the road."

"Well sure, Garrett."

I settled into the spot at the counter next to Garrett while I waited for Doris to fetch my card. I felt the older man's gaze on me as I tried to figure out what to say.

"You gonna follow me to the auction too?" he asked after Doris brought his coffee. " 'Cause I'm headed there next, in case you need a heads-up."

"Well, I am headed that way in a bit. I'm meeting Calliope."

"The cousin with the purple hair." Garrett poured some creamer into his to-go cup. "Colton Hayes gonna be there too?"

A handful of customers rushed through the door before I could answer.

Doris seated them at a booth on the side opposite us.

"Whew!" Doris fanned herself with a menu as she approached. "Lots of out-of-towners today for that auction. It's gonna be crazy in here." She glanced my way. "You hungry, kiddo?"

"I mean. . ." Whataburger could wait.

"You like your eggs scrambled or fried?"

"Sunny-side up."

"White or wheat toast?"

"Whatever you say."

"You're too easygoing." She gave me a pensive look. "Bacon or ham?"

"Is that even a real question? Bacon. Duh."

"You're feistier than I gave you credit for." She turned toward the kitchen then glanced back. "Hash browns?"

"Why not. Go big or go home, right?"

"Speaking of. . .where is your home anyway?" These words came from Garrett.

"Jefferson. I brought my mare down to Lickety Split to breed with—"

"Doris! Check!" He rose and dabbed his lips. "Gotta get over to the pavilion to see a man about a horse."

And just like that, Garrett Stone bolted.

I spent the next few minutes trying to come up with a workable plan to find Sunshine. Should I make flyers with her picture on them? Put them up around town? Doris would probably let me hang one up in the window of the diner.

Maybe I could also reach out to the local paper to run a story. That might help spread the word. People could be on the lookout.

I made a list of ideas to tackle after the auction, then made quick work of eating my breakfast. I finally asked Doris for my check but it turned out, Garrett had already taken care of it. Crazy. Never saw that one coming. I grabbed my purse, ready to head out. Maybe the auction would distract me from my worries about Sunshine.

I didn't realize Doris had followed along until I got to the front door. She rested a hand on my shoulder, and I turned to face her.

"Hey, I thought you'd like to know something."

"What's that?" I slung my purse strap over my shoulder.

"I know that Colton sent the cops around to talk to Garrett about your mare, the one that went missing."

"How do you know that?"

Doris let out a knowing chuckle. "It's a small town, honey. Anyway, between you and me, I was with Garrett on Thursday night, and he was nowhere near the Hayes place."

"Oh?"

Her cheeks flushed pink. "No one knows, but he asked me out on a date." A little pause followed, and the edges of her lips curled up in a smile. "It was our first."

"Oh, I see."

"He picked me up at five, and we drove into Houston to the Livestock Show and Rodeo. We didn't even get back to Magnolia until almost midnight."

"Thanks for letting me know."

"You know, Garrett's kind of a curmudgeon. He's been like that since his wife died and his kids moved off to Louisiana. But it didn't take me long to figure out he's just lonely. When we're together, he's a completely different fella."

"Well, that's good."

"And he would never hurt an animal, a horse especially. That man loves his horses. I had to practically drag him to Houston Thursday night, and even then he spent half the evening texting back and forth with his hired hand to make sure they were okay. I'm telling you, he's an old softie when it comes to the animal kingdom."

I understood that. I loved my animals too.

"You tell Colton that he's wrong about Garrett, okay?" She gave me an imploring look. "I don't like folks thinking my fella is some sort of bad guy when he's not."

"I will." And I meant it.

I thought about her words all the way to the pavilion. Garrett did seem like an old sourpuss, but life sometimes did that to people.

Maybe I needed to extend more grace, like Doris said. And maybe I would buy his lunch next time. If I stuck around.

When I arrived at the arena, I had to find a spot in a field far beyond the parking lot. This place was insane. I made the trek to the arena, past the pop-up vendor booths, beyond the 4-H kids selling baked goods, and went from stall to stall, checking out the various horses.

I grabbed a catalog so I could learn more about them. And heavens! What a show of breeds. Shimmering hides, beautifully braided manes, velvety coats. I saw horses in every size, shape, and color, each one prouder than the last.

I loved the working horses. Quarter horses were most popular for a reason. And those Paints took my breath away, especially the little filly in stall fourteen. But the most impressive horse of all?

Wow. I stopped in my tracks, jaw slacked, as I stared at the most remarkable Clydesdale I'd ever seen—a noble fellow standing over seventeen hands high. Broad chested. Muscular. Majestic. This fellow might've been bred for farm work, but standing there, in stall seventeen, he looked better suited for a job in a Hollywood commercial.

Locating my cousin wasn't easy, but I finally found her in a stall with a Shetland pony. Dr. Anderson was too busy to say much, but I didn't mind.

"We're almost done here." Calliope looked up from the paperwork in her hands. "See you inside in a bit?"

I nodded and kept moving.

By now the crowd was a little too thick for my liking. I needed to get to the pavilion to look for Colton.

And that was when I happened upon the great Southbound Fury in stall twenty-one. My breath caught in my throat as I clapped eyes on the stallion. He was even grander in person, all 16.3 hands of him. His muzzle was gorgeous—velvety, even. But those snow-white socks! Perfection!

"Oh. You. Are. Spectacular!" I walked his way to run my hand down his muzzle, and he nestled into me, as if he belonged with me.

I flipped through the catalog and read all of his specs and suddenly understood why everyone in town wanted to get in on this action. Southbound Fury was the kind of horse that could change a breeder's life—and business—forever.

A man in faded jeans and dusty button-up approached and took the horse by the reins. "He's something else, isn't he?"

"Unbelievable."

"Want to watch him in action? I'm about to take him out to the riding area to saddle him up."

"Really?"

"Sure. He still moves like a knife through butter."

I tagged along behind him as he led Southbound Fury out to the central dirt ring, where potential buyers looked over the horses as they showed themselves off.

Colton approached and settled into the spot next to me at the fence. "Well? What do you think?"

I released an exaggerated sigh. "He's everything you said and then some. It's the weirdest thing, Colton. When I petted him, I felt the same way I felt when I first touched Sunshine. Like he was—"

"Family?" The look he gave me was so tender, so heart-felt, that tears sprang to my eyes.

I pushed aside the lump in my throat to whisper, "We've got to find my girl."

"We will. I promise." Colton reached to grab my hand. "We won't stop looking."

We stood in silence for a few moments, and I realized, much to my surprise, that Colton still had his hand around mine. I didn't mind a bit. In fact, it felt completely natural. Together we watched Southbound Fury move with grace and speed around the warm-up ring.

That coat—gleaming in the midmorning sunshine—was enough. But the muscles rippling underneath really caught my eye. This magnificent horse moved in perfect rhythm, a specimen so fine, so perfect, I couldn't take my eyes off of him. And I knew at once that the Hayes family must have him. No matter what.

Off in the distance the announcer's voice crackled through the speakers, some sort of important announcement I couldn't quite make out.

"Southbound Fury's group is up next." Colton released his hand from mine. "We've got to get inside."

Moments later we worked our way through the crowd in the pavilion. I located Colton's parents seated in the bleachers nearest the center of the ring. They waved for us to join them.

My gaze traveled up to the banners flapping in the wind, promoting Magnolia Weed & Feed, the diner, Las Fuentes, and half a dozen other places. The scents of horses, hay, and anticipation merged into one heady scent.

I searched the room and wondered if Asher was here. If so, would he bid against Colton?

I didn't see him, but I definitely saw Garrett Stone as he took a seat on the bleachers opposite us. He carried a bidder's paddle and wore a tight all-business expression on his face. He and Mr. Hayes exchanged tense looks.

The bidding began, and I was caught up in the excitement as horse after horse entered the arena for their turn at bat. One of the wranglers was a bit of a showboat, making a spectacle of himself.

"That's Jake." Colton offered a curt nod. "In case you didn't recognize him."

"Oh, right." I zoomed in on him through my phone's camera. Yup. Same handsome guy I'd seen in the gas station parking lot a couple days back.

The auctioneer did his thing as the horses came and went from the ring. The Hayes family watched quietly.

When Southbound Fury entered the ring, the whole pavilion seemed to come alive with an energy we hadn't felt before.

Mr. Hayes, Rose, and Colton all sat up straight, as if ready to dive into action. Calliope appeared next to me, just in time. And across the way, Garrett Stone clutched his paddle, ready to dive in.

In that moment, with dust hanging in the air over the pavilion, I ushered up a prayer that the right owner would end up with Southbound Fury.

The auctioneer's voice sounded over the loudspeaker, animated and ready to go. "Next up, folks, we've got lot number eighteen, our much anticipated six-year-old registered Thoroughbred, Southbound Fury."

A cheer went up from the crowd, and the horse put on a glorious display as he entered the ring with a prance in his step. Jake used the lead rope to calm him and bring him to a halt, center ring. Southbound Fury was composed. Well-handled.

Across the way, Garrett reached for his phone and gave it a glance, as if reading a text. He scoped the audience, clearly looking for someone. Was Doris joining him, perhaps?

"Standing at 16.3 hands, this proud boy is a top-five derby finisher out of Velvet Horizon and sired by the great Crimson Tempest."

A cheer went up from the crowd.

"Don't let Southbound Fury's retirement from the track sway you, folks. He's a runner determined to produce runners. He's got the bloodline to pass on stamina, speed, and a mighty fine name to boot."

Southbound Fury kicked up some dust, still in show-off mode as Jake gave the lead some slack.

"Check him out, friends," the announcer called out. "Now *that's* a stallion you can write home about. He's got the look. He's got the line. And he's got the temperament. Best of all, he can be yours today when you place the highest bid!"

A roar of anticipation went up from the crowd.

"So, who's going to start the bidding at twenty-two thousand?"

Colton's hand went up, and before long we were off to the races, a handful of locals vying for their chance to own this inspiring beast.

Another handler took over for Jake, who seemed to be more interested in the audience than the horse. I reached for my phone, ready to snag a few pictures when the Hayes family won him.

Up and up the bids went, from the twenties to the thirties, and eventually tapping the low forties. Wow.

My breath caught in my throat at numbers this huge. But then again, we were talking about a derby runner. Garrett was all in and so were the Hayeses, but I knew they could only go so high.

I noticed Jake move to the rails on the south side of the ring. He was still scoping the audience, as if looking for someone. I followed his gaze, and my breath caught in my throat as I saw Asher Brooks move his way then lean in to holler something at him.

Asher Brooks from Jefferson. . .knew Jake Owens from Magnolia?

I snapped a picture of the two of them, my hands now trembling.

The bidding continued with great excitement from the crowd. I watched as Asher reached for his phone and appeared to be making a call.

Which Garrett Stone answered seconds later.

And just like that, Garrett Stone upped his bid to forty-six thousand. . .

Winning Southbound Fury.

CHAPTER TWELVE

And in that moment, I knew.

I knew they were all in cahoots. . .working together, not just to win the coveted Southbound Fury but to outsmart the Hayes family and destroy their business. I also suspected they'd been up to much more than that.

The auctioneer declared Garrett the winner, and the crowd offered a mixed response, some cheering and others offering a collective sigh. I snapped a couple pictures of Jake and Asher talking.

"Well, that didn't go as expected."

I turned when I heard Colton's somber words. He rose and shoved his phone into his pocket. "Let's get out of here."

I needed to share my suspicions with Colton and his parents. Pronto. "Colton, listen—"

"I didn't realize Garrett had that kind of money to spend." Mr. Hayes rose, pulled off his Stetson, and rolled it around in his hands, looking more than a little downcast. "We did the best we could, Son."

I had just opened my mouth to share my suspicions when Brody approached, worked up about another horse he thought Colton might be interested in. Seconds later, Colton and his parents took off with Brody, headed toward the stalls, which left me alone with Calliope.

I turned her way, completely overwhelmed.

"You okay? You look like you've seen a ghost."

"I have." I shot a glance at Garrett, who was being escorted out of the pavilion by a man with a clipboard in hand. "I have a lot to tell you. But not here. Are you free to leave?"

"Sure." She rose and stretched. "I'm ready. It's been a long day."

"Late lunch?"

She nodded. "Where?"

"Las Fuentes."

"They have great queso blanco."

"So I've heard. But that's not the only reason we're going. I've got to get the answer to one lingering question before I talk to Colton about what I just saw."

Her forehead wrinkled. "What did you see?"

"I'll tell you when we've got a bowl of queso blanco in front of us."

"O–okay."

We followed at a distance behind Garrett as he was escorted to the sales office. He went inside to sign the purchase agreement and arrange for payment. I knew that Southbound Fury couldn't leave the grounds until he was paid for, but I suspected Asher Brooks would have to involve himself in that process.

Sure enough, Asher disappeared into the sales office seconds later.

"Hey, isn't that—" Calliope pointed at Asher and then looked my way.

"Yes. Let's get out of here."

We headed to our respective vehicles. Then, less than ten minutes later, we met up again at Las Fuentes, where a young server seated us at a booth. Five minutes later we were drinking Dr Peppers and shoveling down chips and queso blanco. I quickly shared the tale of all I had witnessed between Asher, Jake, and Garrett Stone back at the pavilion, and my cousin's mouth fell open.

"Oh, Jessie!" She dangled a cheese-covered chip midair. "Are you sure?"

"Yes, and I just had it confirmed when Asher went into the sales office with Garrett. They were in this together all along."

"So are they mutual owners now, or what?"

"Could be they plan to share ownership of the horse. That happens all the time. But I don't know for sure."

"And you really think they have Sunshine too?"

"It's just a guess, but I'm about to find out for sure."

I called the server over, ready for answers.

"Were you working last night, by any chance?" I asked.

She refilled our tea glasses and nodded. "Sure was."

"Do you know this guy?" I pulled up one of the photos of Jake I'd just taken at the auction.

She nodded. "Yup. I know Jake. He used to come in here a lot. Didn't see him for a while, and then—"

"He showed up Thursday night?"

"With some guy I'd never seen before, yes. They had more than a few Margaritas." She paused. "I already gave the police a copy of their receipt."

"I saw it, actually."

Her eyes bugged. "You a cop?"

"No. But I'm pretty sure I know the guy he was having dinner with. Did they both leave together?"

"No." The server set the tea pitcher down on a tray behind her. "Jake took off first."

"Did you mention that to the deputy?"

She shook her head. "No. They just asked for a copy of Jake's receipt, which I gave them."

"So the other guy stuck around, and—"

"He looked nervous, especially after he got a phone call. I wasn't deliberately listening in, but he was arguing with someone. He was talking really loud."

Asher had always been loud. And obnoxious.

"What was the argument about?"

She shrugged. "Something about a code?"

And there it was.

I pulled up a picture of Asher from his social media profile and showed it to her. "Is this the guy who paid the check, by any chance?"

"Yes." Her eyes widened. "That's the bigmouth. Should I be worried?"

"No." And for the first time all day, I wasn't worried either.

I had a pretty good idea who had taken Sunshine, and even had some thoughts about where she might be.

We ended our meal and headed out to the parking lot, where I called Colton.

"Hey, can we meet up at your place?"

"Sure." He paused. "I'm almost done here. We didn't end up bidding on the other stallion. Everyone's feeling kind of down in the dumps, so I think my parents will be happy to head home."

"Call Deputy McAllister. See if he can meet us."

"What's up, Jessie?"

"I have news, and I think we all need to be together when I share it."

We arrived ahead of the group, and Deputy McAllister pulled in behind me. Brody arrived on his tail, and the Hayes clan pulled in moments later.

Standing in the driveway, I shared everything I had witnessed at the auction and the conclusions I had drawn.

"Whoa, whoa." Deputy McAllister held up his hand. "You're saying Garrett Stone and Jake Owens have been working together all this time to make sure you guys didn't get your hands on that new stallion?"

"Looks that way," Colton said.

"That can't be right," Mr. Hayes said. "Jake can't stand Garrett."

"But they have a mutual enemy now," I countered. "You all. They don't want Lickety Split to succeed."

"I never saw Jake talk to Garrett at the auction," Colton said. "Not once, and I kept a pretty close eye on him."

"He didn't," I said. "He talked to Asher, who talked to Garrett. I doubt anyone in the room noticed but me."

"Asher, the guy from Jefferson?" the deputy asked.

"Yes. All three of them were working together to produce the highest bid on Southbound Fury, which makes me believe they were working on something else too."

"Like what?" McAllister asked.

"All three men linked arms to steal Sunshine."

"To what end?" Mr. Hayes asked.

"Place the highest bid on Southbound Fury. Steal Sunshine. Merge the two family lines and produce a runner so fast they would pocket the money from the offspring for years to come."

"Makes sense to me," Colton said.

"If we're going to prove any of this, we've got to bring Jake into the conversation." Deputy McAllister got on his radio and put out a call to his officers to round up Jake Owens and bring him to the Hayes home as soon as they could.

In the meantime, Rose insisted we go inside the house, and a short time later we were in the kitchen, drinking coffee while she mixed up a fresh batch of Snickerdoodles.

"So you really think all three men were in on this together?" Rose asked as she set the sugar bowl on the table in front of me.

"I do. And the auction definitely gave Asher the perfect excuse to be here."

"I still can't figure out how Asher knew to contact Garrett Stone though," Mr. Hayes said.

"Asher knew I was headed to Lickety Split. So I'm guessing he googled other top breeding services in Magnolia and saw that there were a few on the list, just under yours. Probably figured y'all were competitors."

Calliope reached for her coffee cup. "So he reached out to Garrett and offered to cut a deal to co-own the offspring with him if Garrett would help him steal Sunshine and acquire Southbound Fury? Is that it?"

"As best I can figure, yes."

"So Garrett hired Jake, the best wrangler in town." Mr. Hayes shook his head. "If this is true, then my former son-in-law is a bigger scoundrel than we thought."

"He's desperate, Dad," Colton said. "I think he would've done anything to get some cash after losing his job here."

"Katy did say he was flashing money around when he stopped by her place," I reminded him. "So somebody was paying him."

"But what about the part where Jake has an alibi?" Brody asked. "He was out to dinner until seven thirty on Thursday night, right? There's a receipt."

"Saw it myself," Deputy McAllister said.

"Yes." I nodded. "There's definitely a receipt showing the bill was paid at 7:29 p.m., but Calliope and I just talked to the person who served them, and she said that Jake left the restaurant before Asher paid the check."

The deputy scribbled something on his notepad. "I see."

"So Jake had plenty of time to come over here and nab Sunshine," Mr. Hayes said.

"But we never heard a thing." Rose pulled a fresh tray of cookies from the oven. "That's unsettling."

"Yesterday morning I noticed the fence was down by the grove," Colton said. "I'm guessing he had his truck back there, ready. Complete with trailer. It was just a matter of sneaking her across the property in the dark."

"But where did he take her after that?" Rose asked.

I was about to answer when the police arrived with Jake in tow.

I felt pretty sure I had the final piece to this puzzle in my purse, so I reached inside and pulled out the scrap of paper I'd found in Sunshine's stall on Thursday night.

Jake's face paled the moment he saw it.

"0258." I spoke the numbers to Jake, who looked like he might be sick.

"Wh–what?"

"0258. I'm guessing that's the code for the gate in front of Garrett Stone's property. Am I right?"

Jake looked back and forth between Deputy McAllister and me. "I don't have any idea what she's talking about."

"You dropped this paper in Sunshine's stall on Thursday night but didn't realize it was missing until you got to Garrett's place. So you called Asher Brooks, who was still at Las Fuentes, to let him know you'd messed up. He lost his cool with you. So then you texted Garrett at the rodeo where he was on a date with Doris."

"Wait." Rose put her hand up. "Doris and Garrett are dating?"

"That's supposed to be a secret. But she told me he was preoccupied that night, worried about something going on back at his place with his horses."

I peered down at the paper, giving the letters on top a closer look. In full light, I could almost make out a *B* in front of the *L* and the *F*.

BLF.

Brooks Legacy Farm.

I'd been holding Asher's new letterhead in my pocket this whole time.

But I still had one lingering question, which I posed to Jake.

"Asher said he couldn't leave town until he held up his end of the bargain. What was his end of the bargain, exactly?"

"Putting Garrett over the top with his bid on Southbound Fury."

"And push that pesky Hayes family way down the totem pole." Colton glared at Jake, whose gaze shifted to the floor. "Was that the idea?"

Jake offered no response.

"And Cosmic Sunshine?" I asked.

Jake looked my way and offered a little shrug. "According to Asher, giving you grief over that mare was just the icing on the cake."

CHAPTER THIRTEEN

It took less than an hour for the police to track down Garrett and Asher and haul them up to the station for questioning. And one hour after that, Sunshine was home.

Well, not *home*, exactly. But back in her premiere stall at Lickety Split, where we all greeted her like a prodigal returned to the fold. I couldn't stop the tears from flowing as I threw my arms around that beautiful neck and embraced her with joy flooding over me.

A couple of stalls down, Like the Wind nickered softly. All was right with the world.

When we got Sunshine settled, I made a call to my parents to share the news. I put them on video chat to show proof that God had, indeed, performed a miracle.

Mama offered up a couple of "Praise the Lord!"s and said she couldn't wait to contact the prayer team at church to spread the word.

My dad tried not to get too emotional in front of the Hayes family, but I saw tears glistening in his eyes.

"So now what, honey?" Mama asked when the celebration died down. "When are you coming back home?"

"Well, I have yet to pay for—and receive—the services I came for." I laughed. "We still have to take care of that or the whole trip was in vain."

"I suspect it was *not* in vain." Mama gave me a little wink and then shifted her gaze to Colton, who now stood beside me. "God is *always* up to something behind the scenes, that's what I say."

"Amen to that!" Rose chimed in.

Calliope jumped in front of me to chime in with her thoughts. "We want her to stay a few more days in Magnolia, Aunt Lucy. We're having so much fun."

"You do that, Jessie," Mama said. "Take your time. You deserve a little vacation after all you've been through."

"Just keep a close eye on Sunshine!" my father added.

To which Colton responded, "Security cameras are fired up and ready, sir."

We ended the call, and my cousin—still giddy—threw her arms around Brody's neck, gave him a kiss on the cheek, then released a rowdy, "Woo-hoo!"

"What was that for?" he asked, all smiles.

"I'm celebrating. The return of Sunshine, my cousin's decision to stay a little longer, and a little dog named Peanut that I've decided I'm going to adopt!"

And just like that, she talked Brody into driving her back up to the vet's office to fetch the adorable little rescue dog. Heaven help us when that poor innocent pup would meet Taquito for the first time.

Mr. Hayes received a call and slipped off to the living room to take it. We heard the front door open and then close.

After a couple of minutes, Colton got curious and decided we should follow him outside.

We located Mr. Hayes on the front porch, deeply engrossed in the call.

Up above, the star-lit Texas sky twinkled merrily.

When the call ended, Colton's dad looked our way.

"Well, that was interesting."

"Who was it, Dad?" Colton asked.

"The director of the auction. It seems Garrett pulled his offer on Southbound Fury an hour after it was placed."

"He did?" Colton's eyes widened. "Seriously?"

"Yeah. Asher Brooks never produced the money for his end of the bargain, so Garrett fell short. Way short."

"Are you saying Asher swindled his fellow swindler?" Colton asked.

"Sounds like it." Mr. Hayes shoved his phone into his pocket.

"So, does that mean..." Colton shot a hopeful glance my way.

"You were the second-highest bidder, Son." Mr. Hayes patted him on the back. "Looks like we'll be picking up a new stallion sometime around noon tomorrow." It was his turn to glance at me. "After we take care of a little business with a certain mare from Jefferson."

Mr. Hayes disappeared back into the house, leaving us alone.

Colton took my hand, and we began to walk toward the barn, the stars above us still dancing in the night sky. He dove into a conversation about how good God was, about how the Lord always provided just what we needed when we needed it.

"Sounds like you've secured another winner," I said.

Colton stopped walking and turned to face me, still holding tight to my hand. "Oh, I secured a winner all right."

But when he grabbed me to plant a toe-curling kiss on my lips, I felt sure he wasn't just talking about a horse.

And in that moment, as the stars danced over us in the gorgeous Texas sky, it occurred to me that Mama was right.

God really *was* up to something, wasn't He?

JANICE THOMPSON, who lives in the Houston area, writes novels, nonfiction, magazine articles, and musical comedies for the stage. The mother of four married daughters, she is quickly adding grandchildren to the family mix.

YOU MIGHT ALSO ENJOY. . .

SECRETS BETWEEN THE SHELVES

MYSTERIES LEAP OFF THE PAGE

MURDER AND MAYHEM HAUNT FOUR NEWLY OPENED BOOKSTORES.

***Murder in the Mystery Section* by Cynthia Hickey**

Amber Swanson's dream is coming true as she opens an Alice in Wonderland–inspired bookstore with tearoom. But her first customer accuses Amber of stealing a rare book, then the woman ends up dead in the mystery section of the store.

***The Secret Passage Bookshop* by Linda Baten Johnson**

Abby Scott, a retired ski instructor, opens a bookshop in a quaint Wyoming town. During renovations, a secret passage is discovered to be housing a missing teenager and exposes a dark secret in town.

By Hook or by Book **by Teresa Ives Lily**

Lily Carter is excited to open her pirate-themed bookstore on the Maine coast. But when someone is seen sneaking around her property, then a man in pirate costume is found dead, Lily must seek answers.

The Missing Chapter **by Marilyn Turk**

When Kelly Stephens opens her shop, Artistic Adventures, next to Bayside Books and Reading Room, she witnesses a suspicious death. Kelly wants to prove the pleasant bookstore owner innocent, despite the rumors that he killed his wife years ago.

Paperback / 979-8-89151-031-9

YOU MIGHT ALSO ENJOY. . .

DEATH BY FOOD TRUCK

FOOD TRUCKS CAN BE MURDEROUSLY GOOD

GET A TASTE OF MURDER AND MAYHEM IN FOUR COZY MYSTERIES.

Birch Tree, Maine, is experiencing a rash of deaths, all mysteriously linked to food trucks that frequent Birch Point Lake. Mey's noodle truck was her ticket to a new life, until her ex-boyfriend threatened to take it away. Angel's new donut truck was doing great, until deathly rumors started. Shanice thought she had customer support when taking over her grandpa's potato truck, until one started complaining. Marissa's taco truck was a fixture in the park, until linked to a food judge's death. What could have led to such foul-tasting murder and mayhem in an idyllic community?

Paperback / 978-1-63609-594-3

Little Red Truck Series of Cozy Mysteries

By Janice Thompson

Breathe in the nostalgia of everything old red truck in a new cozy mystery series.

Book 1: Tracking Tilly
The Hadley family ranch is struggling, so RaeLyn, her parents, and brothers decide to turn the old barn into an antique store. The only thing missing to go with the marketing of the store is Grandpa's old red truck, Tilly, that was sold several years ago. Now coming back up on the auction block, Tilly would need a lot of work, but RaeLyn is sure it will be worth it—if only she can beat out other bidders and find out who stole Tilly after the auction ends. Hadley finds herself in the role of amateur sleuth, and the outcome could make or break the new family venture.

Paperback / 978-1-63609-908-8

Book 2: Sabotage at Cedar Creek
The Hadley family's new antique business is open and running well with Tilly, the red antique truck, as its mascot. RaeLyn Hadley is happy to see her friend Tasha open a new bed-and-breakfast inn to accommodate the area's growing tourism, but a fire threatens to spoil all Tasha has worked for. RaeLyn immediately gets to work sleuthing out who could be behind such an act of sabotage. Could it be the nearby resort owner, the daughter of the house's former owner, a neighbor, or a squatter who had been living in the house before renovations? RaeLyn is determined to solve the mystery for her friend.

Paperback / 979-8-89151-026-5

Book 3: Mistletoe and Mayhem
RaeLyn Hadley's family business, old red truck, and location of her upcoming wedding are threatened by a wildfire of mysterious origins.

Paperback / 979-8-89151-172-9

Christian Fiction for Women is your online home for the latest in Christian fiction.

Check us out online for:

- Giveaways
- Recipes
- Info About Upcoming Releases
- Book Trailers
- News and More!

Find Christian Fiction for Women at Your Favorite Social Media Site:

 Search "Christian Fiction for Women"

@fictionforwomen